T0277258

"Sometimes you just need to check speculation at the door and sink into an utterly absorbing tale, taking you to a dreamy place (Italy), introducing you to fascinating people (time-travelers) and casually learn about a time period you might not know much about (medieval). Diving into the deep end of this first book in the Oceans of Time will bless you with a refreshing 'break read,' as well as a restorative opportunity to consider how families are sometimes uniquely brought together by God . . . a theme close to my heart."

— **TRICIA GOYER**, bestselling author of 80 books, including *A Daring Escape*

"*Estuary* will whisk you away into a richly woven world of danger and beauty—and sweeping romance. Full of twists and intrigue that will keep you turning pages, this riveting tale delves into the ties of family that span centuries and the parts of ourselves we discover in long-forgotten places. Fans of the original River of Time series— as well as new readers, diving in for the first time—will discover charm, heart and courage brought to life in a breathtaking new way. This spellbinding novel a must-read. Highly recommended!"

— **KARA SWANSON**, Christy Award-winning author of *Dust* and *Shadow*

"Lisa Bergren weaves a beautiful story in this unique time jump novel. Medieval Italy provides the backdrop with knights, battles, and strong women. A definite recommendation for both those who love her River of Time series and fantasy."

— **MORGAN L. BUSSE**, award-winning author of The Ravenwood Saga and Skyworld series

"Fabulous and utterly satisfying! *Estuary* is a glorious return to Bergren's much-beloved River of Time series. Beautiful portrayals of love, betrayal, and courage are as gorgeous as the Italian countryside in which they're set. This story will delight Bergren's longtime fans and have new readers searching caves for that portal back to medieval Italy to meet the infamous She-Wolves of Siena. Nock your arrows and get ready to ride—this is one story you won't want to miss!"

— **RONIE KENDIG**, award-winning author of the Droseran Saga

RipTide

Books by Lisa T. Bergren

The Oceans of Time Series
Estuary
Rip Tide

The River of Time Series
Waterfall
Cascade
Torrent
Bourne & Tributary
Deluge

River of Time California
Three Wishes
Four Winds

The Remnants Trilogy
Season of Wonder
Season of Fire
Season of Glory

The Gifted Series
Begotten
Betrayed
Blessed

View more of Lisa's books
at lisatawnbergren.com

OCEANS OF TIME | BOOK 2

LISA T. BERGREN

For Brielle Barton,

who loves these books

so much, she wanted

to be *in* the next one.

1

LUCIANA

*S*truck by Lightning and Lived to Tell About It.
    That's the headline that ran through my mind as I lay on the tomb floor, trying to remember to breathe. Cascading through time felt—especially when we released our hands from the prints—like a shock wave going through me. I groaned and turned my head to see Ilaria and Domenico to my right, gradually coming around.

We'd made it. *All* of us had made it. Back to the right time? And . . . Giulio?

I pushed up on an elbow, looking around.

Lady Adri was asleep at the edge of the tomb, with a blanket below her and another on top—as if she had been camping out.

Sensing our movement, her lovely light-blue eyes opened, and she rose with the three of us, face aglow. "Oh, you did it!" She rushed to Ilaria and bent to examine her wound, just as Ilaria herself did. The scar upon her skin—while covered in dried blood—appeared as if it had healed years ago.

Lady Adri gripped the young woman's shoulders, grinning, and hugged her close, then turned to Nico and me to do the same, kissing us each on both cheeks as the Italians do. "Well done, my young cousins. Well done!"

"How-how long have we been gone?" my brother asked.

"*Toscano, per favore.*" Ilaria touched his arm, wanting to

understand too. *In Tuscan, please.* Meaning, their medieval dialect of Italian.

"You were gone three days," Adri returned in the native tongue. "You were swift," she added in admiration. "Was it about three minutes?"

"About. But we weren't quite swift enough," he added ruefully.

She lifted a brow. "Oh?"

"Doctor Manero and two men were in the tomb when we arrived. One saw us appear. They tried to grab us. I think all three of them saw us disappear. Maybe a fourth."

Adri's eyebrows rose. "Oh."

"What happened?" Ilaria stared down at her blood-soaked gown. "I remember getting hit by the arrow. But little after, until. . ." She looked at me and my brother. "Where *were* we? Who were those people?"

Nico rubbed the back of his neck. "That will take a bit to explain."

"Well, then, please. Begin." Ilaria crossed her arms.

"Has anyone seen this happen before?" I asked, turning Adri aside as my brother began to tell Ilaria the truth about our ability to travel through time—and the tunnel's ability to heal.

Adri put a hand on her head, thinking. "No. A number have seen us emerge from or disappear into the tomb, but we've always been able to explain it away. None but family have actually seen it occur."

"Will they chalk it up to a dream?" I asked hopefully.

Her eyes narrowed. "Not Manero. He will conduct a very thorough investigation. Mayhap even do damage to the tunnel in his desire to discover what is transpiring."

My pulse picked up. "Would he dig into the wall? Isn't that against all the archeology rules?" My thoughts ran in two different directions at once—I had really wanted to come back. To the Forellis. To Giulio.

But to not have the option to return to our own time? Ever?

"I hope not. But I've seen Manero's desire for fame push him to take shortcuts that most of our peers would condemn." She took my hand, understanding in her wise eyes. "Do not fear. Should you wish to return, I believe there is another tunnel. The Betarrinis who previously visited us arrived via a tomb near Firenze."

Nico and Ilaria rejoined us, Ilaria blinking rapidly, as if trying to absorb it all. "What is this?" She lifted a hand. "You do not intend to remain?" She looked to Nico. "After all that has transpired to bring you here not once, but twice?"

He glanced at me. "I-I believe we do. At least for a while?"

I bit my tongue. I was ninety percent sure I wanted to stay with the Forellis. To figure out where this thing with Giulio was going. But to promise forever? I wasn't ready for that. After all, things hadn't turned out so well for my parents and their marriage. What did I know about forming something strong enough to go the distance?

I saw the wall go up in Ilaria's pretty brown eyes when I didn't respond. Still, she took Nico's hand and then mine, looking at both of us. "Thank you, my friends. Thank you for saving me. I-I believe I was dying."

"You were," Adri said gravely.

"Tell us what has happened since we left," I said, eager to catch up on the news.

We followed Adri out of the tomb. No one was within view, to my relief. But also my disappointment. Where was Giulio? The others?

"We received word yesterday that Marcello and Gabi, Fortino, Luca, and Lia are all in Firenze. There is to be a hearing soon."

I took a breath—so glad they were all alive—but her tone implied a trial was dire news indeed.

"Tiliani, Giulio, and every available knight are on the hunt for Sir Ercole and his companion. Our only hope is to find them and force them to confess to the Fiorentini at the hearing. With so many dead . . . we fear the very worst outcome."

What did that mean? Would they hang them? Chop off their heads? I bit my lip. "What of Lord Paratore? Will he help us?"

"Gabi sent word to tell us he is conflicted. Torn between believing that we had nothing to do with the murders of his fellow citizens and the circumstantial evidence that we were instrumental in the bloodbath. He faces incredible pressure from his fellow countrymen to be as vengeful as they."

"He can't possibly . . . not after spending so much time among us!" It caught me—how my use of *us* so easily slipped from my tongue. "Has Tiliani spoken to him? In person?"

"She shall," Adri said, as we moved as rapidly toward Castello Forelli as Ilaria could manage. While my friend appeared healed, she was still pale, perhaps as affected from the shock of time travel as her wound. "But our priority needs to remain on finding Ercole and his woman, a former castello maid named Rosa. If one of them— or the mercenaries they hired—can testify that the tunics they wore were not Forelli-issued, but fake, 'twould aid us."

"If Tiliani could speak to Aurelio, I am certain she could convince him." Ilaria wiped perspiration from her forehead. "He seemed genuinely fond of her."

"Be that as it may, Luca and Lia are reluctant to let her anywhere near the border. As am I. There are already enough of us trapped on the other side. You know how mob mentality goes."

We all paused to take in her words. They genuinely feared we would lose those already in Firenze.

"What of Benedetto?" Ilaria asked.

Adri's elegant brows furrowed. "He is abed with a fever these last two days. None of the remedies Chiara and I have tried have given him relief."

"Was he wounded in the battle?" Ilaria asked, her hand moving to her own scar. "Is it infection?"

"Nay." Adri shook her head, clearly troubled.

"Back to aiding those in Firenze," Nico said. "What if we find some of the men who aided Ercole on the road? Those who wore the stolen Castello Forelli tunics and attacked the Perugian patrols?"

"We are on the hunt for them as well," she said. "But mercenaries more readily slip into the shadows."

"I saw Ercole and the maid in Siena," I put in. "I think I might recognize them both again. I should be on the hunt too."

"We shall all join the effort," Nico said.

Four knights rode up to us at the forest's edge. Sir Fiore's weather-rimmed eyes flicked over the three of us, and his brows lifted in surprise. "You have . . . returned. And Ilaria—you are *well*?"

"Indeed," she said, placing a hand over her wound as if it still pained her. "The Betarrinis aided me in the forest, hiding me away and tending to my wound."

"God be praised," he said faintly, as if he wasn't completely buying it.

Had he heard that she had been pierced through in the battle? I knew he was truly glad to see Ilaria up and about—but I'd be wondering too. And not appreciate being kept in the dark.

He dismounted. "Please, Lady Ilaria." He gestured to his gelding.

Playing the part of a wounded maid, she allowed him to lift her up and onto the saddle, and in gentlemanly fashion, he looked away from the bare skin of her calves as her skirts rose. She kept her hand over her chest the whole time, but as she shifted, briefly let go to settle her skirts. Had Fiore glimpsed what I had? The slashed-open bodice? The puckered but clearly healed skin? Or only the dried blood?

He looked a good bit shaken as he took the reins and led her forward. What else had he witnessed over his years of serving the Betarrinis and Forellis? Surely this was not the first time he had encountered something mysterious.

Two other knights offered Adri and me their own horses, but we decided to walk. One moved to lead our small procession forward, Sir Fiore remaining beside Ilaria, and the other two behind us. It was a beautiful summer midafternoon—not too hot, even though this was usually the warmest part of the day.

I took a deep breath as we neared Castello Forelli, my nostrils filling with the scent of pine and eucalyptus and lilac. I was eager to be inside the castle's walls and hoped Giulio had returned from his search. While to my mind, we had been apart for only a couple of hours, it *felt* like the full three days he had experienced. Would he be gone until nightfall? No one was going to let Nico and me grab some horses and peel out on our own search. Nor would that be wise. But I was itching to do something to help, and quickly.

I scanned the woods, finding it hard to believe we were not still under attack. Three days had passed. Three days, in a matter of minutes! What would've happened had Manero succeeded in waylaying us? Separating us? Hours could quickly mean years here. How long had passed when Gabi and Lia traveled back each time? I wished they were here so I could ask them.

My mind returned to the tomb and the possibility that Manero would do some harm to the wall—and therefore the tunnel—in his quest to figure out just what they had witnessed.

He had become somewhat of an adversary to the Betarrinis over the years. Would he be obsessed with discovering if that's why they had disappeared too?

Adri, walking beside me, seemed to read my thoughts. "It is a great deal to contemplate," she said quietly, in English. "Remaining here. Forever. 'Twas something the girls and I wrestled with for a long time."

"How did you know? That it was right for you?" I returned.

She looked up at the castle and moved around the opposite side of a boulder on the dirt path, then emerged, chin in hand. "In the end, it was simply the only answer. Once we had Ben with us, and Gabi and Lia had found their hearts entwined with the Forellis, it was just *right*. And we found we were together here as a family like we'd never been before."

"Nothing like fighting for your lives to bring a clan closer, huh?"

She gave me a rueful smile and bent closer. Nico was directly in front of us, so he could hear, but not the two knights on horseback behind us. "There was that, yes. But it was more. The communal nature of the castello. The connection to others went beyond our nuclear family, which was so different than what we'd experienced in America. We'd long witnessed it among the Italians, of course. They are famously clannish. But here? In this time? It's even more prevalent." She walked a few steps farther. "Once we were one with them—experiencing this fierce love they share—we could not imagine separating from them again."

"Did you fear losing Ben had you traveled again?" Nico asked over his shoulder.

"We knew not what would happen, but it was a factor. However, I don't think we would have left. This became our home. Our place. Our people. As it might become yours."

"Why?" I asked. "Why would God send us here? Why *us*?"

"That's a question for Father Giovanni." She took my hand and gave it a brief squeeze. "And for each of you, as it was for each of us. 'Tis an important step in deciding. Do not fear speaking to him. He has been our confidant—in *all* matters—for years."

The priest knew? Everything?

"Lady Adri at the gates!" called a guard, spotting us. He grinned and leaned over the parapet as if he could not believe his eyes. "And more—Lady Ilaria and the Betarrinis! Open the gates at once!"

His command echoed below, and we heard the creaking slide of the iron crossbeam, then watched as the patched doors opened—giant, new, pink wooden beams between the old weathered-gray ones now—where it had been broken through by the Perugian battering ram. As two knights pulled them aside, I looked to those gathering in the courtyard, alerted by the castle gate guard's delighted call. There was Cook and Tomasso and the archers, Otello and Baldarino. I smiled with them as they hurried forward to greet us all.

But it was Ilaria they were most concerned about, of course. They'd probably all thought they'd never see her again, since when we carried her away, it appeared as if she was dying. I was thankful we had been gone at least three days. What would have happened if we'd reappeared after only one? It was already hard enough to explain how Ilaria was upright and able to sit on a horse.

She bent her head, letting her hair fall over most of her face.

"God be praised!" cried Cook, going to Ilaria's side as Sir Fiore aided her in dismounting. "What is this miracle?"

"I found them in the Fiorentini forest," Adri said, loudly enough to be overheard. "The Betarrini twins discovered a medicinal moss and packed her wound, seeing her through the long days and nights between us. God be praised, Lady Ilaria appears to be on the mend. But we must get her to her quarters. Cook, please send two buckets of hot water. Tomasso, please fetch my tincture chest. Luciana, would you be so kind as to aid me with Ilaria?"

"Of course."

Chiara emerged from a turret and ran toward her sister. "Ilaria!" she cried, her face awash in relief.

"I must tell her," Ilaria whispered to Adri when Chiara was halfway across to us.

"She knows," she returned. "She was with us when you went."

Ilaria wrapped an arm around Luciana's shoulders and kept her hand on her chest, curling in as if in pain, for the sake of the others around us. Chiara reached us and put trembling hands on her sister's cheeks, gazing at her with tearful wonder. "You are . . . here. And well?"

Ilaria smiled and nodded. "I am on the mend. But please, I must rest. Might you help me to my room?" We were all feeling the heat of so many eyes—and the need for frank conversation.

"Yes, of course. Come at once." Her sister scurried to wrap her arm about her waist.

But as soon as Ilaria sat down on her bed and the maid closed the door behind her, Chiara went to her knees beside her, clutching her hands. "Ilaria! Ilaria!" she cried, tears rushing down her cheeks. "I cannot believe . . . I mean, we so hoped—"

"I am well, sister, *well*." Ilaria smiled, tearing up too. "Examine me yourself."

Chiara's long fingers traced over Ilaria's face as if verifying she was real. "I saw you . . . disappear," she said with a ragged breath. "I feared I might never see you again!"

"And yet here I am." Ilaria sat up. "Whole and hale. See?" She spread apart the fabric of her bodice so Chiara could see the healed wound.

Chiara's fingers went to her mouth as she paled. "How? How is this possible?" She looked from her sister to Adri to us.

"'Tis the miracle of what certain Betarrini siblings are able to do," Adri said. "'Tis how Gabriella was saved from her poisoning."

"Nay." Chiara made the sign of the cross over herself and gazed at her sister as if she were an apparition. "'Tis a miracle of God."

"That too," Adri said with a smile.

Could it be? I wondered. Could God have really used us to do such a thing? Did he want Ilaria alive for some purpose? And why had we been chosen? We were nothing more than two regular college kids.

I had to admit I was moved by the gleeful reunion of the sisters. Had we not agreed to go, to take Ilaria through, there was no doubt she would have been dead within minutes. Her bright smile, her fierce loyalty, her draw to my brother and him to her—gone within a breath's time. The thought rattled me.

I glanced at my brother. Tears streamed down his face, too, as he watched the sisters. He cared for her, deeply cared. Because Nico never cried. Since we'd been kids, I'd see it happen only three times—when the Yankees won the World Series, and when our mother and grandmother each breathed their last.

He turned toward me and wrapped an arm around my shoulders, still gazing at the sisters hugging each other tight. "Thanks, Luci," he whispered, kissing me on the temple. "For going. And for returning."

"Better that than captured by Manero and interrogated for days," I muttered.

"Sure," he said with a knowing smile, crossing his arms. "That was *totally* the reason you came back."

"Well, yeah." I grinned impishly, thinking of Giulio. "What other reason would I have?"

2

TILIANI

Conjecturing that our enemies had sought to poison our neighbors against us, we mapped out their next potential target. They had succeeded with Fortebraccio and Belucci to our eastern border, and now with the Fiorentini to the north. With Siena to our southwest, our only remaining open flank was to the northeast, so we concentrated on visiting neighbors there, affirming our intent for ongoing peace, and searching their woods for our enemies.

Now, after a week of lining villagers' and merchants' purses with Forelli coin, we were finally on the trail of a band of mercenaries camping in the woods near the border—one of them reportedly in possession of a golden tunic.

After searching all day, we at last saw the spiraling rise of campfire smoke in the distance. Communicating through hand signals, we agreed that Giulio would lead twelve men directly toward them, while I would lead the other twelve off the road and go around to cut them off should they try to flee. I left before Giulio to find good spots for my archers. But I knew he wouldn't tarry long, fearful that our presence would be detected.

I urged my mount to move faster through the trees, my heart pounding. Did we finally have them? We needed to capture at least one alive—someone who knew of the intrigue—in order to clear the Forelli name and free our family from the Fiorentini's nets. Their trial was fast approaching, and it would take a day and a half just to travel there. We had to find our witnesses, and quickly.

I gestured to Iacapo and Falito, urging them to take up position in trees on either side of the road. Then to Gaspare and Agostino, to do the same farther along the road. Four swordsmen moved toward the wood on the road itself, remaining mounted. Two more hobbled their horses and stood their ground before me. The last two flanked me. We were ready.

I prayed each man remembered their charter to not kill, only maim. I prayed we would find the one we needed. *Just one, Lord. We need but one. But two would be better.*

Was Andrea Ercole amongst them, or one of his hired men? Was the girl, Rosa, with them too? Ideally, we would capture them—for they were surely instrumental in the Fiorentini bloodbath in Siena. Luciana and Domenico had given them chase. If only they had succeeded in bringing them down!

I thought of my time-traveling cousins, and of Ilaria, disappearing with them. Would they ever return? Giulio and I had both been in dismal spirits since they departed, fretting that we might have lost Ilaria forever. But what choice had we? She had been about to die when the twins took her. According to my aunt and mother, it could be days, or weeks—or even years—before they returned. If they were able to return at all. It all depended on what they encountered on the other side.

Nona thought it highly probable, given her experience with my aunt and mother. I rested in that—her hope that the twins would return our beloved Ilaria—and chose to ignore the fear that lined Chiara's eyes.

We waited, straining to hear men coming our way, my mount dancing beneath me with the tension. And then I thought about taking a witness to Firenze, clearing the Forellis' good name . . . and seeing Valentino Valeri. He had gone with Lord Aurelio Paratore, his only recourse as his captain. But now, with him on the far side of the border, it seemed as if he was as cut off from me as I was from Ilaria. As if an insurmountable wall had risen between us.

If I saw him in Firenze, would we be able to find a moment? To speak? I shook my head. This was not the time to be lost in fanciful dreams.

"M'lady," Agostino said under his breath, nodding toward the wood.

I heard it at the same time. A cry, a shout, the clang of swords. The whinny of a horse.

"Steady," I growled, as much for myself as the men about me.

They emerged then, riding fast. A pair together, then a single rider, then three more. From the sound of it, the others were battling with Giulio's men amongst the trees.

My first line of archers shot at the leading pair, but in their efforts to maim but not kill, missed one and shot the other through the thigh. He managed to keep his seat and kept on riding. The second line of tree archers took out the one they had missed, shooting him in the shoulder at such close range that the force of it sent him wheeling over the back of his mare. Seeing us ahead, the next man rode wide and into a field.

"Go after him," I said, sending one of the horsemen at my flank.

Without hesitation, he was off.

Iacapo and Falito descended from the trees to capture the wounded man. But the masked trio riding past them—and rounding toward the woods—stole my breath. One wore Forelli gold! And the smaller one had to be a woman. Rosa?

But they were escaping.

"With me!" I shouted to Agostino, still on his horse. "To your mounts and follow!" I cried to the swordsmen. We gave chase, granting our horses enough rein to find their own sure path as we galloped behind the three fugitives.

We gained on them by riding beside the edge of the forest, glimpsing them between the trees, until the wood became too thick. I saw one riderless horse, then a second, and belatedly realized they had abandoned their mounts where the woods grew thicker.

Agostino and I circled back and studied the wood, frequently pausing to listen for the telltale sign of those bushwhacking their way through—or trying to stealthily slip away. But we heard nothing beyond the labored breathing of our own horses.

Where had they gone?

With a grunt of frustration, I dismounted and slapped Cardo's rump, sending him away, frustrated that his heaving breath might be disguising our enemy's escape. Agostino did the same. Together, we held our own breath, listening for any sign of them. But there was nothing. Had they gone to ground? Were they but a few paces away, hidden in the thick foliage?

Forming a protective arc, somewhat flanking one another, Agostino and I cautiously moved left, where the woods seemed less daunting—more passable—and mayhap more attractive for someone intent on escape.

Blood pulsed in my ears. In the distance, men cried out in battle. Giulio had managed to waylay some of them, at least. My eyes darted left and right, searching the wood. *Where, Lord? Where? Please do not let them escape us again.*

I heard the whir of the blade just in time. I dodged left, and the dagger, coming end over end, rammed into the tree beside me.

Agostino and I turned to see a second dagger winging its way toward him. It grazed his cheek, and he winced but concentrated on the two men coming our way, swords drawn, cloths across their faces in an effort at disguise.

Masked or not, I knew the taller one was Andrea Ercole.

Agostino drew his sword. I pulled the short sword I wore in a hilt between my shoulder blades, my bow useless in such close proximity.

"I am Lady Tiliani Forelli," I gritted out, planting my feet and preparing to defend myself when they did not pause. "And you are to lay down your swords and come with us."

They continued their approach, ignoring my command.

When they reached us, they divided and struck at Agostino

and me at the same time. We blocked and parried, then came back-to-back.

"I know who you are," said the taller man across our blades, looking down at me.

"As I know you, Sir," I growled, trying to stab him in the leg, *"Ercole."*

"You saw through my disguise," he said, as if disappointed. He again lifted and brought his own sword down hard. I narrowly lifted my blade in time to block him. Where were my swordsmen on horseback? Had Rosa lured them in another direction?

I heard Agostino swear under his breath, then the clang of their swords meeting, right before mine hit Ercole's.

Andrea Ercole was an adept swordsman—one Giulio had been reluctant to dismiss—and I was now reminded of his prowess. I leaned back and felt the tip of his blade just miss my belly. I turned and stabbed again—the best use of a short sword—but he sidestepped me. His next attempt nearly took off my head. It brushed past my ear and I distantly wondered if he had taken a part of it.

Agostino cried out. I dared a glance in his direction. He staggered, hand to his gut.

Ercole struck again and I blocked him. We stared at each other across our blades. "Let us go, m'lady," he said. "Or you and your man die here today."

I held his gaze. Everything in me wanted to refuse him, but wisdom prevailed. They clearly had us, and to allow him to escape was the wiser choice.

But it burned. Oh, how it burned.

I panted, still trying to think of another way to entrap them, hoping my men would arrive, but neither a stroke of brilliance nor reinforcements arrived.

When Agostino took another blow, I bit my lip and stepped back. "So be it," I said reluctantly. I lowered my sword. "Go. But harm my family no further."

"That I cannot promise." I heard the grin behind his tone.

"Why?" I asked. "What drives you to such lengths? All this murder and mayhem, merely because we dismissed you from your post?"

He laughed under his breath, brazenly ripping away his mask. I knew the maids had all thought his long face with chiseled cheekbones and ample lips handsome, but I could never agree with them. What he did next reminded me why.

He lifted his sword to my neck and let his eyes roam down my body then back to meet my gaze. Bile rose in my throat. I remembered the dishonored maid, her tears. And why I had urged my father to send him away.

"You shall know my reasons in time, m'lady. My post at Castello Forelli was but one rung in my ladder upward. The more I can lay your family low, the easier it shall be for me to claim what is mine."

I frowned in puzzlement. What did he believe was his?

"Mayhap in time, you shall be *my* lady."

I laughed and used my gloved hand to shove away his sword. "I would rather fall upon that blade."

"That can be arranged," he said with a cocky smile. He slapped his companion on the back and the two dived into the brush, making their way steadily uphill, every step audible. I itched for my bow and quiver, the chance to riddle their path with arrows, but honor held me. He had spared me when he could clearly have killed me and my knight. Why? Would it not have been the greatest blow to our house to take me down?

Nay, his purpose was not so obvious. And I found it far more menacing, coming from the shadows. He could not have been serious, with his mention of making me his lady. Could he?

Two of my men rode up at last. "Lady Tiliani!"

I stifled a sigh and leveled a gaze at them, even as I moved to come up underneath Agostino's arm when he faltered. "What waylaid you?"

"The woman," he said, grimacing.

"Did you capture her?"

"Nay! Armando and Benito were after her, but they had set a trap. She sliced through a rope as she passed by, sending a ram into those who chased her. It hit Armando's gelding and he careened into the other. Benito's arm is broken."

"So they anticipated us finding them and giving chase," I said.

"We have spread the word wide," Alessandro grunted. "All know whom we seek."

I stared up the hillside, green leaves of oak and maple dancing in the afternoon breeze. "Where will they seek shelter?"

"They know we shall scour these hills," Baldarino said.

"Indeed. So then the only place they can hide is . . ."

"Firenze," he finished. "Unless they circle back to Perugia or Arezzo."

I pondered it. Ercole still had at least one more Forelli tunic. For what nefarious purpose did he keep it?

"The hour is late," I said wearily. "Let us see if Lord Greco was able to capture any others."

"We do have at least one captive of our own," Baldarino said. "The man Falito shot at the edge of the wood. Mayhap our men were able to capture the other."

"That is good," I said. But it grated at me. Those we needed most were Andrea Ercole and Rosa—and they'd slipped through our fingers again.

Dusk had nearly given way to dark when we met up with Giulio Greco's patrol and finally reached the gates of the castello. "Lady Forelli and Lord Greco have returned! Open the gates!" called Frederico.

We heard his echoed order below, and after a brief wait, the towering gates opened. Our grandmother, Adri, awaited us, and

I fought not to hang my head in failure as we neared her and dismounted. But she was not as grim faced as I anticipated. Nay, her face was . . . exultant. "What is it? Have you had good news from Firenze?"

My grandmother's smile faltered. "Still no further word from Firenze. But some from those of *Britannia*." She turned partway, and Giulio and I looked past her to the others who gathered. My eyes widened.

"Ilaria!" I cried, already swinging down out of the saddle. "And Luciana! Domenico!"

Giulio rushed ahead of me. We collided as a group, sharing hugs and kisses and greetings. Ilaria held her chest—bound in fresh bandages—as if protecting it, but I knew her well enough to recognize she wasn't as injured as she acted. I could not get over the thought that she was *alive*. When she'd vanished with the Betarrinis, I'd fought to hold on to hope. Fought not to give in to grief, as if she were lost to us forever.

But now she stood here among us. Stood, when only days ago, Nona had said she had minutes left to live.

I turned to the twins, gripping each of their shoulders. "You did it. Oh, my dear ones, you *did* it."

They grinned back at me. "We simply did what we could," Domenico said. "The rest? Well that, we cannot explain."

I glanced around, my smile fading. "Nona, Benedetto still has not risen?"

She glanced at me, her eyes troubled. "Nay. His fever has worsened."

I frowned. I was accustomed to our people responding well to Chiara and Nona's remedies. But in recent weeks, fevers that never abated had taken several lives within a nearby village. Had my cousin come down with the same illness?

Giulio picked up Ilaria and held her close, eyes closed, as if he might never let her go. "Oh, how glad I am that you have returned, sister. I thought . . . I thought we had lost you." He slowly set her down and turned to Luciana. "And your return, m'lady . . ." He put his hand to his chest and partially bowed his head, staring at her with tears in his eyes. "I count myself doubly blessed this night. I cannot express how very glad I am that you are home as well."

"As am I." She blushed prettily under his intense gaze and took a daring step closer to him.

I had never seen my friend so smitten. Beyond them, Ilaria shared shy words with Domenico. *Ilaria.* A woman who never acted shy!

What was this? Were both Giulio and his sister falling for the Betarrini twins? And was that partly why they had returned? As I stared at them—giddy with joy—Nona drew alongside and put a comforting arm around me.

It was as if she had anticipated my feelings before I recognized them myself.

The joy I felt for my friends and cousins intensified my longing for my own love. To be with the one who had first sparked it. The only one who had ever done so.

Sir Valentino Valeri.

"Tiliani?" Nona asked. "We need to hear of the day. What of the two men you brought back as captives?"

"We know not, yet, what they do."

"Leave them to me." Giulio motioned toward four knights to retrieve our captives. "Take them to the dungeon. We shall interrogate them after we sup."

"Come, beloved," Nona said to me. "Let us look in on Benedetto. Mayhap hearing your voice shall rouse him."

"He has not opened his eyes at all?" I asked in alarm.

She shook her head. "Not since last night. Worse, Chiara and I are hard-pressed to get more than a swallow of water down his throat."

"His fever remains?"

"Nothing seems to touch it."

A knight opened the door for us, and we climbed the turret

stairs and entered the family wing. Benedetto's rooms were close, and a knight was stationed outside his door as guard. He bent his head in greeting and wordlessly opened the door for us.

A maid wrung out a wet cloth in a basin and placed it across my cousin's forehead. She curtsied and stepped aside for us.

"Any change?" Nona asked.

"None, m'lady."

"Benedetto," I said, settling on the edge of his bed and taking his hand. "'Tis I, Tiliani. Might you open your eyes, cousin?"

There was no response. Yesterday, he had periodically roused. He had even made a terrible joke, trying to make me laugh. I put my hand to his forehead. He was still so terribly hot.

"He perspires no longer. Is that not a good sign?" I asked.

"Nay," Nona said, settling on the other side of his bed and dousing another cloth in the water. She let it trickle between his parted lips. "I fear he is terribly dehydrated."

"He should be better by now. This fever must break soon."

"It is a stubborn one." She lifted her pretty blue eyes to meet mine. "You must prepare yourself, dear one. Your cousin is fighting for his life."

"His life? But this is no plague," I said, confused. Benedetto was young and hale! The villagers who had died had been old and frail. "If it gets worse, the Betarrinis could take him through the tunnel. Heal him like they did Ilaria."

But Nona was shaking her head. "They were very nearly captured on the other end. We are fortunate they were able to return. We might not be so lucky if they attempt it again."

I stared at my cousin. "But Zio Marcello! Zia Gabi and Fortino!" I said nothing more. My grandmother understood.

If Benedetto hovered on the edge of death, his family ought to be surrounding him. For them to return home to find him . . . gone?

'Twas unthinkable.

LUCIANA BETARRINI

As everyone dispersed, Giulio remained with me. Gradually even the servants gave us our space, leaving us alone in the middle of the massive courtyard. It felt good to be surrounded by the comforting, protective walls again, among our people. But even better to be with Giulio. He took my hand and ran his thumb over my fingers as if trying to verify that I was truly here with him.

"I am not an apparition," I said.

He looked about, and seeing we were alone, lifted his other hand to my cheek, staring into my eyes. "Nay, you are not."

"I am very glad to see you," I said softly.

"No more than I, you." He lifted my hand to kiss it. His lips were warm and soft, and I longed to stand on my tiptoes and kiss him in earnest. But the center of the courtyard was not really the right place to make out. Even I knew that.

I saw Tiliani and Adri exit the turret and walk, arm in arm, toward the Great Hall. Their faces were somber. What was the matter? Was it Benedetto? Was he really bad?

"We should go to the hall," I said. "You are going to give me a bad reputation, keeping me out here in the shadows like this. And Adri and Tiliani will want your report, will they not?"

"Yes." With a heavy sigh he offered me his arm. "But do not leave my side, Luciana. I cannot bear it at the moment."

I smiled as we walked, knowing the guy was scared I might disappear again. But I really liked how forthright he was. And I liked the sense of claiming in his words. I mean, I could leave his side if I wanted to. He wasn't *forcing* me to stay. But Lord Giulio Greco *wanted* me at his side.

Me. Like no man had ever wanted me.

At least he did right now. *Don't get ahead of yourself, woman.*

But I couldn't help myself. I'd dated before, but I'd never

ever had a guy like this so into me. It was hard to not grin from ear to ear.

We entered the hall. A fire crackled in the massive fireplace at the far end. Though it was late summer, the evenings—and the cavernous hall, crafted of stone—tended to be chilly. The fire was a welcome sight as we drew closer to the others. I thought back to my own time, when we stood *inside* that long-defunct fireplace, scrubbed clean of any soot. Here and now, massive logs glowed red, and smoke disappeared up the blackened chimney.

Adri sat on Lady Forelli's chair, the lone presiding elder present. The rest of us stood. In quick order, Tiliani told them all she knew, including the story of letting Sir Ercole and his companion go. "Forgive me, Nona. I failed you and the family."

"You did the only thing you could," she said kindly. "Had you not, they would have likely slain you and *then* disappeared. At least this way, you live another day to capture them."

"I do not know if we can, in time," she said.

"This Ercole dude is getting on my nerves," Nico said in my ear.

"Mine too."

"Guys like that . . . they want to hang around to see what happens."

I thought about it. We'd seen our share of crime shows over the years. Arsonists always stuck around to see the fire. "You think he's heading to Firenze?"

"It's logical," he whispered. "He'll want to witness his moment of glory."

I nodded, then whispered our thoughts in Giulio's ear as Lutterius gave a report of the wounded men they had captured. Both captives insisted they were in Ercole's employ but steadfastly declared they had not been a part of attacking the patrols—they maintained it had been others before them. Ercole had disbanded that group, gave them coin to escape to Spain, and found new mercenaries.

"I shall interrogate them myself," Giulio said. "To be certain they speak the truth." His tone was ominous. What pain tactics would he use? I shuddered at the thought, but had to remember this was a different day and age. Such things were the norm. I remembered Marcello and Luca returning from Perugia, battered after days of their own interrogation.

"If Ercole did as they say," Nico whispered to me, "he's clever."

"Sending the bad guys off to another country? Yeah. He's always one step ahead. But if we can find Ercole in Firenze, we'd have him where we need him most."

"But we will be in enemy territory."

"For a bit," Nico said with a shrug. "Get in. Nab this dude. Force him to tell the truth. And get the heck out of dodge with our family in tow."

"That easy, eh?"

"Easy peasy." But even Nico's bravado could not hide the glint of fear in his eyes.

3

LUCIANA

As we concluded our meeting, Giulio found my pinkie among the folds of my skirts and hooked it with his. Standing as close as we were in the circle, few would've noticed it. And while it was the tiniest touch possible, it may as well have been an iron rod attracting a lightning strike. After a moment, he tugged slightly on it and then released me, giving me a small smile as he headed toward the door. He wanted me to follow. For what? To talk? To kiss? Didn't he have prisoners to interrogate?

"I need to, uh, change for the evening meal," I told Ilaria.

I followed Giulio into the deep shadows between the rays of light cast by torches dotting the walls. He stayed ahead of me by twenty paces, maybe searching for some secret alcove—someplace we wouldn't be discovered.

But when he drew to a stop, it was beside the very well-lit chapel door.

I hesitated. What was this? He didn't think we were going to get married or something *right now* did he?

How fast did medieval couples move on the love-and-marriage front in Italy? I remembered from my studies that in England, it could be an extended courtship or an arranged marriage in which couples met and married the same day. Marriage was an anything-goes concept in this period. Just as it pretty much was in mine. Lots of people spontaneously decided to elope. Was this a medieval version of Vegas's Chapel of Love?

I cocked my head and waited, hands on my hips, as he opened the door.

He gave me another small smile and gestured inward. "Go in, Luciana," he said softly. "There is someone I wish for you to meet."

I followed him inside and saw the small priest, Father Giovanni, on his knees before an altar at the front of the tiny stone chapel. I'd never entered it before, though I'd seen many of Castello Forelli's inhabitants attending services throughout the day. We went to the second row of benches, crossed ourselves, and then sat down, awaiting the priest to conclude his petitions. His head was bowed in earnest prayer, his arthritic-bent fingers running through his rosary beads.

Before I could ask Giulio why it was so urgent I meet the priest, he took a knee, head lowered in prayer. I sat there awkwardly for a moment, wondering what I ought to do. There was a strong urge to follow suit and kneel as well—I didn't want Giulio to think I was a total heathen. And yet I hadn't been to mass since it was required in our Catholic high school. Other than, you know, Christmas and Easter.

Mom and my grandmother had been devout. Dad, not so much. Last I knew, he was on his own "spiritual quest" out in California, which apparently relied heavily on time spent in hot yoga and long swims in the ocean.

So to kneel felt fake. Not that I didn't believe in God. I did. I just hadn't thought about him all that much before he sent me and my brother hurtling through time.

I finally ducked my head and silently prayed, *Lord, show me what this is all about. Why you've brought me here. And if Giulio is truly The One. Because I'm scared he is. And kind of scared that I'm scared. What is that all about? Okay, then. That's it. Oh, and help Benedetto to get better tonight. Amen.*

When I opened my eyes, Father Giovanni was rising with some effort—as if he might have just finished praying for hours—and turned to find us. He smiled warmly, welcoming me with a sparkly eyed nod. He then folded his hands, patiently waiting for Giulio to finish his own prayer. I fought the urge to nudge him. Priests always made me feel uneasy and judged. This one might get irritated waiting on us. But as I dared to meet the small man's eyes again, I saw nothing in him but peace. It let me take a deeper breath and settle in a way I'd never experienced before.

Giulio at last crossed himself and rose. "Ahh, Father Giovanni, forgive my delay."

"There is no delay in God's time, my son," the man returned kindly.

I came to my feet too. We had met before, but in passing. "Father," I said, briefly bowing my head in respect.

"Lady Betarrini." He returned my bow. "You are a welcome sight." He glanced over my shoulder to the door, verifying it was shut. "And I hear that God granted our prayer—your journey healed our beloved Ilaria. Please, sit, sit. Let us talk." He took a seat on the bench before us, and we returned to our own.

"I brought you here, Luciana, for I knew you undoubtedly have questions," Giulio said. "As did I. Lord Marcello sent me to speak to Father Giovanni. He knows everything. M'ladies and their husbands needed someone in whom they could confide. You may trust this man with your secrets, too, and he can assist you in sorting out your thoughts, your direction, and ultimately, your decisions."

I gaped at him. He'd understood something that I had not yet deciphered myself. I needed a neutral sounding board. Not Lia's slightly jaded ear, nor Gabi's slightly sunny one. Nor the irrepressible draw of Giulio's whole being.

Not that I wanted to leave. I'd wanted to remain even before it was our duty to bring Ilaria back. But Father Giovanni might fit my need for a counselor and guide. Someone to help me sort it all out. Because this was . . . *a lot.*

"Thank you." I squeezed Giulio's hand.

He covered my hand with his other. "You are most welcome. I want you to have all that you need, Luciana. If you need anything else, simply tell me. I will do everything I can to get it for you."

He was as generous as he was handsome. But as I tore my eyes from him and returned to the priest, I silently admitted that Giulio—a man I had just begun to know—could not be the sole reason I chose to remain. Evangelia had thoroughly warned me. Medieval times threatened to exact a steep toll.

"You decided to return," the priest began.

"Well, yes. There were many reasons to do so, the most prominent in restoring Ilaria to you all."

"God be praised."

"Yes," I said, absorbing the statement. "God be praised. It is a miracle of sorts, is it not?"

"Not of sorts. A true miracle," the priest returned easily. "I so wish we could shout of it from the parapets, but alas, we cannot."

"So, I suppose that is where I wish to start. Why me, or us? Me and my brother?"

"Why not you?" he casually returned. He leaned forward, elbows on knees, fingers steepled beneath his chin.

I hesitated. Would Giulio judge me for this?

"I have been less than a devout follower," I confessed quietly. "I was here for weeks last time and never even entered this chapel."

He considered me with gentle eyes. "God is a judge of the heart, not of our ways. Of course, he longs for us to honor him with our ways, but we do not work our way to salvation. Faith in Christ alone saves us."

I took that in. This was a different sort of priest than I had ever met. Maybe that's why the Forellis had chosen him.

"I am no one special," I tried again.

"Ahh, but you are. Each child of God is special," he said with a twinkle in his eye.

"But not so special that I should be given this gift."

"God has a long history of choosing unlikely servants. You can either accept it or try and out-reason him, which hardly ever goes well."

I nodded. *Okay.* "So if I accept it and move forward . . . what am I to do? What is my purpose? What does he wish for me to accomplish here?"

He shrugged. "In that you are like every other one of us. It remains to be seen. I advise you to simply walk through the next door God opens to you. The Ladies Forelli became the She-Wolves of Siena, saving our republic with their leadership, time and again. You have already served us in saving Lady Ilaria, and others in daring to enter the fray of battle. That alone could be *purpose* enough, would it not?"

Glancing into Giulio's dark-blue, grateful eyes, I settled on that. It was true. My friend, his sister, might have died. Other knights we helped protect too. They might have all been buried by now, their friends and family in mourning.

"What do you think about us changing history? The Ladies Forelli—it is clear their presence changed the future of the castello. They said that as children it was but rubble, but in the future, it is whole. What about the lives that were changed because of their presence and actions?"

He frowned, chin in hand. "'Tis a grave question, indeed."

"They likely saved lives. But they also took lives, as I have now, too." My voice cracked as I uttered those last words. Giulio put a gentle hand on my back as I fought back sudden tears. "If I remain here with my brother, we will likely save and take others."

Father Giovanni nodded gravely. "Yes."

"So we are changing history. Families. Bloodlines. Is that . . . all right? Acceptable in God's eyes?"

"Apparently," he said, lifting both hands. "Otherwise, he would not have sent you." He heaved a sigh. "Lady Gabriella and Evangelia and I have pondered this for years. I have encouraged them to simply live their lives as God ordains, trusting in his sovereignty. But this notion with Firenze . . ." He looked away from us to the small windows that lined the tiny chapel and shook his head. "Their intention—along with Marcello and Luca—to try and build a bridge between Firenze and Siena was noble, at heart. If Lady Tiliani and Lord Paratore had found their way to love, I might have considered it God smiling upon their plan."

"But they did not."

"Nay, they did not. And now fourteen prominent Fiorentini are dead, their families and republic intent on retribution. And our own risk bearing the punishment, traveling to Firenze."

I bit my lip. "So you think they went too far."

"I think the Forellis tried to get *ahead* of God," he said sorrowfully. "Something I cautioned against." He reached out to put a warm, weathered hand over my own—which I hadn't realized I was wringing. "The Lord brought you here, to us, Luciana. Your presence is bound to change history, as you say. But you cannot second-guess everything— 'twill make you mad with worry. Simply walk through the next door he opens for you, but do not try and forge your own door. Make prayer a habit. Try and *listen* for a response, and follow where he directs you to go. When in doubt over taking a life, choose mercy. When in battle, protect yourself and our people. And trust him with what comes."

I took a long, deep breath. "Thank you, Father. You have given me a great deal to consider."

"I have spent a decade considering such things alongside our ladies," he said. "Seek me out as you wish. I shall always have time for you and keep your confidences."

I smiled, astonished at the relief I felt. "Thank you."

Giulio rose and offered his hand. I took it and he led me out as the kindly priest watched us go.

We paused outside. "He is a good man," I said.

"The finest." He looked down at me. "Do you wish to return to the Great Hall or—"

I shook my head. "I am very weary. I think I shall rest a bit before supper."

"It has been a momentous day," he said, leading me to the turret door that led to my wing.

"Indeed."

"And one of the best of my life." He kissed my knuckles, gazing at me all the while. "I am very glad you saved my sister, Luciana. But I am deliriously happy that *you* returned as well."

"As am I."

"I remain unchanged in my desire to court you. But I shall give you a few days to find your land legs before I begin my pursuit in earnest."

"My land legs?"

He smiled. "You have been at sea, in a way. Any sailor needs a few days ashore before they are quite steady on their feet." Then he bent and gave me a short, soft kiss on the cheek, before drawing away, our hands stretched between us. "I shall see you at supper."

I turned toward the door, half sad that he hadn't kissed me on the lips, half glad. He knew. Somehow, he knew that it would rock me, when he was trying everything to steady me.

And as I really comprehended that—how he was again putting my needs ahead of his own—I fell a little more in love with him.

LUCIANA

A maidservant knocked on my door the next morning.

"Lady Ilaria wishes to see you, m'lady," she said with a brief bob of her head. "She is convalescing in the solarium."

"Thank you," I said. "I shall go at once. Might you lace me up?"

I let her in and turned so she could pull taut the laces at my back. Then she fetched my slippers and helped me slide them onto my feet like I was three years old. It was an odd time. Women were expected to do so much—the ladies of this castello so much more—and yet they also were expected to be fussed over and assisted. It didn't help that some of the clothing forced assistance. And yet there was some sweet connection in it all—this reliance on others.

There are pros and cons wherever you live, I could hear my mother say. *The important thing is to focus on the positives.*

Pulling my bodice straight and fluffing out my skirts, I gave the maid a nod and followed her out, closing my door behind me. I hurried down the hall and through the turret gate, then on down another hall, then up a turret to the second floor where the solarium was. When they were home, it was where the elder Forellis spent the majority of their time, and I could see why. Situated to absorb the afternoon sun—and yet with wide windows open to the courtyard and arrow slits on the far side that permitted good air flow—it was a pleasant place to be.

Ilaria was there, pretending to be hard at work on some embroidery, with her feet up on an ottoman, her body covered to her chest with a light blanket. I swallowed a knowing smile when I saw Nico already there, quietly conferring with Adri and Chiara in the far corner. *Of course he's already here. Didn't take him long.* But as soon as I'd closed the door and it was just us, Ilaria threw the blanket and stitchery aside and rose.

"Luciana." She took my hands in hers. "How happy am I to see you. I owe you a great deal. What you did was—"

"Nothing more than all you have done for me," I protested with a squeeze. "And how good it is to see *you* so well. You were still a bit wan yesterday."

"I feel as well as I did before it happened! But you took a terrible risk in that tomb for me."

"Just as you took a terrible risk once, remaining at Castello Fortebraccio with me." We sat down together. "I assume Lady Adri told you everything you need to know."

"Everything I can take in. I confess, 'tis a great deal."

"I understand. How much longer do you need to pretend to convalesce?"

"I must appear ready to ride on the morrow, for we shall depart for Firenze. We must take word to the Forellis of Benedetto's dire state."

"It is puzzling that we have not heard from them, especially after sending news about how Benedetto ails," Adri said. "It makes me fear the worst."

"He is no better this morning?" I asked.

"He fights to rise to consciousness," Adri returned, her eyes deeply troubled, "but cannot seem to make it to the surface. You must encourage Gabriella and Marcello to return home. Luca and Lia can see through what they must with the Fiorentini."

Ilaria reached out a hand to touch the older woman's. "If they allow them to depart."

Adri's lips thinned. "While you all are away, we shall be gathering more mercenaries and arming them for whatever comes. Tiliani insists she must go north, too, despite her parents' wishes. She feels she may aid in the negotiation, given her . . . *friendship* with Lord Paratore."

"Our best chance to free the Forellis and avoid outright war is to produce Sir Ercole . . . or at least one of the murderers in Palazzo Pubblico," Nico said. "What if Luciana and I go ahead of you? The Fiorentini do not know us as well as they do you and may not recognize us. We can disappear among the streets and tavernas, making inquiries as to where we might find Sir Ercole and his lady or their associates. With a few well-placed coins, we might make greater progress."

"And if they are not there? Or remain hidden?" Adri asked.

He shrugged. "At least we will have tried every alley."

"Men like Ercole enjoy hanging about to see the flames from fires they've set," I said. "Allow us to serve the Forellis in this manner. We can set off immediately."

"Nay. Giulio and I shall travel with you," Ilaria said. "Along with a patrol. The woods are rife with Fiorentini eager to draw Sienese blood."

I nodded, as if it didn't matter either way. Truth be told, I didn't mind the idea of traveling with Giulio Greco at my side.

"But when we reach Firenze, we shall be permitted to enter alone?" my brother pressed. "Otherwise, we might attract additional notice."

"We shall see," Ilaria said, biting her cheek, her eyes shifting as she thought it through.

"You are well used to being my companion and guard," I said

with a smile. "But remember I am fairly adept at handling myself, as is my brother. Together, we are even stronger. And this time around, we're more prepared for what might come our way."

"I shall not let her out of my sight," Nico pledged, hand to his heart. But it was Ilaria's gaze he held, never looking to me. He wanted to do this for the Forellis. Yet it was pretty clear that he wanted to do this for her too.

Chiara left to alert her brother, and Nico and I set off to pack our meager belongings. I'd need a couple of gowns to be presentable, and to find the training outfit I'd used in the woods. It might come in handy to disguise myself as a boy, making us less recognizable in the dark tavernas.

"So why don't we just bust in and *Mission Impossible* the Forellis out of there?" Nico asked under his breath.

"Because I think they want to use, ya know . . . *negotiation*, first. And because there are probably tens of thousands of Fiorentini all around where they're being held. We might bust them loose, but we'd be hard-pressed to *keep* them loose. Or ourselves." I pulled him to a stop and waited until we were alone. "Gabi told me the Fiorentini hauled her to the wall and put her in a cage for days. She almost died. It was only because Lord Greco helped Marcello and Luca and Lia free her that she got away."

He grimaced and rubbed the back of his neck. "All right, all right. I'll keep a level head and do my best to stick to our plan. But if we get painted into a corner—"

"I'll be ready to Tom-Cruise our way out with you," I finished.

TILIANI

I knew my mother and father wanted me to remain at Castello Forelli. They feared for me as their only child. But they were my only parents. And Zio Marcello and Zia Gabi were my only uncle and aunt. So I had convinced my grandmother to let me go with Giulio and the Betarrini twins. After all, 'twas I who had the inroads with the Paratores, and while my union with Aurelio was not to be, we had left on friendly terms. And Valentino? Even the idea of seeing him again made my pulse rise. I would have taken any opportunity, I admitted to myself.

Nona stopped me outside the stables. She looked as if she had been up all night.

"Nona?"

"Take care of yourself, dear one." She cupped my cheek. "I cannot bear to lose another of my loved ones."

"I shall."

She bit her lip.

"Nona. Is it Benedetto?"

She looked to the sky a moment and then to me. Her eyes were bright with tears. "We might be losing him, Tiliani. His pulse is so faint."

I frowned. "I must go to him."

"Nay. I want you to steer clear of his quarters. The last thing we need is for you to become ill too. I was foolish, allowing you to see him last night. I am . . . not thinking clearly."

I put an arm around my grandmother. "You are exhausted."

She nodded and wiped her nose with a handkerchief. "Be swift, beloved. Send his parents, his brother. Send them as quickly as you can."

Her fear made me grow cold. Benedetto might die? It seemed impossible.

A ball formed in my throat. "I shall move quickly," I promised, kissing her on both cheeks and then hugging her close. "We shall get his family home. Having them here, hearing them, shall aid his recovery."

"I pray that you are right," she said, smiling through her tears. We parted, and I walked into the stables, feeling a bit dazed.

Giulio watched me approach the stall, his face falling when he saw my expression.

"'Tis Benedetto," I said, a knot forming in my throat. "He worsens."

He nodded and set Cardo's saddle across the gelding's back. "Are you certain this is a wise decision?" Giulio asked quietly, passing Cardo's saddle strap to me as I took position to help him finish the process.

"Nay. But I do believe it is the only one I can make. To remain here would be . . . untenable. We must aid my aunt, uncle and cousin in escaping the city and returning to Benedetto's side. Mayhap if he heard their voices, he would fight harder to return to us."

"So it is only for Benedetto that you go?"

"And to hunt for Ercole."

"And?" He crossed his arms and lifted a brow.

"Very well," I said in irritation. "Would you remain home"—I glanced around to make sure none were in earshot—"knowing Luciana was elsewhere and you might see her?"

"Never," he said with a grin.

"Exactly." My friend knew what it was to long for another who might not possibly be his. But if Luciana decided to return home, she would be far further than Firenze. Did the thought of it terrify him?

I finished saddling Cardo and slid a bit into his mouth. We had packed our finery and elected to all wear plain gowns and jerkins and tunics, endeavoring to blend in along the road and secret the twins in through Firenze's gates without them being identified. We had gone as far as adding a mule loaded with carpets, crafted by a local weaver, so that when Domenico and Luciana reached the gates, they would appear as nothing more than merchants, eager to hawk their wares.

But when Luciana emerged from the stable gateway, I had to stifle a laugh. Giulio glanced past her and then did a double take.

Luciana had stuffed her long hair beneath a cap with sides that hung down and covered her ears. It was warm for the season, but it hid her hair well. She had donned my cousin's leather jerkin and tunic, which she'd borrowed for practice in the meadow, as well as someone's knee-high leather boots. If one didn't study her for more than a moment or two, they would assume she was a boy.

Giulio took her arm and pulled her deeper into the stable shadows, looking anxiously over her shoulder, then back. "Nay. This cannot be done."

She frowned and pulled her forearm from his hand. "It already has been done."

"You do not understand," he said. "'Tis a crime for a woman to masquerade as a man."

She gave him a look as if she thought he jested, but then after I gave a nod of assent, sobered. "Well then. It will be more convincing than ever that I am but a man. No one would take such a risk, right?"

Giulio's mouth dropped open.

"She is correct," I said to him, recognizing the genius stroke. "'Twill be all the more convincing. And we need every opportunity to ferret out Ercole and his woman. Mayhap she is the cleverest of us all. If I dressed the same, we would be less likely to be identified, pursued, or attacked on the road."

Giulio turned to me with a scowl. "You cannot possibly—"

"I believe I shall," I said with a grin. "Give me a moment, and I shall return in equal disguise." I finished saddling Cardo, then raced out of the stables and back to my quarters, ignoring Giulio's call.

When I returned in my costume, the three of them were mounted and ready. Ilaria too. Giulio stiffly sat atop his mount, lips clamped shut. Seeing me dressed as a man plainly made him all the more furious. Luciana gave me a half-guilty, half-jaunty smile. Mounting Cardo—so easily done in male clothing—I smiled too. This reminded me of stories my mama and aunt had told me over the years of their adventures. Of when they were young and more . . . fearless. And it made me feel better prepared to face the Fiorentini.

"Let us be off, Lord Greco," I called.

He held his mare's reins tightly as if he wished it were *us* he could rein in. "Tiliani, I beg you to reconsider this course. You already endanger yourself by going to Firenze, against your parents' wishes. Do you—"

"Giulio," I gritted out. "This might allow us to reach Firenze without harassment or attack. We cannot afford further delay. I am decided. Let us go."

He stared hard at me for a long moment, then wheeled his mare around and led the way out.

Knights to the left and right studied us, but it was with some glee that I noticed few seemed to recognize either Luciana or me. 'Twas more like they were trying to puzzle out when these new young men had arrived . . .

Captain Mancini was the first to meet my eye. He walked alongside us as we went to the gate and awaited its opening. "A She-Wolf disguised as a ram, eh?"

"Indeed," I said to him. "Better able to enter the flock." I nodded forward to Luci. "Two of us, in fact."

"Just like the old days with your mother and aunt." He broke into an admiring grin. "Go with God, m'lady. We shall be here, protecting what is yours."

"Thank you, Captain."

Others around him were catching on now, gaping at Luciana and me, half horrified, half intrigued.

The gates opened, and as we exited, Captain Mancini let out a wolf howl. When the others echoed him, I could not keep my smile from spreading across my face.

4

TILIANI

We circumvented the main roads, avoiding any Fiorentini eager to ensnare more Forellis. We then took one game trail after another northward, Giulio leading the way. Like their father had been before them, both Giulio and Ilaria were gifted trackers and able to keep their bearings in the densest forest. My cousins and I had given up playing hide-and-seek with them as children, simply because they readily found us, and when they hid, it took us hours to find them.

We formed camp that night, mayhap two hours short of Firenze, and discussed our options. I disliked the idea of the twins entering alone, and the Grecos readily agreed. We decided that Giulio and Luciana would enter her gates in the morn alongside other village merchants. Ilaria and Domenico would enter with the throngs of visitors to the city. Once inside the city, they would divide up—Giulio and Luciana concentrating on the northern side, Domenico and Ilaria on the southern. We would all reconvene that night at Palazzo Paratore—after Luciana had donned a proper gown, of course. Giulio would be less recognizable separated from me, and he had purchased a wide-brimmed hat that he wore low on his brow. He might pass as a merchant, but I worried that his famously handsome visage would be too much of a draw for tavern maids and attract others' attention in turn. He'd be more liable to be recognized among Firenze's elite and their protectors than the locals, but if there were some of Fortebraccio's mercenaries among them . . . I sighed, weary of fretting.

I suspected Giulio agreed to our plan because he wanted to be near Luciana, and yet I knew it grated at him, allowing me out of his sight. He and his sister had always been my protectors. That noted, neither of us could deny the Betarrinis' prowess in a hand-to-hand fight. On the battlefield I would still want Giulio beside me. In a taverna? The twins' particular fighting prowess would be preferable.

And while we cooked our supper over open fires, twenty-four knights from Siena arrived at our rendezvous point a half-mile distant, sent by Lord Enici to watch over me. I breathed a sigh of relief as we saw smoke rise from their fire. I would likely need every one of them.

Circled around the campfire, we each stared up through the trees in silhouette, looking to the canopy of bright stars above. "Does everyone in your time know how to fight as you do?" I asked Domenico.

"Nay," he said. "We are . . . unusual."

"In more ways than one," Giulio said dryly.

"A small portion of people in *Britannia* train as we do," Luciana said. "The method is called jiu jitsu. But few pursue it for as long as we have."

"Why not?" Giulio asked tentatively, as if reluctant to have this conversation and yet unable to ignore his curiosity. "It seems to be of good service."

"Lessons are expensive," Domenico began.

"You must pay to be trained?" he asked.

"We do. All must, unless you happen to befriend a teacher."

"Then why do not all befriend a teacher?"

"It is rather like hiring a tutor here in Toscana," Luciana explained. "We are educated for free, but we must pay for other kinds of education."

"That is odd," Giulio said.

"And we think it odd that you must pay for your education and yet you are freely taught to fight."

"Is that because you live in a more peaceable time?" I asked.

"Yes." She paused. "And no. We have peacekeepers for our streets, called police. Knights who go to fight for our countries, but we call them soldiers."

"Mercenaries?" I asked.

"Some of those too."

"So it is not so terribly different," I said.

"No. And yes." She huffed a laugh. "Some things will always be the same, I think. People, mostly. Greed and pride and fear and lust will always be among us, as will goodness and grace and kindness and peace."

"Do women dress as men in your time?" Giulio groused.

Luciana laughed softly. "More often than you would believe."

Giulio let out a dismissive noise, but it seemed only to amuse her further.

"Some men even dress as women," Domenico said.

Giulio rose to an elbow. "You jest."

"I do not."

"Do you do such a thing?"

Domenico laughed. "Nay. I do not."

That seemed to appease my friend, but he was still stiff in his actions as he lay down on his bedroll again.

"I wish I could have spent a day in your time," Ilaria said. "To see it for myself."

"I would have enjoyed showing you," Domenico said. "Except that remaining would have probably landed us in a prison cell."

"Why? Is that why they attempted to waylay us?"

"They'd rightfully claim we are trespassing. But they'd mostly want to hold on to us because we *appeared through a wall*," Domenico said dryly. "We cannot explain it, nor can they. So they would want to study us. Dissect us—as much as they could—examine our blood, our brains. Figure out how we do what we do."

"There is no magic in what you do?" Giulio asked.

"No magic," Luciana said quickly, as if to reassure him. "No incantations. We simply place our hand on the prints, and God opens a door. Just as he did for Evangelia and Gabriella and the Betarrini brothers after them."

"Seems naught but a dream." Giulio murmured. We were all weary from the long day's ride and growing sleepy.

"A very good dream," Luciana said happily.

LUCIANA

As we rode toward the giant gates of Firenze's Porta Romana and joined a queue of about two hundred people leading mules or pushing carts full of food and wares, we'd already divided into two pairs. Giulio and I entered first. My brother and Ilaria would follow behind in ten minutes. Tiliani later in the day. Nico had patted my back and whispered in my ear, "See you tonight, sis."

"Tonight," I whispered back, holding onto his hand as he tried to pull away, making him promise me.

"Tonight," he agreed, solemnly holding my gaze.

We'd all agreed this was the best plan, splitting up. But now that it was actually happening, my pulse raced. We were about to enter an enemy city of about fifteen thousand people. If our true identities were discovered, we weren't going to be able to ninja our way out of it, especially separated. But our whole goal in returning was to aid our family. And somewhere about, Sir Ercole—or someone who knew him—had to be lurking. We just needed to find him, capture him, make him confess. Then we could all hopefully depart in peace.

I walked on the far side of the mule from Giulio, as most of the other peasant pairs did before us. Horse-drawn carriages and cargo gathered before the massive central gates. Merchants and pedestrians lined up at either of the flanking smaller passageways. As we neared the stiff, irritable armed guards and secretary taking names, I was thankful that Giulio was there to speak for us. Though I was rapidly picking up medieval ways of speech, I knew the locals noticed there was something just a little off—like my accent was a bit wrong or something.

"Giulio Matanesco and my brother, here to sell carpets in the market," Giulio said.

I tensed. The secretary briefly flicked his eyes over me, the mule, then back to Giulio. "From where do you hail?"

"The village of Paterno," Giulio said.

The secretary dipped his quill again and finished the entry in his log. "See that you are out of my city by sundown, Signore Matanesco."

"We intend to spend the night with a cousin, then leave on the morrow."

"His name and street?"

Giulio gave more false information, and with a nod of approval from the secretary, we moved through the small gate and into the wider plaza beyond. I dared to take a full breath and we shared a short look. *That was the easy part,* I reminded myself.

We moved down the already-crowded street, with established merchants opening doors and shutters and setting out their wares, then past a towering cathedral and stonemasons building a new palazzo. I paused beneath a hand-carved sign with the simple word *Libreria*—knowing it was a bookstore—all the volumes likely leather-bound and in a locked cabinet on the far end. Only a single massive volume, open on an ornately carved stand in the center of the store, gave one a glimpse of the treasures that might lay inside.

Once we'd reached the market piazza, and spoken to the dismissive coordinator, we quietly set out our carpets in the chalked-off portion assigned to us, numbered XXXII. We were flanked by a basket maker with questionable skills and a woman selling chipped, secondhand pottery. Watching the clean-dressed and happy merchants toward the front and center of the plaza, we were clearly third or fourth tier, but that was fine with us. We didn't wish to draw attention.

As arranged, I picked up a woven bag and fingered the small purse at my hip, intent on making my way through the whole market as if shopping, while Giulio remained here to talk up our neighbors and any shoppers who came by. The carpets we'd brought were decent, but not top-notch. Our goal had been to attract the middle and lower class—those who might be more willing to share the local gossip with strangers. Later on, as the day faded, we would slip into the tavernas to eavesdrop, hoping to gain word of where Ercole or his men might be.

Giulio caught my eye as I departed, and I gave him what I hoped was a reassuring, small smile. I could feel his gaze as I meandered my way down the first row. I truly wasn't scared. The whole feel of the marketplace was friendly, people already bantering and laughing, others bartering.

I made minimal small talk with the merchants, pretending to be shy as I smiled at them and then ducked my head and listened in to their conversations. Some griped about the rising taxes in the city, some of which had been dumped on the street merchants. The vintners talked about the slow growth of grapes this summer, blaming it on a late spring.

I paused before a blacksmith with an impressive array of daggers, kitchen knives, and a few swords, hopeful that those who came to chat with him might be more within my target range.

"*Buongiorno,*" I greeted him, trying to sound like a man. "*Sto cercando un pugnale come regalo per mio amico.*" *I am looking for a dagger as a gift for my friend.*

The man immediately frowned and squinted his eyes as if he wasn't sure he heard me right. Then he crossed his beefy arms and looked me up and down. "Do you wish bad luck on your friend?"

It was my turn to frown. What was this? A man wasn't allowed to buy a knife for his friend? "Of course not," I returned. "But he lost his in the wood."

"Then send him to me to replace it. I shall not have any part in bringing evil spirits his way." He leaned closer to me, as if I myself wasn't the sharpest knife in the drawer. "If I did, the evil eye might turn upon *me*. Now move along. I want no part in it."

I rushed away, knowing by the heat of my face that I was blushing. Within ten minutes, I'd already blundered and attracted attention. All I'd wanted was a reason to hang around his stall, and now he'd marked me as foreign and odd. *Stellar sleuthing, Betarrini,* I said to myself. *Forget any idea of working for the CIA.*

There was a whole row of vintners with barrels of wine. It seemed that the rule was that for every ceramic growler they filled for shoppers, they poured a cup for themselves. I'd have to circle around and return when more sales had been made and their talk might be a bit looser. Safely out of view from the previous blacksmith, I stopped at another's stall. His swords were more finely wrought, his daggers accompanied by beautiful leather sheaths.

I took a deep breath and thought of Ilaria and Tiliani and how they wore a sword as a backup to their bows. "*Buongiorno.* I am in search of a short sword to wear on my back."

This middle-aged merchant, too, looked me up and down and sniffed. "You cannot afford my prices, boy."

I should have moved on. But his superior attitude irritated me. I swallowed a sarcastic retort and said meekly, "I have been saving for some time. I need a decent weapon. I intend to join my brothers in the next fight against the Sienese."

The man considered me a moment before turning to the far end of the stack of short broadswords. "If it is the Sienese you intend to fight, then I shall give you a bargain on this one." He lifted it and looked down the shaft as if admiring the plane, shining in the sun, then with a neat flick of his wrist, tossed it up and caught the tip, handing it over to me to examine.

I took hold of the leather handle, crafted for a slightly larger hand but reasonably comfortable in my own. Then, as Giulio and Ilaria had taught me, I turned it in an arc one way and then another. I flipped it to the far side, examining it further. "*Quanto*?"

He named a sum greater than what I had in my purse. Maybe he'd been right—I couldn't afford his wares. But this was also not my first time bartering in a Florence marketplace.

I gave him a doubtful look. "Come now. I could purchase this from you, or I can purchase one from your competitor across the market. Give me a fair price."

"That is a fair price, boy," he said with a superior snort.

"Nay, 'tis not. I shall give you half."

The man laughed as if I had offended him, but he was willing to overlook it. He crossed his arms and squinted at me. Then he named a sum twenty-five percent off his original demand.

I talked him down to sixty percent. "And I'll need a sheath to wear between my shoulders."

The man gave me a very hard look indeed. I refused to drop my gaze. After a moment, he glanced around and then slowly focused back on me. "Eh, the market is quiet this morning. 'Tis better to sell to you at a slight loss than to not sell at all."

I handed him the coins and settled the sword into the sheath. Now that the sale was done, he became a bit more friendly, helping me adjust the straps and the sheath between my shoulder blades. "Whom shall be your captain, boy?" he asked.

"I know not," I said honestly. "I arrived only this morn from Paterno. Whom do you recommend?"

He tapped his chin. "There are several who recruit mercenaries out of Taverna degli Assi. Go this eve and watch them for a while, see how they treat their friends and newly hired, before you enlist."

I paused. "My mother is very sick. I need to make the greatest amount possible to pay for her treatment. Who pays the best?"

He laughed and patted me on the shoulder. "You shall need far more experience before such men would consider you, pup."

He lowered his tone. "Besides, men that pay the best are either lords or those employed by lords for nefarious purposes. You want nothing to do with them."

"I understand," I said soberly, as if chastened and grateful. "I shall steer clear of them. Where do they recruit their men?"

"The southern area of town," he said, downright fatherly in his tone now. "Nay, you head farther north to Taverna degli Assi. I'd wager Adriano Sordi would be the best boss for you. He'll give you minor responsibilities in battles until you cut your teeth. Once you're a man with molars, he'll give you greater responsibilities. And he pays decently."

"*Grazie.*" I gripped his arm in thanks.

"*Prego.*" He glanced down and seemed to be taken by my arm's slender form. I was strong, but I was still a woman. "You watch yourself, *boy,*" he said, giving me a hard look as if lamenting his choice to aid me.

5

TILIANI

The Sienese knights accompanied me into the streets of Firenze. I had left most of my men behind at Castello Forelli—despite Nona's disagreement—knowing Giulio and Ilaria would be in the city with me and Benedetto unable to lead them. With every elder Forelli now in Firenze, that left our home a viable target. Thankfully, Lord Enici had also sent a hundred knights to camp about the castello, making it less appealing. I knew from their one and only missive that my family was under house arrest with Lord Russo. I turned onto Via Roma, heading to where Aurelio had described his palazzo's location. He would know how my family fared and how best to approach Lord Russo. Better yet, he might have discovered a path out of this dire situation by now.

Fourteen of his friends and comrades from Firenze had been murdered in Palazzo Pubblico more than a sennight past. Fourteen men—young and old—each with influential families and friends. Fourteen men with families and friends now bent on seeing the Forellis pay a price for those forfeited lives.

Dressed again in a proper gown, I carried a white flag myself. Moving at a trot and armed to the teeth, we passed dumbfounded knights at the gates and made our way quickly into the city. People gave way to our entourage but hissed and shouted behind us as they identified us by our Forelli gold. As we pulled to a stop beside a palazzo with the Paratore's crimson flags, I glanced back. Sienese knights toward the end of the line were getting pelted by rotten fruit. Some drew swords when the crowd surged toward them.

Sir Fiore dismounted and rammed on the door with a huge iron knocker fashioned into a dragon's head. I looked up. A tall tower extended above the main palazzo, where four stationed guards peered down at us. A fifth guard opened a tiny door in the massive gate, showing only part of his face. "Who goes there?"

"Lady Tiliani Forelli wishes to call upon Lord Aurelio Paratore," Sir Fiore said gravely.

The man drew back, visibly surprised. "I shall see if m'lord wishes to accept her." He sniffed.

I leaned forward in my saddle. "I suggest you do not dawdle, man. The Fiorentini are hassling my own, and there is bound to be bloodshed here in the streets momentarily. I doubt your master wants that right outside his door."

Someone ran up behind the guard gate and whispered something in his ear. Grimacing, he shouted, "Open the gates! Prepare to receive armed visitors!"

Without further word, he slammed the tiny door shut, and we heard the slide of a barrier rod, then the creak of the giant oak doors. I dared to take a breath, relieved that Aurelio might grant us even temporary sanctuary. I glanced back as the gates opened. Four Sienese knights now slashed downward or lifted threatening swords. Each time, the growing mob shrank back, gathered themselves, and tried again.

With relief we began filing into the courtyard, one at a time, then two as the doors opened wider. I turned and waited beside the gate until the very last man entered, the mob shouting lewd and foul names at me, lifting daggers and swords. *Murderess. Temptress. Whore.* Hate fairly dripped from them. As the gate was closed and secured again, I discovered Aurelio beside my gelding, rubbing Cardo's head.

"So much for peace between our republics, eh?" he asked wryly.

I smiled with him, relieved for a bit of levity, and accepted his help in dismounting, though I did not need it. I looked up into his green eyes, refusing to search beyond him for Valentino. "Thank you for allowing us sanctuary," I said.

"Why not?" Aurelio lifted his hands. "'Twould be difficult to further damage my reputation at this juncture." He gestured toward a hallway leading into his home.

I glanced back at Sir Fiore and the other men, who were all systematically disarmed, as expected. They would remain in the courtyard, under guard. No respectable Fiorentini—least of all Aurelio—was about to allow a takeover from within by Sienese. But I hoped they might be given access to the well at the center of the courtyard. Each carried a week's supply of dried meat and fruit in their bags, as well as a bit of bread. I needed them restored from our long ride in order to face whatever lay ahead of us. I walked beside Aurelio as we entered his home, Sir Fiore the only one allowed to accompany me.

He did not offer his arm, nor did I resent him for it. 'Twas enough to allow us sanctuary. I understood why he did not need his men to see him making anything but polite overtures. We passed a fine library and what appeared to be a small butlery. There were gorgeous tapestries on the walls.

'Twas odd to think that this once might have been my home, too, had things worked out differently. We walked through the large central hall, with a barrel-vault ceiling and numerous beautiful tables for dining, then through a narrow passageway. We then climbed up a turret, walked down a hall, and entered an intimate, luxurious meeting room. There was a low, central table, already set with a jug of wine, cups, and a wide platter with bread and cheese and fruit. Open windows allowed me a fine view of the city wall and beyond it, the green-wooded hills that climbed away from the far side of the River Arno.

I wondered again where Valentino might be. Mayhap he was on an errand. I sat down while Sir Fiore took his station beside the door, staring dead ahead as if he could not see or hear me and Aurelio.

Aurelio poured me a cup of wine and handed it to me. "Please, eat and drink. Sate your thirst. Fill your belly. You must be famished after your long ride."

"I bid you thanks, but hunger is the farthest thing from my mind." I took a sip and then set the cup aside. "Please tell me what you know of my family."

"They are well enough," he said with a sigh, settling into his soft chair and rubbing his face with both hands as if unaccountably weary. He looked me in the eye. "Trust me when I say I am doing all I can to aid them."

"And how do you fare in that endeavor?"

"I have made headway with some, but some refuse to even receive me." He took a sip of his own wine. "I must tell you that you do not aid my cause by coming to call."

I swallowed hard. Had I truly erred in coming here?

"But fear not. I shall figure out a way to spin it in our favor. I may have to claim you are begging me to reconsider our betrothal, but I will refuse you. It shall make my fellow citizens feel superior, and that might partially appease them."

I hesitated, but he plainly jested. Any hope of our nuptials uniting our republics was gone. He leaned forward, elbows on his knees. "Any luck in finding Ercole or his men? A witness?"

I shook my head. "We captured two of his men, but they were newly hired, able to tell us nothing. Ercole himself seems one with the shadows. Every time we pick up his trail, he goes to ground. But there are some who believe he might be on your very streets, eager to watch my family laid low."

Aurelio nodded in agreement. "It could be. So you are here to search for him?" He cocked his head. "I do not believe you shall get very far, dressed in your Forelli finery. I am thankful that no one shot you en route."

I thought of Luciana binding her breasts and dressing as a boy.

Mayhap she had found the only way for a woman of Castello Forelli to freely search these streets. Mayhap I should have remained in my own costume.

"I am here as an emissary for my family, backed by the might of Siena. Should anything happen to me, Firenze would bear the wrath, just as we are bearing the wrath of Firenze for your lost friends."

He gave me a rueful look. "You took a terrible risk, Tiliani. We lost some of Firenze's finest."

"I had no choice. We have not heard from our family in days and feared they are not receiving our missives. My cousin Benedetto is terribly ill. And I might bear witness at the hearing on the morrow. You and I are at the very center of this. Neither of us had any knowledge of what was about to transpire. Mayhap if I dare to testify, your Grandi shall take me at my word."

"The odds are not in your favor." He took another swig of wine.

"And yet at least there are odds." I thought back to my conversation with Luciana.

Ercole will not be able to stay away, she'd said. *And if you are there too? Daring to march right down the street and into the heart of the city? He'll take it like a slap to the face. He will arrive as fast as a shark to blood-filled waters. And we will be there, waiting for him to surface.*

I prayed she was right.

LUCIANA

Giulio trailed me, maybe ten people between us. I took to pausing at each corner, making certain he could keep track of my progress. Because as much as I wanted to blend in and not be seen, I also didn't want to lose him. *Good grief, I'm already so far from Nico . . .* the thought of Giulio not having my back sent a little shiver of panic down my neck.

I paused and took a deep breath, remembering my training. *I'm strong. I'm a good fighter. And I'm smart.* I undoubtedly had ten times the education most of these people around me had. But then they were medieval-street-savvy like nobody's business.

Ahead, men and a couple of women entered and exited Taverna degli Assi, if I was reading the soot-smudged sign right. I pushed my way inward, then after letting my eyes adjust to the dim light, edged my way to the bar.

The portly man behind it poured twelve ceramic cups in a line full of wine, not stopping, just letting it splash between—surprisingly, not spilling much. When he got to the end, men cheered and slid a coin across the bar in exchange for one. I fished out a coin of my own and, at next pass, took a cup and then slowly eased past one table and then another, eavesdropping on conversations.

It didn't take long to know Tiliani had arrived—"marching as bold as you please up to Palazzo Paratore." Apparently, Aurelio had taken her and her knights in, which didn't sit well with the locals.

I stood at the far wall, no longer able to linger without attracting attention, sipping on my wine. Giulio had arrived, and it was his turn to take a cup. He casually looked around, but never in my direction. I tried not to look his way, but having him in the same room comforted me.

"*Stai cercando lavoro, ragazzo?*" said a man as he came to rest beside me. *Are you looking for work, boy?* "I saw you meandering about the tables, among the bosses."

So much for my skills at covert intel. And this was a room full of bosses? "*Nay, sto cercando qualcuno.*" *No, I'm looking for someone.*

"And who is that?"

"Someone to whom I owe a debt. His name is Ercole. He travels with a woman."

The middle-aged man eyed me a moment. "I know of this man. What do you owe him?"

"My gratitude and mayhap my service."

The man pursed his lips and nodded. "You wish to try your hand as a squire, then? A knight such as Andrea Ercole rarely hires anyone other than seasoned mercenaries."

I latched on to the idea. "If he would allow me to be of service."

The man drained his cup. "You are old for such a position. But mercenaries are oft not in the best position to pick and choose." He clapped me on the shoulder. "'Tisn't a bad idea. More than one boy from this city has made it to greater wealth and glory, beginning as a squire. Head to Coquinarius on Via Santo Spirito. His kind is more likely to frequent that taverna and those around it, rather than the working men here."

"*Grazie mille*," I said, as he moved back toward the bar for another cup. I paused a moment, not wanting to look overeager—and to give Giulio a chance to glance my way—before I shoved off the wall and made my way to the door.

A hard hand grabbed my arm, and I tensed, narrowly resisting the urge to wristlock him. I glanced down at this other man, who swayed on his stool. Six empty cups were stacked on the table before him. "*Ho bisogno di qualcuno che trasporti il rock domani*," he slurred. *I need someone to haul rock tomorrow.* "You look like a strong boy," he went on. "You need work, right?"

I hesitated. If tonight didn't pan out, it might be a good cover, and a chance to learn more town gossip. "Where and what time?"

"Piazza Santa Croce, *alba*." *Dawn.*

"I am off to find a lord and ask to be his squire," I said. "But if he denies me, I shall see you in the piazza. *Grazie.*"

"Eh," he said, waving me off. "Just like all the rest. So eager to give your life in battle! With masonry work, we build instead of destroy."

"True. I shall think on it."

I continued making my way outward and saw Giulio had been watching our exchange. He looked away, letting me pass behind him without turning his head.

Out on the street, it was getting busier, everyone finished with work now. Men and women were strolling together before supper, stopping to talk with friends. People milled in and out of the tavernas and the finer osterias. Some stopped at tiny bars for a small glass of wine and a bite of bread and cheese, then moved on.

I asked a woman the way to Via Santo Spirito, and she pointed to my left. "Up to the next corner, then turn left, then take your first right." I thanked her and moved on, hoping that Giulio was out of the taverna by now and following. Men moved down the street, setting ablaze one torch after another, replacing those too burned down to reignite. The flickering light cast ghostly shadows and I rubbed my arms, feeling the sudden, surprising evening chill.

But as I turned left at the corner, I felt a wave of *heat* wash over me.

Because directly ahead of me—three people between us—was Sir Ercole and his female companion, Rosa.

6

LUCIANA

I hesitated a moment, shocked, remembering that fateful night in Siena when Nico and I pursued them, and I ended up clotheslined on the ground. I'd narrowly escaped with my life. Just the memory of it made me pause and rub my neck.

"You are attracting attention," Giulio whispered as he passed me, clearly having spotted them too.

I grimaced and slowly set out after him, letting him get ahead of me and more people between us. I could no longer see Ercole—I hoped he could. Giulio took a right and I followed.

Ercole gripped Rosa's arm and appeared to be dragging her along. They turned the corner. Evening shadows couldn't cover Rosa's black eye. Torches revealed her tears. Lips curled, Ercole leaned down and ferociously whispered into her ear. Then he shook her a little, looking about as if worried he'd be seen.

They didn't enter the taverna with the carved sign that said Coquinarius. Rather they went through an unmarked door—after glancing left and right again—toward the end of the block. Giulio had disappeared between us, perhaps because he feared Ercole would identify him. Our adversary looked right at me and then beyond. I tugged my hat further down on my head and walked past his doorway as if I were heading elsewhere, not daring to look inside. Had he left it cracked open? Had he been watching?

I turned into the next alleyway and waited for Giulio to come.

When he barreled into the small space, I took a relieved breath, but when he forcefully hustled me deeper into the alley, I got scared.

"Giulio!" I whispered, yanking my arm from his grasp. "What is wrong?"

I couldn't see his face in the dark, but I could see his stance in silhouette, felt his fury. "You," he growled, leaning closer, "are dressed as a man, but you are still plainly a woman!"

"Wh-what?"

"On the street," he spit out in a whisper. "Touching your neck, the way you asked directions—from another woman, rather than a man. Back with the blacksmith, allowing him to see your slim wrist. At least three or four have already identified you as potentially female. If the wrong one does, they could haul you to prison. And I could not get to you there, Luciana."

He *feared* for me. That's what drove his anger. He was scared I'd be taken and he could do nothing to stop it. And I figured that prison would be the very last place I wanted to be in medieval times.

"Very well." I lifted my chin and folded my arms. "I made a couple of mistakes. It shall not happen again. But did you see Ercole? We cannot remain here! What was that door? What if he is slipping away even now?"

"He is not slipping away," he said, tiredly rubbing his face. "That was the servant's entrance to Palazzo Vanni."

I stilled. "Palazzo *Vanni*?"

He nodded and glanced over his shoulder as a drunken man turned into the mouth of the alley and relieved himself, never looking our way.

"But Lord Vanni was one of the victims at Palazzo Pubblico," I said slowly, remembering the name.

"His son was." He rubbed his temples now and paced. "Which begs the question—was Ercole in his employ before? Or did his family hire him afterward? Was he an accomplice in a greater intrigue that fateful night?"

"Can we slip inside ourselves? See what the servants are gossiping about?"

"Nay," he said. "'Tis too great a risk. I cannot go in there. Ercole would know me with but a glance."

"But not me, dressed as I am. The last time I saw him, I was in a gown."

He paused.

"Here." I grabbed a crate of rotting onions that had been thrown into the alley. I turned a few, bringing the best sides to the surface. They were pretty bad, but maybe if no one looked too closely . . . "I could go to the door with a 'special delivery for the cook.'"

"No respectable cook would accept those."

"Nay. But I shall disappear into the halls before I see her," I said.

He crossed his arms. "So you would walk directly into the lion's den."

I turned a few more onions. "If you do not enter the den, you cannot hear them growl and purr. And tonight is critical for the Forellis. If we do not find out what's really happening here, they might find they are on their way to the gallows, right?"

He clenched his teeth. I knew it terrified him, thinking of me inside without him.

I perched the crate on my hip and reached out and put a hand on his forearm. "I can fight, remember? They shall not take me."

He looked down at me and let a humorless laugh escape through his nose. "There 'tis again," he said, gesturing angrily toward me. He leaned closer and whispered, "Men do not have hips."

I bit my lip and cocked a brow. "Noted." I shifted my load and attempted to pass him before I lost my nerve.

But he blocked me with one arm.

Slowly, I looked up into his face.

"I shall give you a quarter hour. After that, I shall pound on the door, demanding to know if anyone has seen a street rat pretending to be an onion delivery boy."

"But what if Ercole is there? What if he sees you?"

"I do not care, Luciana. You are my charge. *You*," he said, more softly, bringing a knuckle beneath my chin. "If it comes between deciding between you and capturing Ercole, I shall choose *you*, trusting that God will show us another way to deal with *him*."

"Then I best get in, get what we need, and get out."

"Indeed."

I considered him. "Give me half an hour. It might take me a quarter hour to even reach those inside."

"Nay," he grunted.

I took his hand. "You put me in greater danger, should you burst in. That should be our last resort. Give me half an hour."

I left him before he could think better of this plan. Or I talked myself out of it. I had no idea how he was going to count the minutes—no one had a watch in this era—but I decided he had been speaking figuratively. While they had few clocks, everyone seemed to be more attuned to the daily rhythms of life, and therefore the passage of time.

At the edge of the alley, I looked at my onions and grimaced. In the torchlight, I could see they were riddled with mold and maggots. I picked up a disgusting, discarded handkerchief from the ground and cracked it open, doing my best to spread it across the vegetables, while praying I wasn't picking up some horrible medieval plague.

Down the street, I paused at the back door to Palazzo Vanni, fighting a dry mouth, then distantly watched as I lifted the heavy, circular knocker. I dropped it twice, as I'd seen Ercole do, then stepped back and angled myself against the nearest torch, hoping to cast my crate in deeper shadow.

This time, I remembered to hold it directly before me, rather than perch it on my hip. I hoped Giulio noted that I was a fast learner.

A haggard, middle-aged servant came to the door and looked at me askance. "What is it, boy?"

"Delivery for the cook," I said, lifting my crate slightly. "She sent word she was in need of more onions right away."

He frowned, paused, then turned sideways. "Very well. In with you, then. I must return to the master at once. Make haste."

I scurried inside and paused, waiting as he turned and bolted the door, then closed an additional barrier and bolted that as well. I fought to keep my shoulders loose, to not bite my lip. I remembered how my coach taught me not to let my opponents know I feared anything by keeping the expression on my face neutral.

"You know the way to the kitchens?" he asked, pushing me a little ahead of him. "I do not think I have seen you before."

"Nay. I am new to town, taking this position only three days past."

"Hmm. Turn left here. A right at the end. You shall see the kitchen then. A kitchen maid shall see you out."

"*Grazie*," I said with a bob of my head as we paused before a corner candelabra. I moved down the hall before he could take a proper look at my crate. I could hear the muffled sounds of conversation, but I never paused, aware that the man watched me go. I had to appear as if I had one mission and one only—to deliver these onions.

Two men turned the corner ahead of me—guards—but they barely looked at me as I passed. I turned, relieved no one else was in view for the moment. At the far end, women and men in the kitchen were in the throes of cooking supper. A maid came out with a tray and turned to her left, never seeing me. With luck, I could drop my crate and then slip away. Passing a torch, I grimaced again. The cloth atop the onions was smeared with grease, grime, and a substance I didn't care to really think about further. And the onions . . .

Hurriedly, I set the crate down in the corner of the hall and looked in the direction the maid had gone with the tray. Was it destined for Ercole and his companions?

"Who are you?" A female servant paused in the doorway with another tray, this one with a jug of wine and six goblets made out of real glass—a rarity in this era.

"Delivery boy, miss," I said, with a slight bow. "I came with onions." I gestured back toward my crate.

"Well remain right here. Cook will notice you in a minute and come and pay you."

I thanked her, and she went on her way. I quietly slipped out of view, watching as she walked halfway down another hall and turned left. Kitchens were typically toward the back. Was that a central drawing room? Their Great Hall?

The cook shouted at an underling for burning the soup. The last thing I needed was to face a harried, irritated superior with those disgusting onions . . . so I set off with a decided step, trying not to look as hurried or scared as I felt.

TILIANI

Even I could admit Palazzo Paratore was lovely. In classic fashion, it stood four stories tall, each wing open to a courtyard with an ornately carved stone well at the center. On the far side, a formidable tower climbed into the darkening sky. In the corner was the wide entry to a neighboring stable and quarters for the knights, large enough to accommodate half my knights. Half of them would remain awake anyway, ready to answer my call, rotating with the others through the hours of the night.

Aurelio had sent me to the courtyard, not wishing me to be present when ten of the Grandi arrived to call, obviously alarmed when hearing word that I had come. I had reluctantly agreed, eager for the opportunity to convince any willing Fiorentini to hear our side of the story, to understand that the last thing I had wanted to happen was this . . . and that my parents, aunt, uncle, and cousin should not be kept from leaving. But I also understood that Aurelio knew his people—and their current mood—better than I.

Trust that the Lord shall make a way for you, when the moment is right, Father Giovanni had counseled right before I departed.

Please, Lord, do make a way for at least one of us to speak the truth. And give them willing ears to hear. I touched the nearest beautifully carved granite archway that helped form a cloister around the courtyard. On the ceiling above were ornate frescoes, bucolic scenes from the countryside. Birds and deer. Green hills and castellos. Round and round I walked, waiting for Aurelio to summon me again. We had not yet had our supper. Would the visitors remain all night? When could he take me to my family?

"Lady Forelli," a man said from the shadows. He moved quietly toward me, and when he reached the light, my breath caught.

Valentino.

I glanced past him, then over my shoulder. We were not alone. Men stood in groups of two and three all about the courtyard. I returned my gaze to him, endeavoring to look unaffected. "Captain Valeri."

He perused me from head to shoulder, and I felt his gaze like a caress. "You are well, m'lady?" he asked softly. He gestured forward, indicating that we should walk, perhaps to get me farther out of earshot from the closest men.

"As well as I might, considering my loved ones are languishing as Fiorentini prisoners."

"I hear they are under house arrest with Lord Russo. It could be worse."

"I fear it might soon become worse, should not the hearing go as it ought." I pulled to a stop. "They are innocent, Valentino," I whispered, resisting the urge to reach out to him. "They had nothing more to do with the bloodbath than I myself did."

"I believe you," he said, his solemn gaze a pledge.

I longed to fling myself into his arms. To feel the warmth of his chest. The reassurance of his steady heartbeat beneath my cheek. But I did not have to look around to know we had drawn more than a few men's attention.

"And yet surely you knew, m'lady," he asked gently, "that your presence here would only exacerbate tensions."

"I had little choice," I said. "I had to deliver a message to my family. And we believe Sir Ercole—the same man who brought the wrath of Perugia down upon us—was instrumental in the murders of your countrymen too."

We resumed our walk. "It seems an extreme measure," he said. "Even for a man such as he. Vengeance was clearly served after setting your house up against Perugia. Lord and Sir Forelli suffered greatly. The castello and her people did too. Surely that was enough to satiate his need to right the scales."

"Agreed. Unless he is a madman."

He lifted a brow and tucked his hands behind his back. "You think he has been pressed to madness?"

"How else would one explain it? He intimated that he anticipates gaining from all of this. And yet we cannot decipher *how* he might gain financially, unless he is receiving funds in exchange for his efforts. But then who might pay him? The Perugians lost patrols, and many more in the battle."

He paused for a moment as if considering how candid he wished to be. "Do the Forellis have enemies in Siena? Those who would like to see you displaced? Or Sir Luca's position with the Nine usurped?"

His words were like a slap to my face. The Sienese? I resisted a quick, defensive retort. At this point, all potential answers to our dilemma deserved examination. Not everyone in Siena was as close as kin to us, of course. There were some who vied for power, others who disliked the Forellis' propensity toward quick decisions. Still others who resented our cellars and barns, stacked high with barrels of wine, wheels of cheese, and ample hay for our cattle. But after several bountiful years, were not all better off?

I remembered Stefano Rondelli, Flavio Bartolini, and Andrea Donati the night of the ball. Cornering me and questioning me. Was not Flavio's family better off in times of war, given that they made their fortune on arrowheads and armory?

I turned toward the well and grabbed for the dipper, suddenly unaccountably thirsty. Had we looked among our own for such explanation? My father and uncle, mother, aunt, and cousin had left, steadfastly determined to represent Sienese innocence. But had they departed before really differentiating friends from enemies?

Valentino hovered beside me. "M'lady? Did something occur to you?"

"Indeed. I need to speak to my family. Might I see Fortino, if not the elder Forellis?"

"As I understand it, you may see them all. They simply must not leave Palazzo Russo."

I nodded my head. "Can your men take me to him?" I asked. "If Aurelio approves it?"

"Of course," he said.

"Then let us go to him at once."

7

LUCIANA

I moved down the hallway, head up, as if I had nothing to hide—when everything in me wanted to scurry along, hovering periodically in the shadows. I forced myself to maintain my pace as voices rose, and I spotted two guards ahead, on either side of a closed door.

"Who are you?" asked one, as I heard a man shout inside the closed-off room.

"Only a delivery boy," I said.

"Where are you going?"

I forced myself to pause. "I am seeing myself out, sir. The maids and cook are busy getting supper finished for m'lord and his guests." I dropped my tone, relieved that I seemed to be going in the right direction to exit and they didn't doubt me. "It smells quite delicious. There is roast hen and boiled turnips and more than one meat pie, from what I could see." I kicked the ground, summoning my inner Oliver Twist. "Do you think if I wait around, they might give me scraps afterward?"

The nearest guard sniffed. "This is not an almshouse. Be on your way, boy. But be certain someone is there to lock the door behind you. If not, return to us."

"Yes, sir." I turned to go. At the end of the hall, I veered right, knowing I'd made it around the perimeter of the house and the back door was this way. But I doubled back through an interior servant's hallway, hoping it might lead toward the Great Hall, where the men were meeting—and arguing.

I bit my lip. More than five minutes had surely gone by. Ten? Admittedly, it felt like more than an hour, and I fought the desire to flee. But I had made it this far.

Hearing the creak of a step, I backed up and hid partially behind a door and partially behind a tapestry. A manservant passed by with a thickly padded, embroidered chair, barely making it through the doorway. I watched through the crack as he opened another door—disguised to look as but one panel in the next room—and entered, leaving it open behind him. I followed him, glad no candles burned in these interior rooms. But ahead, light streamed through an ornate panel of latticework. I edged toward it and gazed into the hall, where six men gathered by the fire, four in chairs, two standing.

"Ahh, Santino, *grazie mille*," said an older man, hand to his lower back. "My rheumatism fairly demands a softer perch these days," he said apologetically to his companions.

A man rose and pulled his chair wider in order to make room for the new chair.

Sir Ercole.

I gasped, and he immediately glanced in my direction. I whipped to the side wall. Had he heard me? Or had it been happenstance? Was he coming my way, even now?

I tensed and eased around to peek, this time taking care to be out of the light from the room and in the shadows of the room behind me. Ercole was sitting down again, but the butler-dude headed my way. In terror, I glanced around, looking for a place to hide. It was maybe six-by-six, apparently a servant's station to either deliver or collect food and plates. At the last second, I scrambled to sit on the far side of a table, pulling my knees in tight and ducking my head.

Thankfully, Santino paused only to shut the door and then went on his way, leaving me in the dark. I rose and bent to rub my trembling knees. I was right where I wanted to be—in place to hear their conversation. But would I be able to hear anything over the thunder of my own heart? And how long before Giulio came tearing inside after me?

Please, wait, I thought, knowing it was crazy, thinking I could somehow *will* him to wait. *Please, Lord,* I prayed. *Please make him wait. Tell him to trust me.*

Maybe, maybe if God had truly been the one to send me here, now, he was listening. And if he knew I was trying to help, he'd make a way for me. *Oh, and once I hear what I need, help me escape?*

I steadied my breathing and tried to quiet my thoughts in order to concentrate on their conversation. They spoke in undertones, as if wary, until a point of contention arose. I rose and dared to peek inward again.

"Press for death, I say," said a man, slapping his fist into the palm of his other hand. "A life for a life! Siena would still owe us a debt!"

"They came freely," said another. "Unarmed and with their heir, as a sign of their good intentions. They have been steadfast in their claims that they knew nothing about it."

"Trust me when I say they knew," Ercole put in.

"What evidence have you?"

"None as of yet," he gritted out, "but fair little occurs in Siena or her territories without a Forelli having a hand in it."

Wait, what? They had hired *him* to dig up dirt on the Forellis?

"The hearing is on the morrow. Where are your witnesses? You have already been discredited by the Forellis. There must be more to back up your story."

"I have received word that two men are due to arrive this very night from Perugia."

"Two is good," said a man. "Ten would be better."

"I could find another ten . . ." Ercole led suggestively.

"Nay," said Lord Vanni, identifiable by the color of his tunic. "I want justice for my son. Not a setup. *Justice.* And if a Forelli is put to death, the Sienese will have to be presented irrefutable evidence. To date, all is circumstantial."

Put to death? I thought this was a hearing!

Ercole sat back and shrugged. "If my two witnesses are not enough, then it is out of my hands. But if they are, and the Forellis are hanged, you all must follow through on your promise. The castello shall be mine. You know by rights it *should* be mine."

The castello? Castello Forelli? That would be his reward?

Their tones dropped again, and I leaned closer to the lattice, hoping to catch more of their conversation. My hand was sweaty, and as I leaned, it slipped on the polished wood of the table, making an odd, squeaking sound. Ercole rose, staring my way as I slipped backward into the shadows. *Time to go.*

He moved across the marble floor toward my hiding place, even as I searched for the knob in the dark.

"Andrea, 'tis only a servant," said a tired lord behind him.

"Then it shall take only a moment to make certain you are correct," he said. "Who is there? Come out!"

I closed the door behind me, just as he opened his, and hoped it would have disguised the sound of the latch. I backed up slowly, praying he didn't come through the second door. I looked left and right for the best avenue of escape, when firm hands grasped my shoulders.

"You! What are you doing here?" asked one of the guards.

Another came my way from the left, scowling. It was the one that I'd promised I was just seeing myself out. Worse, the doorknob before me jostled. Ercole was coming through.

"Gotta go," I muttered in English, turning to grab the man's wrist behind me, then twisting my body to throw him over my shoulder. He landed on his back with an audible *oooph*, blocking Ercole's door. I took off, praying it was the way toward an exit. *Front door, back door, any door. I just need a way out.*

The other guard shouted and tore after me, Ercole hollered an alarm, and a minute later, the whole palazzo was on alert. I ran down the central hall, but four armed knights headed my way, all with swords in hand.

Okay, the front door is out.

I barreled back, turned a corner, and then spotted the stairs.

They wouldn't expect me to go up. They'd search the main floor first, suspecting I'd try and get out.

But as I took them two at a time, my heart sank. There wasn't going to be any escape through a second-story window. This was a medieval palazzo, designed for defense. If there was going to be a window, it'd be three or four stories up, and likely fortified, so it'd take some time to open . . . plus, what was I going to do then, rappel down with a bedsheet?

Men clambered up the stairs behind me. I ducked into the first room I found, closing the door with the quietest click possible, and then eased the lock into place.

"Who are you?" demanded a feminine voice.

I whirled, eyes wide. *Oh, no. No, no, no . . .*

She was maybe fourteen or fifteen. I had little choice. I went to my knees and clasped my hands and mouthed the words, *"Per favore,"* shaking my head. *Please.* *"Misericordia,"* I whispered, as a guard tried her knob and then knocked hard on the door. *Mercy.*

Then I did the only thing I could that might tip the scales. I pulled off my hat and let my long hair fall to my shoulders.

The girl's eyes grew wide, and she looked from me to the door and back again.

"M'lady! Are you in there?"

"I will not harm you!" I whispered. "I need only to escape. I have stolen nothing!" I showed her my empty pockets.

"M'lady!"

"I am here!" she called, staring into my eyes. "'Tis only me and . . . my maid!" She moved to the door. "We are frightened! I shall keep the door locked until you return to me and tell me all danger has passed."

"So be it," grunted the man outside. "Do not let anyone in but a house guard, m'lady."

"As you say."

She turned to me, looking a bit ashen, eyes wide. "Who are you?" she whispered. "If they do not chase you as a thief, what have you done?"

Oh yeah, that.

That . . . was going to be hard to explain.

TILIANI

Aurelio would not allow us to go alone. He insisted that four of my men, as well as four of his own, accompany me, including Captain Valeri.

"M'lord, we would likely blend in far better if it was only your captain and me," I tried.

"M'lady," he said, giving me a rueful smile. "By now, there is not a Fiorentini in the city who is not aware that the youngest She-Wolf has come to call." He shook his head and dropped my hand to rub his forehead. "Nay, if you wish to reach Palazzo Russo unmolested, kindly do as I ask." He snapped his fingers, and a maid hastened forward. "Find the lady a plain house dress and cloak, so she might not be so. . . noticeable."

"There are some in the city who already demand that you should be placed under arrest, along with the rest of your family." Valentino faced me with Aurelio, every inch of him the commanding captain of the guard. "You must deliver your message and then make your way home at once."

"Do they not realize we could have *all* remained safely at home?" I asked. "That our mere presence here is a testament to our goodwill?"

"Some do," Aurelio said with a heavy sigh. "Even as others purport that you play on our own goodwill. Pretend to be innocent by taking this bold stance."

I clenched my fists, frustrated. I wanted to blame the Fiorentini as narrow-minded, failing to see truth for what it was. But I knew if the situation were reversed—if fourteen Sienese had been murdered on Aurelio's watch—my fellow citizens would likely react very much the same.

"Our only chance," I said, "is to find Ercole. And mayhap if word reaches him that I am about on the streets, he will come to see it for himself. Find me. Stir up further trouble."

Valentino nodded. "If he dares to show his face, we could capture him. Force him to confess his duplicity."

"If we are right in assuming he is behind all of this," Aurelio grunted. "But I am loath to use Lady Tiliani as bait. See to it that she is closely guarded all the way there. And arrange for four more of our men to follow behind in pairs. None of you should be dressed in Paratore or Forelli tunics, but rather common clothes. Those who follow shall come to your aid if something untoward transpires."

"Yes, m'lord," Valentino nodded. "'Tis a wise course."

"None of this is wise," Aurelio grumbled, running an agitated hand through his hair.

A footman arrived, announcing the arrival of two new guests, so we took the opportunity to slip away and down the stairs.

"Is Palazzo Russo far?" I asked, taking Valentino's offered arm. "Shall we fetch horses?" I tried not to get too distracted by the fact that I was *touching* him. Touching *Valentino*, smelling his clean scent of leather and linen again, as I had longed for ever since we parted.

"Nay," he returned. "'Tis but a few blocks. I think we shall attract less attention and move faster if we are on foot."

I readily agreed, wishing again that we could go alone. The city seemed as if she were teeming with cats ready to pounce on the first mouse to cross their path, the air charged with a mix of hungry anticipation and pain-fueled, righteous anger.

He led me to a guest wing of the palazzo, each room with its door open, pristine, and prepared. "The maid shall come to you with the plain dress and cloak. I shall go and change as well, find the men I wish to accompany us, and meet you in the courtyard shortly. Agreed?"

I nodded, hating that this was all so *formal*, while at the same time hating my girlish fantasies of him taking me in his arms and claiming a kiss, as he had on the rooftop in Siena. He turned to go.

"Valentino," I dared, reaching to gently take his hand and stop him.

He paused as if I had struck him, then looked over his shoulder. Down his arm, to our intermingled fingers. Then slowly, ever so slowly, up my arm, my neck, to finally meet my gaze.

"We cannot," he whispered, his tone ragged, turning. He tore his eyes away, glancing down the hall in either direction, plainly alarmed that we might be seen.

I dropped his hand, my own palm awash with sweat now. What had I been thinking? Of course we could not pursue this now, here.

Not with everything else that was happening. Mayhap not ever.

He was Aurelio's captain. More a brother than friend. And I was . . . Sienese. His republic's reviled enemy. Today, more so than ever.

I turned to enter the room, concentrating solely on escaping my mortification.

"M'lady," he said, misery in his eyes, stepping toward me as I began to shut the door.

I shook my head, the heat of a terrible blush on my cheeks, a lump in my throat. "Say no more, Captain." I forced a small, close-lipped smile and a nod in his direction. "The courtyard, shortly?" I managed.

He drew back a step and, as instructed, said nothing more. Only pivoted on his heel and strode down the hall. But I watched him through the crack before closing the door, not wanting to miss a moment, even if he did not wish the same with me.

At the end, I saw him clench his fists, draw to a stop, and look up at the ornately painted ceiling above as if seeking God's counsel. When he turned to glance back toward my door, I let it close with a quiet click. But as I leaned my forehead against it, I smiled, even as tears rolled down my cheeks.

While we were still outwardly apart, we were still inwardly *together*. He clearly felt the pull between us as much as I did.

But the question remained. How were we ever to bridge the divide?

8

LUCIANA

The girl stared at me, hands on her hips, waiting for my explanation.

Honesty. That was the word that flashed through my brain. My only hope.

Slowly, I rose and took a step back with my hands cupped, wanting her to know I would not harm her. "I am Luciana Betarrini," I whispered.

"Betarrini," she repeated slowly, frowning. "From *Siena*?"

I nodded. "I am chasing a man we believe is responsible for the deaths in Palazzo Pubblico. He and a woman were there that night. And now that man is downstairs, speaking with your . . . father?"

Her frown deepened and she bit her cheek. "Why should I believe you?"

I lifted my hands higher. "Why else would I be here? I am desperate to exonerate the Forellis, as well as any others who have been wrongly accused."

"My brother died that night," she whispered, tears gathering in her pretty eyes.

"And for that, I am terribly sorry." I remembered it well. I had been outside with Giulio when the assassinations took place, but I had heard the screams, the shouts. Seen the bodies. And this, this was the sister of the young man who had died, the youngest of the fourteen slain. "It should not have happened. I beg you to believe me when I say the Forellis had nothing to do with it. They wanted only to build a bridge between Siena and Firenze. But others wished to tear it down."

She stared at me. "My brother wanted that too. He was so hopeful—hopeful that it meant something would change for us. But now my father . . ."

I nodded. "He is understandably enraged." I dared to take a step closer. "But that man downstairs—Sir Ercole—had something to do with it. Do you know why he has come?"

She shook her head. "I was dismissed and sent to my room as soon as he arrived."

"Where is the woman who came with him?"

"She appeared injured. She was sent to the guest quarters to convalesce while the men conversed."

Injured? So I *had* seen a black eye.

"She was crying."

"When she arrived?"

"Nay. Moments ago."

Now I was seriously confused. "How do you know?"

She wrung her hands a moment, then decidedly moved to a trunk and opened it. "These were my sister's, when she was about your size." She glanced back at me, then back to the clothes within. Seconds later, she handed me a plain day dress. "Make haste. Put this on and I shall see to your hair. If you are to escape the palazzo, you must appear as I claimed . . . my maid."

I ducked behind a screen and hurriedly pulled off the tunic and shirt but left the braies on beneath my skirt. If push came to shove, I could unlace the skirt and leave it behind me in a fight. The bodice was a bit big, thankfully—nothing like the one I'd been assigned at Palazzo Fortebraccio. This one at least gave me room to breathe. And fight.

Part of me still couldn't believe I'd lucked out and found this girl—anyone, really—willing to help me. But then I'd seen it in her eyes. She had believed in the whole build-a-bridge dream, like the Forellis and Aurelio Paratore had. Part of her *still* believed in it.

I came around the screen, and she handed me a brush, which I rapidly pulled through my hair, while she laced up my bodice from behind. "What is your name?" I whispered, hearing another couple of men run by her door.

"Simona," she said. "Sit."

I did as she directed, and with expert hands, she quickly braided and pinned my hair into a neat knot at my neck.

"Come." She moved to the corner of her room. There, she pressed on a panel, and a secret door popped open.

My mouth dropped open in surprise. This, this was how she knew about Rosa crying. "Servant's entrance?" I asked.

She nodded, looking grim. I could tell that she was torn—wondering if she was aiding either a friend of her brother's killer, or the one that was truly trying to find the guilty. I followed her into the narrow passageway, and we moved along the edge, passing peepholes that I assumed peered into each room. At the corner she paused, glanced back at me, and then pushed.

We emerged inside a lovely corner bedroom with an ornate four-poster bed on the far side, a woman tied to one of them. She startled, alarmed by the squeaking door. Her cheek bore the mark of a slap, and now I could clearly see her eye was horribly bruised and swollen shut. "Who—what—" she said.

Simona shushed her with a finger to her lips, and we drew closer.

"You," Rosa said, forehead wrinkling in fear as she recognized me. "You are from Siena."

"Yes," I said. "The night you tried to kill me."

Simona glanced back and forth between us, surprised and alarmed now.

"But," I whispered, gesturing toward the leather strap that bound her, "I am guessing we now share a common adversary. Was it Andrea Ercole who so abused you?"

She ducked her head, as if she'd forgotten about it until now. "He-he did not mean to hit me hard."

I swallowed my rage. "That he hit you at all was a poor decision. What was his . . . reasoning?" *Excuse*, was what I *wanted* to say.

"I misspoke. Questioned his coming here." She glanced to the window, through which we could see the dome of a neighboring church. "I thought we had done enough. Made you and the Sienese suffer enough. I wanted only to be away from here. From both Siena and Firenze. But he had other plans."

"Why did he tie you?" I asked. "Was he afraid you would run?"

She nodded, head ducked again. "He fears that I shall share the truth. This close to the hearing . . . he cannot risk it."

This was it. If we could not capture Ercole, Rosa might exonerate the Forellis on her own. But I knew women in abusive relationships were often tangled up in their thoughts and emotions.

"Men like him," I said, daring to untie her, "do not act in a loving manner, regardless of how they feel. If he has hit you once, he shall hit you again."

She frowned and looked at me with her one good eye. She did not defend him as I expected. There was doubt within her already, just as there had been hope in Simona.

"Rosa, do you know why he is here?" I asked.

Simona reached for a ceramic goblet of water on the bedside table and handed it to Rosa. She drank thirstily. "He wishes to collect from both sides."

"Both sides?"

"He pretends to be an ally to both Perugia and Firenze, offering to help both bring down the family that stands between. The Forellis."

Perugia. "And you went along with him on this?"

She gave me a doleful look. "He said he loved me."

"As he did the other maid he accosted at Castello Forelli?" I asked her, my voice hard. I had to give her a dose of reality. She was still wavering. And I needed this girl to come with me. Now.

"She was nothing to him." Rosa sniffed, lifting her chin.

"But this"—I gestured toward her eye—"is how he treats the one he *truly* cares about?"

She grimaced as if I had hit her, and then her lips trembled, and the tears began again. "Mayhap not. Mayhap he never truly cared about me." She shook her head slowly, glancing from me to Simona. "But I have done terrible things for him. Terrible things," she repeated, her voice cracking.

"You were misguided." I reached for her hand. "Deluded. Ercole is clever and evil, used to getting anything he wants. But you can help us." I knelt beside her, still stubbornly holding her hand when she tried to pull away. "You can help us clear the Forellis' name and bring him to justice."

She swallowed hard. "I do not know . . ."

"The first thing is to help you escape so he can never harm you again." I rose. I had to force her to move before she got sucked back into the Ercole Vortex. She was the key to this whole, complex puzzle! "Come with me. Lord Greco is outside, waiting to aid us. Simona, you have a way out?"

"I do." She lifted her skirts and opened the servant door again. "Follow me."

We could hear men open the door in the room next door and roughly search it. Others headed to this one.

The knob turned but did not give way. "Who locked this door?" a voice thundered.

"No one is inside but Sir Ercole's mistress."

"Let us be certain! Bring the key!"

Rosa's good eye narrowed, and her lips clamped together.

"Come," I urged, slipping into the passageway behind Simona. *C'mon, c'mon, c'mon!* I screamed inwardly. "If you remain, you agree to allow Ercole to harm you further." I gestured for her to follow.

She rose and was halfway across the room when a key entered the lock. Rosa glanced in fear toward me, but the moment seemed to galvanize her. When she was two paces away, I reached forward and bodily hauled her into the passageway. Simona closed it with a quiet, blessedly squeak-free click.

My mouth dry, I looked through the peephole as two men

entered, glancing around in surprise. "Was not the woman put in here?" asked the first. "The one who accompanied Sir Ercole?"

"Mayhap the servants placed her in the guest room on the far side," said the other. "I shall check." He ran out.

The first man did a slow three-sixty, taking in every bit of the room, then leaned down to lift the leather band. He glanced at the cup as I left my perch, tiptoeing down the passageway behind Simona and Rosa. We had just turned the corner and put our backs to the wall when we heard the telltale squeak again.

He'd opened the secret door.

Simona leaned forward and whispered in my ear, "Go halfway down this passage, then take the stairs down to the kitchen. I shall wait here in case he comes."

I nodded, gratitude practically making me choke on my own sob. I pulled Rosa onward, wincing as she tripped on a warping floorboard and her boot made a loud sound with her next footfall. I rushed on, even as a man thundered behind us.

"Who is there? Identify yourself!"

Simona gave me one last glance and then turned the corner. "Giorgio, it is only me!" she called.

"M'lady!"

"I was frightened by all the commotion and thought it best to hide!"

We did not stay to hear the rest of their conversation. We found the curving stairwell. I rushed down it, hoping Giulio was on the other side of that kitchen door. Or that I could find him soon.

TILIANI

I arrived in the courtyard to hear Valentino gruffly issuing orders.

"'Tis imperative that we avoid notice as much as possible," he said. "With that in mind, I want you men in pairs. Endeavor to appear like nothing more than two out for an evening stroll, on your way home to your wives, or heading to the closest taverna. Understood?"

Solemn nods came from the seven others present.

"If Lady Tiliani is discovered, we might encounter significant threat or even attack. We are but three short blocks away from Palazzo Russo. Let us escort her to her gates without pause."

Sir Fiore looked over Valentino's shoulder, spotting me. "M'lady."

He bowed, and all the other men did the same, except for Valentino. A show of independence? Separation?

"What is the plan?" I asked, stepping up beside him. More of my men circled around, listening in. I knew all itched to attend me. But the last thing we needed was a war erupting because of this outing.

"We shall move out, two by two," Valentino said. "Four before us, in pairs, searching for any potential threat, then periodically falling back in pairs to allow others to take the lead, reducing the chance of others seeing us moving as an organized group." He dared a glance at me. "You and I, m'lady, shall find things to attract our interest, allowing them to shift. We shall pause over pretty flowers. Examine pottery at the corner. Consider a stop for wine or cheese. Simply follow my lead."

I nodded primly. "Of course." My knights were well armed, as were his. I myself wore a sword beneath my cloak, as well as daggers at my waist. While I did not wish to start a war, I also had no desire to become another Fiorentini captive or victim.

Valentino glanced at me and gestured to my cloak. I covered my hair with the hood, not knowing if I would draw more attention—given the heat of the evening—with the cloak than I would have by leaving my dark-blond hair exposed. But he and Lord Paratore were doing me a great favor when they already suffered for coming to our defense.

Again, I took his offered arm, and we turned toward the front gates, following four men. The guards there allowed the first two pairs out, then us. The other four would follow.

We eased into the flow of pedestrians, the streets busy with people returning to their homes after work, shopping for meat and bread before the butcher and baker closed for the night. At the corner, we passed one pair of our guards and Valentino eased me to a stop, asking for a bunch of fat grapes from a fruit merchant's stand and fishing a coin out of his drawstring purse to pay for it—even as another pair of guards passed us.

We were almost to the second corner when a man paused and called to Valentino. "Captain Valeri!"

"Keep moving. Do not look back," Valentino said, his arm stiffening.

But the man pursued us, calling out louder. "Captain Valeri! *Valentino*!"

Grimacing, Valentino pulled me to a stop and glanced over his shoulder. He gave the man a wave. "*Buonasera*, Cassio," he called. "Forgive me. I would stay to chat, but we are late for a meeting." He turned to lead me forward again.

"A meeting? With whom?" said Cassio, a bit out of breath as he hurried to follow us. "And who is your lovely companion?"

Heaving a sigh, Valentino stopped again and reluctantly turned to face the man. Two of our guards hovered a few paces away, faces tight. Valentino opened his mouth to speak, but the man's eyes grew wide.

"You-you are . . . you must be . . ." His face shifted from excitement to confusion. "My friend, you must not be seen with this one! She is one of them!" He backed away as if I had sprouted plague buboes. "I thought you had more sense than to fraternize with a Forelli!"

Two men in fine tunics and jewelry paused at the sound of my name. Members of the Grandi, judging by the gold rope they each wore at their collars.

"Or are you as weak-minded as your lord?" Cassio spat out.

More men paused to face us, distracted from their shopping by the commotion.

"I shall speak with you later," Valentino gritted out, then took my elbow and hastened me down the street again.

"It is her!" cried one of the Grandi. "Lady Tiliani Forelli!"

We doubled our pace.

"Murderess!" cried a man.

A woman gasped and pulled her child close, as if I might attack them as we passed.

"How dare she come here!" cried another woman.

Our men closed in, forming a wall before and behind us. But someone grabbed a corner of my cloak and yanked me from Valentino's side.

Two of our guards unsheathed their swords in tandem with Valentino. He whirled and pointed his blade at the burly man who now held my arm in a painful grip. "Release her!"

I did not draw my own sword, waiting. The two nearest Paratore knights had their hands on the hilts of their swords but did not draw either.

"I am escorting the lady to her family," Valentino said loudly. Still others joined the crowd around us. "You shall allow us to pass peaceably."

"Why should we?" asked the man holding me. "They did not treat our own with such kindness, did they? Mayhap we need a bit of justice of our own!"

"Yes! Slit her throat!" jeered a thin man. "Let the Sienese feel a measure of our own pain! Lord Vanni's son was about her age. A life for a life!"

"A life for a life!" repeated a woman. Others began to chant the same.

The remaining Paratore knights drew their swords then, pushing the crowd back. "This is for the courts to decide on the morrow!" called one. "Not for the people of the streets!"

I itched to reach for my dagger and plunge it into the belly of the man who held me, but if they were already calling for my life, killing another would only push them into a frenzy.

"Bury her alive!" yelled a man. "If her kin are proven innocent on the morrow, we shall dig her up again!"

"Now *that* sounds rather unpleasant," said a familiar voice. I turned in surprise to see Domenico. He grabbed hold of my captor's arm as well as his head and threw a knee to the liver. When another moved to apprehend me, he struck the man's temple, sending him careening away.

Fighting began in earnest, our knights pairing up with those who had waylaid us, but grievously outnumbered. Ilaria grabbed my arm, and we began running down the street, Nico right behind us. Ilaria and I were fast, even in our skirts, and our decisive move surprised the others. We had to be close to Palazzo Russo. Valentino said it was only a few blocks away, and we had passed two already. It would likely be well guarded, given that my family was inside and public temperament was as I had just witnessed.

We turned a corner, and I spotted the knights in full armor outside the massive palazzo. "There," I grunted, taking the lead. "I am Lady Tiliani Forelli," I said to the first one we reached. "I am here to speak to my family."

His dark eyes moved past me to the crowd turning the corner, a man pointing, shouting. He rammed his fist on the door. "Open up! Swiftly!"

We heard the bolstering bar slide back, agonizingly slow. The door slipped open, and the knight shoved us through, just as the mob reached us. The three other knights held them at bay, swords menacing in an arc, while two knights inside rammed the door closed and the bar back in place.

"You are truly Lady Forelli?" asked one, a bit pale.

"I am." I pulled back my shoulders and smoothed my skirts as I waited for my heart to cease pounding. I prayed Valentino was safe, as well as the other knights with them. That no one had been hurt. That no one had died. That I had not sealed my family's fate by coming here, let alone my own.

"Tiliani?"

I turned toward my mother's voice, then raced into her arms. She hugged me, as did Zia Gabi after her, relief flooding through me.

"What are you doing here?" Mama asked me, pulling back to better see my face.

"I had to come," I said. "I have urgent news from home. I so feared . . ."

I turned to my aunt and took her hand. "All I could think of was your story of being hung in a cage from the city wall. When we did not hear from you, we feared the worst."

Mama shared a long look with my aunt, then gestured to all of us. "Come along," she said wearily. "Your father and Lord Marcello shall want to hear what you have to say too."

9

LUCIANA

I paused at the open kitchen door, glad to see cooks and bakers and their minions rapidly moving back and forth, wholly absorbed in their task of preparing dinner and not yet alerted to the fury of our pursuit.

Heavenly aromas emanating from a boiling pot over the fire—as well as roast pork turning on a spit—briefly distracted me. But my eyes had seen the far door, which might lead to an outer door . . . and Giulio.

Please, God, let Giulio be nearby and not trying to storm the palazzo.

"*Cosa stai facendo qui?*" shouted a cook, shaking her wooden spoon at us, asking what we were doing here.

"We are on our way out," Rosa said, lifting a hand. "Pay us no heed."

I kept moving, not daring to look back. I hoped no guards had heard the cook.

"The men!" shouted a male servant at us. "They are searching high and low for a delivery boy. Have you seen him in the halls?"

"Nay," Rosa said. "None but us."

"And you are?" asked the cook.

I ignored her and pushed the latch, and we were outside, in a narrow corridor between the palazzo and their neighbor. From the ash, I assumed it was where those who kept the fires blazing made their daily trek to dump cold coals in the alley. Stepping forward, I grimaced and belatedly smelled something foul. It was also an open sewage drain.

"Ugh," I groaned. "C'mon," I continued in English, grabbing Rosa's hand. "Let's get this over with." I didn't care that she didn't understand my words; she'd understand my action well enough.

We ran down the V-shaped path—trying to keep our skirts out of the muck—to the heavy, fortified door at the end. I paused and glanced up the twenty-foot face of it, with metal bands across it every two feet. But in the center was a small door for dumping. Rosa nervously looked back over her shoulder, but the corridor remained empty. Apparently, the kitchen staff was too busy with dinner prep to sound an alarm over two girls.

I unlatched the dump door—about two-by-two feet—and peered outward. Passersby glanced my way but paid little attention. Could I get through that with all my skirts? Rosa was smaller, less curvy than I. She'd probably fit. But the last thing I wanted was to get stuck.

"*Devi andare,*" I said, telling her she must go. "Feet first." I directed, moving behind her to wrap my arms around her chest. If someone saw her climbing out headfirst, it would undoubtedly attract attention. But if we could get her out and immediately on her feet, and if people didn't happen to be looking our way, we might have half a chance. *Please, God, don't let people be looking our way.*

"*Aspettare,*" I grunted, urging her to wait while I reached down to wrap her skirts around her legs as tightly as I could. I tucked the end between her ankles. "Hold it there. Now go through. Quickly!" I then hugged her back against me, and she pulled up her legs and pushed them through the hole. I thought she was going to get stuck at her hips, but with a little wriggling, she was halfway through, then, by curving her shoulders inward, she was out.

She turned back to me, fluffing her skirts. A couple women

glanced our way, but then shook their heads as if to say *it's not our business*, and moved on.

"Look for Lord Greco," I said, taking a panicked breath. There was no way I was going to fit through. Not with my curvy hips and broad shoulders. "He is out there someplace. He will help us."

For the first time, I worried she'd run.

I was unlacing my skirt when I heard a shout from the back side of the palazzo. But it was behind me, near the kitchen. Not out front.

"Come, quickly," Rosa said, waving me out.

"I will not fit," I said. "Please. Go to the nearest alley and wait for me or Lord Greco. I am coming *over* the wall."

She looked up and then back to me with her one good eye, skeptical. But I slammed the dump door and tied my now-freed skirt around my waist. I'd still want it on the other side to blend in. With one last look at the wide, massive blocks of the palazzo to my left and the rough, smaller bricks on my right, I jumped up and jammed my feet outward. I breathed a relieved sigh as my boots caught on either side. Then I shimmied my way upward, scrambling higher and higher.

Twelve feet up, my left boot slipped a little and I gasped, heart pounding. I closed my eyes and had to force myself to continue, relieved when the next shift upward was accomplished without incident. I talked to myself as if my coach was speaking to me, urging me onward and upward, pushing me to ignore my fear.

I had nearly reached the top when I heard two men coming. I froze. Were they pointing an arrow at me, even now? Drawing swords?

But no, they were swearing, grumbling as they splashed along the sewage line. Their entire focus seemed to be downward. One lamented the sacrifice of his new boots. The other, the hem of his tunic.

How could they not *see* me directly above them, regardless of the deepening shadows?

My heart was in my throat as they reached the end and continued to curse their lot, forced to make sure this section was secure.

"How long must I serve before the captain will trust me with more?" the first gritted out, opening the small dump door and peering out. "I have obeyed his every order for three years."

"Mayhap another three, and you shall have proven yourself worthy," said the second. He clapped him on the shoulder, then turned to go. "Come, let us make our way out of this stinking mess."

I panted shallowly, desperate for oxygen after my rapid climb and fearful they might hear me, directly above them. But they had been so engrossed in their own frustration that they had failed to fully do their duty. I laughed silently. Maybe it'd take 'em more years than three to earn their captain's approval when he learned that I'd just evaded them.

But my legs, spread-eagled as they were, began trembling. I had to start climbing again or I risked falling.

Carefully, I looked over my shoulder and watched as they turned the corner of the palazzo, leaving the gully blessedly empty again. I forced my legs to move, shifting my right and then my left, refusing to look down at the ground, now twenty feet below me. In another minute, I reached the top and carefully peered over the edge.

People walked by in either direction, intent on returning home. It was likely suppertime for most. I hooked a knee partially over the top of the thick gate, relieving the pressure on my aching muscles, and gave the street a closer perusal. I glimpsed Giulio in a nearby alleyway, peeking around for me. Thank God! Did he have Rosa?

I needed to get across this gate and to the street ASAP. The trouble was—there was no way to shimmy down, like I'd managed to shimmy up. The gate was at the corner of the building, extending out past the neighboring building. The only option was to hang over the edge and drop.

But hovering there, at the top of a twenty-foot gate, made my heart pound. I'd never liked heights. Could I hang and drop from the equivalent of a two-story building without breaking my legs?

At the corner, two men shouted, gesturing for others to join them. I looked up, aware for the first time that there were guards atop the palazzo, keeping watch. Thankfully, they were too intrigued by whatever commotion was happening on the street to notice me yet. This was my chance.

Memories of my jiu jitsu coach came back to me. Encouraging me to breathe and trust my next move. To rely on what I knew to be right, rather than what I feared might happen. Before I could overthink it, I scrambled over the edge, caught a grip, and then lowered myself to hang for a moment. Even as I thought, *what have I done?* I forced myself to release my handhold, trying to remember to keep my knees soft for impact. It was a half second longer than I expected, causing me to expel my breath—as well as let my ankle curve—when I slammed into the cobblestone.

I gasped and careened to my left, half exhilarated that I was free from Palazzo Vanni and half chagrined that I had not landed in a perfect Olympic dismount.

Giulio was there immediately. He hauled me up from the stones, hooking his arm around my waist. Rosa came to my other side, giving me equal support, and using her skirts to at least hide part of my improper dress. Giulio hustled us down the street, turned right into an alley, then pulled us into a covered doorway.

He turned to me, his hands cupping my shoulders. "How badly are you hurt?"

I grimaced as I tentatively rolled my ankle around, still trying to figure it out. Rosa untied my skirt and shook it out.

"Luciana, how bad is it?" he said, more urgently.

"I don't know," I muttered in English, still assessing. I switched to Italian. "My ankle . . . it's definitely sprained. But not badly."

Rosa looked anxiously back to the mouth of the alley. "We need to get farther away." She took hold of Giulio's forearm. "He might find me here. With you. If he does . . ."

He shook her off, as if irritated by her intrusion, his focus solely on me. "Luciana," he breathed, leaning his forehead toward mine. "I was so worried."

I was torn between them—equally relieved to be reunited with

Giulio, but Rosa was clearly scared to death. For good reason. "I am well." I gripped one of his hands, looking into those beautiful blues. "Other than a twisted ankle, I am well. Now we must get Rosa someplace safe."

He glanced in disdain toward her. "She is an accomplice to untold evil."

It was my turn to grip his face between my hands as he tried to turn away. "Giulio, she is a witness. *A witness to the Forellis' innocence.* That's why I brought her."

He had been so focused on me, on Ercole, that he had failed to think of Rosa and what her presence meant. His eyes widened with sudden understanding, and then his jaw muscles stiffened. "I shall get you both to safety. But first, my love. Put on your skirt?"

I glanced down and laughed. "I wager that's something you never thought you must say to me."

And when he smiled, oh, man, when he smiled . . . I didn't care that we were still within reach of utter disaster.

Making Lord Giulio Greco smile might just have to become my job, I thought.

TILIANI

I hugged my uncle and cousin, then my father. They turned to greet Domenico and Ilaria too.

"So, you thought we might be having such a merry time you could not resist joining us?" Papa said, putting an arm around my shoulders.

"If only that was the sole reason for me to come." I smiled ruefully. "We had no further word from you after your first missive about the upcoming hearing. And when we sent word and did not receive a reply, I had to come."

We sat down together around a long, low table.

"Benedetto is gravely ill," I said, looking to my aunt, uncle, and cousin. "Nona and Chiara have done all they can, but we do not know how much longer he can battle the ague. He grows progressively weaker. You must return home at once."

"The hearing is on the morrow," Zio Marcello said. "If God smiles, we shall be home in two days' time."

I shook my head slowly, hating what I had to say next. "'Twould be best if you leave this very eve. Escape the city during cover of darkness. Make it home by nightfall on the morrow."

The frown on his handsome face deepened. "'Tis truly so dire?"

I remembered the earnest, worried expression on my grandmother's face. How Benedetto did not rouse, even when I called to him. "You must. Nona insists. She . . . fears the worst."

Zio Marcello rose and paced, rubbing his face with both hands, then going to rest them on Zia Gabi's shoulders. She looked pale, thunderstruck. They knew my grandmother was not given to panic.

Fortino rose. "We cannot leave. It shall appear as if we fled, regardless of our excuse! It shall unravel all the good we proposed to weave, coming here."

"There is more," I said. "We hope Sir Ercole might be in the city. Luciana and Giulio are hunting him as we speak. If we can capture him, we might be able to force him to tell the Fiorentini the truth." I turned to Ilaria and Domenico. "Did you find any trace of him?"

"Only word that he is indeed here," Ilaria said.

"Firenze?" Zia Gabi said. "Why would he come here?"

"To witness the spectacle of the Forellis on trial," Zio Marcello said bitterly. "Is there no end to that man's vendetta?"

"'Tis not a trial," Mama said defensively. "'Tis a hearing. A moment for all to be heard, including us."

"*All* to be heard." Papa rubbed the back of his neck, then crossed his arms. "'Twould be a challenge to force Ercole to tell the truth. In fact, he might emerge to further his campaign against us."

"What matters most is that you get home to Benedetto." I sank to my knees beside Gabi. "I shall remain in your place. Give my testimony as to his poor health. They cannot argue that I took a great risk coming here. I was nearly overtaken on the streets when they realized who I was." My voice broke on the last words, and Mama came to rest her hand on my shoulder. It surprised me, as did my own trembling hands. I had not stopped to think about how close we had truly come to the very worst thing possible. The people on the street had not wanted to capture me; they wished to slay me.

I looked to Ilaria and Domenico. "They saved us. I have no idea what became of our knights. Or Aurelio's." *Valentino.* Where was he? Had he been harmed on my account? Was he bleeding in the streets? Or safe at Palazzo Paratore once more?

Tears rolled down my cheeks as I looked to my family. "This city loathes us. *Loathes* us. We Forellis are the symbol of all that has harmed them. The symbol not only of what transpired at Palazzo Pubblico, but also of all their losses beyond. And I am at the heart of that hatred, the almost-bride of one of their own. My father, one of the Nine. The Nine, guardians of Palazzo Pubblico, where fourteen of their own—emissaries of peace—were cut down. Surely we three shall suffice." I shook my head bitterly. "It is genius, Ercole's plan. He could not have played this game any better."

"Except that we have a witness against him," said a man from the corner of the room. I turned in surprise. *Giulio!*

We all turned to watch Luciana and Giulio approach, a battered young woman between them. Luciana limped, but her expression was victorious. As they approached the light of our candles, I recognized their companion.

"*Rosa,*" Mama said, her tone a mixture of horror and glee. If Rosa was here, she was *not* with Andrea Ercole. She gestured to a settee where the girl could rest.

"Please," Zia Gabi said, waving a servant to come near. "Might you fetch a poultice for her eye?"

"As well as a soothing tincture tea?" Mama added. "For both

her and Lady Luciana?" Papa went to aid Giulio in supporting Luciana, as Mama and Zia Gabi sat down on either side of Rosa.

Rosa shifted uneasily. "I am so very sorry, m'ladies," she began as the servant left. "M'lords as well. I do not deserve to be in your company, given how I left my post without word."

"Fret not over that." Mama reached for her hand. "Sir Ercole charmed many." She paused, then reached up to trace her swollen, bruised eye. "Did he beat you?"

Rosa nodded. But she was crying now, great sobs racking her slender body. "This was his doing, yes. But . . ." She dared to glance around at us with her one good eye. "But I am—I am as beastly as he. I deserve no mercy."

We all held our breath.

"Rosa," Mama said gently. "Tell us what you must."

"I-I . . . murdered for him," she sobbed. "I . . . believed him. That we were doing something right. Something . . . just. *Righteous.* He had me—" She completely broke down then, unable to go on.

Mama sat down beside her and wrapped her arm around her shoulder, handing her a handkerchief. She looked up to Papa.

But Papa had a spark of renewed hope in his eye. "This girl," he said quietly to all of us, "may be our salvation." He turned to Marcello. "If she is able to testify, she shall exonerate us. Tell all that we had nothing to do with the massacre. That it was all Ercole."

"No woman's testimony," my uncle returned reluctantly, "equals a man's."

Zia Gabi groaned. "Again, with this nonsense." She turned to her sister. "I shall never get used to it!" she added in English.

Mama turned to her. "My child is here, Gabi. Yours is at home and in need of you. Let us take it from here. You must go. If Benedetto fares so poorly . . ."

The sisters faced each other, their hearts in their eyes. I knew Mama was thinking of my lost little brothers—as was Zia Gabi.

"Let us see this through." Mama squared her shoulders and faced the others. "You three must return to Castello Forelli."

Papa stepped up beside her. "Agreed. You all know how I feel about bad odds. Bad odds, more glory. And while the girl might be discredited by her womanhood, she is a voice of truth. 'Tis the first bit of true hope we've had."

I smiled through my tears. Even though it terrified me, remaining behind, I felt enormous relief at the thought of them getting home to Benedetto. Mayhap if they arrived, it would bolster him, bring him back to health. I could imagine nothing other than both Fortino and Benedetto beside me in the years to come. And if the worst happened—if we three were imprisoned or killed—at least some of our family would survive.

Papa reached for his cousin's hand. They clasped, then hugged for a long moment.

"You are certain?" Zio Marcello asked him, drawing back.

"Your son ails. You must return home. Lia and I shall see this through."

"As will I," I said. I felt a strange sense of pride. All my life, my cousins and aunt and uncle had led us, represented us. Even after my father took his seat as one of the Nine, he had always lived in Zio Marcello's shadow. And with no brothers, I fought the sensation that I was almost worthy. The third in line to serve as the head of the Castello Forelli. But with no husband beside me? Few would honor me as such.

Here, now, we had the opportunity to serve as representatives of Castello Forelli. Of Siena. To testify to our innocence. To lay Ercole low.

And then get home. *Oh, how I long to be home . . .*

10

LUCIANA

I helped Rosa to get to her room, waited until a maid saw to her injured eye and helped her into a nightshift, then settled her under the covers. I sat down beside her on the bed and took her hand. "No matter what comes on the morrow, Rosa," I said, "I shall be at your side. You have done the right thing. The only thing that will bring rest to your soul."

Confession. Would it bring her a death sentence? I knew now that she had killed not one, but two of the Fiorentini in Palazzo Pubblico. She thought Ercole had killed four others, his hired men murder the rest. But he had friends here. People who believed in him and had something to gain, supporting him.

I had seen it for myself. And the Forellis' reaction to Rosa being our witness? It left me less than assured that a slim, young housemaid might be a winsome witness. This was not the 21st century.

"The Ladies Forelli," she whispered, "must wish me dead."

"Nay." I shook my head. "You are their only hope." I took her hand in mine. "You have decided as they might. To fight for right. To confess what you have done wrong. And to accept the consequences. God will see you through."

I thought about that. About my words, even as they left my lips. I was getting absorbed into this time, this philosophy, this family's theology. It was becoming mine. She was facing the consequences of her actions. And I believed that God—a God who sent me and my brother hurtling through time—would see her through. Even as he was seeing me through.

"Those consequences might mean I hang."

I wanted to deny it—to tell her some miracle would happen—but knew I couldn't. Chances were, we were all in deep weeds. "You may," I admitted. After seeing the mob on the street, I knew it as truth. "But at least you die with a clean conscience." *We might die with nothing to confess at all.*

"Was I but a common idiot?" Rosa asked through her tears.

I reached for a clean handkerchief on the table beside us and handed it to her. "Common?"

"Was I a simpleton? To be so deluded and taken with him?" She turned to her back and shook her head, staring at the rafters, then laid her wrist across her forehead. "I left my position at the castello—highly regarded by so many in my village—to follow him. After he accosted another."

I took a breath. This was key to her testimony. "Why? Why did you believe him over another woman?"

She closed her good eye and winced. "I did not wish to believe her. I wanted only to believe what he had told me. That she was . . . and I was . . ." She dissolved into sobs.

Some things never change. User-men were always user-men. "Not all are like him," I said, thinking of Giulio, as she partially regained her composure.

"No," she returned wearily. "But many are."

The key, I thought, *is to wait for the one who isn't.* But I refrained from sharing that with her. She was too raw. Too exhausted from the fight. And on the eve of possibly paying a very steep price.

But before we faced what might come tomorrow—we had to get some of the Forellis on their way home. *Home,* I thought. I wanted to know we had a home in this distant time. If we did not have them, and *that,* then why were Domenico and I here at all?

I squeezed Rosa's shoulder. "Try and get some sleep," I said. "You are not alone."

She nodded and turned her back to me as tears dripped down her face. With a sigh, I rose and slipped out the door. Tiliani, Giulio, Nico, and Ilaria awaited me. A hall torch sent flickering shadows over us all.

"So?" I asked in English. "How are we getting them outta this palace, let alone the city?"

"We wait until all are asleep and even the guards fight dozing," Nico said in Italian, nodding at Ilaria. "Two-ish," he added in English. "The Zombie Hour."

"Roger that," I returned.

"We shall assist them in escaping over the far side of Palazzo Russo and into her alley," Giulio added, ignoring our exchange in English with but a raised brow, assuming what we discussed. "They shall repel down and get to the river. M'lords and ladies have escaped the city before, using a boat."

"Any news of Lord Paratore? Sir Valeri? Might they aid us?" I dared not look at Tiliani.

Giulio shook his head. "No news. Hopefully, Sir Valeri got back to the palazzo safely. With Tiliani inside, the mob probably lost interest in any true fight."

Tiliani leaned forward. "Luciana and Domenico, I know this is a risk for you," she said. "To remain here, with me. As well as aiding my family in escaping this night. Mayhap you and Domenico should escape the city with them."

"Those are risks I am willing to take," I returned. "Nico and I can testify that we saw Ercole and Rosa in Siena that night, running away. *Fighting* to get away. I heard him speaking with Lord Vanni and others, making plans. I can expose him. Tell how he is playing everyone he meets in order to get a castello for himself."

"A castello?"

"Yes," I returned grimly. "I believe he thinks the Fiorentini shall grant him Castello Forelli if he succeeds in bringing you all down."

Tiliani's mouth dropped open, and she shook her head, blinking slowly as she absorbed that information. "Unfortunately, my friend, that leaves us with two female witnesses. And you heard what my father said. Both might be discounted."

I sighed heavily, wishing women's lib wasn't a good six hundred years away. It was a definite con on the Pro/Con List between Medieval Times and The Future.

"If I understand this right, you and your mom and dad are going to take on the equivalent of a firing squad on the morrow," I said. "Nico and Rosa and I will stand behind you. Maybe Aurelio. But that will be it. You need us. Every one of us. Even if some of us are women."

Til gave me a rueful grin. "My father likes bad odds. Mayhap you are the same?"

"Guess we have no choice," I allowed, smiling. "Let's do this," I added in English to my brother.

"Oh, yeah," he said, in English too. "Let's totally do this. Because I, personally, can't wait to see this Ercole dude forced to tell the truth at last."

LUCIANA

We all turned in early, eager for the palazzo guards to settle down and get sleepy. Our crew weren't truly prisoners, even if the Grandi had placed them under "house arrest." The Forellis had ridden into the city as emissaries for Siena, eager to try and assuage the fury of the Fiorentini. Lord Russo, who was still sympathetic toward the Forellis' cause—and impressed by their magnanimous gesture in attempting to restore peace—had offered his home more as sanctuary than prison. He stationed guards out front and on the roof—as much to protect us all as to keep us in. And when he heard that Benedetto ailed, he immediately agreed that Marcello, Gabi, and Fortino must make their way out at once, regardless of the consequences. His largesse was especially moving, given that when it was discovered that they were missing, he would likely take some significant heat.

But we had not expected him to dismiss the roof guards before we got there. Nico and I looked around in disbelief, as we'd been ready to take the four men out as quietly as we could, using chokeholds to render them unconscious, then pass them along to Ilaria and Giulio to gag and tie up.

"I'm liking this Russo more and more," Nico muttered.

"He probably didn't want the guards hanged for not stopping us," I said.

"Clearly not all Fiorentini are bad." He opened the door and gestured for the others to follow.

I crept to the wall and looked below to the alleyway, then along the streets. Aside from some pods of drunk men, making their way home late, the entire city appeared to be enjoying their slumber. More worrisome were the neighboring towers of other palazzos, the nearest half a block away. How tired were their guards? Asleep at their posts on this quiet night or bored and ambling about, eager for any diversion possible—including what might be happening at Palazzo Russo?

With that in mind, I moved to the corner of the back wall that would be most hidden from any curious eyes in that tower and waved the others over. Giulio and Nico tied the rope around a pillar and dropped it over the side.

Marcello peered over and let out a big sigh. "I sincerely hope my shoulder is healed enough for this."

I shivered as I looked over the edge, glad I wasn't going with them. My ankle—and heart—might give way.

"Allow me to go first," Fortino said, easing over the parapet and grabbing hold of the rope.

"One hand below, one above," Marcello said. "Take your time. I would rather be captured than see you fall."

"I know, Papa," he said. "Do not fret. Mama taught me."

Marcello cast a rueful grin at Gabriella, and I smiled with them. How awesome was that? Growing up with a mom who could teach you how to rappel? My mom might've done something similar had she been in medieval times. In fact, I was pretty certain Mom and Gabi would have been friends. The thought of it pulled at my heartstrings.

Despite his father's warning, Fortino was down the wall in under a minute. Marcello began his descent as Gabi wound her skirt up through her legs and tucked it into her belt. "Take note, Luci," she said with a grin. "Never climb without tucking your skirts first. The men here don't like it much, but it's better than plunging to your death."

"Noted," I said dryly.

She paused on the other side of the wall—as if she didn't hover forty feet from the ground—and looked at us all. "We leave our beloved family in your care. If the Fiorentini turn feral, find your way to escape and return home. Agreed?"

"Agreed," Giulio said. "Our prayers shall follow you every step of the way."

"*Grazie*, dear one." With but those few words, she descended as we watched. Apparently, medieval times didn't require more than shorthand speech. She rappelled five feet at a time, and reached the ground in short order.

"She did that as easily as if she'd done it a hundred times before," I whispered to Ilaria, watching as Gabi took a few steps away from the rope on the ground and settled her skirts about her as if she had just risen from a chair.

She smiled. "There is a reason they are called She-Wolves."

"Luca told me she has rappelled down the side of more than

one building," Giulio put in, as he hauled up the rope, gathering it in a coil. "One of them was Castello Greco."

I thought about those towering walls. Had that been necessary in escaping the elder Paratore? Or in their fight to claim the castello as their own?

Once Giulio had brought up the whole rope, he stashed it where he had found it, among other supplies on the roof. The others disappeared inside the house, returning to their quarters, but Giulio and I dared to linger. Ilaria closed the door with a knowing smile on her lush lips.

I returned to the wall and looked in the direction of the River Arno, glistening in the waxing moonlight. It was unfortunate that the river flowed toward the sea, because if they could ride it *upriver*, it'd take our family almost all the way home.

Our family, I mused, repeating the phrase in my head. Why had I never thought of our family in New Jersey the same way? They were closer, biologically, than these people. But these people were somehow. . .what? *Closer to my heart*, I thought. From the get-go. How was that possible?

"So when they get clear of the city, how will they make it the rest of the way?" I asked, re-focusing. "Their horses are here."

"They shall travel on foot to a neighboring village, and Fortino shall purchase new mounts, while Marcello and Gabriella remain in hiding. There are many who might recognize m'lord or lady. And if Firenze realizes they have escaped and raises an alarm . . ."

"Let us hope they are far, far from here before that happens." With luck, it wouldn't be until tomorrow, when we reached the Palazzo Vecchio—which I'd learned was called the Palazzo della Signoria in this era—the main public building for Firenze's ruling body. There the Forellis would face the Priori, Firenze's nine ruling members, chosen from among the city's Grandi. I supposed the only good thing in all this mess was that it had been members of the Grandi who had died in Siena's Palazzo Pubblico, rather than any of the main Priori dudes. Had that happened, I supposed we'd already be at war.

Giulio interlocked his fingers with mine, and we stood for a while, staring out toward the river, as if we could somehow hasten the Forellis' steps home. Above us, a canopy of stars—more numerous and dense than I had ever seen—covered us. He turned partially toward me. "On the morrow, Luciana, I think you should stay back. You and your brother can resume your hunt for Ercole if you blend into the crowd."

I nodded. "Until you have need of my testimony."

He shook his head. "Luca and I discussed it. We do not believe it shall further our cause to have you share what you heard Ercole say. 'Tis only a supposed promise from the future. And it shall only draw a new mark on your back as well as ours. With luck, if the worst happens, you and Domenico can escape the city and get back to Castello Forelli."

I tried to make out his expression in the near dark. Was this about keeping me safe? Or because my testimony would be discredited?

"It seems to me that additional testimony—regardless of how it is received—would help. Even a bit of help is better than none at all. I saw him in Siena, Giulio."

He turned so he could fully face me and tucked a strand of my hair behind my ear. "I do not want you to do anything if it endangers you further." He took my other hand in his. "When you disappeared into Palazzo Vanni for so long . . . Luciana, I nearly went mad. And watching you dangle from the gate, so high. Suffering your injury?" He shook his head. "Nay, you have given enough to this cause. You did enough in finding Rosa."

"Rosa will want me there. I do not think she can summon the courage to testify if I am not with her."

"She shall have Tiliani with her."

"Mmm." I shook my head in doubt.

"Please, Luciana." He pulled one of my hands to his lips and tenderly kissed the tender flesh of my wrist, sending delighted shivers up my arm. "Please. Do this for me. Ilaria and I shall have enough to consider, watching over the Forellis. If we might know that you and Domenico are safely in the shadows—ready to come to our aid if we call—but not at the center of every Fiorentini's attention—'twould aid us greatly."

When I still hesitated, he pulled me in his arms until my head rested under his chin and I could feel the steady beat of his heart. He kissed my head and then leaned down to whisper. "Can you hear my heart? *You* are my heart, love. Please. Do this for me. If anything was to happen to you, I do not know how I might go on."

"So be it," I said with a sigh, unable to deny him anything when he was being so tender. I pulled away a little and poked him in the chest. "But I am keeping *you* within my sight at all times too."

"Very well." I could hear the smile and relief in his tone. "You should know . . . Ilaria and I have proposed something to the Forellis. 'Tis our hope that it will end this madness at last and we shall *all* be able to head home on the morrow, peace restored."

"Oh?" He had my attention now. "And what is that?"

"On the morrow you shall know." He looked to the river again. "On the morrow, all shall know."

11

TILIANI

I awoke with a start. And then gladness. Relief.

My aunt, uncle, and cousin were on their way home, to Castello Forelli and hopefully to be at Benedetto's side as he healed . . . either on this side of heaven, as Father Giovanni said, or the other.

I sank back into my pillow. *Please, Lord, let him live!* I prayed. I found some solace in the thought that at least some of my kin would survive this day to fight for right. *Lead me, Lord,* I prayed.

I knew a deep sense of peace that I had done what I ought. No matter what I faced this day, my extended family was on their way to where they must go—even if my nearest and dearest were not.

Mama. My beloved mother, who had lost so much. *Papa.* Who pretended to be braver than he could possibly feel. Giulio and Ilaria. And now Luciana and Domenico too. Rosa. Might we all perish in the face of the Fiorentinis' wrath when they found out our relatives had escaped?

Mama strode into my room, unannounced, already dressed as a lady. She wore not her Forelli gold, but a gown that made her appear regal from head to foot. Her golden hair was wound in a demure knot, bound in mesh at the nape of her neck. She was in a deep-blue gown, enchanting and yet not evocative.

'Twas not her own. Had Aurelio had it fashioned for her? Or Lord Russo?

She turned and gestured a maid in through my door. This one carried a seafoam-green bodice and skirt. With a nervous glance toward me, the maid laid it out on a settee at the edge of the room and disappeared through the door again. The dress had a wide neckline of ivory pearls embroidered upon it, as well as along the wide skirt hem.

"A gift from Aurelio," Mama said of her gown, "as is this." She gestured toward mine.

"He did not trust us to choose our own clothing?"

She paused, fingering the pearls on my bodice. "Men oft struggle in such situations. He likely felt moved to do something within his power. Even if he could not assure the outcome of this hearing."

"Generous to the last," I said, sitting up, shaking my head. How was it, that a spurned lover had become such a treasured friend?

Mama sat down beside me.

"Shall we survive this day?" I dared to meet her eye.

"Father Giovanni says the Lord has brought us this far. What else might we do but trust him?"

"Gabi, Marcello, and Fortino are safely away?" I asked in a whisper.

"Hopefully halfway home by now." She took my hand.

"Home sounds so nice," I said.

"Yes, it does." She patted my hand. "We have seen worse, Til. We can get through this."

I smiled and nodded. "Yes, Mama. Together. The Lord hasn't brought us this far, only to see us perish."

Her beautiful blue eyes were ringed in wrinkles, wrought from the years, but they turned to smile lines then. "You testify to me, child. You teach me. You lead me, even in your young years. How is that possible?"

I placed my palm against her cheek. "How is it possible? Because you have lived your life as a testimony to me every day." I leaned my forehead against hers. "Every day, Mama. Every day. I have seen your sacrifice. I have seen your example, in the manner you waded through grief, time and again." I pulled away. "And I shall honor it for every minute I have left on this earth."

A single tear dropped from her eye and over her cheek. "I love you, Tiliani. No matter what comes. You have filled my heart and life with love."

"As you have, for me," I said. We embraced, weeping for several minutes.

It had been years since I had felt this close to my mother. Somehow here, now, I was in the depths of her heart—a heart she had kept partially closed—and she, to mine.

I knew her better now, somehow, glimpsing threat, even unto death. Knew her as an adult. The potential depth of loss laid it bare. As well as the potential of life we had yet to live . . . so much hoped-for *life*.

Valentino, I thought wistfully. What stirred in my heart for him had awakened hopes and dreams in my future, when heretofore, I had been all about my present. Was that where Mama had periodically become so lost? Somewhere between her hoped-for future with my brothers still at our side and our present as a family of three? Or somewhere in her unlived future, when all of this might not have happened at all?

I understood her dilemma anew—at least in measure—because every thought of Valentino Valeri made me long for the man. Yet right then, he seemed further from my future than ever. And that made me even more bereft.

LUCIANA

We slipped into the streets well before the Forellis did, our goal to find any trace of Andrea Ercole. If we could find him and bring him to the hearing, force him to tell the truth of his duplicity before one and all, maybe this whole nightmare would end. We'd all return home to the beautiful Castello Forelli, settle into medieval life, and Giulio could—

"*Luci*," my brother said, leaning close. Obviously, he'd been trying to get my attention for some time.

We stopped in a little alcove to the side of a tiny fruit store.

"I can cover twice the territory you can, with that limp. Why don't you go set up surveillance near Palazzo Vecchio—"

"Palazzo della Signoria," I corrected him.

"You know what I mean. Remember that place to the side where they had all the statues in our time?"

I remembered it well.

"Set up camp somewhere there, and I'll find you. That should give you eyes on all who enter and exit."

"I doubt Ercole will arrive until the bitter end," I said.

"Agreed. But just in case he slips in earlier, you follow. If I don't see you at our meeting spot, I'll assume you are on him like a parasite on a host."

"Eww, really? That's the best analogy you could come up with?"

"I thought it was pretty good. But that's how I want it, Luci. If you find our man, you keep him almost in arm's reach, understood? Then I will find my way to you, and if it's right, we'll take him down together. Present him to the Priori, the whole nine yards."

"That simple, huh?"

He flashed me a grin. "As always."

"What makes you think he will tell the truth?"

"My well-placed dagger will encourage him to do the right thing." With a wink he was off, leaving me to hobble my way down the street, hang a left, and then settle into the flow of the larger avenue leading to the Piazza della Signoria.

It comforted me to see some familiar buildings that would still be standing in seven hundred years, to feel like I somehow *knew* part of this city. Some of the buildings felt familiar. But the streets in this time were stinky—rotting food and sewage carted away to the nearest canal that led to the River Arno. And there were a good eighty or ninety towers in the city. It felt . . . So. Different.

Most palazzos were owned by wealthy merchants who conducted business on the first floor and lived on the second or third, just as the Romans had. Some of them were topped by towers, but most of the new ones rose only six or seven stories above the ground.

In the fourteenth century, Firenze began a campaign to make the city *il più bello che si può*—as beautiful as possible. This included decreasing the height of some of the city's towers to make them uniform and adding stone cladding. There were holes high up that were used for scaffolding to hold balconies or awnings, a welcome respite from the sweltering summer sun. And while in a century or two, some of the towers would be topped by elegant loggia for entertaining and soaking in the view, in this era, they were predominantly crenellated—ready to defend.

At ground level, iron rings hung from the stone so people could tether their horses, as well as brackets for torches and horizontal bars on which the wealthy hung tapestries or their coat of arms. It was nothing as glorious as it would be in the coming Renaissance, but my inner history-nerd was thrilled to be walking the streets in 1372.

I was soon in the piazza and passed where the Gothic-style Loggia dei Lanzi would eventually be built, housing tons of statues in our time, but originally constructed for public gatherings and hearings. Now it was only a warren of tent-covered merchants, selling their wares.

I sighed. My throbbing ankle begged me to find a perch on the wall in the shade, my back against a cool stone column, leg elevated as I kept watch for Captain Evil. I searched for an alternative and finally found it in a small, temporary *enoteca*—a man selling bite-size bread, cheese, and preserved meats along with tiny cups of wine.

I settled on a stool and accepted the rounded wooden trencher they handed every person, without asking. Clearly, if you were taking up space, you were buying what they were selling. That was fine with me—it was a blessed relief to be sitting anywhere. I just wished I was back home at Castello Forelli. While Lady Adri and Chiara wouldn't have the ibuprofen and the ice pack I dreamed about, they'd likely have another way to bring some relief.

Wincing, I turned a bit on my stool.

"*Sei firito?*" asked a kindly old man as he poured my wine, wondering if I was hurt.

"*Mi si è storta la caviglia,*" I returned, telling him I'd twisted my ankle.

"*Ah, si, si.*" He held up an arthritic finger, went to the back and fetched me a second cup, then poured wine into that one too.

I smiled. He meant well. But I was on watch—the last thing I needed was to get tipsy. Still, having two cups of wine would give me more time. The man then went to find another stool and insisted I put my foot up.

"*Dio ti benedica, amico mio,*" I said, sighing. *God bless you, my friend.* I bit into my first little bite of pecorino cheese and dry bread and watched as noble men and women began filtering into the Palazzo della Signoria. My eyes narrowed as I saw two guards checking scrolls for names as each person entered. Was this an invitation-only sort of deal? How was I supposed to follow Ercole if he made it inside? Or the Forellis? Giulio had asked me to stick to the shadows. My brother, right behind Ercole. Neither was going to work.

I glanced along the formidable palazzo wall and wondered about slipping in through a side or back entrance, but I doubted any of them would be unguarded. Especially today, with the Forellis soon to be brought forth. Would Ercole arrive with his buddies from Palazzo Vanni? Or come alone? Would he want to get settled someplace inside, to watch the proceedings from the edges, or boldly enter the crowd, daring them to see him?

He seemed more like an edge-man to me. After all, he had been acting all paranoid when I was spying on him.

My eyes took in every man who passed by the osteria tent and every single one who climbed the steps of the palazzo. A few times my breath caught, as I recognized similarities, but none was the man I sought. A customer came in and gestured toward my stool, irritated that I was using it to rest my foot, but the proprietor shooed him away, telling him to leave me alone.

"Do you not see she's ailing? What sort of man are you?" the merchant chided.

But people beyond them gathered in a crowd, their chattering growing in intensity. I heard the name *Forelli* mentioned several times, as well as *Lupa. She-Wolf.*

Then armed Fiorentini knights on horseback came down the cobblestone street, preceding, surrounding, and following Luca, Evangelia, and Tiliani on their own horses, as well as Giulio and Ilaria, who flanked Rosa. At least here, now, the people were not pelting them with rotten fruit, though a fair number jeered and raised their fists.

I rose to watch, and the disgruntled customer hit his companion on the arm. "Where is the other She-Wolf, Lady Gabriella? I heard the whole family was here, not half."

"Mayhap she tucked her tail and ran!" laughed his friend, folding his arms in satisfaction.

"Leaving her sister behind? Nay. I wager she's prowling about, even now," he said with a shiver, glancing around at the crowds behind us.

I laid a coin on the table for the kindly wine merchant and slipped through the crowd, following the Forellis. The armed guards pulled up in front of the palazzo and formed a half circle, allowing them to dismount in peace and regally climb the front stairs, ignoring their hecklers. There was no way I could get to Giulio in time to ask him to let me in with them. The crowd was pressing in.

"No sign of our friend, eh?" Nico said, somehow beside me.

I glanced at him, relieved. "Nope."

"Let's wait a bit," he whispered. "See if he follows them."

"How are we going to get in?" I asked. "Looks like it's by invitation only."

"No worries. I got the golden ticket."

I gaped at him. "How'd you score one of those?"

"Don't ask." He winked.

"You stole it?" I mouthed.

"I prefer to think of it as borrowing."

I shook my head, smiling. Some poor member of the Grandi was madly searching his pockets about now. "There's nothing that identifies who we should be on that paper?" I asked, still not able to believe it'd be quite this easy.

"Nope. It's just a general invitation with an official Priori stamp."

"But they were checking names, earlier."

"Maybe that was for the main guests. Front row seats, that sort of thing. This appears to be an all-access pass."

"Well done," I said, breathing a sigh of relief. We settled in to watch for a while longer, edging closer and closer to the steps, keeping some people in front of us. While Ercole had only glimpsed us in Siena at night, he might have as good a memory of our faces as we did of his. And the trick here, of course, was to find him before he found us.

TILIANI

I did not like the sentiment in the room as we entered the grand salon. It was already sweltering in the windowless room, the torches and candelabra sending smoke up to the soot-soaked ceiling.

The nine Priori sat in ornately carved chairs set in an arc, and it appeared that all two hundred of the Grandi were intent on making their way in as well.

Mama took my hand, hidden amongst our skirts. "Courage, dear one. Shoulders back, chin up. We have nothing to hide. There is nothing to fear, because we have done nothing wrong."

I tried to swallow, finding my mouth dry. I wished we could have a bit of water. I thought longingly of the public fountain we had passed, flowing freely. That was an advantage Firenze had over Siena—a wealth of water. Siena was perennially dry.

But the Priori did not appear to have our comfort or hospitality in mind. Not one of them was under the age of my father. All appeared stern, some hateful. I was prepared to encounter animosity, anger. I was not prepared to encounter loathing.

There is nothing to fear, because we have done nothing wrong; Mama took comfort in those words. But these men did not seem ready to hear truth. They seemed to have already decided much about us. I glanced at Rosa, wringing her hands beside me. Then I looked for the Betarrini twins, hoping, praying they had found Ercole. When I at last spotted Luciana, she gave me a sorrowful shake of her head.

"Where are Lord Marcello and Lady Gabriella Forelli? And their heir?" asked the Priori in the center of the arc, a balding, strident man with hollow cheeks. "We were told that you all were here to attend this hearing."

"M'lord and lady had to return to Castello Forelli," Papa said, taking a step forward. "Our nephew, Benedetto, is gravely ill."

This set the crowd murmuring and groaning. Some shouted.

"I received no reports of their departure." The head of the Priori glanced at Lord Russo.

"They did not wish to create a fuss," Papa said. "Or potential skirmishes on your streets. So they departed with as little fanfare as possible."

"You mean they sneaked away," said another Priori.

Papa ignored him as people laughed. "You shall see that I have with me my wife, Lady Evangelia Forelli,"–he reached for her hand as she stepped forward, taking it–"and my daughter, Lady Tiliani." I joined them. "We have come to represent the family, as well as Siena herself. As the branch of the family instrumental in seeing a potential marital union as a bridge between our republics–the reason your beloved friends and fathers were in Siena–we believed we would suffice."

"We have also freely come on this peaceable errand," Giulio said, stepping forward. "I am Lord Giulio Greco, and this is my sister, Lady Ilaria."

"And who else is that with you?" sniffed the man, nodding at Rosa.

Giulio glanced back at her. "A friend and a witness that I think you would like to hear out."

"That remains to be seen," sniffed the head of the Priori. "I do not know what your practices are in Siena, but we entertain few women as 'witnesses' in this hall. We find they are frequently given to . . . *hysteria*, seldom providing reliable testimony."

Giulio did not flinch. "I believe you shall wish to hear from this one, m'lord–?"

"I am Lord Pagolo Piccolomini."

The men among us bowed, and we women curtsied, though it was hardly a formal introduction.

"We have freely come to you, m'lords," Papa said, "as emissaries. Passed a hostile border in our earnest desire to restore peace. For no one was more grieved than I when your beloved citizens were murdered in our own public hall. Indeed, I had endeavored to build bridges, pledging my daughter's hand to your own Lord Paratore, in order to further that effort. My cousin and I desire peace between our republics, for no one gains from threat of battle or war, other than mercenaries or weapon-makers."

He turned and looked at the crowd, then back to the Priori. "Most of us are guildsmen, dependent on the land for wool, grapes, or grain. Some of us are merchants, depending on cities full of prospering citizens, to buy our wares. Peaceful times benefit us all."

"And yet your own have committed an act of war," Lord Piccolomini said evenly, settling back against his chair, "murdering our own peaceful emissaries."

"Interlopers," Papa corrected him carefully, "assassinated them. Someone—or numerous people—sought to derail our efforts. And did so most effectively that night through one of the most heinous acts I have ever witnessed." He took a deep breath. "M'lords, I say this in all honesty. Not one of my friends has Fiorentini blood on his hands from that fateful night."

"Then who does?" scoffed another lord.

"Call for the the Perugian witnesses!" cried another.

Luca hesitated before he had no choice but to turn. He looked over his shoulder to Rosa.

"You, girl?" said Lord Piccolomini. "Are you telling me that you are the only one who can tell us who are to blame?"

Rosa stepped forward, trembling from head to foot. "I am, m'lord," she whispered.

12

LUCIANA

"What was that?" asked Lord Piccolomini, cupping his ear. "Speak up, girl!"

"I am, m'lord," Rosa repeated, a bit louder this time.

I was so proud of Rosa, daring to raise her voice! I wanted to go smack the little, rude lord at the table. Couldn't he see she was doing all she could? That she'd plainly been abused? That she was scared out of her mind?

"Was it Lord Forelli who damaged you so?" asked the man. "Leaving you with that swollen eye? Did he force you to come here today?"

"No, m'lord," she said.

"You came on your own volition?"

"I did."

"For what cause?"

She bit her lip. "To clear the Forellis' name. They had no hand in the Fiorentini's deaths that night in Siena."

"Then pray tell. Who did?"

"I did," she began, wringing her hands again. "I killed two of your beloved sons that terrible night."

"*You* did," he said doubtfully, settling back in his chair and steepling his fingers. "A mere wisp of a girl."

She nodded. "On the behest of–"

"M'lords do not truly intend to believe the word of a whore," called a man from the corner.

"I am no whore!" she cried.

The man, young, dark, and dashing, stepped through the crowd. "Did you not leave your post at Castello Forelli and travel with a man who was not your husband?"

Rosa blushed painfully red and put her hands to her cheeks. "A thoughtless act for which I have apologized to my ladies. I-I thought I was in love."

"There you have it," said the young man, lifting his hand. "Is this truly a credible witness or but another thoughtless girl, looking to make a name for herself?"

Lord Piccolomini narrowed his eyes. "This 'thoughtless girl' just confessed to murder."

"And for that she should be hanged," said the man, lifting his hands and shifting back into the crowd.

"She is no credible witness!" cried another.

"Let us move on with it!" called a man from the other side.

"Order, order!" shouted Lord Piccolomini, slapping his hand on the wooden table. "I demand you all be silent!"

"You must hear her out," Luca shouted. "She knew she risked the gallows in testifying as she has. Let her tell you who led her to this heinous act."

"Sir Andrea Ercole," Rosa shouted quickly, before anyone else could interrupt. "He convinced me that it was for the best if we stopped the Forellis' efforts."

"He convinced you to warm his bed is what he did!" called a man from the back.

"Order!" Lord Piccolomini shouted as the crowd erupted in laughter.

I tensed. This was not going well. Not at all.

"This knight, Andrea Ercole, set us up with the Perugians," Luca said, pacing slowly before the Priori like a proper lawyer. "Perugians who savagely beat Lord Marcello and me, attempting to coerce a confession, which we refused. *Because it was a lie.* Ercole was dismissed from Castello Forelli for accosting a young maid, then convinced this one"—he gestured to Rosa—"to run away with him. He is obviously persuasive. We believe he persuaded or paid mercenaries to help him murder the rest of your fellow citizens that night in Siena, then promptly shipped said mercenaries off to Spain. He persuaded Perugian lords to attack us. As he may be attempting to persuade some of your lords now to back him."

Lord Piccolomini stared at him. "My brothers, have any of you been contacted by this Ercole fellow? Have any of you conversed with him, or received emissaries from him?" He looked left, then right, then out to the Grandi, but all shook their heads. He lifted his hands. "So he has not infiltrated our ranks, Sir Forelli."

"That you know of," Luca dared. "What of Lord Vanni?"

Lord Piccolomini's eyes narrowed. "You dare to invoke the name of one of our brothers who has lost a son?"

"I have it on good authority that Ercole met with Lord Vanni and others, not more than two days past."

"M'lord, if I may," Giulio said, edging in. "We have done our best to track down Andrea Ercole, but he has evaded us." His words reminded me of my mission, and I scanned the crowd for any sign of the man. There was a gallery above too.

"You lost many treasured men that evening in Siena," Giulio went on, and I saw Aurelio Paratore step forward with him. My heart surged with hope, as well as admiration for Aurelio. Even now, he dared to support us! "My sisters and I hold the title to Castello Greco," Giulio said, "once Castello Paratore."

A rumble rolled through the crowd again, and I felt the collective anger against us like a tangible threat.

Ilaria took her place at Giulio's side. "We were willing to give our inheritance to the cause," she said, voice raised. "To freely give our castello and her lands to Aurelio Paratore when he took our lady Tiliani Forelli's hand. 'Twas to be a gesture of peace, proof that our two republics could stand side by side, even when separated only by a creek and a few miles."

Giulio gave her a small smile, and in that quiet encouragement, my heart melted a bit more. I loved that he had allowed her a moment. That he had given her voice merit. He turned back to the Priori. "As reparations for your losses, we again offer our castello and lands to Lord Aurelio Paratore, who has agreed to watch over it all and share a portion of her profits with the fourteen families who lost men that fateful night in Siena."

The crowd hushed, and I tried to absorb the import of his words.

He glanced at me, briefly.

Why? Because he feared I might turn from him, if he was not lord of his own lands?

Not a chance, Handsome.

Did he not realize that he meant so much more to me than a big, old castle?

He and his sisters had offered everything they had—*everything*—to make this whole, awful mess somehow, possibly *right*. And gosh, that made me fall a step farther in love than ever.

TILIANI

Giulio gave the barest nod to Luciana when she smiled at him, eyes shining. People from the future were truly different—what sort of woman fell for a young lord who was willing to give up his entire inheritance? But then. . .

I searched for Valentino Valeri. He had to be somewhere near, given that Aurelio was here. I finally found him, hoping for a shared look of longing, connection, as I'd noticed between Luciana and Giulio, but he only looked away. Had his feelings for me cooled? Or was he wrestling with the idea that he and his lord might live only a short distance away from me—and yet be further away than ever?

Lord Piccolomini tapped a long fingernail on the highly polished wooden table. He leaned left and conferred with the man next to him. Then he leaned right, whispering in the next man's ear, and listening as the man said something in return, nodding all the while. He straightened in his chair and eyed Aurelio Paratore. "On behalf of the families who suffered terrible losses in your very own Palazzo Pubblico, we accept this gift of Castello Greco, given back to the family who once guarded her gates, and who shall now shepherd her wealth as reparations for said families."

I held my breath, taking that in. Castello Greco was now gone, again in Fiorentini hands. And not because I married her master, but because we needed to reconcile with his people. The depth and breadth of what Giulio, Ilaria, and Chiara had given up was staggering. And proof that they were more loyal kin to me and my cousins than any others.

He turned toward Rosa. "You, daughter of Siena, as the only confirmed assassin we have in custody, shall be hanged at sunrise for your crimes against us."

Rosa gasped and fell back. I took her arm, willing courage into her. She had expected nothing less, truly. But to hear those fateful words uttered . . . no one was likely ever prepared. I began to tremble myself.

"Call for the Perugian witnesses!" shouted a man.

"Hang the Forellis too!"

Lord Piccolomini rose and lifted a hand. "Be at peace!" he bellowed. "We, your Priori, have decided how best to proceed. Guards shall escort you out, if you dare to speak again." The room quieted.

"You Forellis"—he pointed from Papa to Mama to me—"Lord Greco's generous offer has appeased a portion of our rage. But it was because of you and your enticement of Lady Tiliani's hand that our people were in your city at all. You three must bear some of the responsibility."

"But, m'lord—" Giulio began, stepping forward.

"Nay, Lord Greco." He raised his palm. "Your offer has assuaged our need for recompense. It shall keep us from amassing soldiers and mercenaries to pillage your city on the morrow. But fourteen of my brothers still cry out to me from their graves." He glanced left and right, and as he did so, the other Priori came to their feet as well. "And their cry must be answered."

I stiffened. What was this?

Mama's hand again covered mine.

"We understood this was a hearing, not a trial," Papa said.

"Indeed, it is. Therefore we shall leave it to God to try you himself. The Lord shall take his vengeance, or he shall show mercy," he said.

"M'lord, we came as but emissaries to—"

"You have three choices, Sir Forelli," said Lord Piccolomini grimly. "You and your family are to endure the Lazarus test."

"Nay, m'lord." Papa grew visibly pale. "Take me, but leave my family—"

Lazarus test? I thought. *What is this?*

Judging from Papa's reaction, 'twas dire indeed.

"Might there be another way—" Aurelio began.

"It shall be all three of you." Lord Piccolomini raised his voice. "Three, in exchange for fourteen. Given that we have a mighty She-Wolf and the She-Pup among you, as well as you, one of the Nine, Sir Forelli, I deem it a fair exchange." He looked out beyond us, among the crowd, which had hushed. Apparently, they deemed it a good exchange too.

Then I thought, *Thank you, Lord, that Gabi, Marcello, and Fortino are safely away!* What if we had *all* been caught in this trap, while Benedetto ailed? What if the Fiorentini had captured Castello Forelli as well as Castello Greco? What then, for Siena?

But his next words sent a shiver down my spine. "What say

you, Sir Forelli? Shall you run the gauntlet, endure the cage, or choose the coffin?"

I knew of a gauntlet—running through streets lined with angry citizens, all attempting to beat us to death. And I knew of the cage, based on Zia Gabi's tales. But what was this threat of a *coffin?*

Papa turned to us, searching our faces, distress making him appear far older than his years.

"We cannot survive the gauntlet," Mama whispered. "Nor do I think I can endure the coffin."

Papa turned back to the Priori. "Cage," he said, gritting his teeth.

"So be it, so be it," called Lord Piccolomini over the crowd's noise. "Cast them into the cages at once. Should they still live in four days' time, we shall declare it the Lord's mercy and send them home to Siena. And should they perish, we shall toss their bodies into the river."

13

TILIANI

Four days. Four days! I finally understood what *Lazarus test* meant—the time that Lazarus had been dead before Jesus brought him back to life. But Jesus was not here—not as he had been for his old friend. Could he save us too?

Rough hands grasped my arms. Giulio and Ilaria shouted, fought, but were quickly overcome.

Fiorentini guards held back the knights who had accompanied us. Disarmed as they entered, several moved to try and reach us at least.

"Stand down!" Papa shouted. "Be at peace!"

Rosa was hauled out another door—presumably heading toward the dungeon.

Aurelio dared to draw near me, Valentino behind him. "I shall speak to the Priori." It was all he could say before I was bodily hauled past them.

He would *speak* to them. In order to do what? See if they would reduce our sentence? Release us before the four days had passed? Or avoid the cages altogether?

Papa was between two guards before me, and Mama behind. Papa kept looking over his shoulder to make sure we were still together, half relieved that we were, half chagrined. "Think of it this way," he said to me as we turned the corner. "Your Zia

Gabi will not have sole bragging rights over surviving this particular Fiorentini specialty."

"I never thought I wanted to contend with her claim," I returned, our grim humor buoying me as he'd intended.

"*I* was quite content for her to have it all to herself," Mama added.

We reached the front gates of the palazzo, and outside, the crowds parted for us. People laughed and jeered. Some spit. Others tore at our skirts, our bodices. A woman left long, bloody scratches on my right shoulder. Only the presence of the soldiers kept them from taking us apart. We exited the gate of the old wall of the city and moved five more blocks to the new wall that had extended the city. Three fresh cages were passed over the heads of the crowd that amassed around us, word of our sentencing spreading. Fiorentini knights drew their swords on their own people, demanding they press back, as our semicircle narrowed.

Knights on the wall threw down heavy ropes, and I gaped up at the corpses of other prisoners farther down the way, left there as a tangible warning to their former fellow citizens to stay in line. How long had they suffered before they died? I clenched my teeth and looked neither left nor right as our cages were attached to the ropes. I would not give the Fiorentini the pleasure of seeing an ounce of my terror.

"There's my girl," Mama murmured. "Chin up, shoulders back. We shall get through this. Together."

I smiled at her, grateful I was not alone in this like Zia Gabi had been. And then I mimicked her stance. It was an act, of course. I had entered the Palazzo della Signoria already thirsty, and I remembered how Gabi spoke of thirst being the very worst part of this torture. Three days was as long as a body could stand to go without water. And by order of the Priori, we would need to withstand four. Would any of us be alive in four days? Papa had only recently recovered from the Perugians' torture. And Mama was strong but getting older. The last thing I wanted was to survive—after watching them perish.

Papa's cage was ready first, and his guards led him to it. He shook off their hands and stepped inside as if he relished the opportunity.

"I hear the view is unrivaled in all of Firenze," he said to one of the knights with a grin.

"You shall soon find out," muttered the man, shutting the door and tying it closed.

Mine was next. The cages were oblong, reminding me of eggs crafted out of vines. Mayhap they grew grapevines expressly for this purpose, shaping them as they matured, weaving them together and pruning away limbs to create the perfect prison for some future, unlucky soul.

I did as my father had and shook off the knights' hands, willingly entering my cage and turning to face the crowd with as regal and defiant a stance as I could manage. The Priori arrived as Mama took to her own tiny prison, the crowd parting for their solemn entrance. My hands gripped the vines before me, and I longed to rip it open and race toward Lord Piccolomini to wring his neck. How dare they do this! We had come freely, expecting to reason together. To find a solution, the true villains behind this crime. Make amends, the best we could. Giulio, Ilaria, and Chiara had given away their very inheritance! *Castello Greco.*

And still it was not enough.

There was good reason for us to continue to treat the Fiorentini as our enemies, despite witnessing some good souls among them.

Lord Piccolomini raised his fist, silently demanding the crowd fall silent.

When they did, he called, "What is the time?"

A young man behind him said loudly, "'Tis half past the noon hour, m'lord."

"Half past noon!" repeated Lord Piccolomini, looking to a priest.

"Half past noon," the priest acknowledged, hands clasped before his ample belly, a trio of other clerics behind him. "We shall return in four days' time, at precisely this hour. And we shall see if the Lord on High has deemed you worthy to live another day or condemned you to death."

"'Tis not He who condemns us," Mama growled toward Lord Piccolomini. "'Tis you and your distorted sense of justice. You cage a She-Wolf. May you be haunted by nightmares of me and my sister coming to tear you apart for this."

"And her daughter behind them," I added, glaring at him.

"And her husband as well," Papa said.

Lord Piccolomini raised a gray brow and huffed a laugh. He pointed toward us. "'Tis oft said that wild animals become feral when caged." Others around him laughed.

"Send them up, m'lord!" cried a man.

"To the wall!" called a woman.

"Make them pay for our brothers!"

Lord Piccolomini stepped closer. "In four days' time I doubt any of you shall be any threat to me or mine. Lady Gabriella escaped her cage, but mark my words, *you* shall not. Guards shall be on duty day and night. The only Savior you shall find is our Lord."

"May our prayers be answered, and not yours," I said, refusing to let him see that he'd touched on my greatest fear—surviving alone. *Any of you* . . . What if Mama survived, alone? I did not think her heart could take it, after losing my brothers. What if it was me? Or Papa?

Lord Piccolomini sniffed and glanced at Mama, then Papa. "Four days. May God have mercy on your souls."

He lifted his hand, and I immediately felt my cage shift, lift, and turn. I looked up to see my rope winding around a winch, visible through a small trap door along the wall, and prayed that the rope and knots would hold. Because with each turn of the rope, we got higher and higher. When we stopped at last, we were but four feet beneath the trap doors, and we could easily see over the three- and four-story buildings below us, over to the River Arno and the hills across it. I fought dizziness and nausea, being so high.

The trap doors closed, a neat hole for each rope between them. Below us, men and women cheered. Some danced. Others shook their fists or made lewd gestures at us.

"There. You see?" Papa said, waving to the horizon. "One of the finest views in all of Firenze. When Gabriella was caged, she was on the old wall. So already our story is better than hers."

"Must you, Luca?" Mama asked, her face pale. She shifted her slippered feet along the slanting limbs of her cage floor. I already felt the discomfort too. Standing on them created a pressure point on one-third of our feet. And yet there really was no way to sit or lie down either.

"Are they truly going to keep us in these for the full four days?" I asked.

"They are," Papa said, any trace of humor gone.

"And hasn't Zia Gabi said that had you not freed her on her third day, she would have likely perished?"

"She has." Mama leaned her forehead against a vine. It was hot, but at least at this height, there was a bit of breeze off the water.

"Didn't Zio Marcello say he had to carry her out?" I continued to press. "So weak was she?"

"He did," Papa said.

I shook my head. "All of Firenze must know this tale as well as we do. That they had a She-Wolf in hand, caged and on the wall, nearing death when she was rescued. They shall not allow that to happen again."

"Nay," Mama said.

"So what shall we do?"

"There is little we can do," she said, "other than pray. Like you said."

I had thrown it in the Fiorentini lord's face. That our prayers might be answered over his.

Was I willing to believe they might be?

LUCIANA

My brother and I gaped at the cages.

"Yeah, this"—Nico shook his head—"is not one of my favorite things about medieval times."

"I'd say it's definitely a con on my Medieval Pro/Con List," I said.

"They might not survive two days up there, let alone four. No food, no water, no shelter?"

He wiped his mouth. "It's bad. It's really bad."

"Maybe we can find a way to get them supplies."

His eyes traced the wall, a guard tower every hundred feet. "I doubt they'll let us cruise on up there."

Seeing a commotion, he pulled me back through the crowd. Lord Piccolomini shouted orders to his knights who surrounded the Sienese.

"Are they—"

"Yeah," Nico said, glancing over his shoulder. "They're either getting sent out of the city or into prison. We don't want to be in that mix."

"What if they discover we're missing?" I hissed. "Will they try and hunt us down?"

"Maybe. But let's try to make them forget we were even here."

We turned into a small alley. "Maybe we're better off staying with the men. Maybe they're about to send them all home to Siena. Or Castello Forelli. It could be our escape route."

"Maybe, but Luci, think," he said. "Who will want to come and taunt the Forellis? Thumb his nose at them?"

My eyes widened and I gripped his shoulders. "Yes. Of course." If he hadn't come to the hearing, Ercole would show up. Tonight. Tomorrow. Or the next day. But he would most definitely show up. "So we need only evade capture until—"

"Until we can find him, capture *him*, and force him to confess."

I took what felt like my first full breath in hours. Here at last was hope. *Some* measure of hope.

"Come on." I took his arm and eased into the flow of pedestrians leaving the piazza. "We gotta get out of here before they realize we're not in their bag of netted fish."

We moved down the street and ducked into a tiny wine bar, little more than a stall and table one could stand beside for a few minutes. Nico ordered us two glasses of watered wine and some small bites. Once again, there was no menu. You got whatever the "chef" decided to make. Not that I felt like eating after all that had come down. But we'd need energy if the fight came to us, so I shoved down some gamey, chewy meat on top of bread, refusing to decipher what it *really* might be. *Protein*, I thought. *Carbs. Fuel for the fight.*

"Did you see if Giulio and Ilaria were nabbed?" I whispered to him.

"No. But I doubt they escaped too."

I hoped he was wrong. It'd relieve me, knowing that the fate of the Forellis wasn't solely in our hands. "Should we go back to Palazzo Paratore? Seek out Aurelio's help?"

Nico shook his head. "I'd bet they're watching his place now, since he tried to defend them. We need to give it a wide berth. Only go to him when we have Ercole."

"So where are we going to sleep tonight?"

"We'll find an inn. A little out of the city center, but not too far. If they discover we're missing, the hunt may be on."

"Agreed. And we need new clothes. We might have been seen in these."

"Good plan." He looked me over as the proprietor set down two more ceramic glasses and a plate with what looked like crostini smeared with pâté. "Think you could put on boy clothes again? They'll be looking for a man and woman . . ."

"Absolutely," I returned, grimacing as I forced myself to eat one of the tiny toasts. I hated pâté. "Better to fight in pants than a dress."

Nico cheerfully downed two other crostini. "Although I do find it highly amusing to watch you tuck your gown in your belt. It's kind of like seeing my sister in a big diaper."

I smiled and nudged him, but my smile quickly faded as I remembered the Forellis hanging up in those cages. The idea of them dying, becoming withered corpses like those farther down the wall . . . No. We had to find a way to free them. Or at least aid them. We might be the only two friends they had left in the city.

A group of six Fiorentini city knights crowded in behind us, ordering over our shoulders, jabbering on about the glory that had just unfolded at the wall. "'Tis a sincere pleasure," said one, "to personally see one of the She-Wolves in a cage. This round is on me, friends."

"And her husband and daughter alongside her!" said another, clapping him on the back. "The next is on me!"

We forced back the rest of our watered wine, and Nico grabbed the last crostini as we ducked and moved through them, praying they eyed only our vacant space at the table—and the proprietor arriving with a pitcher of wine—rather than our faces.

I was nearly clear of them when one grabbed my arm. I looked back in alarm, and he raised his hands, as if showing he meant me no harm. "Forgive me. But you have such a beautiful face," he said. "Would you not stay? Share a cup of wine with me?"

Nico turned to us and frowned, manifesting his whole Medieval Big Bro. "We do not know you," he said. "How dare you make overtures toward my sister, without proper introduction!"

The man lifted a brow and raised his hands. "Again, forgive me," he said, bowing toward Nico. "I did not know that you were nobility, here in a lowly establishment such as this."

I smiled, and brushed my fingers over the man's arm, trying to soften Nico's harsh tone and defuse the situation. "No harm done. But we must depart at once. We have errands to complete for our parents before *riposo*," I said, referring to the midday rest time.

But the man again dared to take my arm as I turned to leave, walking beside us now. He peered at me a bit closer. "Have we met before? You and your brother look familiar."

"Nay," I said brightly. "We have just returned to the city after several years away." I gave him a brief curtsey, neatly dislodging his hand. "Good day."

"'Tis a fine day," he said, following me, "now that I have met you. Might I have the pleasure of coming to call?"

"Unfortunately, it would not be permitted," said Nico, a little more kindly this time. "My sister's hand has been promised to another for some time. Buonasera." With that, he pulled me out the door and we set off down the street, not daring to look back.

14

TILIANI

"I suppose that next time we tell you to stay home, you shall listen," Papa said, smiling tiredly at me.

I smiled back at him. The sun was setting now, the heat of the afternoon finally easing. It was a blessing, but I knew that come nightfall, we might be shivering. Neither Mama nor I had left Palazzo Paratore with a cloak. Papa had the benefit of both a shirt and tunic and, because of the ceremony, had worn a more formal, light coat atop them. He'd taken it off during the afternoon and used it as padding for the bottom of his cage. Mama and I had ripped out our underskirts and done the same, giving our feet—and our rumps—a place to rest. It was possible to sit, but only with my knees tucked to my chest.

"I would do it all over again," I said. "In order to give Benedetto a chance to see his family . . . again." Not *one more time,* I told myself. Surely after all we had gone through, God spared my cousin.

He would be there when we got home. When we all made it home. He had to be.

"Of course you would." Mama shifted again in the endless effort to find some comfort. "You are as stubborn as your aunt."

"And as loyal as her mother," Papa said.

"We are proud of you, Tiliani," Mama said. "Know that always. You are a fine young woman, always willing to make sacrifices for those you love. There is no finer attribute."

"We *are* proud of you." Papa rubbed his face with both hands and then rested them on his knees. "I hope you can forgive us for getting you into this rat's nest in the first place. If we had not set out for Firenze, intent on building bridges . . . If we had not met Aurelio and begun thinking about how a marriage might be the very best sort of bridge . . ." He looked to the sky. "Much would be different."

"Mayhap," I said. "And yet, only God knows how it might have transpired. Mayhap we would have had to deal with some other sort of pain. Firenze's agitation has grown over time. We might have come to a crossroads with them anyway. And Perugia? Ercole would still have been dismissed and likely done the same. So the only thing that is truly different is that we've landed in these cursed cages."

"We should never have decided to pursue Firenze in order to try and preserve future generations of our family," Mama said with a sigh. She looked up to the clouds. "We are not God. We should have trusted him to do what he would, when he willed it. Instead, we attempted to control it all."

I tried to lick my lips, but my mouth was already bone dry. "It makes sense, Mama. Losing Rocco and Dante as we did . . . I can see why you and Zia Gabi wanted to do what you could. Why Papa and Zio Marcello did what they did, too, to help protect Siena. Everyone wants to protect their children and grandchildren and great-grandchildren. And that desire is born out of love."

"But we did not give you the same choice that Gabi and I had. To choose the one you love. I hoped . . . we hoped in time you might come to love Aurelio."

"I might have," I admitted, "in time. He is a good man." *If Valentino Valeri had not been his captain,* I added silently.

"I suppose next time, you shall want to be the one to decide," Papa said.

"Without question."

If there was a next time. If I lived to love another.

I scanned the quiet piazza below us, many people already home for the evening meal. Where was Valentino? Would he come to check on us? Try and speak with me?

I thought not. Aurelio was already under suspicion, trying to defend us against the Priori. He likely endangered his seat with the Grandi in raising his voice. *Wolf-lover,* I'd heard someone grumble, when he came near. And if his captain was seen here, speaking to us? That would not bode well for him either.

"Do you think Lord Paratore shall move to Castello Greco at once?" I asked. Were he and Valentino already en route, even as we hung there? Or trying to persuade friends to help free us?

"Firenze shall be eager to take the keys," Papa said. "Though I truly thought the Grecos' generous, selfless offer would likely put an end to this madness."

"It could have been worse," Mama said. "We could have been sent to the dungeon, awaiting the gallows, as Rosa is."

We paused, somber.

"What did they mean by the coffin as one of the Lazarus tests?" I asked.

"They bury you alive," Papa said. "If you still breathe when they dig you up again, they figure you are innocent."

"You might be breathing," Mama said with a shudder. "But you will surely have lost your mind. I would have."

I shuddered too. "A fine choice, these cages," I said, appreciating the breeze anew. "And how many have survived the gauntlet?"

"Running from Palazzo della Signoria to the Arno? I have heard of only a few. But then they drowned in the water, too battered and broken to swim."

"Well then, again, I applaud your choice of the cage."

"I hope you shall say that come morning," he said wearily. "And the next. And the next. And the—"

"Let us take it one day at a time, Papa. Shall we? To think of more . . ." I left the thought unfinished. Surely none of us really could comprehend what we'd have to endure, ahead.

"To think of more is to borrow trouble," Mama said. "Each day is enough for us to manage. And together we will. Somehow. Some way."

I awakened in the night to a terrible cramp in my calf. I cried out, half asleep, belatedly remembering where I was.

"Tiliani?" Papa asked.

"It-it is well," I gasped as I frantically rubbed the muscle, trying to ease the pain. "Only a cramp."

I shifted and then shifted again, feeling my aching back and hip, which were perched against one side of my cage. I had tried to sit on the bottom, with my legs propped up, but they'd fallen asleep. I'd stood and moved from side to side, easing the pressure from one foot to the other, until I'd collapsed, drifting off. Now I sat again, drawing my knees to my chest and continuing to rub out the cramp in my calf. Gradually, it eased, but it felt as if it might be bruised from ankle to knee by how it ached.

"How did Zia Gabi manage this?" I asked.

"One day at a time," Mama said groggily. "One hour at a time."

"Mayhap one minute at a time," Papa said, his voice as dry and raspy as my own.

I sighed and looked around the empty piazza, the torches dying in the wee hours of morning. By sunrise, they would have sputtered to a stop. No one was out, given that it was past curfew and even the drunks had stumbled to their homes, the beggars finding a place to perch for the night. For the first time, I found myself jealous of them, able to stretch out, turn at will, then chastised myself. I was truly in a dismal state if I was wishing I was a beggar on the streets, rather than a captive in the cage.

My eyes moved up the formidable wall beside me to the skies. Clouds still dotted the expanse, blocking the blanket of stars, and in the distance, a crescent moon peeked and then hid behind another bank.

"I always find a crescent moon hopeful," Papa said.

I glanced over my shoulder, surprised. "More than a full moon?"

"Indeed. A full moon has reached her apex, only to wane again. A waxing crescent moon? Mayhap God has allowed us to see it this night to remember we are not forgotten. That we have reason to hope. There shall be more light on the morrow. And more light still, the night after that."

"I like that." I stared up again at the moon, watching as it emerged and submerged in the bank of clouds. "But I also like a big, fat harvest moon. Watching it rise, casting the trees of the forest in silhouette. Rising higher and illuminating the hills around Castello Forelli." I paused a moment. "Do you think we shall live to see that again, Papa? Truly?"

"I do."

I shook my head. "Why?"

"Because somehow, some way, we Forellis always find a path forward. I do not believe God brought us through battle and plague to perish here."

"But four days, Papa. *Four.* If it were but three, I might hope."

"There is always hope, *mia dolce.* Always. We are to hope until our dying breath that we might live. And if we perish, we have hope in heaven. There we shall find relief, peace, and reunion with all who have gone before us. Rocco and Dante will be there first, running to meet us. My cousin Fortino. Rodolfo Greco . . ."

I could hear the smile in his voice and smiled with him. "You almost make me long for it."

"You do not?" he asked.

"Not yet. There is too much life here I wish to experience."

"And yet Father Giovanni tells us that our life here is but a sliver of a very big cake we have yet to eat."

I thought about that. It did comfort me, the thought of seeing my precious little brothers again, as well as friends who had died through the years of illness or accident. 'Twould be a fine reunion indeed. But now . . . I thought of Ilaria and Giulio and Chiara. My grandmother. My aunt and uncle and cousins. And Valentino . . .

Nay, I was not yet ready to leave this earth. "I look forward to heaven, Papa. I do. But for now, I want to fight to remain. My life— our lives still feel like bunches of grapes on the vine. A vine that is growing, spreading. Getting closer to the harvest."

"I like that image, sweet girl. May it be so. May we see the harvest and squeeze every single bit of juice from our grapes, see it aged to perfection in a barrel, and share it at a feast—before our earthly days are over."

"May it be so," I whispered, leaning my head against a long-dead vine and watching the moon peek and disappear. At last I let my dry, heavy lids fall over my eyes again.

It seemed seconds later that I awoke, but by the numbness in my legs, I knew it had been hours. Men were calling out and chiding one another as they carried timbers into the piazza below. It cheered me a bit—this semblance of normal life—until I realized what they were doing at work before sunup.

They were building gallows. Outside of the gate, where we could see it. Where we would watch Rosa die. As if *we* had convinced her to murder their fellow citizens ourselves.

I groaned and closed my eyes. Her hanging would draw a new crowd. More to yell and curse us. More to stare at us as we tried to find some sort of comfortable position in these horrible, tiny prisons.

Grasping hold of the vines on either side of me, I pulled myself to standing, despite the fact I could not feel my legs. I managed to flop my feet into new positions and was reasonably certain my knees were locked before I released some of my weight.

I was wrong. My knees collapsed and I would have crumpled to the bottom had I not caught myself again. I let go of one handhold and tucked my skirts between my legs so that the leering workmen below could not catch the view they were hoping for. We had already endured the indignity of having to relieve ourselves yesterday, given there was no garderobe in which to retreat. That was the sole positive aspect of dehydration and lack of food. There would be little need to do so again.

One man had the audacity to whistle a merry tune as he walked to the pile of lumber and dropped his heavy beam. How could he? Regardless of how he felt about Rosa and whomever else was to be hanged this day, how could he *whistle*?

Mayhap if one was charged with constructing an instrument of death, 'twas the only way to manage. To concentrate on the task, the blessing of work and payment, rather than on the death that was to come.

I had seen more than one hanging in my life, but I was not anxious to witness another. I did not understand the impulse of the crowd to gather for such a gruesome event. Was it because they considered how it may very well be them, instead? Did it remind them of how fortunate they were in contrast, regardless of their circumstances? Or was it curiosity that drove them to watch a person take their very last breaths?

I supposed we were blessed in this regard. Should we still be alive in four days' time, there would likely be little spectacle. I had assisted Chiara and Nona enough with the ailing that I knew we might very well be unconscious by the third day, which would hardly be entertaining for those watching.

As I rubbed my finger over a lip splitting from the dry, I thought it might not be so bad to slip into unconsciousness. 'Twould be a sort of blessing. A blissful slip into sleep, half alive, half dead, only awaiting the Almighty's decision as to whether we might recuperate here on earth or be revived in heaven.

LUCIANA

We eased through the gathering crowd as guards dragged Rosa and three other condemned prisoners from the bowels of the prison, then marched them to the city gates.

I wanted to be anywhere else but here. But I could not bear to think of her dying alone. After all, I had gotten her into this mess. She could have slipped away. Disappeared. Not helped us at all. Lived on with Ercole—as miserable as it was. Instead, she had confessed, done her best to clear the Forelli name, and unburdened her soul. She would pay a price for her crime, but it had been Ercole who had convinced her to do it. It should be he in chains! Him walking to his doom!

Fury flowed through my veins, and I vowed again to find that man and make him pay for all the damage he had done. To the Forellis, to Siena, to Perugia, and now to Rosa. She looked tiny between the men before and behind her, all chained together as they trudged through the crowd, many spitting at them. Nico and I shoved our way through the groups, and circumvented others, but we stayed in step with Rosa.

I willed her to look my way, not daring to call her name. If the Fiorentini found out we knew her—or dared to support her— they would likely turn on us, and with such savagery, and in such numbers, no jiu jitsu would save us. But she kept her head down, moving only to shy away from the spittle or mockery of those she passed. The crowd bottlenecked at the gate, and it took some time to catch up with her, but Nico and I made our way toward the front. When they led Rosa up to the platform, there were only three people between us.

But her eyes went up to where the Forellis hung in their cages. All three stood, fingers wrapped around the vines, peering down at us.

"Forgive me!" Rosa cried to them.

"Be silent!" shouted a guard, stepping forward and raising a hand as if to strike her.

"Rosa!" Evangelia cried, her voice raspy. "Rosa!"

And in spite of themselves, even the guards quieted and looked up to the cage.

"We do not hate you!" Evangelia called. "We forgive you!"

The crowd grumbled in complaint, but there was no shushing

those above. And it seemed that those around us half wanted to hear what they had to say.

"You were persuaded to do evil, but we know who was truly behind it!" Luca shouted, his own voice gravelly. "Andrea Ercole and others he deceived! Confess to the Savior, and he will receive you in peace!"

"Andrea Ercole convinced you to murder those men!" Tiliani resumed.

"He did!" Rosa shouted back. "While he and other hired mercenaries murdered the other Fiorentini!"

I smiled at their brilliance. Here, now, they were getting to say what they wished to the masses. Making their case. If Andrea Ercole was among them, he had to be squirming. I wished we had taken a perch somewhere higher, where we could see the crowd, maybe spot him. If I were him, I'd be pulling up the hood on my cloak about now.

I scanned the people around me and sensed Nico doing the same. But I belatedly realized that if Ercole was here to watch his girlfriend die, he likely was on the outskirts, somewhere he could easily escape. Nico seemed to come to the same conclusion.

"Should we split up?" he whispered.

"No. We need to stay together. No matter what happens, *we need to stay together.*"

"Got it. Follow me." He turned and waded through the people, many grumbling and frowning at us as they pressed into their neighbors to give us room to move past. I looked back at Rosa, feeling guilty for leaving my post as her sole friend in the crowd, and realized our movement had caught her attention. She seemed to recognize me, even dressed as a boy.

I paused, put my fist to my chest and gave her a single nod. *You can do this*, I thought. *It will be awful, so awful, and then it will be over.* I willed courage into her, hoping she had heard the Forellis' words and taken them to heart. I hoped she would be received by God on the other side.

"*Brother*," Nico whispered, tugging at my elbow. Reluctantly, I turned and followed him, listening as the crimes and sentence of the first prisoner were read aloud from a scroll—a robbery witnessed by several others. I was just thinking *they kill people for robbery here* when the crowd booed and hissed, and I heard the squeak of a rope as it was hauled upward. I glanced back and froze in horror to see the man dangling, his legs pulling up—as if struggling to free himself. Wasn't hanging an instant death? I'd always thought so. But maybe it had to be a sudden drop—not this slow haul upward.

I glanced at Rosa and saw the terror on her face.

"*Brother*." Nico gripped my hand. "We can't change it," he whispered urgently in English. "The only thing we can do for her is find the one responsible for all of this."

Two men frowned at us. *Best to keep to Italian,* I thought. I immediately followed Nico, not pausing again until we'd made it to the edge of the crowd. Rosa's crime of murder was announced and the crowd cheered. Not seeing Ercole anywhere, we stopped and looked back at her. Terror had evaporated, and she appeared resigned.

"Receive her, Lord," I whispered, praying she had done what the Forellis had shouted and made her peace.

As the last word left my lips, the executioner hauled up on her rope. I closed my eyes, not wanting to see the agony of her death, while the crowd erupted in cheers again. When I opened them, I looked up to the Forellis. "We can't let them die too, Nico," I said to him.

"Then let's find Ercole."

We glanced left and right. "If I were him, I wouldn't be down here," I muttered. I looked up to neighboring buildings that surrounded the city wall.

And that's when I spotted him. On a roof, five buildings down. Turning to go, now that Rosa was swinging from a rope.

"Nico," I said, desperately pulling at his sleeve. "I *see* him! C'mon!"

15

LUCIANA

We ran toward the building, the crowd distracted by the third execution. But as I glanced up, I saw that Tiliani tracked us, her eyes wide with hope. She said something to her parents that made both of them straighten.

We entered the building—a wine shop—as Ercole came down the stairs. He appeared shaken. Even a little sad, which surprised me. Nico and I divided up, going either way around a large communal table. A couple people sat there, the hour being early and most outside to observe the execution. Even the proprietor had been outside and followed us in, probably curious why we'd want anything when there was another execution to watch. But our attention was solely on the man now just thirty feet away.

He looked up and saw us, his sorrow turning to fear. He immediately pivoted and ran back up the stairs, two at a time. We charged after him, passing through the empty living quarters on the second floor. Ercole slammed open the door to the roof and kept running.

Where did he expect to go? As we reached the top, too, he leaped to the next building.

"Oh no," I muttered. *You're not getting away that easily.* I chased after him before Nico, knowing he hated heights just as much as I did, and figuring it was better not to see what was below before jumping the five-foot chasm.

It wasn't until I landed that I remembered my sprained ankle. I gasped in pain. But adrenaline was my friend at the moment—along with my determination to capture this guy at last. *If mamas can lift vehicles off their children in an accident, I can do this.*

Ercole kept going, leaping to the next building, and Nico passed me up to leap after him. I didn't stop to think. I leapt after him. There was no way I would leave my brother to try and take this one down alone. It'd take both of us.

The buildings outside of the city wall had none of the tall towers, but some had tents atop them, either for cool sleeping quarters during the hot summer nights, or additional living or storage space. The third building had two tents, and I briefly lost track of our adversary. I glanced left and right but saw nothing.

"Go right." Nico shouted, rushing past me. "The Forellis see him!"

I looked up and saw them pointing out directions. "Our own surveillance helicopters!" I said with a laugh.

"That's right!" Nico leaped to the fourth and then the fifth building. We slowed there, thankfully. Because I didn't think my ankle could tolerate one more leap. This was a bigger building, with four separate tents on the roof and lines of laundry, pinned and drying in the breeze. I looked to the Forellis and Tiliani had a hand up, palm facing us. *Stop.*

"He's here somewhere," I whispered. We split up to warily walk around the first tent, glancing inside to see pillows and lounge chairs, then around a second, a sleeping pallet at its center. I was almost around the third, belatedly seeing my shadow against the tent's side, when a dagger slashed through and raked down my arm.

I cried out and jumped away, gripping my wound. Nico charged inside, taking him on, while I examined the damage. It was deep at the top—maybe half-an-inch—and gradually grew more shallow as it went down my arm. I grabbed a stocking from a nearby clothesline and hurriedly wrapped it around the worst of the wound, using my teeth and opposite hand to tie it tight, then hobbled around to back up Nico.

The two circled each other, Ercole's dagger stained with my blood. I had a new appreciation for the phrase *seeing red*.

"This guy needs to go down," I muttered in English.

"Oh, yeah," Nico said. "*È finito, amico. Resa.*" *It's over, man. Surrender.*

Ercole's lips clenched in defiance. "I think not."

I helped Nico flank him, but he'd hurt my dominant arm.

Acting on instinct, I pretended to move, capturing Ercole's attention. Nico grabbed his wrist, trying to put him in an armbar and take him down.

But Ercole was strong. He stepped forward, hooked Nico, and bodily lifted him, slamming him to the ground. He was on top, with his right arm on top of my brother, dagger still in hand.

I grabbed his free arm, hooked my legs around his chest and rolled him to his back atop me, freeing my brother. Nico scrambled to his feet as I struggled to hold on to our adversary.

But in a move that surprised us both, Ercole twisted and wildly stabbed. The blade rammed into my right pectoral. He savagely pulled it out, scrambling to his feet.

I tried to stand but the full force of my wound caught up with me then. I grew dizzy and stumbled backward against the side of the tent. It tore as I fell to my back.

"Luci!" Nico cried.

I gasped for breath as the ruined tent wall fluttered around me, my vision tunneling. For a moment, all I could hear was the fabric flapping in the breeze. All other sounds faded.

"Luci!" Nico said again, kneeling beside me.

"Go, Nico. Go get him," I panted.

"No." He pressed his hand to my fresh wound. "I need to get you to a doctor."

"Nico, go get him," I said, utterly frustrated. We were so close! So close!

"No," he said angrily. "We're sticking together. Remember? And you're not exactly in fighting shape anymore."

I let out an exasperated breath. But that's when I noticed it. I was breathing okay. I was shaky—probably from the shock—but I was breathing. "He missed my lung."

"Well, that's good. But you're bleeding like crazy. We gotta get you to a doc," he said. "You're gonna need stitches."

I winced as his other hand brushed the wound on my right arm. "Just . . ." I panted. "Just give me a sec." I sat up, grimacing, and leaned against a pillar of the tent, pressing against the wound.

Nico looked in the direction that Ercole had fled and wiped blood from the corner of his lip with the back of his hand. "I really hate that guy."

"Me too," I groaned, starting to feel my wound's pain supersede my shock.

Nico went to grab another piece of laundry from the line and came back with leggings that he tore in half. He ripped off a smaller piece and placed it over the wound, then wound the longer piece under my armpit and across to tie it on the far side of my neck.

I looked down. Blood was already seeping through.

"Yup, gotta get you stitched up," he grunted.

The door to the rooftop slammed open, and Giulio and Ilaria charged through. Giulio had his sword in hand, Ilaria daggers.

"Giulio," I whispered, relief flooding through me. If Ercole was still around, surely my brother and these two could take him down.

They ran to us, grimacing over my wounds. They looked wildly about.

"He's gone," Nico said apologetically.

Giulio knelt beside me, his beautiful blue eyes searching mine. He gripped my hand.

"You came back," I said.

"*Ovviamente*," he returned, tracing my face. *Of course.*

I belatedly noticed they wore nothing that would identify them as Sienese or of Castello Forelli. They had traded their beautiful tunics for the clothing of peasants.

I took a firmer grip on his hand. "We must find a way to free the Forellis. Even if we cannot capture Ercole."

He nodded solemnly. "Agreed. But first, we must find you a surgeon."

He shifted and then lifted me in his arms. The motion made my head spin anew.

"Do you know where we can find one?" my brother asked, following him to the doorway.

"We shall ask," Ilaria said. "But we must say you were attacked in the alley by robbers. Two of them, both men. Say nothing about Ercole. We don't want anyone summoned who will recognize the four of us. Understand?"

"Understood." Nico twirled a finger and pointed, urging them to go. "*Andiamo.* She has lost a great deal of blood already."

Liquid warmth ran down my chest, my side, soaking Giulio's shirt, too, and for the first time, I really got worried. There were no transfusions in this era. Bleeding out was a serious concern.

Giulio rushed me down the stairs and then into the street before anyone noticed us. The crowd was just now breaking up, the hanging complete.

"What is this?" blustered a man before us, spreading his arms wide. "What has happened?" Others stopped around him.

"We were attacked!" Giulio motioned with his head. "Two alleys back. Two men in black shirts!"

The man called out to others, and as a group, they ran toward where we had indicated, leaving the women behind.

"Please," Ilaria said. "We need a surgeon barber."

"This way," said the younger woman, gesturing for us to follow. "With luck he will be home."

We hurried down an alley, then took a right on a crammed street, circumventing people and wagons full of goods. A boy flicked a stick at a small herd of pigs, eating the scraps thrown from windows, and other things I didn't want to really think about. I felt a wave of nausea and tried to breathe slowly.

"Make way!" cried the young woman, parting the people for us.

Half a block farther, we paused by a door as she lifted the heavy metal knocker and let it fall, again and again.

"Giulio," I said, "please. Put me down for a moment."

"Are you certain?" he asked.

I nodded, and after a moment's hesitation, he gently set me on my feet. I leaned a hand against the stone wall and blinked, trying to get my swirling head to settle.

No one was answering the door.

But while the others conferred on where to go next, I wavered and knew I could not stop myself from vomiting.

Giulio caught and held me partially upright as I emptied my belly. He pulled my hair back from my face, winding it around his hand. Something about that moved me. *So tender. . . so caring,* I admired, as if from a distance.

Panting, I tried to wipe my forehead of sweat and then cried out when I belatedly realized I'd attempted it with my wounded arm. I looked at him and my eyes drifted down to his chest, his shirt covered in my bright red blood. *Blood,* I thought. *So much of my blood.* My vision tunneled, and I felt my knees give way.

But Giulio picked me up in his arms again, consternation etched into his face. "We shall get you to a surgeon, beloved," he said. "Do not give up."

"I-uh. I . . ."

"Make haste," he grunted to the others, and it felt like I was very far away when I recognized that they now ran.

TILIANI

I sank to my haunches, utterly dismayed.

From my peripheral vision, I knew my parents did the same.

"I so hoped . . ." I said.

"As did I," Mama said.

"And now—"

"Things are even worse," Papa said.

We had watched the Betarrini twins catch sight of Ercole and give chase across multiple buildings. Then, when the Grecos had arrived, we had pointed them toward the building we had last seen them—the last building we'd watched Ercole leap to. He had emerged at ground level and, with a smug little bow toward us, ducked down an alley and disappeared.

But there had been no sign of the twins. We watched in terror, fearing the worst. Shortly afterward we saw Domenico and Ilaria appear, then Luciana in Giulio's arms. She was bleeding so much she had left a red trail along the street behind them. They rushed away without even a glance in our direction.

"Does Firenze have as many surgeons as Siena?" I asked Papa, leaning my aching head against the vines.

"I assume so," he said grimly. "Let us pray there is one nearby."

I closed my eyes, feeling both utter disappointment of being so close to capturing Ercole again, and fear for Luciana. Might she die? Might we all?

I looked to the gallows, the four bodies twisting in the slight breeze. The people had left, flowing from the piazza like water through a sieve. The sun was climbing. How long would they leave the bodies there before cutting them down? Were we soon to follow Rosa into death?

I had a crack on either side of my mouth now, the skin splitting as I spoke. My eyes felt as if there was a layer of dust beneath the lids. And my head ached, oh, how it ached.

And this was but day two.

"We shall not make it to day three, let alone day four," I muttered in despair. "Why would God allow this to happen to the Betarrinis? To us?"

"God allows us free choice," Papa said, after a moment. "'Twas our choice to come to this city. Yours too. The Priori's choice to condemn us to the cage. God directs us all, but in the end, we all must choose whether to follow his lead."

I shook my head and then immediately stilled, finding it made the pounding worse. "But have we not suffered enough?" I asked. "Losing Rocco and Dante? Our friends over the years?"

"Life is rife with suffering." Mama leaned her head back against a vine. "But I have been thinking on that today, and something Father Giovanni told me once about oysters."

"Oysters?" I said blankly.

"On occasion, a bit of sand or other irritant gets beneath the mollusk. Over time, the mollusk rolls that irritant over and over, coating it with a secretion that eventually covers the thing in concentric layers. In time, it becomes a pearl."

I thought on that. "So you are saying that in time, things that irritate us become something good?"

"I am saying that pain can become a pearl in time," she said wearily. "And I believe I have not allowed much of my own to become that. Instead, I work and work and work over my pain, like something still stuck under my own tongue." She lifted her head and looked to me and Papa. "For that I am sorry. If we ever escape these cursed cages, I want to be . . . different."

"We have borne a great deal of pain, beloved," Papa said.

"But Rocco and Dante"—she sighed, leaning her head back again and closing her eyes—"would want us to live. *Freely. Fully.* To accept the pearls. I feel as if I've lived with my grief like a badge of honor for them. That to give up the kernel of sand, to allow it to become something different, would feel like I was somehow forgetting them."

"We shall never forget them," Papa said.

"Nay, never," I said.

Mama took a deep breath and let it out slowly. And in that moment, it felt as if she was lighter, relieved of a heavy burden, for the first time in years.

"We have *one another* today," she said, looking over at us.

"And if on the morrow we perish, or the next after that, we shall be reunited with our boys again." She smiled, and I winced as it made her own lip split. She wiped at the trickle of blood. "Life has been a fine adventure with you, Tiliana. With you, Luca. I love you."

"You shall have my heart forever, beloved."

I felt a knot form in my throat, listening to what sounded like a farewell between my parents. I thought of Valentino, of how we might have had a love like theirs. How we might have married and had a child of our own in time.

I looked to the glistening Arno, then to the outskirts of the city, heat rising from her sunbaked, red-tile rooftops. I closed my eyes, feeling the burning rays on my cheeks, knowing I should try and cover my face, but lacking the strength to do so. I lacked the strength to do anything at all but pray.

16

LUCIANA

I came to, screaming.

Giulio and Nico held me down on either side. Ilaria helped a gray-haired man by holding my flesh together, while he rammed a needle through my skin with another stitch. I screamed again. Ilaria splashed clear *grappa* over my wound . . . an attempt to sterilize it?

"Bite down on this." Giulio placed a weathered piece of leather between my teeth.

I was just wondering how many others had had it in their mouths when the needle again went into my skin and out the other side.

I clenched so hard on the disgusting leather that I dimly worried I might crack a tooth. *I don't want this guy to have to pull a tooth out too.* I concentrated on breathing slowly, in through my nose, even as tears rolled down my cheeks. I spat out the leather and exhaled through pursed lips, then drew another in from my nose.

The doctor peered at me again, his eyes weary, as if he had seen a thousand such wounds. "Who of you will tell me," he said, stabbing me again while I panted through it, "why this woman is dressed as a man?" He pulled the heavy sinew through the other side.

My friends and brother remained silent a moment. I wished they would talk, say anything, because I thought I could *hear* the thick needle enter my skin—or was that the pull of the sinew? The room began to spin again.

"We would like that to remain a secret." Giulio pulled a purse from his waist and casually set three, then four coins on the side table.

"Secrets cost more than that," the surgeon said, not looking at the coins. "There will be soldiers here shortly, inquiring about the alleged crime."

Giulio added another coin to the stack. "I shall put three more on this pile if you can get her sewed up and we leave before they arrive."

The physician perked up and picked up his pace.

"I don't know if the speed makes it better or—worse," I said to Nico, panting as the doctor pricked and pulled, pricked and pulled. "How many more?" I managed to ask, wondering how long I must endure.

"Maybe four or five," he said. "Hang in there."

The surgeon cast me a curious glance. "What language does she speak?"

"We are from Britannia," Nico said in Italian. "English is our native tongue."

"Are you spies? Is that why she is disguised as a boy?" he asked. He straightened and looked from Nico to Giulio and then Ilaria.

Nico laughed. "We are not spies."

"Why else would she dress this way?"

Giulio walked back to the side table and lifted the coins and let them drop. "Time is passing quickly. Do you truly want answers, or do you want more silver?"

The surgeon let out a mirthless laugh and waved them away. "Three more should do it." He jabbed me again, and again, and again. I felt as much sweat flowing from my temples, forehead, and neck as I did blood from my wounds.

"Why did you not . . . cauterize it?" I asked, this time, in Italian.

"My fire was not hot enough," the man grunted as he knotted the sinew. "And your wound too deep. But now it might be hot enough to tend to your arm."

Belatedly, I remembered my other wound and looked over to my bicep, the stocking bandage dripping blood. I groaned and my head began to spin.

"C'mon, Luci," Nico whispered in my ear. "It will be the coolest tattoo ever."

I grimaced at him. "We always wanted *twin* tattoos," I ground out. "Why don't you get the same one?"

He laughed. "I think I shall wait for something more artistic."

The doctor stretched my arm onto a board that swiveled out from the table. Giulio and Ilaria moved to hold me down when I reacted, wanting to bolt.

"You must stay still, beloved," Giulio said. "There is no other way. You have lost so much blood."

"It will be but a moment," Ilaria said.

Nico sprawled across my legs, pinning them to the table as the doctor strapped down my arm with leather bands from beneath. I gazed in terror as he went to the fire and then returned with a red-hot poker.

"Nico!" I shouted.

"*Aspettare*, Luci!" he cried, telling me to hold on. Hold on? Was he crazy? This was a nightmare!

The doctor pushed up on the underside of my arm with his left hand, bringing the flesh together, and quickly lowered the poker to my flesh.

It took a second for the pain to register.

Another for a scream to form in my throat.

By the third, I faded again into oblivion.

And oh, how I welcomed it.

TILIANI

I could not feel my legs, yet I did not have the strength to pull myself up on the vines for the twentieth time that day. Distantly, I knew

I ought to do it, to allow the blood to flow. But 'twas a painful, prickling process. Truthfully, I did not know if my arms had the strength to hold me up any longer while my legs remembered their purpose. I forced myself to raise my aching head and look about the empty piazza below. There was no one present other than the four corpses, casting massive, ghostly shadows to the cobblestones before them. With the sputtering torchlight, they seemed to eerily dance.

I looked away from them to the crescent moon, unfettered by clouds this night, thinking about Rosa, Rocco, and Dante all in heaven now. Dancing. It made me smile, that promise. In the midst of such dismal failure and pain, there, there was a bit of hope. Always hope.

I stared at the moon and prayed. *God, do you see us? Or do you attend to others, knowing you shall soon be welcoming us home to heaven?*

This was but night two. I doubted we would survive a third. And the thought of it left me bereft. I had so much more to do here, on earth! I wanted to live and work beside my cousins at Castello Forelli. Hug my nona again. See my mother and aunt on horses, in those fine blue tunics embroidered with the golden wolves. Fall in love with a man, a good man. And if Valentino Valeri could not be that man, mayhap there would still be another.

Might I have avoided all of this if I had not kept Aurelio at arm's length? Fought my parents' wishes? Fancied myself falling for his captain instead? There were many nobles who married upon meeting. What if I had done the same? We would not have given Ercole time to sow his thorny seeds. Or he still might have moved against us, but then Perugia would have found both Siena and Firenze coming to our defense. And in fighting together we would have swiftly laid low any thought Arezzo or Pisa might have of coming for us afterward.

There is no profit in thinking about the road not taken, Nona often said. *Only how you might make better decisions next time.*

I closed my eyes and heavily sighed. If my head had been aching before, now it was making me nauseous, even with nothing in my stomach. *Too much thinking,* I told myself. *I need only to sleep. Mayhap come morn . . .*

The sound of the trap door opening above me, as well as those above my parents, startled me. I looked up, seeing nothing but darkness. What did they want? To see if we still lived?

Fury spurred me to lift myself a final time. I did not want to be seen, unable to rise. "Mama," I whispered. "Papa."

But as I reached a trembling standing position, I saw the fat waterskin lowered on a rope. I dared to release one of my handholds to grasp it and pull it through the vines above me. Looking over to my parents, I saw they had the same at their fingertips. But Papa was still asleep.

"Papa!" I whispered.

"Luca!" my mother said.

"Shhhh," said the man above me, even as my father roused. "Make haste. Untie it and drink. We must be away in a moment."

I strained to make out his voice. Was it Aurelio? Valentino? But the thought was lost to me as the urgency of bringing the skin to my lips, assuaging my thirst, became primal.

With trembling hands, I unclasped the metal spigot and tipped the round skin to my parched lips. I began with a sip, running it around my mouth before carefully swallowing. As if I had forgotten how! Then I took another sip, and then a gulp, feeling it wash down my parched throat. And then another, and another until the skin shrank in my hands. Too soon, the bag was empty. I tipped it back, trying to get the very last droplets, but the man was already pulling on the rope. *Retrieving the evidence,* I thought. *Why could he have not given us more? And a bit of bread?*

As if on cue, my stomach rumbled. And then I knew. He had given us only enough to survive. He did not want it too evident, this angel of mercy, that someone had given us aid. My mother and father finished their skins, too, and the depleted vessels were drawn back up, the doors coming to a swift close. I listened for evidence of battle. A skirmish. But the angel—or angels—disappeared as swiftly as they had appeared.

I winced as the familiar prickling in my legs returned. I glanced at my father. "Did I dream that?" I whispered.

"Nay," he said, rubbing his lips in wonder, as if wanting to remember the sensation of drinking too. "Clearly we have at least one friend remaining in this city."

"Think 'twas enough to sustain us to the fourth day?"

"I have hope again. Do you not?"

I nodded, noticing how my headache had receded to a dull pounding again. "I wish there had been more."

"If there had, we might have vomited it all," Mama whispered.

"And we cannot appear *too* revived," Papa added.

"Do you think it was—" I began.

"Do not utter any names," Papa rushed to say. "Mayhap even the guards do not know who it was. And we do not want our friends in any trouble."

"How did they get past the guards?" Mama asked.

"I suspect . . ." He made a rubbing motion in the dim moonlight, the signal for payment.

I smiled, feeling the prickling pain reach my feet as a small triumph. Of course they had been paid off. The city was at a heady point against us—against all of Siena, really. And the only thing that could top loyalty, in the end, was bribery.

I searched the piazza below, hoping I would catch sight of Valentino. That it was him, or Aurelio, behind this act that might very well have saved us. A patrol of six Fiorentini guards marched through, making me fear for our deliverer, but there was no shout of alarm, no sign of them giving chase.

A guard coughed above us and then blew his nose, a familiar sound. Was he the one who had been paid off to step aside for a moment? To look away? Mayhap he needed the money to pay for medicine. Or mayhap he had loved ones at home who were ill.

I prayed a prayer of protection for him and any others who had been part of our relief this night.

For I did feel it as relief. We still needed to survive until the end of the Priori's sentencing. But with a bit of water in my belly now, yes now, I had the first tiny bit of hope. *Thank you, Father, for this grace and mercy. Preserve us, Lord. Sustain us. And be with Luciana and our loved ones in Siena.*

My prayers said, I settled back in my seated position, tucking my arms around my legs, a bit chilled now. And then I prayed for sleep—hours of sleep that would catapult us closer to the end of our trial.

17

LUCIANA

I awakened to a fist ramming against the doctor's door.

"Firenze guards!" cried one. "Open up!"

The doctor paled and looked to Giulio.

"Buy us a minute," he growled. "And when they enter, tell them only that this *boy* was stabbed by robbers in an alley."

The doctor slowly walked to the door, shouting that he was coming. "*Sto arrivando!*"

Giulio leaned toward Nico, even as he pulled a blanket up to my chin. Ilaria swiftly covered my head with a stocking cap. "Describe Ercole as the main man you remember. Mayhap they can find him if we cannot."

Then he turned to me and kissed my forehead. "We shall be out back. If there is any trouble, call for me. Understood?"

I nodded, sweat beading on my lip. What if these soldiers figured out I was a woman? I remembered well the warnings of it not being allowed for women to dress as men, or vice versa. Would they put me in a cage too?

"I've got this," Nico whispered as the doctor slowly opened the door. "Let me do the talking. You keep your eyes shut."

A soldier slammed open the door and pushed past the doctor. "Who is this?" he asked gruffly.

"My patient," said the man. "He was stabbed quite viciously. Had to sew up his chest and treat his arm."

The soldier stepped up beside me, another on my opposite side, pushing a protesting Nico aside.

They peered down at me. "A report was made to us late last night. You are the two attacked by men in black? Were there not two others with you?"

I groaned, as if I hovered on the edge of unconsciousness.

"We were attacked in an alley," Nico said. "Robbed of our meager purse. When we tried to fight them off, they stabbed my brother. He moved in time for it to only rake down his arm. But then the other stabbed him in the chest. Those two others were Fiorentini who came to our aid. I do not know their names."

"Will he live?" grunted one knight to the doctor.

"I believe so. He lost a great deal of blood. He may not be completely conscious for a day or two. But he needs rest, not an inquisition."

"If there are robbers in this city, we aim to capture them now," said the leader, turning toward Nico. "Can you describe them?"

"I can describe one. He was the one who spoke to us. After he struck my brother, my attention was on him."

"Understood. What did your assailant look like?"

"About my height," Nico said. "A bit more slender. Lighter brown hair tied at the nape of his neck. Well-defined, high cheekbones. He carried both daggers and a battle-axe on his back. He has not shaved for a few days, and he wore a black tunic."

I thought of that small mercy . . . at least Ercole wasn't still wearing a Forelli tunic.

"What did they steal?" asked the second man.

"All we had. Only a meager purse."

"Would you recognize him again if you saw him?" asked the first.

"I would."

"And be willing to testify against him?"

Nico paused. "Of course. But we are traveling through. As soon as my brother is on his feet again, we shall be on our way."

"See that you remain for at least two days," said the captain. "With luck, we shall apprehend these men and you can identify them."

"As you say," Nico said, with a deferential duck of his head.

That worked out for us. We needed to remain here for a couple more days anyway—for me to get well enough to travel *and* to see the Forellis through their torment.

"You shall give them food and a place to sleep," the captain said to the doctor. He paused near the side table. "What is this?" My heart sank as I remembered Giulio's pile of coins.

"Payment for my services," the surgeon returned.

"I thought you said you were robbed of your meager purse?" he said suspiciously to Nico.

"Indeed," my brother said smoothly. "A good Samaritan stopped by and agreed to pay for the surgeon's services. Are all in Firenze so kind?"

The captain huffed a laugh. "Not all." He picked up the stack of coins and dropped them one at time into his other palm. "Have your prices gone up of late? I recall bringing one of my wounded men for half this sum."

"Well," said the surgeon, in a wink-wink, nudge-nudge way, "that was for *you*, Captain. You keep our streets safe. Protect our noble city." He lifted both hands and shrugged a little. "Can you blame a man for asking a bit more from a wealthy benefactor?"

The captain gave him a hard stare. "Taking advantage of a good Samaritan, eh? While I shall look away"—he set the coins down on the table again—"God shall not. Mind your step."

The surgeon readily agreed.

"Who was this benefactor?" he pressed.

"I do not know. I had never seen him before. He was likely another traveler, only in our city for the day. He certainly was not from this *contrade*," he said, referring to his neighborhood.

"He discovered us outside the surgeon's door," Nico said. "Mayhap he was simply grateful that it was us and not him."

The captain considered him for a long moment. "Mayhap. Crime has increased of late, in this contrade outside the gates. The Priori wish to see it curtailed."

"That would be good for all," the surgeon said. "Thank you for your efforts."

I was shivering now. From the loss of blood? Or fear that we hovered on the edge of disaster? The captain stepped toward me again and took hold of the blanket.

I froze, fearing he would lift it and glimpse my bound breasts beneath the bandage. But he only brought it closer to my chin and patted my good shoulder. "We shall find who did this to you, son. And your brother shall aid us."

I fought not to open my eyes wide in surprise. Instead, I grimaced and moved my head, focusing on the pain I truly felt, maintaining my act of semiconsciousness.

"May I not remain here, with my brother?" Nico tried. "I give you my pledge that I shall not leave this building."

"Do you not wish to aid him further? Patrol the streets with us. If you glimpse your assailant, we shall give chase. Mayhap we shall find him within the hour, if we move quickly. It could be that he is in a nearby taverna at this very moment."

"Ahh, yes. That is a good plan," Nico acquiesced, clearly seeing no way out of it. He turned to me and put his hand on my good shoulder. "Rest well, brother. I shall return to you as soon as I can."

With that, they all tromped out the door, the doctor closing it behind them. He leaned his head against it, visibly pale, while Giulio and Ilaria slipped back inside. Ilaria stepped up beside me, and I looked up to her, teeth chattering. She put a hand on my forehead. "She burns with fever," she said accusingly.

I groaned, infection immediately coming to mind. I thought of the surgeon's needle entering my flesh again and again. Had it even been washed since his last patient?

The man waved off her anger and came to me, pulling back the blanket. Giulio turned his back, giving me privacy, given my state of undress. The surgeon untied my shoulder dressing and peeked beneath it. "She may need leeches," he said.

That brought my eyes open. "Nay," I said, pleading with Ilaria. "No leeches." I shuddered at the thought.

"Lady Adri and Chiara use leeches and maggots at times," she began, trying to reassure me. "'Tis good with infection."

"No maggots either," I insisted. "At least until Lady Adri or Chiara directs it."

Seeing my determined expression, she looked to the doctor. "Honey. Our women at home are adept healers, and often use honey to fight infection."

"I have no honey," he said.

"Then I shall obtain some," Giulio growled. He glanced back and, seeing me covered again, turned and took my hand in both of his, frowning at my chattering teeth. "I shall return soon."

His voice and my trembling reminded me of that moment weeks ago, when we had hidden away in the crevasse of a rock, our enemies hunting us. How he had held me tight when I was falling apart. I wished he wasn't going away now, but knew he had to. Because apparently, honey was not just a good match for peanut butter, but also for wounds.

18

LUCIANA

The crackle of a fire startled me awake, but I was so tired I could barely move beyond a single blink. I saw the doctor's table and knew, with relief, that at some point in the last day, I had been freed of it. Now I was directly before the fire. I shifted a little and felt the firm but welcoming form of Giulio behind me. He reclined against the wall, slightly snoring, his legs on either side of my own, his arms gently surrounding me. Following my movement, he tensed and tightened his hold.

"Giulio," I whispered.

"Ah, my love," he whispered back, feeling my forehead. "Has your fever broken?"

"I believe so," I said. "What-what are we doing on the ground?"

He laughed softly. "You were trembling so, I could do nothing but hold you."

"Oh," I said, feeling the heat of a blush and glad he could not see it in the relative dark.

"I can . . ." He started to shift away.

"Nay." I put a hand on his thigh to still him. I leaned back against his chest. "You bring me comfort," I said simply.

He paused, then pulled my braid around to the other side of my neck, then lowered his nose and lips to my shoulder. I noticed then that someone had put a fresh, white shirt on me. But the heat of his breath passed right through the soft woven cloth to my skin.

"I am so glad you are better," he whispered in my ear, kissing me right behind it, sending shivers down my neck. "I thought I might need to track down Domenico and get you back to the tomb."

"I am glad it did not come to that." I settled back, loving the feel of his chin against my head, the connection between us. Despite what I'd been through, the thought of leaving him again was the last thing I wanted to do. "Where is Ilaria?"

"On a pallet on the far side of the table," he said. "Can you not hear her?"

I listened, then heard a most ladylike, soft snore, and smiled.

"The surgeon wanted you to remain on the table. To tie you up so you would not mess with your wounds and bandages. I told him I had a better solution."

I placed my hand over his arm, wrapped around me. "I much prefer yours."

"As do I." He kissed me again on the side of my head. "Especially now that you are improving. I was so worried, Luciana. So worried that you had returned to me, and I was about to lose you again. I prayed for you constantly."

"How long was I unconscious?"

"Unconscious?" he repeated.

"Asleep?"

"Ahh, *insensate*," he corrected me. "More than a day," he said. "The surgeon blames the loss of blood as well as the infection setting in. You battled on two fronts."

"So this is . . . come morning 'twill be . . ."

"The day of the Forellis' reckoning."

"Do they . . . are they . . ."

"They live, as of late last night. Ilaria went to check on them."

"'Tis a miracle."

He cocked his head to look at me and ran his index knuckle down my jawline. "It apparently takes a great deal to take a Betarrini down."

"What of a Forelli or Greco?"

I could hear the soft smile in his words. "They can hold their own as well, by the grace of God."

"What of Domenico? Has he returned?"

"He is well," he assured me. "Ilaria spotted him on patrol with the guards in the center of the city yesterday afternoon. They stopped by last night, but given that you were still *unconscious*," he said, testing out the word, "demanded that he remain with them for another day. They shall likely allow him to return shortly."

"How long have you sat like this, holding me?" I asked quietly.

"About five hours," he said. "I finally had had enough, watching you shiver so on that cursed table. Ilaria made you presentable, set you in my arms, then finally gave in to her own slumber."

"Five hours?" I tried to sit up, then gasped at the pain. "You must be in need of your own slumber."

"Hush now," he said, gently shifting me so that I could partially see him. But I was utterly secure in his arms. "Surely you know that I would not give up this stolen moment for a purse full of gold."

"Thank you," I said, running my left hand over his long, finely muscled forearm to his hand. "I am so grateful."

He lifted his palm, and I interlaced my fingers with his.

"No more than I am that you are here, Luciana. Still with me."

I sat there a moment, trying to really absorb the fact that the big, handsome knight really wanted to be exactly where he was. On the cold, hard ground, holding me. That he had prayed for me through the night, holding me as I shivered and sweat through my fever. Belatedly I touched my forehead and hair. "I must be a sight."

"A most beautiful one at that," he said.

I laughed softly and shook my head. "Clearly, your standards are low."

He gently turned my face toward him again. "They are not. Luciana, you captivate me, and it goes far beyond your appearance."

We stared into each other's eyes, and I was just wondering if I might be able to bear the pain to turn enough to kiss him, when Ilaria groaned and sat up.

"You do understand that we shall have our hands quite full this day," she said, stretching. "If the Forellis are freed, we might have to battle our way out of this city, and Luciana is hardly in fighting shape. She should be *resting*."

"Be at peace." Giulio lifted a palm to his sister. "We are celebrating the fact that she is on the mend. Mayhap you should go and scout the piazza again?"

Ilaria rolled her eyes, recognizing he simply wanted her out of the way. And as soon as she'd sheathed her sword and was out the door, he carefully moved around me so that he could take my face in his hands and kiss my lips, my cheeks, my temples, my eyelids with such exquisite, slow tenderness, I almost felt my pain disappear.

Almost. Because the pain? The pain was pretty bad.

That's another con for the List, I thought. *No Urgent Care on every medieval corner. Or Walgreens. Or CVS. And the apothecaries are probably highly suspect.*

Giulio moved to kiss me softly on the lips again.

But that's a pro.

Yes, that most definitely is a pro.

As his kiss deepened, I moaned and gently pushed him backward, feeling my head swirl.

"Oh, Luciana, forgive me," he said, lifting me and placing me back on the table. He covered me with a blanket and then pushed the hair from his forehead in frustration. "I forgot myself."

"It is all right," I panted, lifting a hand, struggling to breathe as the pain came roaring back. "Did the doctor—the surgeon—give me some sort of medicine for the pain? Because I think it might be wearing off . . ."

Giulio nodded. "I shall fetch him."

"Yes," I panted. "Please. Do so. Now."

19

I opened my eyes to the tinge of light on the horizon.

We had made it! Made it to our fourth day. Impossibly, we had made it.

But when I tried to move, I found I could not. I truly felt the way Lazarus might have in the grave, wound up in graveclothes. My hands and feet refused to obey me. Sometime in the night, I had managed to position myself in the very bottom of the cage on my side. In terror, I tried to move again to no avail. Was I paralyzed? Or had I lived through these hellish days of captivity only to find myself dying within reach of freedom?

My head could turn, I realized with relief. I lifted it and glanced at my parents. Both appeared asleep, nestled on the bottoms of their cages. Skin tears crisscrossed the soles of my feet given the constant, unrelenting pressure of standing on the narrow vines. My mother and I had tried to give them respite, standing on our toes for a time, our heels another, but it never lasted long. We'd given up and either sat or curled up.

Curling up was a mistake, I belatedly realized. Not that I had been thinking clearly. I fought to think at all now. I remembered how my legs continued to go to sleep. That was what had happened. I simply had to find a way to move now, even a little, to revive them.

"Papa?" I tried, as my cage turned in the breeze toward him.

He lifted his head from his knees, as if startled. His eyes were unfocused, distant, but at least he moved. "Tilly?" he said, using my childhood nickname.

"I-I can't move," I said.

He blinked again, more rapidly this time. "'Twill be well. You need only a bit of water," he rasped. "Some bread."

"And room to move," groaned my mother, her voice strangled.

But Papa smiled. "We have made it, my girls." He gained strength with each word. "Made it to day four. Today we shall be released!"

"And then what?" Mama asked, managing to partially sit up after some struggle.

I pinched the fingers of my left hand together, feeling some life returning to it. Then I clenched my fist.

"We shall find our way out of this city and return home," Papa said.

"They shall let us walk out, unfettered?" Mama asked.

"Or ride. We have passed their Lazarus test. To not allow us to drop our graveclothes and walk would be impossible."

"Domenico and Luciana are here somewhere," I rasped. "As are Giulio and Ilaria. They shall come to our aid." Speaking, with my throat so dry, felt like pulling tiny knives along it.

"How long shall they wait?" Mama asked, looking downward.

Yesterday, they had taken down the rotting corpses of Rosa and the other three criminals, wrapped them in burlap, and unceremoniously dumped them in the back of a wagon. I knew all three of us had wondered if they would treat our bodies with similar disdain.

"Mayhap until half past the noon hour," Papa said. "Exactly four days since our sentencing. They took note of it when we entered."

"They shall not give us a few hours' grace?" she asked dully.

"Nay. They do not *want* us to exit these cages."

"They want us to die. Expected us to die," she said.

"But my She-Wolves have beaten death yet again."

"Which will make them hate us more than ever."

"And make your own people love you all the more on the morrow."

Mama sighed and managed to more fully sit up. I gaped at her.

She had the sort of inner strength that I could not quite summon myself. "We shall see about the morrow. All I care about is this day. Tiliani"—she frowned—"are you unwell?"

"You mean, other than starving and thirsting for four days?" Papa quipped tiredly.

Mama ignored him and leaned her face against the vines. "Til."

"I am well enough," I groaned. "I think—I think my whole body is cramping or asleep."

"Try and move."

"I am." What did she think I had been trying to do all this time? I could move my left arm now, and I reached out to grasp a vine, but I couldn't find the strength to clasp it and pull myself upright. However, with my arm lifted, I concentrated on moving my left hip and shifting my leg a bit, willing the blood to flow again.

The sound of boots against cobblestone drew our attention. The city gates opened, and twelve soldiers marched in, surrounding two of the Priori.

The sun was not yet peeking over the horizon, only warming high clouds in the sky. Why were they here when the city still slumbered? Did they intend to release us early, as an act of mercy?

But as my cage began to lower to the ground, I tensed, thinking of another answer.

In our weakened state, we could not put up much of a fight.

And if their intent was to murder us, they would not want it witnessed.

LUCIANA

Someone pounded on the door before the morning sun illuminated the street outside. Giulio went to the door and cracked it open. I forced myself to get to my feet, realizing for the first time that they had bound my sprained ankle while I was unconscious. There was a poultice and thick bandage.

"Domenico," Giulio said gladly, allowing him to enter.

"Luciana!" Nico said, moving forward, eyes only on me. I saw that he meant to embrace me.

"Not yet." I put my hand up. "A hug might kill me."

"Oh, right." He took my hand. "I am so glad to see you awake, even upright!"

"I am glad to see you too."

He turned toward the others. "Something is happening in the piazza outside the gate. A couple of the Priori and their knights have gone to the cages."

Giulio frowned. "At this hour? Their four days are not up until noon. There is to be a public ceremony."

"Unless . . ." Ilaria's forehead wrinkled.

"Unless they intend to *not* allow them to rise as Lazarus did," Giulio ground out, staring at his sister.

Not allow them to rise? As in, *kill* them?

"I will go for Lord Paratore," Ilaria said, already at the door. "Only he can stop this. And fetch our horses."

"We shall try and waylay them," Giulio said, "and give you time to return."

She left without further word. Giulio turned to me as the surgeon emerged from the sole bedroom, sleepily rubbing his face. "Who is here?"

We ignored him. "I want you to remain here, Luciana," Giulio said.

"Nay. If the Forellis are released, we shall need to leave the city immediately. You will not have time to come and fetch me." I shook my head when he opened his mouth to argue. "I shall remain on the outskirts of the piazza. Come. Let us go." I moved through the door, not waiting for them, moving as fast as I could, fighting to hide my dizziness and the lingering pain in my ankle.

Giulio and Domenico came to either side of me. "Go. Run ahead,"

I urged them. "I have the worst feeling about what's happening with the Forellis. Please. *Go.*"

They shared a long look and then, clearly feeling the same, ran ahead, disappearing around the corner. We were but three or four blocks away. I hobbled onward, feeling utterly forlorn and panicked.

Because even that short distance didn't guarantee they'd make it in time to stop whatever was about to come down.

TILIANI

We tried to call out, scream, as they lowered us, but our voices were so weak 'twas nothing more than the bleating of baby lambs. *Like lambs going to the slaughter,* I thought distantly. Our cages hit the cobblestone. Guards moved forward to untie our doors.

"She shall live 'til noon," said one quietly to Lord Piccolomini behind him, as he examined Mama.

"So shall he," whispered the one beside my father.

"And this one shall too," said the guard who opened my door. He crouched beside me, peering at my face as if trying to ascertain *how* alive I truly was.

Papa managed to crawl out of his cage but could not rise. I was still trying to find the strength to sit up.

"Resolve it," grunted Lord Piccolomini under his breath, making a twisting motion with his hand. "Make haste. The city awakens."

My guard frowned and then hesitated, looking at me.

"*Per favore,*" I pleaded. "Mercy. Mercy!"

"At once," Lord Piccolomini hissed.

Belatedly, I saw the knight stretching out his hands. At first, I hoped he meant to help me rise. Instead, he covered my mouth with one hand and pinched my nose with the other. I wanted to struggle, fight, but could barely move my arms.

They would put our suffocated bodies back in our cages and return at noon to declare our deaths God's own judgment.

"*Fermati!*" cried a voice across the piazza. "Halt at once! You must not do this!"

Valentino. He was here. Watching over us. Had he been here all along?

"Stop!" cried another from the other direction—Giulio?

My assailant released me and sat back on his heels. I gasped for breath and then panted, wary that he might attempt it again. Fear galvanized me, and I managed to sit up, glancing in terror at my parents. The one strangling Mama was last to let go, but he finally did so.

From one side of the piazza, Giulio and Domenico charged in. From the other, Aurelio and his knights came galloping in on horses, their hooves clattering atop the cobblestones.

"What is happening here?" asked an older man, and with relief, I saw that Valentino had a priest with him. Not the one that had presided over our Lazarus judgment, but another, his hair still on end as if he had left his bed in haste. Mayhap another in attendance at the sentencing?

Lord Piccolomini gritted his teeth. "We are doing what must be done. For the good of all Firenze."

"Nay." The priest clasped his hands before his belly, utterly calm in his decision. "You invoked the Lazarus test before my bishop, Lord Piccolomini. And God has seen fit to allow these people to live. To take matters into your own hands is to claim that God does not know what is best."

"There is no possible way these three should still be alive," Lord Piccolomini said. "They must have had food and water at some point."

The priest looked up to the top of the wall, where the guards stood. "Did you men give these prisoners any food or drink during their confinement?" he shouted.

"Nay, Father," returned one. "Not a one of us!"

"As God as your witness?" the priest pressed.

"As God as our witness," returned the guard. The others nodded, fists to their chests in solemn pledge.

Other Fiorentini emerged from houses and shops to see what caused the commotion.

The priest lifted his hands and cocked his head, as if that was the end of it.

"There remains some hours of their sentencing," Lord Piccolomini said. "Haul them again to the wall!"

My heart lurched in terror. *Nay. They would not take us up again, would they?*

"M'lord," Aurelio's mount danced beneath him in agitation, "have mercy on these souls. They have survived this long. They shall survive a few more hours. Allow them to return to Siena at once. In the name of peace."

"I concur," said the priest. "'Tis only just, after what you attempted. I can only be thankful that your soul shall not have to bear the burden of three murders."

"These three"—Lord Piccolomini jabbed a trembling, livid finger at us—"are responsible for many Fiorentini deaths."

"These three," Aurelio said loudly, "attempted to secure peace between our republics, at great personal cost. They have paid the price you demanded for the murders of our brethren in Palazzo Pubblico, a price they should not have had to pay at all, given they were no more than innocent bystanders, framed to appear guilty. So now, Lord Piccolomini, you must free them. 'Tis over. The Lord has preserved them."

"'Twas you, Paratore," the man returned, squinting in fury. "You somehow aided them. Mayhap you became more Sienese than Fiorentini during your sojourn with them."

"I am Fiorentini to the marrow of my bones."

Lord Piccolomini let out a dismissive sound and shook his head, hands on his hips.

"I assure you, I have no greater love than for those of my own fine city." Aurelio put a fisted hand to his chest. "And it is for the good of my city that I beg you to send the Forellis home at once. Anything else might cost us more lives on the battlefield in the months to come."

"Mercy, my son," said the priest to Lord Piccolomini. "'Tis time for mercy."

He stared at the priest, then over to us. "So be it," he returned bitterly.

I stared at him as if seeing him from a great distance. Had he truly agreed to it? Were we free to go? Was it over?

Valentino rushed to my side as the city guard moved away. "Tiliani, may I aid you?"

"Please," I said. "I cannot move."

"Will it harm you if I pull you upright?"

"I may cry out, but it shall not be your doing. My muscles are seizing."

"Lack of water and food," he grunted, pulling my arm up slowly and wrapping it around his neck. "'Tis barbaric, what they have done to you."

"But *you* saved us, did you not?" I whispered, as he helped me sit up straighter. "Twice over?"

He did not respond, but in that, I had my answer. He had found a way to bring us water. And if he had not been watching over us this morn and brought the priest, we might not be having a conversation at all.

He gave me a moment's rest. "Ready to rise?"

"I-I think so. But you must not trust me to stand. My legs . . ."

"I understand." He looked into my eyes. "I shall not let you fall. And I shall see you to safety. Aurelio bid me to do so."

Hope flooded my heart, akin to a shaft of light entering a dark room as shutters were flung open. *Does he mean . . .*

But he quickly shook his head. "Only to the border," he said softly. "Aurelio does not know my heart when it comes to you. I cannot find it in me to tell him."

Aurelio himself came up behind him then, and we fell silent. "Tiliani. Here. Allow me to assist." He lifted me from the other side, his arm interlocking with Valentino's behind me.

"Wait." I bit my cheek as the slow burn of blood circulated through my feet and hands again, a thousand pinpricks. "Allow me a moment." I concentrated on breathing slowly, trying not to gasp or cry out. More and more Fiorentini approached.

I glanced over to my parents where the Grecos assisted Mama, and the Betarrinis—or at least Domenico—assisted Papa. It was reassuring to see them both on their feet, as well as Luciana, so gravely wounded when we last saw her. She appeared ghostly, wavering a bit, but smiled at each of us, clearly celebrating our release.

"Come"—Aurelio motioned toward my gelding, Cardo—"we must get you clear of the city before a mob forms."

20

TILIANI

More spectators gathered around, grim and somber at seeing us alive. There were no tears of gratitude, no cheering as there must have been for the real Lazarus, walking out of his grave. But then, I could barely keep my feet.

"Tiliani cannot walk, let alone ride," Valentino said to Aurelio.

"Agreed. You must hold her," he said.

Valentino hesitated. "Mayhap one of her men—"

"Nay. I trust her to no one but you. Go to her gelding. I shall pass her up to you." With that, he bent and effortlessly lifted me and followed behind his captain.

"Booo!" called a man, seeing him carry me. Others joined in. The crowd was shifting, their hatred and dismay growing palpable.

"Bah! Boo!" cried others.

"Forgive me, Tiliani," Aurelio murmured against my ear. "Forgive all of us. 'Twas an unjust sentence. I did what I could."

"I know it." My eyes met his. "I am grateful. More than I can say."

"I shall come and call upon you when we reach Castello Paratore. Somehow I shall make this right."

I blinked at his mention of the castello with his name—it sounded utterly foreign to my ears—and looked to Giulio, helping Mama settle before him in the saddle. My father was shaking off his knights' help, taking tentative steps toward his mount, but then had to acquiesce and allow them to assist him up.

What had Aurelio said? He was going to come and call upon me? For what purpose? How could anything between us ever be made right again? Castello *Paratore*? I had heard Giulio say the words, knew what it had meant, but now. . . it did not seem real.

He passed me up to Valentino, who handled me so tenderly, so reverently, it was liable to break me wide open. After days of no care at all, his touch made me want to weep with relief—regardless of how the others around us jeered and shouted.

Lord Piccolomini reluctantly ordered the Fiorentini knights to flank us, so after exiting the piazza, we saw little further trouble. We wound down the serpentine streets, taking deeper and deeper breaths as we progressed. Once on the outskirts of the city, people looked up in surprise as they encountered us, mayhap not knowing who we might be. They pressed to the building walls on either side.

The Fiorentini knights repeatedly shouted, "Make way!" Undoubtedly knowing the faster they took care of this responsibility of seeing us to the border, the sooner their torment would end.

I writhed as my limbs came fully awake, gasping against the pain, but Valentino held me tight. "Do not fear," he said in my ear, one strong arm across my upper chest, the other around the curve of my hip to hold the reins. "I shall not let you fall."

I wanted to look past him, to make certain my parents were well and with us, but I could think of little more than the excruciating pain in my legs and arms now. I crumpled forward, but his bicep tightened, pulling me close to his chest.

"It hurt my heart, Tiliani," Valentino said, as I sat upright again, "to see you suffer so."

"Thank you." I panted a moment, struggling to gather myself. "And also," I said, testing my theory, "for preserving us."

He paused, letting my horse cover several paces before responding. "I was there, but 'twas Aurelio's doing," he whispered in my ear. "'Twas his purse that made the guards turn to the opposite wall for a few minutes. I . . . have not the funds he does. What I might have gathered would have been met with laughter."

We fell silent as a Forelli knight—one of twelve awaiting us outside the city—rode up and passed me a waterskin, a small loaf of bread, and a bit of hard cheese. "Take it slowly, m'lady." He moved on to distribute more to my parents.

I bit into the bread, the first food I had had in days. It was a battle not to wolf down the entire small loaf. I took a long drink from the waterskin. "And yet you *were* there," I said, returning to our conversation.

"I was there," he said in my ear. "As I was in the shadows, every day. I prayed for you and your parents, like I have never prayed before. I so feared . . ." He left the rest unsaid, but the tensing of his muscles around my torso illuminated understanding.

I breathed in and out, taking pleasure in his warm breath at my ear, as well as his broad chest behind me—while enduring the nerve-twinging pain of my limbs returned to life. They had saved us. Aurelio and Valentino. As had the priest and Giulio and Domenico. I had no doubt. If they had all not intervened, we would not be here today, riding out of Firenze. But what Aurelio and Valentino had risked . . . I thought back to the priest shouting up to the wall guards.

"How did they not know you?" I asked when we were clear of passersby. "Are you not in danger?" For the first time, I realized that if one of those wall guards testified against him . . .

"Fear not. We were masked," he whispered. "And the only one who could betray us is one of the guards, who accepted a *bribe*. They shall remain silent in fear of hanging. And there is no need to confess. They told the truth. Not a one of them opened those trap-doors and gave you anything."

My body gradually settled, and as the pain receded, I relished every movement from ankle to wrist I could take. And yet I did not want him to think I could keep my seat without his support—because I loved the feel of being so close to him.

His protective, supportive stance almost felt proprietary, and in that moment, I realized I wanted to belong to Valentino Valeri. As I had never belonged to another.

I settled back against him, so very weary. I felt inwardly tied to him, and him to me. *Is this love?* I wondered. Then I shoved away the unwelcome second question: *Even if it is, how might we ever be together now?*

"Tiliani, we are moving," he whispered in my ear, hours later. "Coming to your border. M'lord asked me to deliver you and then return."

I was still weak, so weak. The scant sleep I had managed over the last four nights conspired against me, robbing me of precious time with this man.

"Leave me not," I begged. "Come with us." I turned toward him, my face against his neck, inhaling his scent of sweat, leather, and a bit of sage, reminding me of foraging for herbs with him. "Please, Valentino. I know what I ask. But is this not our chance? Can you not remain with us?"

He stiffened even as our mount carried on for several paces. He did not meet my gaze or whisper any encouraging words. I glanced up at the firm line of his jaw, then watched as his hazel eyes surveyed the hillside. But they did not really seem to see.

"Tiliani, I owe Aurelio and his family everything," he said, a note of helplessness in his tone.

I sat up straighter, feeling his arm drop away from me at last. I had pressed when I ought not. He was in a terrible position. And he had already done a great deal to aid me.

But it also made me angry that I had at last found a man that had captured my heart, only to discover I was not enough to make him change his course.

"To leave my position—" he began.

"Nay." I choked on the word. "Say no more. I understand."

"I do not think you do," he said softly. He dared to meet my eyes. "Aurelio has wondered aloud about you. Said that mayhap this is the Lord's doing, moving us to your neighboring castello again. With but a couple miles between you, he thought you could revive your dream of building a bridge between our republics. In time, of course."

I tried to swallow, found my mouth dry, and took another long drink from the skin. Aurelio Paratore intended to court me again?

"What if we go to him?" I tried. "Tell him the truth? Why can it not be *you* with whom I build our bridge?"

He shook his head and ran an agitated hand through his dark hair. "The Fiorentini would never forgive me. 'Twill appear to all as it is, a covert courtship, a betrayal, which shall only add more dry tinder to the fires they have set against you. If you married Aurelio, Firenze might consider it a victory. Even before our plans went awry, they thought of it as 'forcing the wolf to heel.' But if I abandoned Castello Paratore in favor of Castello Forelli? Stole you as my prize?" He shook his head again.

"'Tis desperately unfair," I said, fighting tears.

"'Tis," he said simply.

He pulled up while the others began picking their way across the border creek, the water unusually high after a recent rainstorm.

"So we are to never have another moment like this?" I whispered. "Though you be but a half-hour's ride from me?"

"'Twill be best," he said. "For us and for our people." He dismounted and untied his gelding from Cardo's saddle.

I looked down at him. "Please do your best to dissuade Aurelio from further thoughts about me." I settled my feet in the stirrups and sat up straighter. "There shall only be but one Fiorentini in my heart," I whispered.

He reached up and briefly covered my hand with his. "As there is but one Sienese maiden in mine."

I pulled on the reins and wheeled Cardo toward the creek, not wishing for him to see the tears that ran down my face as knights moved to flank me on either side.

LUCIANA

"So did they just break up?" Domenico grunted in English. He had turned the mare we rode to check on Tiliani before disappearing into the woods with the others, given that Giulio rode with Evangelia, and Ilaria beside Luca. Four knights had respectfully pulled to a stop a short distance behind Tiliani and Valentino, keeping watch. And while I wasn't really in fighting shape, ready to protect her, I suspected she might need a friend, more than anything.

Valentino turned and rode away. *Away.* Like *off into the sunset.* There was a note of finality in the way he held his body erect.

Tiliani crossed the creek, wiping her face of tears as she slumped in her saddle. My heart went out to her. The poor girl had gone through so much already. It wasn't fair.

By the time she turned to glance after him, he was galloping over the hill. Did he move that fast so he could get back to Firenze before nightfall? Or because he fought the urge to turn back?

"Talk about Romeo and Juliet," Nico muttered.

Romeo and Juliet—characters that would not be written for almost two hundred years, I thought with a start.

Nico urged our mare forward so we could fall into step beside Tiliani.

"I hate that he hurt you," I said.

"'Tis not him." She wiped another tear as we rode on. "'Tis our republics that keep us apart." She laughed mirthlessly. "One of the reasons I am drawn to him is because of his fierce loyalty. But that loyalty shall keep us apart forever."

"You never know," I said. "Once he is right across the creek . . ."

She shook her head. "He shall be vigilant, endeavoring to keep far from me. Avoiding any temptation."

We rode on a while in silence.

"Are people kept apart in *Britannia*, too, for reasons such as this?" she asked at last.

I thought about that. "For a long time, people were kept apart for reasons of race or religion."

"Or class," Nico said.

I shrugged. "But now, it's rather rare."

"You have no enemies among other republics?"

I glanced over my shoulder, but the four knights now trailed us at a respectable distance, probably glad we were dealing with Lady Tiliani's tears. "In our time," I said softly, "republics have generally become larger, unified countries. Your own is one—from the heel of the 'boot' on your southern coast to north of Milano."

She gaped at me. "All one?"

I smiled gently. "All becomes Italia. A most beautiful country. And while in our time, not all are friendly, I think that if two people fell in love from enemy countries, not even their fellow countrymen would try and keep them apart."

"Well, in some cases, one would have to leave their country for the other's," Nico put in.

"True," I amended.

"Yet it would not be considered a betrayal of one's own countrymen?" she asked.

I considered that. "Mayhap by some. But not the majority."

She sighed heavily. "Mayhap I should travel with you to that time. It makes far more sense to me."

Except I don't think I want to go back, I thought. *Not with Giulio and my brother here.*

"There are other things you might not find acceptable," I said.

"Such as?"

"Many marriages end in divorce and families are split apart. Our own father left us when we were young," I said.

"Left you? That is terrible," she said, incredulously.

"'Twas," I agreed. "I think that was what drew me to all of you. The Forellis, Betarrinis, and Grecos are one big family. And I have always wanted to be a part of a big family."

She reached out and touched my good arm. "You belong with us."

"I know," I said with a smile. "I feel that."

"You have already proven yourself, fighting on our behalf. And now this . . ." She waved toward my bandaged shoulder. "When we saw you carried away, bleeding so, we feared for your life. 'Twas Ercole, who harmed you?"

"'Twas."

She shook her head. "When shall it be enough for him?"

"Unfortunately, his quest to bring your family down shall not end anytime soon. I think he believes he knows enough about Castello Forelli to claim her. I listened as they talked of making it his."

She considered that. "What happens if he stirs the pot to boiling? Shall we face Aurelio and Valentino on the battlefield? The very men who came to our aid? Defended us in Firenze? Kept my parents and me alive?"

I blinked, taking that in. "How did they keep you alive?"

She sighed. "On our second night, they bribed their way past the guards and slipped us each some water. Without it . . ." She looked up to the canopy of trees closing in above us and then slowly shook her head.

I shuddered at the thought of it—them dying in those awful cages—but also facing either man on the battlefield. From my experience, it was utter chaos. There was little time to pause. And yet if they were attacking the people of Castello Forelli or those about us, how could we not fight back?

Even if it was to strike down the one whom Tiliani loved?

21

LUCIANA

We rode through the gates of the castello, and I exhaled as Benedetto stepped from among the Forellis, looking pale, but on his feet.

"*Benedetto*!" Tiliani cried, dismounting in a swirl of skirts and staggering toward him, best she could. She flung her arms around his neck, and I smiled. After all this family had gone through, I'd held my breath in fear that they would be dealt another blow upon our return.

Benedetto laughed and held her close, barely keeping his feet. "I am well, cousin! I am well!" He leaned back and gazed at her with some consternation. "But what of you? You look terrible!"

Her brows arced. "There is reason for that. We shall tell you why. But first, I am in need of a long, hot bath, a good meal, and bed."

"Make that three of us," Luca called, assisting his wife to the ground. "We smell as foul as wild boar."

Giulio dismounted and moved immediately toward me, but Nico was already helping me down. I shoved away the silly disappointment.

"We should get you to Lady Adri and my sister right away," Giulio said. "They must examine your wounds."

"I like Tiliani's plan better. Mayhap an examination *after* a bath and a meal?" I wavered on my feet, woozy after the long ride.

Giulio took my elbow, but then Adri was there too. "What happened?" she asked in English.

"Ahh, you know. Our favorite person slashed my arm and then stabbed me in my pectoral. Then some quack stitched me up."

Her eyes widened. "Come with me." Her tone brooked no argument.

"Do you need me to carry you?" Giulio asked, as we followed her across the courtyard.

"Nay," I said reluctantly, knowing it was best. "It feels good to walk. And be out of that cursed saddle."

"Agreed. 'Tis a long way to Firenze."

I leaned into him, glad to both keep him near and have his stability. "Will Captain Valeri ride all the way home this night?" I asked quietly.

"He will likely bed down part way home."

"Before they return," I said, "I would like to see Castello Greco."

He peered down at me. "It truly does not pain us, letting it go. 'Twas my father's bounty, not mine. As I have said, our home is here." He opened the door for Adri.

"Be that as it may, I would still like to see it. And mayhap," I added as I passed, "we can secure a secret entrance. Or exit."

He lifted one brow, surprise and admiration intermingling in his expression as I left him. I suppressed a grin, recognizing it.

We entered a cozy, warmer room that Adri and Chiara used to treat patients. A fire crackled in the corner, pushing away the chill of the castle's stones. Giulio greeted his older sister, kissing cheek to cheek, and then pulled her into his arms.

"I am so relieved to see you," she said. She turned to me, observing my bandaged chest and shoulder, bulging beneath my tunic. "And you as well, Luciana. What manner of mischief did you manage to get into?"

"She tangled with Ercole and a rather nasty dagger." Adri turned to Giulio and gave him a twirling motion with her finger. "Outside, please. We shall see to this one."

He reluctantly turned. It was a bit silly. After all, he'd seen plenty of my bare skin as the doctor in Firenze stitched me up. But no one argued with Lady Adri, including Giulio. "I shall be just outside. Please call me if I may be of aid."

"I am all right," I said in English to Adri as she closed the door and patted the bed, and I obediently sat on it. "More tired than anything."

"Let's see what they did to you. What sort of 'quack' stitched you up?" she asked in a low tone.

"Someone they called a barber-surgeon?"

She grimaced. "Unfortunately, that's the best they could do. Did he sterilize any of his tools?"

"I think Ilaria might have doused them in grappa. My skin too."

"Good girl," Adri muttered, helping me pull off my tunic and shirt.

I grimaced as I saw the bloody cloth that was wound around my breasts, evidence of that terrible night.

"You lost a great deal of blood?" she asked, leaning close to study the stitches.

"Enough to make me feel pretty woozy."

"I would imagine." She lifted my arm and carefully unwound the bandage. There were a few stitches at the top, then the area he'd cauterized, but the bottom part of the wound wasn't as deep, so it had only required a bandage.

"Any sign of infection? Any fever? Pain?"

"At first. But then it has been all right for the last two days."

She put a hand to my forehead. "You may have a low-grade fever. That's probably what's making you feel a bit light-headed. Or the blood loss. It can take more than a month for the red blood cells to replenish."

"The seven-hour ride right after surgery didn't help either. And we didn't get a whole lot of sleep in Firenze."

"Indeed. It all conspires against your recovery." She turned to Chiara, and they debated which poultice to use, agreeing at last. Chiara left to go mix it up.

Adri turned and sat beside me on the bed and took my hand in both of hers. "Thank you, Luciana, for doing what you could for our family. I assume you were trying to capture Ercole?"

"Yeah," I said. "But we flubbed it. We were *so* close."

"He is quite the adversary." She looked me in the eye. "But I want you to hear it from me—we do not expect you to risk your life to capture him. It is not a price you must pay to remain here."

"Believe me, I didn't plan on this." I put a hand to my shoulder wound. "I'm not super fond of stitches without a hefty dose of lidocaine."

"Me either," she said, with a grim smile.

"Do you think it will be okay?" I asked, looking down at the red, angry gash. "I suppose it's going to leave a nasty scar."

"I'm afraid we're far from the skills of a plastic surgeon," she said with a sigh. "But yes, I think you will heal well. We'll take out the stitches in a week or so."

I grimaced. "That sounds like it's gonna hurt."

"It is unpleasant." She leaned closer to examine my wound. "But I am more concerned about infection."

Chiara arrived with the poultice, and I saw Giulio peeking in. Adri did too.

"You may return, Giulio." She covered me with a blanket and left just my shoulder exposed. "She might like some company as she sits with the poultice." She packed her herbs on my chest and gave me a small, knowing smile. "I have never seen him so smitten," she whispered in English.

"I kinda think he's awesome too," I returned.

"He has waited a long time for the right woman." Adri took the wooden bowl from Chiara.

"Tuscan, please," Giulio groused, pulling up a chair. "Why must I ask? Or are you telling secrets?"

"No secrets," Adri said mischievously. "I was only telling Luciana that you have waited a very long time for the right woman."

"That he has," Chiara chimed in. "And he has turned away his fair share of eligible brides."

He half grinned and half scowled at them both. But then he smiled at me. "It seems I needed to wait this long, because I was waiting for another She-Wolf."

Adri spread the herbal goop on my wound, thick enough to cover all the stitches. "Sit still with that for a good hour. I shall return to clean you up and bring a tub and gown then. For now, we must check on the others."

"Thank you," I said, as she and Chiara turned to go, leaving me alone with Giulio.

He pulled his chair closer and took my hand, gazing at me like he couldn't *see* me enough.

I gazed back at him, from our intertwined fingers to his eyes. How was it possible? That I had come through time and found a man like this?

I sighed and settled back more fully on my pillow. "It feels so good to be back here. To be *home,* and with all three of the Forellis with us. Benedetto up on his feet again too."

"Agreed. I think we may have a bit of a respite from the Fiorentini, after they exacted such a steep punishment."

I thought of the three Forellis, up in those cursed cages, and shivered. Then I thought about Tiliani and how she pined for Captain Valeri. "You said you have been waiting for a She-Wolf," I said. "Was your heart never drawn to Tiliani?"

"Nay." He shook his head slowly and stared into my eyes. "She has always been as much a sister to me as Chiara and Ilaria are. We are her guardians, her closest friends. But nay." He covered my hand with his other. "I truly believe I have been waiting for you, Luciana. Do you not feel the same?"

I felt the magnetic draw between us. "I do. I can't quite believe it."

"Nor can I." He brought my hand to his lips and kissed it slowly, then the inside of my wrist, looking into my eyes all the while. "I want time to properly court you, Luciana. Time to ride beside you and show you our lands, introduce you to our people. Dance with you. Feast with you. Talk with you. There are not enough hours in the day to suit me, because sleep takes you away from me for far too long."

I teared up. "You honor me."

"You honor *me*, allowing my courtship. You are as beautiful as you are skilled in battle."

He thought *me* beautiful. Did he know he belonged on magazine covers? But I smiled over his words. "Apparently I am not quite skilled enough." I gestured toward my shoulder.

"You *are* skilled," he said, kissing my knuckles again. "That fiend merely managed to surprise you."

"Which will not happen again. Next time—"

"Next time," he said, "we shall bring him down. Together."

TILIANI

I agreed to Mama's plan to have two baths drawn for us, in my room, leaving my father to bathe alone in theirs. "I do not want you out of my sight for too long yet," she explained shortly. "After. . ." Her voice broke and she covered her mouth, staring at me with tear-filled eyes.

"It is well, Mama. I know." We embraced. We had endured much together, over these last days. No one but us would likely ever know what it was to endure four days in the cages. Not even Zia Gabi.

Gabi and Nona followed us, as if wanting to watch over us both. My aunt asked the maids to fill the tubs extra deep, and then they gently helped us disrobe. We were both exhausted and hurting from head to toe. As I slipped into the steaming water, lavender floating atop it, I saw why. In our efforts to find relief and respite, we were bruised all over from the cruel vines.

Seeing me wince, Nona asked to see my feet. She grimaced. "How did that happen? Did they strike your soles with a rod?"

"Nay," I said. "'Twas simply the pressure of standing on vines for hours. There was no way to find a place to sit or stand that did not hurt us."

"'Tis a devilish new design," Mama said to Gabi. "Trust me when I say you do not want to be in one of those things again."

Zia Gabi shuddered. "Never. Once was enough for me."

I gingerly let my feet slip back under the water. After a moment of sting, it felt soothing.

"We shall wrap them tonight," Nona said, moving to look at my mother's feet too. "And you must elevate them."

Gabi lathered my hair, while Nona saw to my mother's. We went under, rinsing, and when I emerged, I set to washing every inch of my skin. I wanted every speck of Fiorentini dust off me, away. It was like I could not get clean enough. As if in scraping my skin, I was scraping away the terror, the hurt, the grief, the pain.

After some time, Zia Gabi stilled my hand and eased the sponge from my fingers. "It is enough, Tilly. You are clean now, thrice over. Scrubbing any harder shall only hurt your tender skin, not heal you. Only time shall heal you."

I looked into her eyes. She knew. Of course she knew. She had experienced it too.

"I thought we were going to die," I said, tears rising in my eyes.

"As did I," Mama said soberly.

"You did?" I whispered. "I mean, it sounded as if you were saying farewell to Papa, but you never said it."

She gave me a gentle smile. "You never asked."

"Would you have told me if I had?"

"Probably not," she admitted with a small laugh. "Sometimes a mother has to say what she *hopes* is true. If it aids someone she loves. You needed hope, Til—nothing but hope—in those cursed cages."

Nona nodded and began pulling a thick-toothed comb through my mother's hair, as Gabi did with mine.

"When else have you lied to me?"

"Now *that* shall remain my secret," Mama said with a wink.

22

LUCIANA

I slept for eighteen hours that night, awakening around noon to find Nico dozing in a chair on two legs against the wall nearest me.

"Nico," I groaned, rolling over to nudge him.

He blinked sleepily and let the chair come back to all four legs. "Oh, thank God." He leaned closer to me. "You feeling okay?"

"Yeah." I made myself sit up and slowly rotated my shoulder. "Ya know, for a stabbing victim."

He smiled soberly. "Adri wouldn't let you be alone. She wanted eyes on you twenty-four seven."

"So you've been up all night with me?"

"Nah. Giulio took first shift, Ilaria the second. She woke me at sunrise to take over."

I pulled my legs over the edge of the bed and sat up, wincing. "That was sweet of you guys." It was a little disconcerting, thinking about them all being in here at various times while I was dead to the world. "I didn't hear a thing after I had that bath and got into my own bed. Did I talk in my sleep or do anything embarrassing?"

"You mean, other than drooling so much you soaked your pillow?"

I glanced at him in horror. Had Giulio seen that too?

Nico winked.

I groaned. "Very funny."

He grinned. "Think you're out of the woods?"

I gingerly rotated my shoulder again. "Maybe. Hopefully Adri's medicine is at work. The biggest thing she was worried about was infection, and I don't think I have a fever."

"Right. We all had to check your forehead through the night."

"Did I ever feel hot?"

"Maybe a little. But never more than low-grade."

"I feel a lot better now."

"Eighteen hours of sleep ought to do that."

"We didn't get much sleep in Firenze."

"Roger that." He rose and rubbed his face and stretched. "I'll catch up a bit tonight. Now that I know you're okay, I'm going to go see if I can catch some time with Marcello. He's so happy everyone's safe and home, I think it's a great time to hit him up."

"To talk over your banking idea?"

"If we're going to make this place our home, we need a way to contribute. Especially now, considering they're about to lose Castello Greco's income. But I think we should start with microfinancing. Tiny loans that will aid his sharecroppers, benefitting him in two ways—a little interest on the loan as well as the prospect of a better crop."

"Brilliant. I think he'll like that. Little risk, bigger gains. For him and his people too."

"I hope so." He kissed my cheek and put a hand on my shoulder. "I'm really glad you're better."

"I am too. Can you send a maid to help me dress?"

"Will do. And I don't think you'll be alone for long. Giulio was out in the courtyard at sunup, itching to see you as soon as you awakened."

Ludovica arrived soon after, and I was so glad it was her. She had a sunny personality, her tone "chirpy," as my mother would have said. She reminded me of my favorite grade-school teacher.

"You look like you are on the mend." She pulled the single

shutter over my high, narrow window a bit wider in order to lend more light.

"I think I am."

She helped me out of my shift, and we looked at my wound. Adri had left it without a bandage after the poultice, believing it better to "give it a little air." It seemed a little less angry-red, which gave me hope. After my bath, they'd bound my breasts in clean cloth and given me fresh "underwear," which were kind of like soft-linen shorts with a drawstring. Ludovica helped me rise, but I felt steadier on my feet. I stepped into a long, green-gray skirt, but then frowned as she came at me with a wide-necked bodice. Could I maneuver my arms enough to get into it?

"There are no buttons." She showed me the back. "Lady Adri thought I could tie it loosely about you. Give you a bit of room to breathe, while still making you presentable."

She was gentle in pulling the strings at the back partially taut, then bent to help me slide my feet into slippers. We didn't bother with stockings. She saw to my hair, swiftly braiding it and winding in into a knot at the nape of my neck and securing it with two wooden pins. "There you are. Pretty as a Siena sunrise." She stepped back to admire her work.

"I do not feel much like a sunrise," I said.

"There is a man outside who would beg to differ," she said, giving a wink.

My stomach did a little flip at the thought of Giulio. Was it so plain to everyone about us, how he felt about me, and me about him? But then I felt a pang of guilt, thinking about Tiliani. Would having us around make it all the harder for her?

I thought about her question of what divided lovers in our own time. There were many things that could divide people here. And I was so, so thankful none of them would divide me from Giulio Greco.

At least, I hoped they wouldn't. We still had a lot to find out about each other.

My heart fluttered as I stepped out of the turret and into the courtyard. It was hot, the late summer sun high in the sky, the heat radiating off the dry, hardened soil beneath my feet. I shielded my eyes and looked about. To the right, men went through their daily exercises. To the left, women hauled water up from a well.

"Whom do you seek?" he whispered, close enough to my ear to send shivers down my neck. I spun around. His blue eyes sparkled with delight, reminding me of sunlight dappling across deep ocean.

"Whom do you suppose?" I returned playfully.

He put a fist to his heart as if I'd wounded him and looked down at me with intent. "You mentioned wanting to see Castello Greco while it remains under my care. Are you well enough for a ride?"

"I believe so," I said. "If we take it slowly."

"Agreed. We do not want anything to upset those stitches." He reached out to touch my shoulder but then paused and dropped his hand.

I followed his gaze toward his men, some of whom openly watched us. One hit the belly of another and pointed. Giulio didn't want them to know? Or was he trying to avoid some serious teasing later?

"Do you think Lady Adri would approve of us going?"

"I already asked." He swept his arm toward the stables, ignoring the hooting call of one of the men, the laughter of others, as we fell into step together. "She said she would permit it if you did not have to manage reins. So I can either lead you on a mare, tied to my mount, or you may ride with me as we did yesterday."

I hid my grin as the men continued to stare. "Do you think you can manage the ribbing you shall get if we set off together? Mayhap we best appear a more formally courting couple."

"Ho, Captain!" called Otello, bare to the waist and sweating from his exercises. "Word has it that you ail as m'lords do, with wolf-fever!"

Several men behind him tilted their heads and howled, while others laughed.

"Careful," Giulio growled as we passed. "If you overstep, I shall make *you* my sparring partner on the morrow."

Otello laughed again, but a subtle shadow of concern dropped over his expression. He was a big man, but not as big as Giulio. There was a reason Lord Greco was the Forellis' captain of the guard. I doubted any man present could best him.

I itched to be well and skirmish with him myself. Nico and I had yet to use everything in our jiu jitsu arsenal against the Grecos. They wanted to learn some of our moves. What would happen if I took him down in front of his men? Or brought his men down, one by one, and *then* him?

"Why are you grinning?" he asked, opening the door to the stables for me.

"Oh," I said. "I was but thinking about someday showing the knights of Castello Forelli how wolf-like I can truly be."

TILIANI

My parents and I awakened early, but we plainly wished we had slept longer. I ached even more than I had yesterday, and hobbled about on bandaged feet, bound with herbs. Mine were worse than Mama's or Papa's—Nona had not even bandaged theirs. I must have stood longer than Mama had. And my father's thicker boot soles had been far better protection than our slippers.

I walked past an arrow slit that faced the north woods and thought of Castello Greco, now *Paratore*. Giulio had mentioned Luciana's idea—why not create a secret entrance or exit from Castello Greco before it was handed over to the Fiorentini? I mulled it over as I crossed the courtyard, and when I entered the

Great Hall, I discovered Ilaria, my aunt and uncle, cousins, and parents all discussing it too.

"We have been captives in that castle, held in her dungeon," Zia Gabi said. "Escaped over her walls. Breached her gates. But what if we made it easier on ourselves, in case Lord Paratore is forced to become more adversary than friend?"

Marcello folded his arms and shook his head. "I do not know if we have time to build a tunnel and hide it well enough that they shall not readily detect it. Freshly turned earth or broken mortar would be rather obvious."

"What of the old Etruscan sewage tunnel?" Benedetto asked, still looking pale and fragile on his feet. "As children, we made it a good distance toward Castello Greco through the ruins."

"You did *what*?" Zia Gabi asked sharply.

"Ah, Mama"—Fortino cast me a guilty smile—"we were playing."

I shifted uneasily. All three of us had known we were forbidden to be in that tunnel. It had caved in in several places. "We have not been in it since we were children," I said quickly. "And it ends far short of Castello Greco."

"But we always surmised it led beneath Castello Greco," Benedetto said.

"There is a room off the dungeon that has a few Etruscan frescoes," Ilaria said. "Clearly, the Paratores' ancestors built atop other ruins of the old city, using some of the building blocks in their own structure."

"So let us go and explore it now," Fortino said excitedly. "Mayhap it would take but a couple repairs and a few days of digging to discover if it connects."

"The Etruscans built in grids," Nona said, her own interest piqued now. "And if it's the sewer tunnel, 'twas likely along their main street." Her blue eyes rounded in anticipation. "I would like to map it myself."

"Go with them," Zia Gabi encouraged. "Help them decide if it is worth the time and trouble."

"If any of us lands in that dungeon again," Mama said to my aunt drolly, "'twould be nice to know of an escape route."

"Or an attack route," my father added intently.

I shifted uneasily in my chair. "Is this not acting in poor faith? To do this ahead of Castello Greco becoming Castello Paratore? Might we not hope for the best? That this is the beginning of a new era, between Firenze and Siena, given that it is Aurelio and Sir Valeri inhabiting it?"

Gabi gave me a tender smile. "They may set the tone, dear one, but they shall have to abide by Firenze's decisions. If Firenze demands they attack, how would they refuse?"

I frowned and leaned an elbow on the table before me, rubbing my temple. I could not imagine it. "What we had hoped would bring an end to the discord has created a rather terrible situation. We shall have friends on our border who may be forced to act the enemy." I recalled the last things Aurelio and Valentino had said. "I think Aurelio still hopes to build on our friendship. After this storm blows over."

"An effort I would applaud," my father said. "But in the meantime, we must treat this situation as if the worst of the Fiorentini were taking ownership. For if Aurelio does not capitulate to Fiorentini demands, I have no doubt that they shall promptly replace him." He turned to Ilaria. "Lead six men to the northern border of Castello Greco and keep watch. If anyone approaches, we want to know before they spy what we are doing. Return to us at sundown."

Papa turned to Fortino. "You lead several groups of men to the tunnel and take shovels and buckets with you. Follow your grandmother's lead. I want a report on how much we would need to excavate to make the tunnel passable."

"Take care to disturb as little as possible," Gabi said. "If this works, we do not want it visible to our new neighbors."

"Understood. I can fetch Giulio too."

"I think Giulio has other plans this day," Nona said with a wry look. "Serving as Lady Luciana's escort."

"Ahhh." Fortino lifted a brow. "Why is it that *I* do not have my intended about on a day that might demand excavation?"

"I could assist," Benedetto put in.

"Nay," Nona said gently. "You must remain here to convalesce with your cousin. You and Tiliani have some healing to do yet."

We shared a look of commiseration. I knew we both itched to return to the tunnels that we had explored as youths.

"But you did not demand the same of Luciana," Benedetto tried.

"Luciana has gone for a walk around Castello Greco. She has not set out to haul rock."

"I can help," Domenico said.

"Good," Zio Marcello said. "But first, let us walk together and discuss what has been on your mind."

23

LUCIANA

Giulio lifted me to a sidesaddle and gently settled my feet into the mare's stirrups. "Are you secure?"

"As secure as a woman may be when she's half on a horse and has only one good arm," I said.

He grinned. "The Ladies Forelli rarely ride sidesaddle, but since you are not riding out to battle and cannot manage the reins anyway, I—"

"'Tis well," I assured him. "I simply am used to controlling my . . . direction."

"Mayhap it is a good exercise for you, then. To be led by another."

"Mayhap." I lifted a doubtful brow and he laughed. I watched him move to his gelding and mount up as if it took little effort. The man was like liquid motion. *If I'm going to let anyone lead me,* I thought, *it may as well be him.*

"Your father never led you?" He ducked as he moved through the stable doorway, then glanced back to make sure I made it safely through too.

"Nay," I said, swallowing a smile as the castello knights crossed their arms and boldly watched us pass, giving their captain a hard time. Giulio ignored them. "My father was never truly a part of our lives," I said when we were past our audience. "'Twas my grandmother and mother who raised us."

"What happened to your father?" he asked gently as we waited for the castello gates to open before us.

"He decided to follow a different path. He moved to a far place and began life anew."

Giulio frowned. "Did your mother send him away?"

I thought about that as we exited the castello. "I am certain that in any relationship, there are two sides to the story. It takes two dedicated souls to truly become one, yes? But I fear it is far easier to follow two separate paths when trouble arises. I think our mother hoped for more, but our father chose his own way. And then our mother, another."

"He shall not miss you? In *Britannia*?"

I shook my head, glancing back to see the gates closing. "The way it transpires," I said, somber, "is that it shall take quite a long time for him to realize we are even gone. And when he does, yes, he may be sad. But our hearts have never been entwined the way other families are."

"I grieve that for you."

"Thank you. It once grieved me, too, but I've made peace with it over the years." I glanced back at Castello Forelli. "Mayhap in time, Lord Marcello or Luca shall fill a bit of that gap. That desire we all have for a father."

"They have for me," he said somberly.

I took that in. "Do you remember your father at all?" I asked.

"Nay," he said. "He died while my mother was still pregnant with me."

"That is very sad."

"For her it was. But for me . . ." he shrugged. "Mayhap 'tis worse to know and love and then lose them, than to not know what love you are missing. Marcello and Luca have always treated me and my sisters as their own."

"I expect that in knowing them, you can surmise a bit of what your father was like. Given they were such fast friends."

"Mayhap. There were once twelve of them. All sons of fine

lords. Most of them were Sienese, but a few were Fiorentini. They played together as children, during a long stretch of peace. And as political relations dissolved, they pledged to remain true to one another. They even tattooed their arms with a triangle."

"Why a triangle?"

"'Tis a reference to the Trinity. As the Son serves the Father, and the Spirit serves the Son, so did all twelve of those men serve one another. Even unto death."

I absorbed that. How many had died over the years? Who remained?

"In the end, that was what made my father leave all he held dear in Firenze and align with them. His dedication to them, and they to him, became more important than anything else."

"Have I not glimpsed one on your arm as well?" I asked. I'd glimpsed something on the inside of his arm as he'd sparred in the courtyard.

He glanced at me in surprise. "Indeed." He touched the inside of his right forearm. "I carry it as a memory of him, and for how he stood upon his word to his friends. I want to live such a life of integrity. Regardless of the cost."

Regardless of the cost, I repeated silently. Who thought like that? And how could such a man be falling for me as hard as I was falling for him? "I see you living it out already. In giving your land—and title—away."

He gave me a humble smile, melting my heart a bit more. "As I have said, the castello was truly my father's bounty. My thought is that we should never cling too fiercely to what we inherit. To anything we may lose. What matters most in life is the people."

I thought that over. "What if it were Castello Forelli?"

He paused. "That would be a greater challenge, in that she matters to the people who matter to me. Castello Greco has never been more than a good barrier fortress between us and Firenze. That said, if the people I love all moved to Siena, never to return, I would go with them."

We rode for a while in silence, as I thought about all the friends and families who lived far—very far—from loved ones. But then, back home, we had phones and the Internet to connect us.

Connect us. Maybe that was it. We *thought* we were connected because we could touch base anytime we wanted. Text. Email. Send a photo. But had I ever seen a family connected on a soul-level like I had witnessed here? I thought not. Proximity demanded families figure connections—true connections—out. When you lived with your loved ones, day in and day out, you had to work out the kinks. Iron out the wrinkles. Deal with the trouble so you could move on together in peace. And that was a mutual commitment sort of thing.

I studied Giulio, contemplating all that he was giving up.

"What of the income that Castello Greco generates?" I asked.

He lifted a testing brow. "Do you fear the courtship of a landless man?"

"Nay," I said with a shrug. "Given that said landless man is courting a woman with no dowry."

We shared a long smile and my pulse raced. It felt deliciously sweet to so plainly speak of what we were doing.

"My sisters and I chose long ago to grant any funds our land generated into the general Forelli coffers. It might be a hardship for the Forellis to manage without it, but I suspect it shall all work out in the end."

"You are a trusting, settled soul, Lord Greco," I said.

"Not at all times." He pulled up on his reins and allowed my mare to sidle up beside his. "Especially when it comes to you, m'lady." He reached for my hand and held on to it as he looked into my eyes.

"Out of all of the women who must have fallen for your charms, m'lord," I whispered, with a shake of my head, "why have you set your sights on me?"

He huffed a laugh and stared at me, incredulous. "You are passionate and poised. Beautiful and brave. I find it difficult to find a single thing I would change about you. Other than this troublesome penchant for charging into battle. But even in the heat of it, you are a wonder to behold, Luciana Betarrini."

I stared at him, an embarrassing blush climbing my cheeks. He thought all of that about me? "Well, I *can* be a bit stubborn at times. Some people say that's something wrong with me."

"As can I," he admitted. "Do you think we might find our way? Two stubborn people? Together?"

It overwhelmed me, his intensity. No man had ever looked at me this way. And I felt an odd sort of pressure. I was flattered, sure. Amazed. But also a tiny bit freaked out.

"You are rapidly claiming more and more of my heart, Luciana. Might I hope that you feel the same for me?"

I was still trying to get my head around the fact that the guy—this drop-dead-handsome, caring, loyal man—had feelings for me. Serious feelings.

"Oh, Giulio," I said, squeezing his hand, "you need not hope. You need to *know* that I have never ever met a man like you. I am truly honored that you would court me. And, yes, you are rapidly claiming more and more of my heart too."

His expression was one I'd not soon forget—like he'd won the lottery. Found out a friend on his deathbed had made a recovery. Got his dream job. All rolled into one. He looked grateful. Elated. Flabbergasted. As if I'd honored him, venturing into this relationship.

But what really got me?

Lord Giulio Greco—that big, tough knight—wiped a tear from his cheek as he continued to smile at me. "Whatever is required to win your *whole* heart, m'lady," he said, sobering, "I shall do. For I aim to be your man, and you, my lady. Forever. No matter what comes between us"—he slowly shook his head—"we shall not let disagreements send *us* on different paths. I want to have you by my side until I am old and gray. To have a love like the

Lords and Ladies Forelli have. Marked by dedication. Passion. Joy and hope."

I scrambled for an appropriate response and failed. I could only smile back at him.

All my life, I'd had boys flirt with me, say sweet things. But never ever had a man said such *manly* things to me. And what did I know of a love like the Forellis shared? Could I learn from them? Echo them?

"I doubt I could ask for more," I managed at last.

He smiled. And with that, he moved on, leading me to the castle that he was soon to give away, for the good of the Forellis, as well as Siena.

TILIANI

Benedetto and I watched glumly as two patrols left on horseback with Fortino and Ilaria. Others continued with their daily sparring exercises. Giulio led Luciana's mare out, but their shy smiles toward each other only made me more irritable. My uncle walked with Domenico, intently listening as he shared his thoughts of the future, here in our time—and I wished I could be a part of that too. My parents retired to the solarium for a bit of convalescing as well.

I felt. . . .abandoned. Which was ridiculous. I was surrounded by my people. Even now, I walked with my cousin, Benedetto. But I wanted to be elsewhere. Anywhere. Mostly, with Valentino. What was he doing? Was he thinking of me? Or had he pushed any thought of me aside, endeavoring to move on with his life? As I ought?

I considered doing what Nona asked of me and take up a book rather than my bow and quiver, but as weary as I was, I could not tolerate the idea of being confined for another day. I was agitated, wishing I could don my braies and a tunic and my soft, old boots and take to the deer trail outside the castle, running, running across it. If it were not for my battered feet, it would have brought me the relief I sought.

I was days away from such a physical release. So I instead made my apologies to my cousin, separated, and hobbled across the courtyard to the chapel. The only people present for the service this time of day was Cook, two maidservants, and me. But it mattered not to Padre Giovanni. He would have conducted the service with the same devotion, whether the chapel was full or he was alone.

While he was our family's chaplain, he truly worked for no one but God. That was how Papa and the elders wanted it.

"We do not want any cardinal or bishop meddling in our affairs," Zio Marcello had said once. "But we do want a man of God to lead us along the Way."

Whereas Firenze was beholden to the Pope, Siena had been excommunicated for not obliging the Holy Father as political king and religious leader. Pope Gregory wanted to manage the republics and kingdoms of our land in a way that left his treasury full of gold; the Sienese were too stubborn to allow it. Back and forth they went. Some years we were in the Holy Father's good graces; some years we were not. It mattered little to our chaplain. He had no lofty goals to advance within the Church. He was happy here with us.

After Padre Giovanni finished singing through a psalm, read a brief prayer, and stood in silence for a few minutes, he nodded toward us in smiling dismissal, hands folded over his trim belly. The others filed out. I did not.

"M'lady?" He came to sit on the bench in front of mine. "May I be of assistance?"

"Mayhap, mayhap not," I said miserably.

"What is it, child? Your feet?"

If only it was that. "They hurt, but nay—'tis my heart. My head. I feel as if my thoughts are constantly tumbling. 'Tis as if there is a storm cloud building here"—I touched my chest—"*and* here." I pointed to both temples.

He considered me. "You endured a great deal in Firenze. Such trials oft leave wounds that demand time of their own to heal."

I nodded. "Yet my parents endured the same as I, and they are not here, seeking counsel."

"Your parents have each other. And they have experienced many trials before this."

I rubbed my face. It had been some time since I felt like a child. Weak. And grumpy, like a toddler denied her favorite sweet.

"You are used to physical exercise, responsibility each day."

"Yes. If I could ride out with the others, it would provide some relief—"

"But not all you seek." He paused. "Is it Lord Paratore? Did it pain you, in the end, to not continue your courtship?"

I swallowed hard. Then gave the slightest shake of my head. "Not Lord Paratore," I said bringing my eyes up to meet his.

"Then Captain Valeri," he said gently. I startled and he smiled. "I am a priest sworn to celibacy, but I am not blind to the ways of men with women."

What a relief to discuss at least a portion of my angst! The words poured from me. "I can never be with him, Father. He is devoted to Aurelio. They are like brothers. The Paratore family saved him. Made him a knight. A man of substance."

The priest nodded and patted my hand. "You might be surprised. The Lord oft shows us the hidden path we cannot see from a distance. Lord Paratore is soon to take hold of Castello Greco, no? And will his captain not accompany him?"

A lump formed in my throat. "Yes," I managed, feeling the tears rise, "but 'tis no better than if he were in Firenze. We cannot be together. We cannot. We . . ."

I closed my eyes, and the tears rolled down my cheeks,

remembering him walking away at Palazzo Paratore, looking to the ceiling. Feeling the tearing between us, the longing. How he—and Aurelio—had shielded us as we fled Firenze. How he had held me, even as I slept, on the road home. I could not continue to endure such encounters. Not if there was no resolution in sight.

Padre Giovanni turned more fully toward me and rested his soft hand atop mine. "I grieve over your grief, child. I am sorry you do not think there is a way. But God loves you. He sees you. And I know that he wants your life to be rich and *full* of love. There are good things ahead. You need only trust that you shall see them in time."

"But what if there is not, Father? What if there are not good things ahead? What if my life is solely full of strife, battle, and loss?"

He drew in a deep breath. "There shall be those things too. Undoubtedly. Because this life, here, short of Eden? 'Tis full of pain and darkness. I find the trick is to truly revel in the good, the glory, the love, the *gifts* of this life, every time we spot them."

He touched my chin, and I looked up at him. "Your life is full of those good gifts too. Even in the midst of your pain. That is how your parents cope. I have seen it, time and again, through the decades. They lose, they suffer, but they also gain, celebrate. And they choose to concentrate on the gifts rather than the losses. You, young She-Wolf, must endeavor to do the same."

24

LUCIANA

We rode through Castello Greco's towering twin gates, the guards shouting down greetings to Giulio. He was well loved, and the knights seemed a bit lonely, it made me all the more glad to be here. While a few servants bustled across the courtyard, this was not the home Castello Forelli was. There were people, and there was activity, but no sense of warmth mingled within the cold, stone barriers.

A castle is but a fortress without a family within her walls. Hadn't Giulio said something like that? It made sense now.

He pulled to a stop beside the stables, dismounted, and waved off an eager groomsman, clearly intending to tie the gelding himself. I watched as the young man's face fell and gave Giulio a quirk of my eyebrow and nod toward the young man.

He dragged his eyes from me back to the groomsman, took half a breath, and called him. Giulio clapped him on the shoulder, said something about "only having eyes for m'lady," and suddenly the man was all smiles, taking the reins from his master, shyly glancing my way, then obediently waiting.

Giulio reached for me. His broad, warm hands gripped my waist, and I glanced up to see every single knight on the wall looking our way. I laughed under my breath, placing a hand on his shoulder and allowing him to lift me down.

"Methinks your knights are not keeping to their guard duty,"
I whispered in his ear.

"They are not accustomed to me escorting a lady," he said, "let
alone bringing her here." But he swallowed his own smile and
looked up, all lord-in-command. "Knights on watch!" he shouted.
"See to your duties!"

As one, the twelve knights circling the walls pulled
their shoulders back, and called in return, "Yes, m'lord!"
They immediately resumed their rotation about the wall in
uniform order.

"I shall brush down your mounts, m'lord," said the groomsman.

"Very good, Leo," Giulio said.

Neither his mount nor mine needed brushing after our short
two-mile walk, but the guy was clearly in need of something to do,
and it made me like Giulio all the more for not robbing him of
the task. It reminded me of being at my first job at the Hallmark
store, praying someone might come in to buy a card in a world
full of e-cards.

Is this guy really The One? I wondered, looking up at him.

"Shall we?" He offered his arm.

"Indeed," I said. "Show me the whole of what you are
relinquishing, Giulio. For I know you are relinquishing much,
regardless of how you dismiss it." I strode forward. "This is a
fine castle."

"That it is," he allowed.

"With how many hectares about it?"

"More than seven hundred. Half are sowed or lie fallow," he
said. "The other half are woods."

I took that in. That was the equivalent of 1800 acres in our
time. "And how shall your sharecroppers take to the notion of
again being under Fiorentini rule?" I asked.

He took a few steps, hands tucked behind his back. "Their
parents or grandparents were likely under the same, so I wager
they need not dig too deep to find their way. That said, it might

make some of them a bit anxious. They have become accustomed to the Forellis and their generous ways."

I thought on that. "That is a good thing, yes? Mayhap they shall be less anxious to raise sword or pitchfork against us, in the days to come. Should the worst happen."

"Mayhap." He opened a door, and I climbed up to a room with a window that opened to the courtyard. The furnishings were dusty, the rooms cold, but I paused to consider the view. In a world of castle keeps, it was a rarity. It had to have been built by a man more concerned with keeping tabs on those within his gates, than those without.

"Was Paratore a confident man?" I asked, staring out the window. In all my medieval research, I had never encountered anything of the kind.

"Confident?" Giulio repeated.

I gestured to the view. "Few castellos have a keep with this broad a window to the courtyard. 'Tis easily breached."

"True. Mayhap he believed his walls too steep, his gate too strong, to be too concerned about his keep."

"Mayhap," I said. "And yet it became yours."

"Well, it became the Forellis', which they passed on to my father." He led me on toward the opulent master's quarters, a library, and sitting room and bedroom. We peeked upstairs at several lovely guest rooms. Then he took me down the serpentine stairs to the kitchen and servants' quarters and down a hall. He gestured below. "That is the dungeon. Do you truly wish to see it?"

I paused. "I think we ought to, given that this whole property is soon to pass into the hands of our 'enemies,' right?"

It was his turn to pause. I placed my good hand on his shoulder as he reached for a sputtering torch from the wall and descended the dark stairs, careful to not rush me. "Lord Cosimo Paratore brought Lady Evangelia down here." He lit another dormant torch on a wall. It sparked and caught fire, illuminating the rest of the high, narrow hall, and archaic chains and tools that had once been used for torture.

I frowned. "Did he hurt Lia? Is that what set them all against the Paratores?"

"They had been enemies for decades. And the first time Gabriella and Evangelia traveled to us," he whispered, "they separated at some point, as I understand it. They arrived days apart. Lady Gabriella was rescued by Lord Marcello and Luca, in the midst of a skirmish between the castellos. Lady Evangelia was found by Cosimo days later, stumbling outside of the tombs."

My eyes widened. "How terrifying!" I would have freaked out if I'd arrived without Domenico.

"Indeed." He picked up a rusting, iron cuff to test the heavy length of chain anchored to the stone wall.

"How was she freed?" I asked.

"Gabriella," he said. "Well, she and Marcello and Luca. They found their way in here"—he tossed the chain back to the ground—"and then found their way out."

We stood there a long moment, considering just how hard that must have been.

"There is a reason that they have held this castello all these years," he said.

"Because they do not want to see their loved ones here, in this dungeon, again."

"Yes. But also to keep Firenze more than a day's ride from our border. We have seen skirmishes and attacks of late, but to invite them here . . ." He lifted a hand to the nearest wall and leaned his head toward it, closing his eyes. As if he could feel the future. Or feared it.

"Yet you offered it to them," I said quietly. "Freely."

"We did." He opened those blue eyes to stare into mine.

I still don't get it, I thought. *Not quite.* Seven hundred hectares of land. Tons of farmers or vintners or shepherds reporting to *you.* A *castle.* The Forellis could never repay him.

And yet the Grecos had seen it as a peace offering—an offering the Fiorentini threw back in their faces when they still hauled the Forellis up in those horrid cages.

Giulio led me upstairs, and we wound our way up farther, to the high walls, past two guards. I could see a bit of Castello Forelli in the distance. Her long, golden flags waved in the wind, through a gap in the thick woods between us. We turned a corner and took in the lush hills with shepherds running herds of goats and sheep, as well as vineyards in orderly rows.

I turned to him. "You were willing to give up all of this, for no payment at all."

He clasped his hands behind his back. "'Twas best for Siena. For the Forellis too. Relinquishing this castello likely saved countless lives. Without it, Firenze would have amassed a force and immediately attacked us. As terrible as it was for the Forellis, we might have *all* been summarily hanged in Firenze, just as Rosa was, had we not given it back to them."

"But is it not simply putting off the inevitable? Firenze is not on the attack now, but might they do so next month? Or next year?"

"Mayhap," he said. "I remain hopeful that we can demonstrate to both republics that it is possible to live in peace, side by side. It gives me hope that Aurelio shall be the Paratore taking ownership. We know his intent. Mayhap it shall inspire greater peace between the republics."

I nodded in appreciation. "I did not know you were a peacemaker."

He cocked his head. "I would not go as far as to call myself that. But I am hopeful my future sons and daughters will not constantly be at war."

"Future sons and daughters," I repeated shyly. "How many children would you like to have?"

He put a hand on either of my hips and leaned his forehead down to touch mine. "As many as my future bride would like," he whispered.

Future bride. His words sent a thrill through me. He was talking about *me*. This thing between us was really happening. But was I really ready to be a bride? A mom? *Not for a while,* I thought, grinning shyly and trying to turn away. How long did medieval courtships last?

But he held me fast and leaned down, seeking my lips. I lifted to meet his own, and we kissed softly for but a moment. He did not press in—probably worried about hurting me. Then we walked along the wall, hand in hand, just enjoying being together, touching. "Do you like it here, Luciana? In Toscana? As opposed to *Britannia*?"

"I feel more settled than I have in a very long time," I said, stopping to look out across the woods to the hills with him. "Here with you, the Forellis, it is as if I am more *me*, somehow. All my life I have felt like I was working to get somewhere. And now I believe I was simply longing to be *here*."

He tucked a strand of my hair behind my ear, then cupped my face. "And now I know I was longing for you, Luciana, all these years. Because having you here with me, has made my heart feel as if it has grown threefold."

I liked the way he said that. I understood it, because I felt the same.

"When I am apart from you, I can scarcely think of anything but our reunion," he said.

"As do I," I said, squeezing his hand.

"I think about walking with you, talking with you. Kissing you." He cast me a devilish smile.

"Why, Lord Greco! That is scandalous!" I teased.

"You do not think about kissing me?" he asked with a grin.

Only on the hour, round the clock, I thought. "On occasion," I said.

He wrapped an arm around my waist and leaned close. "Then mayhap I must kiss you more, so you remember well the pleasure of it. Then you shall long for me as much as I long for you."

I wished that my shoulder was healed. Because right then, I

longed to push him into the shadows of the guard tower and kiss him for all he was worth.

But his attention left me. He moved to the wall, and I ambled up beside him. Fortino and the knights of Castello Forelli were already at work, carrying away rocks and timbers and tossing them over the hill, where they would not be readily seen.

"That tunnel truly goes all the way under the castello?"

"To the dungeon or near it," he said. "Those who built this castle a hundred years ago did so directly over the Etruscan ruins."

"So if we can truly excavate the entire sewage tunnel, we shall have access to the castle itself?"

He lifted a dark brow. "I do not know. And if Paratore is worth his salt—or his captain—I doubt what we do will remain undiscovered. But come, let us return below and see what we can ascertain from within."

25

TILIANI

Several days of healing left me stronger—in my head and heart as well as on my feet. I did not know what was to become of my feelings for Valentino or his for me. But it was out of our hands. We simply had to move forward, the best we could, and see if God made a way for us.

As dawn broke, I slipped my healing feet into my soft leather boots and strapped on a leather chest plate over my tunic. I was determined to ride out with the others on patrol and knew doing so would bring me some relief. I needed to return to the familiar.

Besides, the Paratore household would arrive soon, and we needed to serve as scouts for the men completing the excavation today. The Etruscan sewage tunnel did indeed run beneath Castello Greco, but it had been filled with stone and detritus before the castle was built. Our men decided to leave it filled, for the most part, so that it would appear unmolested, but they cleared a crawlspace and excavated twenty feet inward, forming a mining pocket that could be used to bring a portion of the wall down—in the event we went to battle. That crawlspace was to be carefully refilled with rocks at the entrance today. With luck, anyone who discovered it would assume the entire thing remained filled.

When I entered the stables, I was happy to see Ilaria and Fortino already saddling their mounts.

"Cousin!" Fortino flashed me a grin. "'Tis good to see you up and about."

"'Tis good to be so," I returned.

"Are you certain it is not too soon?" Ilaria asked me.

"I am certain I cannot tolerate another day of lolling about," I returned. "I never was gifted at embroidery."

Ilaria smiled. "Neither of us were."

Mama and Zia Gabi arrived. "You are joining us on patrol?" I asked, surprised.

"Indeed." Mama reached for her saddle. "We need every able man and woman keeping the woods clear of Fiorentini while they complete the task at Castello Greco." She, too, wore common riding gear with a leather-armor chest plate, and I saw there was a knit hat tucked in her belt. Zia Gabi donned one too. They intended to avoid recognition, which was wise. After all we'd been through in Firenze, the last thing any of us wanted was to be captured again.

Groomsmen arrived and helped us finish saddling our mounts, then moved on to others for the knights streaming inward. We immediately rode out to make way. I was again surprised to see Nona already leaving through the gates, riding with Giulio and Zio Marcello.

"Where are *they* headed?" I asked my mother.

"To Castello Greco. They shall use your grandmother's archeological skill to put back every stone and cover up our progress."

"So it is finished? They made it twenty feet inward?"

"They did. The tunnel is shored up with timbers and filled with more wood. If we find it necessary, we can either set fire to it—which will hopefully burn so hot it will bring down a section of the wall—or we can remove the fuel and attempt to tunnel up and into the castle courtyard."

I nodded in satisfaction. A ready breach—should Aurelio be forced to turn against us—was reassuring. Both Castello Forelli and Castello Paratore had been sacked through the decades, but not without significant effort, overwhelming forces, and some sort of wedge to begin the break.

We celebrated that night with a fine feast in the Great Hall of Castello Greco. It was a farewell, of sorts, but also an opportunity for every one of our men to study the layout in detail. Giulio had ordered all weapons and supplies moved to Castello Forelli, as well as a number of fine furnishings, tapestries, and books.

"We offered them the castle, not everything in it," he said with a sly smile.

Mama and Zia Gabi ordered the men to dismantle the torture chamber in the dungeon. While Aurelio could easily hire a metalsmith to replace what was taken, I doubted he would. He had a kind heart and would likely seek alternate methods to persuade his enemies. Still, I did not blame them.

After we had eaten our fill and sopped up the meat juices on trenchers with crusty bread, my father stood and raised his goblet. The room settled as all looked in his direction.

"You have accomplished a great deal over these last days, my friends, and I am deeply proud of you. Because of your efforts, we shall have a way to reestablish rule, should our new neighbors prove less than friendly. To a united effort."

"To a united effort!" rumbled the room in response.

Giulio rose next. "I want to thank the knights and servants who have so faithfully guarded this castle over the years. My sisters and I knew that it was often a lonely post, but you all did so faithfully. We welcome you back into the Castello Forelli fold!"

"Welcome!" rumbled the room, followed by clinking ceramic goblets.

My uncle rose last. He gestured toward a number of servants in the back of the room, and they left to fetch something. "You all have seen us through a rather harrowing year, between the battle with the Perugians and the incessant harassment of the Fiorentini. My brother and I have taken it upon ourselves to establish a new coat of arms that shall be unique to our castello and lands."

Mama and Zia Gabi glanced at them in surprise. The servants returned, along with others, each carrying a chest. They stopped at various points in the hall, but one came all the way forward to my uncle and set it at his feet. Marcello crouched and opened the locked lid and smiled at his wife. He passed a blue bundle to my father.

"In honor of our wives, the mothers of our children, the She-Wolves of Siena, our family crest shall henceforth be the howling wolf, and our new color the deep blue of a night sky." He let the tunic unfold, and people began howling as they saw the embroidered golden wolf on the deep-blue backdrop. They matched what my aunt and mother wore to battle. Now we were all to match them as well. I lifted my chin and added my own best howl with the rest, when I wasn't laughing. If Aurelio and his men approached the castello now, what a ruckus they would witness!

"We shall send riders in the morn to all our principal neighbors as well as to Siena, informing them of our family's new color and emblem embroidered on every tunic. Only six seamstresses have been charged with doing this work, and their finesse with needle and thread shall make it difficult to emulate."

"Clearly, I am not one of the six," I whispered to Ilaria as we received our own tunics and admired the beautiful work.

"We shall also inform them that all gold tunics and horse blankets, flags, and battle heralds shall be burned this night. We shall dispose of the Greco colors as well, as our friends fully become a part of Castello Forelli this night, forever. Any tunics or emblems that are found elsewhere—given that every man and woman employed by Castello Forelli is at home this eve—are in the hands of an enemy seeking to further frame us for heinous acts."

I sat back and lifted my goblet to my uncle in silent admiration. 'Twas a stroke of genius. If Ercole was out there, and attempting further framing, he would be hanged by his own golden noose.

LUCIANA

Only some of the men wore Forelli gold in the Great Hall of Castello Greco. I'd noticed the tunics were predominantly worn in battle to help differentiate one side from another, or in celebration, like in Palazzo Pubblico in Siena or for feasts. This preserved them for the important moments, I figured. As I shook out my own tunic and slipped it over my head, I felt the honor of being included with this household of fine people. Marked by the howling wolf. The others around me clearly felt the same, proud to be part of it all.

But as we filed out to the courtyard and watched as the golden tunics and flags were fed to the flames of a hot bonfire, all fell to silence. I imagined they were thinking of fallen comrades, friends and family members who had died over the years, wearing Forelli gold. Yet it also felt momentous, as if this truly was a new chapter in which we were all to take part. Even me and Nico.

We shared a meaningful look. "You look good in blue," he whispered.

"As do you." I ran my hand over the texture of the embroidery. It felt a bit like a uniform might. Or a costume. But it definitely made me feel more the part.

"'Tis fitting for the newest She-Wolf," Giulio said, coming to stand on my other side. "And He-Wolf," he added to Nico. "You are truly part of the clan now."

Giulio's fingers interlaced with mine among the folds of my skirts as the Greco flags were brought down from the ramparts. With a nod from Giulio, servants tossed them on the fire too. They smoldered for a bit and then caught, the threads giving way to bright light and then disappearing in the coals. Giulio observed it all stoically.

"Does it pain you?" I asked gently.

"Yes," he said, still staring at the flames. "It was but a bit I had left of my father. Now it is gone." He swallowed hard and glanced at me. With his handsome face half in shadow, half in flickering light, he resembled some fierce angel. "'Tis what he would have wanted, though. Solidarity with the Forellis over individual family pride."

I again wondered about the power of this family, their ability to so inspire and connect people that they became a part of their own clan tapestry. I felt it myself. I wanted to serve them, protect them, honor them for how graciously they had welcomed me and Nico.

On the far side of the fire, I saw the elder Forellis, each man with an arm around his wife's shoulders. They, too, soberly stared into the flames, likely considering the momentousness of this night.

And yet there was hope in them too. Maybe it was because they had gotten to know Aurelio Paratore. Trusted him, in measure. Maybe they even hoped there still could be a bridge built between Siena and Firenze, with him behind this castle's gates. Maybe they hoped we would enjoy new peace, because with a Fiorentini in charge of these lands again, others were not as likely to venture near to harass the Forellis.

Three knights pulled Nico away for a game of dice, but Giulio and I remained.

"You hand the keys over to Lord Paratore on the morrow?" I asked.

"I do," he said soberly. "Our scout estimates that they shall arrive midmorning."

"And then it shall be done."

"It shall indeed."

Ilaria stood beside Tiliani. They were whispering and smiling together. Remembering some adventure? Or some occurrence within these walls?

"Do you think Captain Valeri shall accompany Lord Paratore?" I whispered.

"Undoubtedly," Giulio said.

"There would be no cause for him to remain behind in Firenze, to protect Palazzo Paratore?" I pressed on.

"That shall be left to another. This is the far more prominent post."

"That is understandable. I only hope . . ."

He followed my gaze to his sister and Tiliani. "Ah, yes. That might prove painful for my friend." He moved behind me and wrapped his arms gently around my shoulders—cautious with my injured one—and I welcomed the warmth of him. "To be so near the one you love," he whispered in my ear, "and yet not be able to touch? I would rather be chained in the dungeon than endure that."

I smiled as his warm breath sent delightful shivers down my skin. "We have to help them find a way to see each other. Mayhap a rendezvous in the woods?"

"They do both enjoy a good hunt for medicinal herbs," he said. "But Valentino is as dedicated to Aurelio as I am to m'lords and ladies."

I heaved a sigh. "Mayhap if Aurelio gave them his blessing?"

He stiffened behind me. "Do not hold out such hope, love. Do not encourage Tiliani. I believe Aurelio might still hope to court her."

I frowned. "But she does not love him."

"Nay. But we are back to where we were. I think she became fond of him, at least. And if it would benefit Siena, the Forellis, and the future, would she be willing to accept his hand?"

"While her heart pines for his captain?" I shook my head in horror. "I hope not. Our future cannot be pinned on one woman. Or man! It simply cannot."

"We shall see. For now"—he took my hand—"come with me for one last turn around the castle wall." He cast me a devilish look as he kissed my hand and held it to his chest, engulfed in both of his. And I, despite my fears of how rapidly this thing between us was sucking me in, eagerly followed him.

26

TILIANI

We rode out the next morning when scouts confirmed that the Paratore household approached. Our knights lined either side of the entrance to the castle. I stood with Giulio and his sisters at the center of our group in the courtyard, my parents, aunt, uncle, and cousins on either side of us.

Aurelio and Valentino rode in first, with twelve knights behind them, four horse-drawn wagons and thirty-six more knights bringing up the rear. While Aurelio and Valentino pulled up before us, Valentino gestured for the others to circle around the courtyard.

I fought to keep my attention on Aurelio as he dismounted and approached us with a genuine smile. "My friends, thank you for welcoming us."

Giulio stepped forward and clasped his arm, drawing him closer for a brief embrace, then did the same with Valentino. "'Tis our sincere hope that this is the dawn of a new era between our republics," he said. "That it will not only soothe the pain of all the Fiorentini families who lost loved ones in Palazzo Pubblico, but that it will also demonstrate how we can live in peace, even when so near a contested border."

Aurelio nodded. "That is my desire as well." He turned to me and my parents. "Have you made a full recovery, my friends?"

"We have," my father said, even though Aurelio's eyes hovered over me. "We owe you a debt of gratitude for not only seeing us safely out of your city, but for doing your best to aid us while there."

Giulio reached for the ring of keys at his waist and lifted them toward Aurelio. "I, Lord Giulio Greco," he said loudly, so all could hear, "do hereby relinquish all rights and claims to this castle and her lands, freely giving them to Lord Aurelio Paratore, trusting he shall be a good steward of the castello, her lands, and her people."

Aurelio took the ring of keys from him with a brief bow. "Thank you, Lord Greco. I shall do as you have bid. Might you do me a further favor?"

Giulio lifted a brow, waiting.

"Ride with me in the coming days, introducing me to the families who work our vines and olive groves, those who shepherd our sheep. Inform me how I might be a good lord to our people."

"I would gladly do so," Giulio said, clearly heartened by his words.

"Excellent. Shall we begin on the morrow, after you complete your morning patrol?"

"Indeed."

Aurelio turned to me. "If you are free to do so, Lady Tiliani, I would welcome your company and perspective as well. Ofttimes a woman notices things a man does not."

I hesitated, even as Mama nudged me. "Of course," I finally said, my heart sinking. For wherever Aurelio went, so would Valentino. Could I tolerate being so near him, yet so far apart?

Mama leaned forward. "We are so grateful for how you watched over us in Firenze, Lord Paratore. Please join us this eve at Castello Forelli for supper."

"You are most kind," he said. "Captain Valeri and I shall gladly attend and bring twelve of our men with us. The others who draw short straws shall have to get used to guarding our new castello."

His men laughed. One hit another across the belly with the flat of his arm. Another whispered in the ear of his companion, while both looked at me. They would be vying for those long straws.

It seemed everyone in this courtyard was interested in what would transpire between Aurelio and me, while all I wanted was a moment alone with Valentino.

LUCIANA

Benedetto, now fully recovered, enlisted my brother and me to teach him some basics of jiu jitsu after we left Castello Paratore. Given that my shoulder wasn't yet healed, I was there mostly for supervision. Gabriella decided to join us, as did Ilaria, Fortino, and Giulio. Tiliani had left on a longer patrol mission with Luca and Marcello.

I thought the distraction might help Giulio put his mind to things of the future rather than things of the past. Because despite his willingness, he had seemed rather somber as we'd ridden away from the castle that had once been his.

It made sense to me. He had joked about being a "landless man," but I knew it was a real concern for men in this era. Would he look for a way to rebuild his own wealth? Or be content to share in the Forellis' gains and losses, come what may? As he rode ahead of us to the meadow where he had taught me to spar and dance, I doubted he would "let much grass grow beneath his feet," as my grandmother used to say.

Even now, he was pointing out boar tracks to Ilaria, mayhap planning a hunt.

Gabriella rode beside me. "He is a talented tracker," she said. "In fact, his father once tracked Lia and me."

I glanced at her in confusion. "What?"

She smiled. "When Rodolfo Greco was still Fiorentini," she said in English, "they used him to track the She-Wolves of Siena down. They were smarting over some serious losses in battle and blamed us. Somehow, we'd become overnight sensations—you know, as far as that works here in medieval Italy." She met my gaze. "You'd be surprised at how word of mouth can rival the speed of social media."

I lifted a brow. "When it's your only source . . ." I shrugged. "Guess it makes everyone a gossip of sorts, huh?"

She laughed under her breath. "Especially when there is so little other entertainment or diversion. Everyone is up in everyone else's business."

We rode a while in silence as I contemplated that. I'd experienced a bit of it, but not the full force. Life hadn't slowed down enough for me to really observe. "Is it a good thing or a bad thing that everyone knows what's up with everyone else?"

"Both," she said, ruefully. "But you wanna know what I love about it? When you find out so much about your neighbor—the good as well as the ugly—you really feel like you know *them*. Everyone has to have an extra measure of grace for others in their world, if you want to live in peace. And that creates a sense of village like I never, ever experienced back in the States."

Was that part of what drew me too? Beyond family, that sense of village? *That'd be a definite pro on the Medieval List.*

"So did Lord Greco catch you?"

She nodded. "He did, in time." Then she quirked a grin at me. "But not before we sorely tried his patience. In the end, Lia got away, and Rodolfo narrowly plucked me out of Cosimo Paratore's hands."

"And that was a good thing, right?"

"A very good thing. While Rodolfo was Fiorentini, he was a fine man. Cosimo was not."

"Your history with the Paratores is very complicated."

"To say the least."

"Do you feel good about this, then? Having Aurelio assume responsibility for the castle after all this time?"

"I think it will help soothe some of the agitation that arose between our republics," she said gently. "But Luciana, there is a reason I wanted to watch you and your brother train the boys and the Grecos. As much as I like Aurelio and trust him—even enough to bless him taking Tiliani's hand—I do not trust the Fiorentini behind him.

They pressed Rodolfo to do awful things . . . which he narrowly circumvented, time and again."

"You think Aurelio shall be pressed to attack us?"

She gave me a thin-lipped smile. "Given all I have seen over the decades we've been here, I wouldn't be surprised. Only the fact that we secured a way to weaken the castello—and removed all torture devices—allows me to sleep at night. These years with Giulio as lord of that place gave me peace. But I also think your method of fighting—jiu jitsu, is it?—might give us another advantage."

"I wanted to ask you about that. Are we not changing history, introducing it now, here? Jiu jitsu didn't really become a thing until the nineteenth century."

She lifted her brows. "We changed things the minute Lia and I stepped foot on this medieval soil. My parents too. And now you and your brother." She sighed. "We try not to have too much impact, but rest in the fact that God saw fit to bring us all here. He knew who we were before he did that. Knew our skillsets and temperaments. And he knew we would use every tool we had to thrive here."

She was right. It assured me, somehow.

"I think we pressed too far," she admitted, "trying to secure things forever by promising Tiliani's hand to a Fiorentini. Or rather, our men did."

"Could you have argued it? Or is that not done here?"

"Oh, believe me, we had some words over it, especially when we learned it was a *Paratore* with whom they had come to terms. But over the course of discussion, we saw the wisdom and hope in it. We thought if this could be done with our age-old 'enemies'— even though Aurelio never met Cosimo—what other mountains could we move?"

We reached the meadow. She dismounted and joined me, walking with our horses to a tree with a long, low branch that was ideal for tying them. "We figured the castello had already been saved. What else might we preserve?"

We tied the horses up and walked toward the others. "Now my

sole aim is to better protect my loved ones here, not secure the future of an entire republic. Because some things are out of even a She-Wolf's hands." She winked and patted my back before turning to walk around the small circle that had formed.

Benedetto stepped toward Nico, looking worlds better than he had a few days ago, but still a bit pale. "I have heard tales of you and your sister flipping men twice your size to their backs. Of you kicking with the force of a donkey, knocking out men's teeth. Of breaking a man's wrist before he could strike you down with his sword. I want to learn all of that."

"As do I," Ilaria said.

"And I," Fortino put in.

"And I," Gabi said.

"The tales are true." Giulio put an arm around my shoulders. "And as they demonstrate those moves for us, know this might be the only chance I get to best this woman, given that she has been winged."

I smiled. He'd meant to pay me a compliment, but he'd made it too easy. Taking hold of his arm, I pressed in with my hip and used my good arm to flip him over my shoulder and to his back. I immediately brought my knee down against his throat. It hurt me some, those moves, but I refused to let it show. I was too busy grinning from ear to ear as he stared up at me in surprise, and the others hooted in laughter.

"I apparently spoke too soon," Giulio said, lifting his hands in surrender.

Laughing, Nico leaned forward and gave him a hand up. Giulio pretended to skirt me warily, smiling with the others. I gave him a smug look. After all the times he had bested me with a sword, it felt good to exercise a bit of my own power.

"Now another way to do that," Nico led, gripping my shoulder, "is to . . ."

"Grab his wrist," I said, "twist, and push with your hip, creating a ramp with your body. You can even do so one-handed."

"Luci—" Nico warned.

But I couldn't resist. With one swift move, he was on his back too.

27

TILIANI

We rode a good eight miles to reach Castello Romano and deliver the word to the last of the Nine about our new herald and colors. I knew my father and Zio Marcello did not need me along for the ride; they'd invited me because they knew *I* needed the reprieve. Because sometimes nothing soothed the soul like allowing your mount to gallop as fast as he could, feeling the churn and rhythm of his gait become your own. I laughed as my father leaned down, clearly trying to race me, and then again as my uncle passed us both. Since he rode the fastest gelding in the greater area, we really never had a chance.

And yet I did not care. It had been years since I had ridden with both men and not been on patrol. It made me feel like a girl again, like when they were first teaching me to ride. Back when I rode with my mother and aunt, too, learning how to wield both a sword and shoot an arrow well. We allowed our horses to settle back into a trot—and our accompanying knights to catch up—realizing that we could not entirely let our guard down. But having my father and uncle on either side of me made me feel as strong as I did when I rode out with my mother and aunt. Together we were a force that would make most enemies reconsider before attacking. And mayhap with Aurelio Paratore here, now, we would settle again into some semblance of peace.

But memories of what Luciana had overheard in Palazzo Vanni in Firenze troubled me.

"Do you think that Ercole will come after us again? After Castello Forelli herself?"

My uncle cocked his head. "Firenze would have to amass a considerable force to do that." He looked to my father. "Do you think Ercole believes he can do so, given that he resided with us for so long? That he spotted some weakness?"

Papa paused. "He did train with us. Learned our tactics. He would have some advantages if we came head-to-head on the battlefield. And he knows every square foot of our castle."

"Best we come up with some new battle plans as a means to surprise him, if it comes to that," my uncle said. "Did you have any idea that he had inroads with the Fiorentini?" he asked my father.

"Nay. He came to us from Siena. Remember when I went to recruit new men, two years past?"

"I do. Who recommended him?"

"Gallo. And Lord Bruno. Iacapo had served with him under Lord Mancini for a year too."

Considering how many men came to us with mere written references, it was impressive that he had several personal connections. Papa could not be faulted for hiring him, despite how he had turned on us.

I thought again of Rosa—how he had so sorely used her— and tensed with rage. Part of me wished we *would* meet on the battlefield. I would like to exact a portion of the vengeance due the girl . . . and others whom he had undoubtedly harmed over the years. Mama always said that abusive men never hurt only one. It was usually a pattern over the course of their life.

"I think Aurelio will advocate for us," I said, "if Firenze wishes to raise arms against us again."

"And yet he is but one man," Zio Marcello said. "The only reason they sent him to take Castello Greco was because his family has historical claim to the castello. Had he not been a Paratore, they would undoubtedly have sent another."

"'Tis true," Papa said. "The way he protected us as we left the city . . ." He shook his head. "It likely did not engender kind feelings from his fellow Fiorentini."

"We had paid our price."

"Most Fiorentini would say we should have paid with our lives."

"Could we not say the same of many noblemen of Firenze?" I returned. "There are about ten families who routinely send men to attack us while on patrol."

"True," my uncle said, "but after Palazzo Pubblico—"

"Which we have atoned for!" my father erupted. "By our suffering in those cursed cages! To say nothing of relinquishing Castello Greco!"

"Agreed," my uncle said. "But sometimes hatred runs so deep, so fast, that it is like a rip tide in the sea. If you wade out into it, you get swept away."

"And the only way out is to swim along the shore," my father mused with a sigh, "until the sea at last releases you from its pull."

"Or you drown," I said soberly. "Is that what we face? An enemy who wants only to see us sink?"

"Mayhap," my uncle said. "It has gone on for many generations, this contention between us. Some of it is because the Pope poisons them against us. Some of it is common greed, wanting our fertile lands and rivers for their own. Some of it is pride."

We rode for a while in silence, all lost in our own thoughts.

"I want you both to know," I said, "that I understand why you wanted me to wed Aurelio. I understand you had the best of intentions."

"And yet we should have warned you. Asked you if you were willing," Papa said. "For that, we are deeply sorry, Til. We simply got . . ." He cast a helpless glance to my uncle.

"Ahead of ourselves," Zio Marcello said. He sighed heavily and then cast me a grin. "So while we may be handsome, we are not always as clever as we wish. Will you forgive us, Tiliani? Truly?"

"Truly," I said, giving them both a smile. "But next time . . . even if Aurelio wishes to renew his courtship, it must be up to me. Yes? Even if it means I *never* marry, it must be my decision alone."

"Agreed," my father said.

"So be it," Zio Marcello said.

We returned home late that afternoon, and I hurriedly bathed and dressed in a royal-blue gown for dinner. It was a bit fancy for entertaining new neighbors, more typical for a feast, but I knew it accentuated my curves. The maid lifted a silent, questioning eyebrow when I chose it, but I pretended not to notice as I bent to fluff out the wide skirt.

I wanted to look my best this night for Valentino. If he insisted on looking past me, I aimed to not make it easy to do so. Once I was in the gown, Ludovica set to working out the tangles in my wet hair with the whalebone comb. She swiftly braided a portion at either temple and then wound them into a bun at the base of my neck. She fit a black net over it and secured it with an onyx comb, tucked into the top.

"A necklace, too, m'lady?" she asked.

"Please. The freshwater pearls."

She hesitated for only a moment, then retrieved the three-strand choker with a piece of iridescent Roman glass set in silver at the center, a gift from Nona. Ludovica settled it around my neck, and I looked at my reflection in the polished bronze disc before me. The neckline skimmed from shoulder to shoulder, dipping just low enough to show my collar bones. The sleeves hugged my arms and came down to a delicate point atop my hands, but then had a generous swoop of fabric hanging beneath. The bodice hugged my torso and hips before dropping to the floor. Given that it was a finely woven silk, the wrinkles were already releasing as I stood. Still, Ludovica did a little more fluffing of the skirt before taking a couple steps away to admire me.

"You look beautiful, m'lady. He shall not be able to keep his eyes off you," she whispered conspiratorially.

I knew she was hoping I'd tell her which man's attention I sought. "Thank you for your assistance," I said with a mischievous smile, reaching out to squeeze her hand. My love life—or lack thereof—was a constant topic among the servants, and little escaped their notice. But I refused to aid them in that endeavor.

She opened the door and I strode out. Giulio, dressed in his new blue tunic, lifted a brow of appreciation. Ilaria was in a fine—if more simple—olive-green gown. My uncle had asked every knight in the castle to wear their tunics tonight. I supposed my choice of the gown might be interpreted as solidarity, versus an attempt to draw a man's eye.

"You are a vision, my friend," Giulio said.

I took his arm and smiled. "And yet I wager you shall consider another twice as attractive as I, regardless of what she wears," I teased.

"Undoubtedly," he readily admitted.

"Things are progressing well between you?" I asked.

He did not try to cover his victorious smile. "Indeed." He reached for the turret door and opened it for me. "I wondered . . . how long do you believe she desires to court?"

I lifted a brow. "Anxious to wed, are you?"

"I would wed her on the morrow if she would have me. But I sense she is somewhat reticent. Might that be due to the fact she is still adjusting to life in the castello? Here. *Now*?"

"'Twould take a great deal to adjust to such a thing," I said, passing by him. "And she and Domenico have been through much while abiding with us. 'Tis best not to rush her."

I thought about Valentino and what it would be like to have

him court me. Whereas I had never considered less than a year's courtship with any of the men who had sought my hand, I believed I was like Giulio in this—I would wed Valentino on the morrow if he asked it.

Most of the people had already gathered in the Great Hall. As Giulio escorted me to the table at the front, up on the dais, my heart skipped a beat. An empty seat—most likely saved for me—was directly between Valentino and Aurelio. Across from us sat my parents, aunt and uncle, and chairs for Giulio and Ilaria between Luciana and Domenico.

All the men rose as Ilaria and I climbed the steps, then bowed as we passed them. I nodded to Valentino—who did not meet my eyes—and then to Aurelio—who did. A steward helped slide my chair in.

"You are worthy of a portrait, m'lady," Aurelio said in my ear, as my father rose, goblet in hand.

"*Grazie*," I said, with a small smile, forcing myself not to glance back toward Valentino.

"We are here," my father said, lifting his goblet, "to celebrate our friendship with Aurelio Paratore and his household. Let this be the beginning of a new era of peace between our households."

"Hear, hear," said everyone in the room, then took a sip of wine.

Servants began to pass the food—trenchers filled with a hearty lamb stew, white beans with sage, and roasted boar. Others followed behind with jugs of wine, refilling goblets.

"You appear to have made a full recovery from your ordeal, have you not?" Aurelio asked.

"I believe so, m'lord."

"I sincerely regret the punishment Firenze exacted. I could do nothing to stop it."

"We understand." I poked a tender piece of boar and placed it in my mouth. I did not want to think about those long days in the cages, nor of how close we came to death. I could feel myself tense and took a gulp of wine to make sure I could swallow the meat. "We know you did all you could, m'lord."

"Please. Can we not return to calling each other by our given names? Now that we are neighbors, I had hoped to revive our . . . friendship."

"I think it best that we return to a more formal friendship, m'lord," I said. "I wish to live in peace as your neighbor." I dropped my tone. "But I fear there shall be nothing more."

He stiffened. My rebuff was far from subtle. "Is this due to the torture you endured?" he asked under his breath. "Did I fail you?"

"On the contrary," I returned in kind. "I credit your household for seeing us safely in and out of the city, as well as watching over us while we were imprisoned in those wretched cages." I met his eye and gave him a small smile. "For that we shall be forever grateful."

We shared a long look, and then he forcibly turned his attention to Giulio. "Sir Greco, might you join me on the morrow, riding out to meet the villeins, as we discussed? If you introduce us, mayhap it shall give them confidence. A blessing of sorts, upon our transition."

Giulio nodded readily. "Of course. Shall we come to you midmorn, after our patrol is complete?"

"That is most agreeable." He picked up his goblet. "But it is my hope, my friends, that with us as your neighbors, you shall no longer feel compelled to run a patrol in your north woods. While we are not Sienese, we intend to abide in peace, and keep any of our fellow citizens from further harassing you."

My father chewed his meat, considering his words. "'Twould be a blessed relief," he said. "What say you, Sir Greco? As captain of this castello's guard, I leave it to you." The table stilled, interest in this conversation gathering.

Giulio glanced at me. I knew my father wanted him to hold on to the patrol, regardless of his trusting words. Did he not?

"I think you are a good man, Lord Paratore," Giulio said,

"with good intentions. I hope you are right and that in the years to come, we might ease our guard. But far more goodwill must grow between our republics before I could agree."

"Of course, of course." Aurelio lifted his goblet. "To coming years of building goodwill!"

"To goodwill!" thundered the people at the table and beyond us.

Aurelio went on to ask Giulio one question after another about the castello. As they became embroiled in their conversation, I dared to turn toward Valentino.

"Is it well with you, Captain? Your new home? Or do you miss Firenze?"

"'Tis well," he allowed. "Abiding here with your family for a time made it clear that there is much to appreciate among these fine hills."

He did not look at me.

"I intend to do some foraging for oyster mushrooms and wild onions in two days' time. Mullein should be flowering by now too." I turned toward Aurelio. "M'lord, would you permit me to continue foraging in your eastern woods? I was telling your captain that a few key herbs and mushrooms should be maturing about now."

"To our east? Of course. Simply send word to let our scouts know you are there by permission." He paused. "Better yet, Valentino should accompany you. He is most excellent at foraging."

"I remember," I said lightly. "After our battle with the Perugians, he was of great aid to me."

"Mayhap you should still take additional knights along. While I can keep the Fiorentini at bay, there is always the threat of new brigands."

"Mayhap 'twould be best to send along some servants to aid her," Valentino tried.

"Nonsense," Aurelio returned. "If our lovely neighbor intends to forage on our lands, I intend to keep her completely safe. I would offer my own services"—he forced a laugh—"but I confess

I am a terrible forager. The only mushrooms I seem to find are either those likely to kill you or make you see God."

Others around the table laughed. Giulio and Ilaria only pretended to do so. They saw through my ruse . . . and they did not like it.

But it mattered not. All that mattered to me was finding out if Valentino felt as much for me as I did for him. If Padre Giovanni was right, and the Lord would make a way for us in time, surely the Lord did not want us to sit in our respective castles. Nay, he would make a way for us by encouraging Aurelio to give us his blessing, in time. But meanwhile, how would we develop any relationship of substance unless we were occasionally together?

I wanted to grin over my small victory, even as Valentino stiffly finished his meal, and Aurelio and Giulio continued to chat. As the servants cleared away our serving dishes and our trenchers, people rose and moved into conversation with others about the room.

I whispered in Valentino's ear as I rose. "Meet me in the stables."

I awaited no response and went to speak to the new bride of one of the knights, a childhood friend. Then, when I moved toward the door, Ilaria took my arm and ushered me through.

"What are you doing, Tiliani?" she asked with a bright smile, pretending her words did not contain challenge.

"What do you mean?" I tried.

"Come now. That was neatly managed, your foraging trip. Is Lord Paratore the only one in this room who cannot see that his captain pines for you?"

"That is just it." I led her toward the door. "I do not know if he still does. Or if he has set his feelings for me aside forever."

"Every time he looks your way, the poor man appears tortured."

"He looked my way?" I whispered.

"He tried not to do so. But I was sitting right across from him. I swear he spent a good portion of the time staring at your hand."

My *hand*. I did not know why, but I found it touching, as well as encouraging.

We walked out into the courtyard, and I took a welcome, deep breath of the cooling air. The hour was late, and it was growing dark. "I shall know this night what he feels for me, one way or another."

"Til," she said, her tone full of warning, as we approached the stables. "This is a dangerous game. Lord Paratore . . . he clearly still hopes you two might court again."

"I made it clear to him," I sniffed, "that all I desired was friendship."

"Mayhap," she whispered. "But what would he say if he found out you two were courting in secret? A man's pride . . ." She folded her arms and shook her head.

"Mayhap there shall be no courtship at all," I said, irritated. "All I know is that I must discover the way of it this night."

"And if there is?" she pressed. "Tiliani. *Think*." "Thinking too much is what has kept us apart," I said. "Thinking I must accept Aurelio's pursuit for the good of my family, for the good of the republic. And then Valentino thinking he cannot go to Aurelio with the truth of his feelings." I threw up my hands. "If he truly has feelings for me at all."

"You know he does."

I remained silent. I knew it. But I needed him to confess it. Not for me. But for himself. If we were to move forward, he had to acknowledge it.

He left the Great Hall then, following two other knights with two women, easily slipping past, given their distraction. But he hesitated, seeing me talking with Ilaria in the shadows.

"Give us a moment," I said to her. "Please. Watch for any others coming our way and knock on the far wall, by Cardo's stable, if they do."

"*Tiliani*," she whispered as I walked away.

I ignored her, forcing her to do as I bid. I hated to act the part as a superior of Castello Forelli—especially with Ilaria—but I could do no other this night. *I must know how he feels. I must.*

A stable boy played with a wooden figure while he sat at his post by the door. "Carlo," I said, smiling. "I thought to come give Cardo a rubdown before bed. If you get to the Great Hall quickly, I believe Cook will have supper for you."

He hesitated, likely fretting over leaving his post more than wondering over me rubbing down Cardo, dressed in such finery. "Be at ease, child. If anyone complains that you are not here, I shall tell them I dismissed you. Just be quick about your meal and return, agreed?"

"As you say, m'lady." He gave me a tiny bow, then shot out the door.

I swallowed hard and moved deeper into the recesses of the stables. Hearing my voice, Cardo edged his tawny nose over the wall, waiting for me, nostrils flaring.

I went to my gelding and stroked his long nose, even as I heard the door creak open again and knew Valentino had arrived. He paused, five paces from me, nothing but a silhouette with his back to the only torch. "You asked me to meet you," he said gruffly.

"Yes." I moved toward him, closing the gap. Closer and closer I sidled, until I was looking up at him, our faces inches apart. I lifted my chin, silently begging him to kiss me.

"What are you doing?" His voice was ragged. I could feel the heat rolling off him. He rubbed the back of his neck and grimaced.

"I told you there is only one Fiorentini I wish to court me," I whispered. "And it is not Aurelio."

He stared at me hard then, as if he could see every inch of me in the dark. "I cannot do this," he whispered, tortured.

"We can find a way." I put a hand on his chest. "If you feel the same for me that I feel for you, we can find a way, in time. In time, we can seek Aurelio's blessing."

He shook his head slowly. "I fear he will not take kindly to the notion. Ever since we were boys . . ." Again, he shook his head.

"There is a sense of competition between us. All is well if he gets what he wants. But if I get what *he* wants . . ."

"Then mayhap I need to find him a wife. Someone far more beautiful and suitable than I. Genteel. A true lady of the castle, rather than a bride on morning patrol. The idea of that never sat well with him."

Valentino held his breath. Was that hope rising within him?

"More beautiful?" He lifted a hand to trace my cheek. "Impossible."

And by his breathless words, I knew he had feelings for me that he could not deny.

I smiled. "But you shall not defend my suitability," I teased.

"'Tis true. He prefers the idea of a woman more intent on seeing to the inner workings of the castello than defending her."

I interlaced my arms around his neck and brought my lips close to his—so close that they brushed as I spoke. "And you?" I whispered.

He closed his eyes for such a long moment that I feared he was summoning the courage to leave me. But then with one swift, sure move, he pulled me close, his hands pressing against the small of my back, his fingers digging in. He then bent his head so that his lips brushed *mine* as he spoke. "What do I want in a woman? To be as close to her as possible, wherever she chooses to be." And with that, he kissed me so deeply, so passionately, and for so long, that when he finally stepped back, I was breathless.

He said nothing more. Simply turned on his heel and left the stables.

I sank to my haunches, dazed, my skirts billowing about me. But I had my answer.

Captain Valentino Valeri had feelings for me. Feelings he could no longer deny.

28

I entered the courtyard as the others returned from morning patrol to refresh their horses and prepare for their tour with Aurelio Paratore. I moved over to Giulio, and he gave me a gentle smile.

"*Buongiorno, amore mio,*" he whispered, greeting me as his *love*.

I returned his smile as he took my hand, and we kissed from cheek to cheek. "Good morning."

He smelled of saddle leather and pine branches. But I decided it was his voice that really got me, every time he spoke. It was a bit gruff, low in his chest, matching the fire in those beautiful blue eyes.

"I wondered if I might ride along with you to Castello Paratore and beyond."

He paused. "Are you truly up to a ride of such length? Has Lady Adri granted you permission?"

"If I am well enough to flip you and my brother on to your backs, I am well enough to take a casual tour. I would like to see more of the lands about us." I leaned forward. "As well as spend more time with you."

He leaned down to touch his forehead to mine. "I would enjoy that as well. However, I fear I shall be mostly conversing with Lord Paratore this day."

"I understand. I will be content to merely be near you. Watch you."

He put his hand to his heart and bowed slightly. "You honor me." He turned to shout at a groomsman to saddle a mare for me.

"Giulio," I said, stopping him as he turned to rejoin the others. "I have a split skirt, as the Ladies Forelli wear. May I please sit a regular saddle today? While my arm is much better, I shall feel more secure. And with you needing to pay attention to the task at hand . . ."

He lifted his hand. "Understood. Come." He gestured toward the others. "We shall leave shortly." With long, assured strides, he passed the group and ducked into the stables to further direct the groomsman.

I glanced up and saw Nico walking the walls with Marcello again, deep in conversation. He'd introduced the idea of microloans, and Marcello seemed interested. I suspected that with the loss of Greco lands and income, he might be more amenable to finding alternate ways to generate funds. It made me glad to see it, because at the rate things were progressing with Giulio, I imagined my brother and I might need to have one last are-you-sure-you-want-to-be-here-forever conversation.

If Nico could get a job of his own going—rather than relying on simply serving as an extra knight to feed—I knew he'd be more content. And while he and Ilaria flirted pretty often, she was playing a lot harder to get than I was with Giulio. She was as strong and independent as Tiliani. Maybe even more so. Was that because she had lost her mother at a tender age? Been forced to grow up faster than any of us wished?

I looked back up at Marcello and Nico, laughing now. Marcello put a hand on my brother's shoulder as they walked—a typical warm, Tuscan gesture in this era—and it made my heart pang. How often had we wished our own father would walk with us in such a manner, talking with us, turning over ideas together! Would Nico get a bit of the father figure in Marcello that he had always needed? I liked Marcello and Luca very much. They were fine men, devoted to their wives, the castello, their friends, and their republic. They were honorable. And if they encouraged Nico to be the same, I would be very glad indeed.

"You are deep in thought," Giulio said, bringing me my mare. He tied her reins to a post and then bent to grab hold of my waist and lift me to the saddle.

"I am," I said.

He looked up at me. "Will you share those thoughts with me later this eve, when we can be alone?"

"Of course."

He handed me my reins and went to mount up himself. Was there anything about me that he missed? Never had a man made me feel so entirely *seen* in my life. I glanced up at Marcello. Certainly not my father. Maybe that's why Giulio's devotion and attention felt so startling. Overwhelming, in a way. If a girl did not have her father's love and devotion, could she really know what she was looking for in a man?

I think I do, I thought. *Someone very different from my father. Someone more like Marcello and Luca. Someone wholly devoted to the one they love.* Was that Giulio? Or was I just another girl with daddy-hunger, looking for love in all the wrong ways?

Going as far as medieval Italy to find love, Luciana? That's some serious desperation, girl.

Ilaria smiled and said good morning, waiting for me as we rode out two by two. Giulio and Tiliani rode before us. Benedetto and Fortino behind us. Somehow I knew that Giulio had arranged this formation for my protection. It warmed me since I could not yet wield either bow or sword. We trotted to the creek, then after picking our way across, slowed to a walk.

"Ilaria, may I ask you something?" I asked quietly.

"Of course."

"Has your brother ever courted a woman before?"

"Nay." She cast me a sidelong smile.

"He had many . . . admirers in Siena. Why has he not?"

She considered that for a bit. "Several have caught his eye over the years. But none had what he wanted *within*. But you do," she whispered.

I smiled. "Do you think he will be a good husband? For, um, someone? At some point?"

That made her laugh. "Indeed. For someone. At some point."

"What are his weaknesses?"

She thought about that. "He learned at a young age that he could trade on his good looks."

"How so?"

"He can give Cook a wink and she'll give him an extra bun," she said in disgust. "He can smile at the hall maids and get a bath filled with two extra pails."

"So he toys with them?"

"Ah, nay, I would not call it toying. Or if I did, it would be with the understanding that all involved know that they are in on the game. 'Tis as I said . . . he learned to trade with those pretty blue eyes and that rare, devilish smile." She shrugged. "If we were bestowed with such beauty, would we not be tempted to do the same?"

I smiled back at her, acknowledging that Giulio was a whole different level of pretty than I was. And yet he somehow thought me beautiful. I mean, when I dressed up . . . I could feel kinda pretty. And what she described was really flirting. Had I not flirted with Renato to find out more about how the Betarrinis had disappeared? Done that kind of thing a hundred times before at school, when I needed the smart kid to help me get through calculus, or on the streets of New York, like when I wanted the roundest, brownest bagel from the old baker on 57th Street? It was more *charming* than *flirting*.

But if Giulio Greco set out to charm an eligible woman? That might be trouble indeed.

"Do not misconstrue what I have said," Ilaria said, brow

furrowing. "I have never seen my brother so taken by a woman. And if you tell him that such moments concern you, I have no doubt he would cease such action immediately."

"Understood. What else might give a lady pause?"

She considered him, riding at the front of our procession. "He is headstrong. Directorial at times. Territorial as well."

"He is the castello's captain, yes? Aren't such ways required?"

"On patrol. On the field. Not with one's sister. Or one's intended."

I nodded. Nico could be relentless when he wanted something. Obsessive, when he got an idea in his head. "Brothers are the best. And the worst too," I said.

"Agreed," she said with a laugh. "But I would not trade my brother for another." She cast me another sidelong look. "Would you?"

It was my turn to smile smugly. "I would not. Are you inquiring as a friend? Or as a maiden with her eye on a man?"

"Both," she admitted with an amused shrug of her shoulders.

TILIANI

The closer to Castello Paratore we drew, the faster my heart pounded. I had barely slept last night, tossing and turning, thinking of Valentino and how he had kissed me . . . kissed me with more passion than I had ever thought possible. How were we to manage being in proximity, sharing such a memory? *Please, Lord. Cover us. Protect us. And please, please make a way for us to be together.*

Trust, Padre Giovanni had encouraged me after morning prayers, giving me a reassuring pat on the back. *Wait on the Lord's timing. He is never early and never late.*

But as we rode up the path to the castle gates, I thought the Lord might be very late indeed.

Valentino sat upon his gelding beside Aurelio, a knight on either side of them. I fought to look anywhere but to him. But I could feel his somber, warm eyes on me. I feared it would send a blush rising to my cheeks and Aurelio might think it for him. So instead I fought to think about cold, awful things—things opposite of Valentino's warm gaze, warm embrace, warm kiss. *The river in winter. The cold castello stones beneath my feet in the morning. The cage outside Firenze at night.*

That aided me in giving them all a cool greeting—only giving Aurelio a demure nod as he bade me good morning. He paused over me for a moment, but then moved on to Giulio, thanking him for coming.

"'Tis no trouble," Giulio said. "If it aids the people, I am in favor of it. For the villeins have no say in the ways of lords or the republics. God would have us look after them with respect."

"Well said," Aurelio agreed. "Let us get on with it before the sun is high and beating upon our backs."

Giulio hesitated. "You intend to ride with only three men?"

"Are you not doing the same?" Aurelio asked with quirk of his lips. "Besides, I have Firenze to my north and friends to my south."

Giulio laughed under his breath and looked over at me, Ilaria, and Tiliani, knowing we had all simultaneously stiffened at the slight. "Clearly you are a brave man, daring to poke them so."

Aurelio gave us an impish grin. "Please, please. I jest. I know that the She-Wolves shall come to my aid if I am in need. We are fast friends now, are we not?"

I forced a smile. Had that been mostly intended for me, given that I had spurned him?

Giulio and Ilaria wheeled their horses around, leading Aurelio and Valentino, with Luciana and me behind them. The two other Paratore knights folded in between us and the Forellis.

"I would not mind if a She-Wolf came to *my* aid," muttered the knight behind me suggestively, and his companion laughed.

I turned in my saddle to glare at them and they immediately quieted. Luciana swallowed a smile but remained facing forward. I itched then, for battle, as the knights often griped through long periods of peace. Battle was an outlet for all the frustration and angst I felt, being so close to something—someone—I wanted, and yet still so far. Even having the excuse to take down the Fiorentini knight behind me would serve as an outlet.

I took a long, slow breath, held it, then released it. I was not like a common mercenary or knight among the barracks. I had been raised for more. Bred to be both a lady and a warrior. And it would take more—much more—to break me.

29

I loved watching Giulio in action over the next hours. With all the people. His kindnesses. Attention to detail. With every stop, I thought I might be falling a little more in love with him. It was a beautiful morning until we got to Signore Colombo's vineyard, and pulled up outside his small, cozy home.

One of Aurelio's knights, Edoardo, and I exchanged idle chatter about his home, Pienza. It was one of my favorite hilltop towns in Tuscany, but given that this was pre-Renaissance, I was curious about what was there now. Eventually, I knew that much of the center part of the town would be razed in order to construct a quintessential Renaissance square, palazzo, church, and more. But who would be burned by that? Gain from it? I was curious.

As Giulio and Aurelio entered the vineyard with Signore Colombo, Edoardo cracked a joke. I laughed. Then he reached up to help me dismount. I thought little of it until Giulio looked over his shoulder. He was in action before I could blink, striding toward us.

Yes, Edoardo held on to my waist a little too long, and was grinning at me—but we had just shared a laugh. Before he knew what was coming, Giulio clamped a gloved hand on his shoulder and spun him aside. His action made *me* stagger back a couple of steps. I gaped at Giulio, but his entire focus was on Edoardo. He stabbed his chest with a finger. "I shall thank you for keeping your hands off my intended."

"Giulio," I tried.

Edoardo grimaced. "Your intended? Forgive me, m'lord, but I did not know. I meant no offense." He lifted his hands in surrender.

Giulio seemed to be growing angrier. "Even if she was not my intended, you kept hold of her overly long. Is this the way of Fiorentini knights?"

"Is it not the way of all knights?" joked Aurelio, stepping in to defuse the situation. "Come, my friend. Come." He guided Giulio back toward Signore Colombo. "Let us finish this business and then break bread together. Pour a bit of wine."

Was that it? Giulio was *hangry*? I crossed my arms. Weren't we all a bit hungry by now?

Giulio glared at Edoardo one more time, then looked to me—as if I were partially to blame—then back at the knight. Ilaria stepped forward and whispered something to him. Giulio took a breath, then a deeper one, then glared at Edoardo. "See that you keep your distance from her, even when my back is turned."

"I shall do as you have asked, m'lord," gritted out the knight, clearly trying to keep hold of his temper, given his employer was present.

But now I was irritated too. What was this? Surely he remembered I could easily defend myself if any knight made a move on me, injured or not. The whole encounter left me feeling like a piece of raw steak between two hungry lions. Like the knight, the only reason I kept my mouth shut was because of the company we kept.

Giulio began to follow Aurelio when he caught my furious expression. He did a slight double take and then turned away, walking stiffly after the others.

Ilaria caught one of my elbows and Tiliani the other. "Come, let us move to the shade." She gestured to a group of three trees on a small hill about fifty paces away.

When we could not be overheard, I growled, "What was that? Why did he react that way?"

Reaching the shade, Ilaria turned, arms folded, but a grin on her face. "That was my brother getting jealous. I suppose you can add that to your list of things that make him less than perfect. I simply have not had the pleasure of seeing it arise in him before."

"Jealous? Of me laughing with another man?"

"And that man with his hands on you."

"Hands on me," I repeated, throwing up my own. "What was I supposed to do? I have only one good arm yet for dismounting, and he'd plainly forgotten I needed help."

"Not that he could have reached you in time," Tiliani said, glancing back at the knights hanging out with the horses. "That one was eagerly available."

I tucked my chin in surprise. "He was simply being friendly."

"Nay," Tiliani said, a small smile on her full lips. "There was more. Giulio spotted it. And did not like it."

I rolled my eyes. "He knows I can look after myself." I lowered my voice. "Had the man not dropped his hands, I could have forced him to do so with one move. With but one good hand."

"Mayhap my brother feels more defensive of you because you are not yet quite healed?" Ilaria said.

"Mayhap. But that was . . . humiliating," I said. "I am not some scrap for two jays to battle over."

"Nay. You are not some scrap," Ilaria said. "You are my brother's *intended*," she added with a smile. "And he will ensure that you are treated with all the honor that affords."

I mean, I appreciated that she seemed happy that Giulio and I were a thing and all, but . . . "Why does being his intended bring me honor?" I groused. "Should I not have honor alone?"

"Indeed," Tiliani said. "But now any affront you face is also Giulio's."

I sighed heavily and put a hand to my head, trying to think it through. I'd grown up with Italians. They were notoriously uppity and ready to tangle, but this was a whole new level. "So this will be the way for the rest of my life? Or will Giulio realize, in time, that I can defend myself?"

Tiliani and Ilaria shared a long look. "Giulio has waited a long time for love," Ilaria said, taking my hand. "He has waited a long time for *you*. And he is passionate and strong-willed."

"And knowing him as we do," Tiliani said, "yes. This will likely be the rest of your life. When a woman gives her heart to a man, she is expected to not look at another."

"Look? Or flirt?" I gestured around. "Gaze about. We three wish to serve with men, out on patrol, in battle if necessary. God gifted us each to be strong enough to do so. How am I to do that without looking? Talking?"

"You will be able to," Ilaria said. "Once you wed, he will settle. I am confident he shall." She looked down the hill at him, bending to take hold of some grapes and say something to Aurelio. "Mayhap you should agree to wedding him sooner rather than later if it bothers you so." She cast me a quirk of a smile, but I did not respond in kind.

Because I was thinking it through. Mama always said to watch out for bad behavior in a man while dating, because it would only get worse in marriage. The question was, was this bad behavior? Or simply medieval behavior?

I shook my head. "You cannot tell me that either of you would be okay with this, if you were in my shoes."

"Okay?" Tiliani repeated, puzzling over the word.

"Settled. At peace with it."

She considered it. "Some of it is a compliment, yes?"

I gave her that. "Yes. But I do not want a lifetime with a partner who thinks of me as territory to be defended."

She bit her lip. "You do not want him to defend you?"

"Well, yes. And no!"

Tiliani took a deep breath. "Think of my father, with my mother. Or Marcello, with Zia Gabi. They are attentive husbands.

Ready to defend their wives. As your father surely defended your mother."

Ilaria nodded at her words.

"My father did not defend my mother," I said, thunder-struck. "At all."

Both women frowned at me. "And that was well with her?" Tiliani asked.

"Nay," I said, blinking slowly, thinking it through. In fact, my father had attacked my mother—mentally, emotionally, verbally. As I had never seen Marcello or Luca do.

"And yet they give them free rein," Tiliani continued. She glanced back to Giulio, who had turned back with the other men. "I believe Giulio shall model himself after them." She put a hand on my arm. "Do not give sway to fear. He knows you are a strong woman. Independent. It was part of what drew him to you. And yet think about what drew you to him too. If you were back in your own time, would you be considering marriage?"

I shook my head. Back in my own time, I'd be focusing on finishing my degree and then applying to graduate schools. Perusing the dating apps, yes, but not thinking *marriage*.

"And yet Giulio is making you consider it now, yes?" She paused. "Why?"

I looked down the hill toward him, smiling now at Signore Colombo's wife, ducking his head in gratitude as she gave him a loaf of bread from her basket and a cask of wine. He was gracious. A leader. Caring. Attentive.

Just sometimes maybe a little *too* attentive.

The other women slipped away as Giulio handed the bread and wine to Benedetto and traipsed up the hill to meet me.

I was silent as his dark-blue eyes looked back and forth over mine. He took my hand. "M'lady. Are you displeased with me?"

"Yes," I said softly. "And no. I am . . . discomfited."

"Because I came to your defense?"

"Nay. Because you did not trust me to defend myself."

He pulled back his head a bit. "You are not yet hale."

"I was hale enough to put you on your back yesterday. Did you think I could not do the same with Edoardo if I felt the need?" I waited for a moment. "I think what discomfits me is that you *knew* I could defend myself. But you felt the need to mark your territory. And Giulio . . ." I paused until his eyes met mine again. "I am not land to be parceled out. Something to be owned. I am a companion. A person."

I reached up to touch his cheek. "You are rapidly claiming my heart, and of *that* you may be protective. But I need you to trust me. To take me at my word when I say there is no room in my heart for any other man but you. Because if you do, there will be no cause for jealousy *disguised* as protection."

He pulled back further, as if I had struck him. Then he took my hand in his, kissed my palm, and then cradled it to his chest. "I shall endeavor to do as you say," he whispered, placing his head against mine. "But you must give me some time to develop that particular strength. Because, m'lady, I have never, ever felt such things as I do for you. And such things tend to take me to the brink of madness."

I laughed under my breath. "I believe they call that falling in love."

"Indeed, they do." Then, as if no one else could see us, he grabbed my waist, pulled me against him, and kissed me for all I was worth.

And as we rode toward home, I realized in doing so, he had both more fully captured my heart *and* staked his territory for every man present. *Well played, mister,* I thought with a mirthless laugh. *Well played, indeed.*

Falling in love with a medieval man was proving complicated. And as we moved on into courtship and day-to-day living, figuring out our life together, I knew there'd have to be some serious negotiations and conversations ahead. As well as a few more kisses . . .

After all, wasn't that what courtship was all about?

TILIANI

Whereas Giulio acted the part of the jealous fool when a man paid attention to Luciana, Valentino again acted as if I was the furthest thing from his mind. Two days later, after two restless nights of sleep, I resolved to go foraging in those eastern woods, as Lord Paratore had given me permission to do. While he had asked me to invite Captain Valeri along, I refused to make it so simple for the man. Nay, if he wanted to see me, he could. I would not throw myself in front of him again, I thought angrily. I would merely make it clear that I was *available* to be seen, should he wish it. And if he did not show his face, mayhap that was my answer, regardless of what I thought had transpired in the stables.

I pulled on the bodice to my split-skirt gown and reached to tighten the laces myself. I wanted a man who was brave, as well as loyal. I wanted a man who followed his own dreams, even if it differed from his lord's. I wanted a man who would choose me, regardless of what it cost.

That thought sent me to my knees at the edge of my bed. I rubbed my face, my temples, trying to ease the tension there. Was I being selfish? Trying to force a path that we might take together rather than waiting on the Lord?

I glanced to the small crucifix by my door. "Do I wait, Lord?"

I listened a moment, but heard nothing but two maids outside, chatting as they moved down the hall.

"Or is this of you? This opening, this invitation to wander the wood where I might see the man who has stolen my heart?"

Again, no answer. Only the sound of what might have been a mouse, skittering and scratching across the floor beneath my wardrobe. Mayhap that was my answer. A mouse moving. Maids moving. Mayhap God was telling *me* to get moving. I rose.

Or was that simply what I wanted to hear?

Grace, Lord. Mercy. Direction, I prayed.

I stepped toward the door and added in a whisper, "If this is not the direction I should take, stop me. Stop Valentino. Keep us from each other this day. Show us, Father."

Out in the courtyard, I paused to speak to Iacapo, a knight who oft rode on my own morning patrol. Given that we had been enjoying the respite Aurelio had promised, we'd taken to giving each patrol two days' rest. This was one of ours.

"Might you do me a favor?" I asked, looking up at the tall, lanky man.

"Of course, m'lady."

"I intend to ride to the woods east of Castello Paratore." I raised a calming hand as he lifted a brow. "'Twas a venture blessed by Lord Paratore himself, as long as we sent word we were coming. My grandmother is in need of some herbs and mushrooms found in a glade there."

"I see."

"Would you please summon a companion and ride to Castello Paratore to inform them? Then meet me on the eastern road by the ruins of that old house to serve as part of my guard?"

"Of course," he said. "Straight away?"

"Straight away. I shall follow in but a few minutes' time."

I turned to go to the armory to pick up my bow and quiver of arrows, as well as a short sword, pleased that neither of my cousins nor any of the Grecos were yet in sight. Might I slip from the castle without any of them knowing? Should Valentino decide to join me in the glade, I preferred to have Iacapo and his companion—whom I could easily persuade to remain just out of sight—rather than my more intrusive friends or kin.

I found Domenico in the armory, trying a broadsword with a sweeping arc. He narrowly missed me as I leaped back.

"Oh! Tiliani!" he gasped. "Forgive me! I thought I was the only one in here."

I laughed under my breath. "As did I." I moved past him to take hold of my weapons, pulling on a shoulder sheath so I could wear the sword at my back, then tucking it inside. I considered Domenico as I lifted my bow from its hook. "Care to ride with me this morning, Domenico?"

"Ride? Yes," he said eagerly, as if weary of idleness. "Where are we going?"

I smiled. "To the woods east of Castello Paratore to forage. I am in need of another guard. If I leave the castello alone, I shall never hear the end of it. But with you . . ."

"But with me," he said, "is that enough? Do they not want you to ride with a full patrol at all times?"

I made a dismissive sound and reached for a quiver of arrows, then turned to walk out. "I ride most every morning alone," I said over my shoulder.

He followed behind, running to catch up. Iacapo and Falito were leaving the gates now, I saw with pleasure. "But is that not at dawn? When none but the chickens are awake?" he asked me quietly.

"Usually, yes." I refused to answer him more fully.

"Should we see if Ilaria wants to join us?" he asked hopefully.

I grinned. "Nay. This day, you simply serve as my guard. You shall have to seek another time for a romantic interlude."

He pretended to be shocked at my words, but then smiled and shrugged. "You cannot fault a man for trying."

Nay, I thought. *I only wish Valentino would try so hard.*

My gelding, Cardo, was already saddled—Iacapo apparently having directed the stableboys. "Signore Betarrini has need of a mount too." I looked over the horses that appeared to be fed and watered already. "Fetch the sorrel for him."

"Yes, m'lady," bobbed the boy, running to do as I bid. A groomsman bowed his head and turned to assist him.

I spotted Giulio and Ilaria leaving the Great Hall and hurriedly pulled Domenico into the shadows. "What is this, m'lady?" he whispered, glancing over at them. "A bit of delicious intrigue?" He rubbed his hands together in delight.

I gave him a wry look. "'Tis a bit of intrigue, solely because I wish to have guardians, not *nursemaids*, this day."

He frowned and fondled the hilt of his sword. "I confess I do not know if I could truly call myself a guardian yet, m'lady. I still have a great deal to learn."

"Learning in the field is the best education for knights," I said lightly. "And I have seen what you can do when the fighting comes to you. You are the perfect guardian for me this day. Besides, the woods are quiet. We shall likely encounter nothing more nefarious than wood sprites."

"Wood sprites, eh? Sounds dangerous. Are those like big mosquitoes?"

"Somewhat," I said with a smile.

The groomsman led Domenico's horse to the stable entrance. When the Grecos disappeared through the turret door—probably seeking me—I shoved away a pang of guilt and mounted my horse. We rode out, and I waved up at Frederico. The gates opened so slowly I bit back a cry of complaint, thinking that at any moment Giulio or Ilaria or my cousins would be shouting my name. But miraculously, no summons arose.

I urged Cardo forward with a click of my tongue and a press of my heels to his sides. Domenico followed right behind me, and I fought the urge to gallop. A trot was more respectable and would draw less attention. And if I went any faster, I might arrive on the eastern road rendezvous point sooner than I intended. I eased up and allowed Domenico to ride side by side with me.

"How is it with you, Nico? Are you settling well, among us?"

"I am," he said, with a nod. "I made my first loan agreement yesterday."

I gave him a look of admiration. "You did? I knew you were

speaking with my uncle and father of this endeavor but was not aware you were prepared to begin. With whom? For what?"

"A woman in the village. She wishes to purchase a second, larger spinning wheel from Siena. She already produces as much wool as she can on the small one her father built. With this new larger one built in Denmark, she shall be able to give her daughter the old one and use the new one to triple their output. She gains, and so shall we."

"Wonderful!" It warmed my heart, that his first loan was to a woman. And I knew of whom he spoke. She was a widow, having lost her husband to plague almost twenty years ago. Their home was in severe disrepair. If this allowed them to take better care of themselves, what a boon it would be! "Who shall be next?"

"We are meeting with a vintner on the morrow," he said. "He sent word of needing new casks in order to make full use of this year's crop."

"Excellent." I looked at him with new appreciation. "You and your sister might not only make us more strategic fighters, but wealthier as well."

"In time," he allowed. "Both wealth and skills take years to develop, yes?"

"Yes. May we have all the years we need."

"May it be so," he agreed.

But as we approached the ruins of the old house and I looked to the Paratore flags fluttering in the morning breeze on the castle parapets, my heart skipped a beat.

Was I about to do something that might rob us of those years? Or make the most of every year I had?

30

TILIANI

When Iacapo and Falito met us at a gallop, I held my breath a moment, hoping Valentino would follow around the bend. But after a few more moments passed, I knew they were alone.

"We were granted permission, m'lady," Iacapo said cheerfully. "Lord Paratore asked only that we grant a portion of what we gather as a gift as we depart." His face fell as he sensed my disappointment, and he looked over his shoulder to the empty road, following my gaze.

"Lord Paratore—he did not wish to send any of his own men to accompany us?"

Iacapo frowned. "Nay. Did you expect him to do so? I believe he trusts us. Is that not a good sign from a Fiorentini?"

"A very good sign," I mumbled. "He only mentioned sending others, as guards against brigands. Ah well. Let us get on with it." I wheeled Cardo around and urged him into a gallop, unable to maintain any semblance of gentility. Had Valentino snubbed me? Or had Aurelio kept him from coming?

My knights quickly caught up, but as I glanced under my arm, I saw Domenico falling behind. I brought Cardo back to a canter, then a trot, waiting on him.

Reaching us, he said, "Are we racing, m'lady? Is there some urgency in this herb-seeking mission?"

"Nay," I said lightly, easing Cardo to a walk. The others did too. "But it is good for our mounts to remember how it feels to gallop, at least once a day. Gets the blood circulating."

"For them and us," he said, brows lifted. He clearly was not yet accustomed to riding, and certainly not at a gallop.

"Forgive me, cousin," I said. "I forget that you are not yet friends with the saddle."

"How is it that you are not?" asked Iacapo, a tad scornfully. "A man of twenty and . . ."

"Two. Twenty-and-two," Domenico supplied. "I was a man of the city. Born and raised walking wherever I needed to go."

"Do you intend to return to the city?" Falito asked boldly.

I regretted bringing up the matter, making Domenico—and mayhap his sister—the center of further speculation.

"I think not. My sister and I rather enjoy abiding here, with the Forellis and Grecos. If they shall have us, my understanding is that we shall remain."

"I doubt Captain Greco would let Lady Betarrini out of his sight at this point," I said with a laugh. "Like it or not, I believe you shall have to remain."

Domenico took a deep breath and gazed with appreciation about the woods. "If I had to remain somewhere for the foreseeable future, this is a fine place to be."

"Indeed." I pulled up before the glade that opened before us. "Now let us see if we can make you as competent a forager as we have a horseman."

He lifted a brow and cast me a quirk of a smile. "So you have high expectations then."

I laughed. "I do. 'Tis all a learning process, Domenico. And I am a patient teacher." It would be good to focus on teaching him this day. A distraction from my disappointment. I turned to the knights. "One of you remain here at the entry point as guard, the other go ahead of us, climbing this small vale."

I reached for my gathering basket and then tossed Domenico a bag. We set out together, passing through the trees and over the rocks that surrounded the bright, bubbling stream. Falito moved ahead of us by twenty paces, then thirty, always keeping us in sight.

"What exactly are we seeking?" Domenico asked.

"Oyster mushrooms. They're white or light brown, about this big," I said, making an oval with my thumbs and index fingers. "It favors the shadows of this glade, as well as the moisture from this brook. In addition, we should come across some lungwort, a moss that grows on the rocks. 'Tis golden in color. Do not pick anything without asking me about it first. We do not wish to disturb foliage that is not yet mature, nor that we cannot use. Mushrooms, in particular, can be deceiving. The oyster grows in tiers."

"How is it used?"

"Nona uses them in poultices and for sore throats. She boils them with white lily roots and linseed, to treat abscesses."

"And what would the wrong mushroom do?"

"Hallucinations. Severe stomach cramps, internal bleeding, sometimes death."

"Well, that sounds unpleasant."

I grinned and began my hunt in earnest. I spied some mullein and harvested some, but wanted to leave enough room in my basket for our targeted medicinals. Nona was counting on me. And Papa had blessed this excursion because he knew what I sought.

"What is that for?"

"Internally, for coughs. Externally, for burns or ulcers."

He nodded and rounded a tree, then another. He crossed the brook, bending to check under the crevices of boulders and rocks on the far side as we made our way up the stream. "So, why did you *really* ask me to come along this day? Instead of one of your closest?"

I met his gaze and saw that he suspected the truth. "Because those closest to me are at times rather meddlesome."

He pushed a low branch out of the way. "You hoped that someone from Castello Paratore would join us too?" he asked quietly.

"I did." Falito was now fifty paces ahead of us, out of earshot.

"I am sorry he did not seize the opportunity. Mayhap he shall later."

"Mayhap." I searched the rocks, the crevices of exposed tree roots, but I had not yet found any wild onion. The brown tree roots only reminded me of Valentino's wavy hair, the moss on the rocks, his hazel, soulful eyes. I remembered the heat of his palm on my face, the intensity of his—

"*Tiliani!*" Domenico cried.

I stopped and looked at him.

He gestured before me. "Are *those* what you seek?"

I glanced down and saw that I was about to step into a dozen oyster mushrooms and laughed, feeling the heat of a blush at my cheeks. "Indeed."

He leaped over the brook and crouched down beside me. "Mayhap I shall prove to be a better forager than a horseman. Any trick to picking them?"

"Cut them about an inch above the ground. They often regrow in the same season."

"Understood."

I busied myself with harvesting them, even though I could feel Domenico's curious gaze repeatedly brush past me. To his credit, he said nothing.

We moved on and, in a few minutes, found another good clump of oysters, then our first patch of wild onion.

"Lady Tiliani!" called Iacapo behind us.

We pulled up and looked down the steep little glade. Two men climbed upward.

I inhaled sharply.

"Captain Valeri has come to see if he might provide aid!" Iacapo called.

"Very good," I managed. "Please resume your position at the bottom as guard."

The knight obediently turned. Valentino stopped and stared at me. "I thought I might come and claim our castello's portion of the bounty."

"You did not trust me to deliver it?" I managed to say, arcing one brow, hand on my hip.

"Nay," he said, continuing his climb. "I know how greedy you Sienese are."

My smiled widened. I glanced at Domenico.

He gave me a wink. "I think I shall move further up the stream. You know, scout out more mushrooms. You should stay here and get the rest of these onions. I'll tell Falito we have company and not to be concerned."

I gave him a look that I hoped conveyed my gratitude and waited on Valentino. He looked marvelous and strong, as utterly at ease and at peace in the woods as I remembered him. Here is where he belonged. Foraging, yes. But moreover, with me. It all felt so right.

But when he reached me, he did not pull me to him for a kiss like I had dreamed. I refused the urge to go to him. "Why did you not come when my men came to the castle?" I asked softly.

"I did not wish to seem too eager. I had to wait for the right moment with Aurelio." He brushed a wave of hair from his forehead. "Please. May we walk?"

We began climbing again together. Domenico stayed an equal distance ahead of us, maintaining our privacy and yet near enough to come to my aid, should I call. Seeing an overhang of granite on the far side, Valentino offered his hand to help me across the stream. Though I did not need the assistance, I gladly took it and then smiled when he did not release it. Hope bloomed in my heart.

We paused beneath the cliff face, about twenty feet high. Tiny rivulets of water washed down the face of it, feeding moss and flowering thyme. When he said nothing, I nervously turned to it, harvesting some of the herb for Cook. He quietly did the same, I thought, but when I glanced at him, he had not the leaves, but tiny lavender flowers in his hand.

I turned, a hundred questions in my eyes. His eyes held only sorrow.

He silently traced my face with the tips of his fingers, then plucked a tiny flower from his left palm. "Cook—my Cook, the one who raised me in Firenze—used to say that the fae left these among the thyme as a blessing." He tucked the tiny flower in my hair at my right temple, sending a jolt through me with his gentle touch. He reached for another and settled it between the strands at my left. "She said they would provide protection."

One after another, he put a dozen of the tiny flowers across my crown, and each time he touched my hair, I fought the urge to fling myself into his arms. But there was a distance between us, something hovering in the air that I was afraid he would explain. When he ran out of flowers, he fingered a strand of my hair that had come loose from the braid, and I remembered how he had said it reminded him of his mother's. It was one of the few memories he had left of her, having lost her as a small child.

"Valentino," I whispered. "Why are you not kissing me?" The tiny rivulet beside me sent a drop of water to my face, but I ignored it, apprehension growing within me.

He brushed the droplet from my cheek and then put it to his lips, rubbing it across them as if he *was* kissing me. "I cannot, Tiliani. We cannot." He swallowed hard. "Leaving Aurelio now . . ." He shook his head and turned half away from me, gazing down the vale. "He is weak, his position tenuous with our republic. Mayhap in time . . ."

I looped my arm through the crook of his then and leaned my head against his shoulder. "Does he . . . does he still have hope in courting me?"

He laughed, but it held no mirth. "Nay. I believe you made your decision clear that first night." He paused. "That is but a part of this tangle. He shall need time to lick his wounds. 'Twas both a personal rejection and the death of that resurrected dream he shared with your father."

"I still believe *our* union might accomplish the same," I said wistfully.

He made a dismissive sound and turned toward me.

"I know," I said. Nobles on either side would see it as an affair of the heart rather than a strategic alliance. They would see it as a slight to Paratore pride. A snubbing. Worse, a Sienese victory. And Valentino could not bear to do that to his friend, his lord, the man who was like a brother to him.

He raised his hands, and I put mine against them, staring up into his sorrowful eyes. My long fingers nearly reached the length of his, but his had more breadth. We stared at each other, neither of us knowing what to do.

Then he said, "Come," and wrapped me in his arms, holding me close, my head tucked in the crevice between his ear and chin. He was warm and smelled of sandalwood and beeswax. I could feel his pulse at my cheek. He stroked my back and sighed heavily, but he did not let go.

"So we are to go on like this?" I asked miserably. "Our hearts one, but our lives divided?"

"For a time." He rubbed my back again and kissed my temple. "For a time," he repeated. "Let us see what comes as the seasons change. Mayhap another woman shall catch his eye come spring. Now that he has the castello, I believe he senses the urgency of finding a wife and producing an heir."

I wet my lips and lifted my head to better see him. "But what if this tentative peace comes to an end before spring?" I drew further back, holding his hands. "What if we come face-to-face on a battlefield? What if your men are killing mine, and mine yours?"

"We must pray against that," he said urgently. "Work against it. Support Aurelio and your father and uncle in continuing to seek peace over war."

His hope moved me. I wanted to agree with him, give in to the dream. But looking into his eyes, I knew neither of us believed it could last for long.

LUCIANA

As August melted into September, we all seemed to melt with it. It had been a sweltering summer in Tuscany, and while the stones of the castle kept it relatively cool indoors, none of us wanted to be inside for long. Castles were fortresses, I'd come to find, not cozy homes. And medieval people had a long way to go in figuring out comfy furniture. The horsehair-hide chairs were not all bad, but I ached to sink into a good, ol' Lazy Boy recliner. Or a bed with a comfort-foam topper. *Definitely a con on the Medieval Life List.*

I paused outside the Great Hall, the morning sun already heating the courtyard like a vast cauldron on low boil. I looked about as servants moved more slowly between the well and the kitchen or about the stables. Even Father Giovanni seemed to be taking his customary morning walk about the circumference of the courtyard—what he called his "prayer walk," blessing each wing, each room, and each occupant—at a much slower pace.

I leaned an arm against the stone wall and stretched, trying to relieve the tension from my back and hips. "Need a good massage?" Nico asked in English.

"Yes," I said with a laugh. "As well as a facial." I fell into step with him as he entered the Great Hall. Breakfast was a casual affair—literally "breaking the night's fast"—with little but a thick porridge and some fruit. Some mornings it was only some bread, a bit of cheese, and water. Today was one of those days, the cooks probably wanting to avoid the fire required to boil the oatmeal.

Nico and I sat down at a long table a few feet from a group of knights, all of whom lifted their chins in casual greeting. It made me feel like we were a part of them now, accepted. And after a month of living among them, it made sense. People seemed to understand we were different, but they mostly chalked it up to our roots in *Britannia.*

"You know what would make a real financial killing?" I muttered.

He raised a brow and tore a hunk of bread from one of many baskets that dotted the centers of the tables. "Inventing the Internet?"

I smiled and cut a piece of pecorino from a wedge, then passed it to him. "That wouldn't be a bad idea. As long as you invented computers and wiring and, you know, *electricity* first."

"No problem," he shrugged. "I'll get right on that. But what were you thinking?"

"Coffee," I whispered, getting a little shiver at the thought of a nice cappuccino with a spoonful of sugar. "Sadly, it does not arrive for another two or three hundred years in Europe."

"So introducing it now would really change history," he said.

I nodded. "But think about it, Nico. An iced mocha Frappuccino. Doesn't that sound good?"

"Anything iced sounds good," he said, "especially in this heat."

"True." I tapped my fingers on the table. "So we can't introduce coffee this early. That'd change trade routes and things. But what if we sail north this winter and bring home a hold full of ice? Bury it in the cellars, like the pioneers did. People might buy that!"

He huffed a laugh and leaned back, chewing. "Are you proposing a business arrangement, sister? Are you seeking a microloan from She-Wolf Enterprises?"

I smiled. "That'd probably take a regular loan. Is that what you are calling your bank?"

"Nah. Marcello insists we not name it at all. These loans are written only as a contract between the people and the Forelli family. He wants to keep it under the radar for as long as possible. Once Siena gets wind of it, apparently, we'll have to jump through a whole lot more hoops."

"So how do you get a piece of that action?"

"I get a percentage of every payment made."

"How much?" I pressed.

"Five percent." He popped another bite of bread in his mouth.

"And have you made much yet?"

He shrugged. "I will, in time. We have more than twenty loans established, with ten more meetings in the coming week out near the country villa."

I sighed dreamily. "I hear the villa is much cooler."

"Let's hope so."

The entire household was moving for a couple of weeks to the

Forellis' country manor, about five miles distant, situated higher in the hills. By all reports, it enjoyed a good, steady breeze by day and much cooler temperatures at night. There was even a small swimming hole along the river. Adri and Chiara had gone on about the neighboring woods and the foraging they could do for herbs and other things. Tiliani, clearly anxious to be away from here—and those inside Castello Paratore's gates—had been all for it.

We would leave behind twenty-four men to guard the castle in shifts of twelve. After a week, those twenty-four would switch out with those coming with us, so all would be given a respite. The knights next to us grumbled about being on "first watch." Apparently they had drawn the short straws.

"Speaking of which," Nico said, rising. "We'd better get packed up. We're due to leave within the hour."

"I'm all packed," I said, lifting my hands. "It doesn't take long to tuck everything you own in a chest." That was another pro for the Medieval Life List. Simplicity.

We walked out of the Great Hall together. "Life is a lot easier here," Nico said.

"And oddly more complicated in some ways," I said.

"How so?"

I looked over to the front gates as Giulio, Ilaria, Benedetto, Fortino, and Tiliani rode through, returning from morning patrol.

"Ahhh." Nico smirked. "Relationships are always complicated. Regardless of the era."

I nodded. "It's both totally simple and oddly complex with him."

"How is it complex?" He leaned against the wall outside the door, kicking a boot up behind him.

I glanced from Giulio, who had caught my eye and smiled, back to Nico. "He likes me because I'm different. But the reason I'm different is because I'm from a different time. And coming from that time makes me wonder if we can really jive long-term. I mean, right now, because he's so different from other men I've known—and I'm so different from women he's known—we're taking *notice*. But what happens if that noticing becomes irritation after a few years?"

Nico moved his mouth left and right, as if swishing. "It worked for Gabi and Lia, right? Maybe you should talk to them."

"Maybe."

"Is there something more that makes you hesitate?" He frowned and folded his arms. "Is there something I need to talk over with him? You know, as the *man* in charge of you? The one who *permitted* your courtship?"

I resisted the urge to drop him. "There. That. Even that is just . . . weird."

He scoffed. "But has it really been an issue, Luci? Not once since I 'gave permission,'" he said in finger quotes, "have I had to intervene or have a discussion or whatever. Seems to me there is a bit more formality to dating here. And as long as you're not set up as pawns between cities or households—love is pretty much in your hands."

"Yeah . . ." I said. "There's just something niggling at me. It can't be this easy, right? Falling in love, yeah, obviously. Anyone can do that. But what about *staying* in love? How do we establish a relationship that can go the distance, when we never saw it modeled between our parents?"

"I think you're letting the heat get to you." He pushed off the wall and wiped his forehead of sweat. Then he moved toward his room to pack, walking backward. "Talk to Gabi and Lia while we're at the villa. They'll have the answers you're after."

"I hope so," I whispered, as Giulio handed his reins to a stableboy and turned my way.

He didn't slow his stride or pause when he reached me. He simply took my hand, pulled me around the wall to the cool shadows, out of sight, cupped my cheek, and gave me a kiss. He tasted of sun and sweat and saddle, and I loved it all.

"Good morning, love," he whispered, stepping back to admire me from head to toe. Boldly. "I have missed you since we parted last night."

In the moment, here with him, I could not grasp even the tail end of whatever was niggling at me. I smiled and grabbed the lapel of his soft, white shirt and pulled him closer. "I missed you too," I said, so close that the movement of my words brushed his lips. But then I released him and walked away, twirling and laughing as he looked up to the skies, as if I'd left him in agony. He was kind, making me think I had that kind of power over him.

But then, maybe I did.

TILIANI

We reached the country manor that afternoon. In all my years, we had done nothing but come for but a few days, my parents having disturbing memories of this place. They refused to discuss it. Repairs had been seen to, restoration complete. The fifteen-foot protection walls had been reinforced. It was certainly no castle, but it was outfitted to not make an attack easy. Not that it had to be. We were halfway between Castello Forelli and Castello Romano, the one owned by Lord Romano, one of the Nine. The manor's fields and vineyards and orchards stopped at a road that marked the division between his lands and our own.

As we toured the inviting, comfortable manor, with wide, open windows welcoming delicious breezes, I wondered for the tenth time why we did not spend months here during the summer, especially in the midst of peace between Perugia and Firenze, as we had enjoyed for most of my growing years. My eyes settled on the Betarrini twins as they gazed at the frescoes that lined parts of rooms, and how they asked Mama and Zia Gabi questions without pause. *They will be able to get the story out of them,* I thought. *Mayhap this very night.*

By sunset, I had convinced them. One or the other would broach the subject as starlight replaced summer's long twilight and we circled around the planned fire. By then, we would all be full from supper and relaxed, glad to be done with our ride and settled in our new abode. It felt so good to be out of the stifling castello, out here in the country. We settled around the big bonfire on blankets strewn across crushed hay at the edge of the field. The newly cut hay smelled sweet, fresh, much like everything else here. In a neighboring field, fat heads of golden grain were ready to be harvested, and I could almost smell the bread they would create in time.

Papa leaned back on one arm, my mother beside him, looking utterly at peace. Zio Marcello brought Zia Gabi's hand to his lips for a kiss, staring all the while at the fire. I caught Luciana's eye and widened my own, silently signaling that now might be a good time.

She bit her lip and glanced at them. "This is so lovely," she said. "Thank you for bringing us here."

"'Tis lovely indeed," Gabi sighed, lifting her chin to watch sparks from the fire rise in the twisting heat, up and up until they disappeared into the dark.

"I am surprised you do not spend a portion of every summer here." Luciana poked a stick into the coals, acting utterly guileless— as if I had not put her up to it. I had counted on her own healthy sense of curiosity to fuel her mission. Mama looked my way, but I pretended not to notice, changing my position on the blanket so my knees were before me, my arms around them.

"Yes, well, matters at the castello are rather demanding," Gabi said.

"Too demanding for a little summer vacation?" Nico asked in English, spreading his arms wide. "If all of this was mine, I couldn't keep myself from it."

Gabi stared at him, then over her shoulder at the villa, then back to all of us. "I fear that as lovely as it is, this place holds some bad memories for us," she returned in Italian.

"Oh?" Luciana asked innocently. "What happened?"

Gabi sighed and glanced at her sister. Lia shrugged, giving her assent.

"Not long after we arrived in Toscana," she said, lifting her chin and looking to the sky, "we were exposed to the plague. A forerunner of the Black Plague to come, terribly similar, but not as contagious.

We knew we could not return to the castello, so Marcello, Luca, Lia, and I came here with the knights with us, so that we could quarantine until we knew who had it and who did not."

She glanced at Luca.

"Luckily for us all, it was I who came down with it," he said proudly, with his customary humor. "And given my superior health, I was able to beat it."

Marcello laughed under his breath. "After I carried you for miles and nursed you back to health like a mother with a baby."

"Yes, well, and that," he said, waving his cousin away as if his efforts were but a trifle.

"We feared we had lost him," Mama said, picking up the tale, glancing tenderly at him, then back to the fire. "We lost others. And that was before we were surrounded, under attack."

"The Fiorentini attacked you here? While you were sick?" I asked.

Mama nodded. "We only narrowly escaped."

"How?" Nico asked, looking into the darkness.

Mama smiled. "There was a tunnel. A secret passageway that led to a cavern where those in the manor could fetch water. We left through it. But then, once outside . . ." She again gazed at Papa, her smile faltering.

"We split up," Marcello said. "We figured we would draw less attention with the fields and forests crawling with Fiorentini. Luca and I pretended to be Fiorentini for a time, settling into one of their camps as this man with 'superior health' moved in and out of consciousness, riddled with fever."

"And it did not take long for Rodolfo Greco to be on our trail," Gabi said. "Lia and I were on the run for days."

"We thought we might never see them again." Marcello squeezed my aunt's hand. He shook his head as if still punishing himself. "We should never have separated."

"You had your hands full with Luca," Zia Gabi said. "You would not have been able to protect us too."

"Oh, of course. Blame it all on the man trying to cheat death," Luca said.

We all smiled.

"It unfolded as it should have," Gabi said, staring again at the fire and the sparks rising from it. "Had it not . . . had we not run across Paratore . . . had not Rodolfo intervened . . ." She shook her head as if to shake the memories away. "Mayhap we would not all be here today. With this new generation of Betarrinis." She smiled at the twins.

We all sat back, considering her words. Life was so complex. One decision affected a hundred others in succession. And each of those, a hundred more. Take, for example, Valentino's choice to not seek me out. I had seen him but three times in the weeks since we had met up in the glade, and each time there had not been an opportunity to speak in private. What if we never met again, alone? What if he married another? What impact would that choice have on me and others about us?

"One thing is for certain," Nico said, pulling me back to the present. "You must show us that secret passageway and cavern before we leave." He switched to English. "Because there's nothing as cool as a secret passageway."

31

LUCIANA

Carrying torches, we emerged from the tunnel and into the natural cavern protecting a freshwater spring. The Forellis had fortified the tunnel, clearing debris that had once blocked it off, and added a protective wall where the cave opened to the hills. I could see that it would be easily breached if under concentrated attack, but the edifices allowed occupants precious time for reinforcements to come from the castello. I tried to imagine my cousins as young women—younger than I was now—on their own and on the run from the Fiorentini.

We exited through the fortified gate, climbed into the hills, and looked back at the villa. We'd gone a surprising distance underground; I could see why the original Forellis had opted to build as they had. Riders in the hills would never suppose that there was a secret entrance to the villa from here. Only the wall gave it away now, and likely local lore. When Lia and Gabi were first here, it would have appeared as nothing but a damp cave with a spring.

"Someone approaches!" a knight called, pointing to the western road, where two riders galloped toward the villa.

"Let us return," Gabi said, and we hurried down the hill after her, Lia, and the Forellis.

When we finally reached the courtyard, the riders had gained access and were drinking water as if parched. Seeing Marcello and Luca, one tossed the ladle in the bucket and moved directly toward them.

"M'lords!" said the one in the lead. The new men both wore forest-green tunics. Marcello and Luca greeted them with an arm clasp, clearly familiar. "We are under attack. More than a hundred Fiorentini are attempting to breach the gates."

Marcello frowned. "For what reason would they provoke Siena so? Attacking Castello Romano is akin to attacking Castello Forelli!"

"My uncle suspects it may be due to a dispute over passage over the trade road and tax collections. He has been in negotiations with Lord Beneventi and had thought it resolved. But Lord Beneventi believes my uncle stole a great treasure and has come to exact vengeance."

Luca took Marcello's shoulder as he turned. "It may be a ploy to distract us," he said quietly. "If it has become known we are away, there might be soldiers closing in on Castello Forelli as we speak."

"Aurelio would not . . ." Tiliani shook her head, but her words fell away as her father and uncle gave her a somber look.

"In the end, he is Fiorentini," Luca said, with a warning shake of his head. "His purpose is to further his republic's goals. We must always hope for the best but prepare for the worst."

Luca turned to Captain Mancini, already on his right. "Divide the men. Send twelve with us to Castello Romano. Send the other twelve to Castello Forelli. If all is well, relieve those on duty there and send them with fresh horses directly for Castello Romano."

"Yes, sir." The knight pivoted toward the group of men that had gathered and waved others down off the walls.

"How many defend your castello?" Marcello asked.

"We had sixty," he returned. "But they have many archers. Before we made our escape, I saw at least a dozen fall."

"Heavy in archers means there are fewer with swords." Luca

glanced at Nico and me. "Mayhap the new skills you have taught our men shall serve us well this day."

I prayed he was right. Would the jiu jitsu be a help to them or merely a distraction? We had been working on those skills for only four or five weeks. I knew from experience that until it became an unconscious skill—second nature to them—it wouldn't be super useful. But if nothing else, it might lend an element of surprise.

"You must remain here," Giulio said to me, not stopping for a response. "With Adri and Chiara."

"What? Nay!" I followed after him as he began ordering men about.

He turned partway to me. Nico was at my side, listening in.

"You are not completely healed," he said. "You do not belong in battle." He turned to Nico. "Keep her here. Protect her. Better yet, retreat to the fortified tunnel and cavern. Take food and stay there with the servants. I shall come to fetch you when this is over."

I wanted to scream as he strode away, as if the matter was resolved. My injury had occurred over five weeks ago! I turned to Nico. "This makes no sense. I'd much rather be with all of them, doing what we can, than sitting here like horror-movie victims waiting their turn to die. Should we add a wall of chainsaws nearby to seal our fate?"

Nico considered me. "You think you're healed enough to fight?"

"Yes." I pretended to have no doubts. "I'd just have to use my left arm, mostly. Avoid my right."

Nico lifted a brow and crossed his arms.

"Okay, I'll be real. I'm at about fifty percent on my right. But on my left? I'm ready to go. If you just stay on my right . . ."

"We could take them down together."

"Exactly."

"Only one problem." He hooked a thumb over his shoulder. "Your big boyfriend just told you to stay put. Both of us, actually. He's going to be pretty dang ticked off if he turns around to find us in the midst of the fray."

I lifted my chin. "Maybe my big boyfriend needs to learn that he can't order me around."

Nico cocked his head. "You sure you want to play it that way?"

"Yes." Once again, I pretended I had no doubts.

The first group was already on their horses and streaming through the gates, heading toward Castello Forelli. The next group assembled. Some men shoved swords into saddle sheaths. Others lifted shields. Six armed themselves with bows and quivers of arrows. The Forellis emerged in their dress tunics, with the golden howling wolf embroidered on each. Seeing them, the men unpacked their own tunics and settled them over their heads and shoulders.

Ilaria and Tiliani led their horses up to us. Adri and Chiara joined our circle. "You will stay here and wait on us?" Ilaria asked us all, but she focused on me and Nico.

Nico shifted and tucked his thumbs in his rope belt. "That was what Giulio asked us to do, though we'd rather join you."

Ilaria mounted her horse in one fluid motion. "Giulio is wise. You are safer here, hidden away in the caverns."

"Especially given that Luciana is still healing," Tiliani added, mounting her own gelding. "She needs a guard. As do the others."

"True," Nico said, agreeing but not promising anything. He moved to Ilaria, took her hand in his, and kissed it, looking at her all the while. "Take care."

"Always," she said, trying not to smile. "Get everyone to the fortified corridor and secure yourselves."

"We shall see to them," he said. "You can count on us."

With that, they wheeled around and tore out. Giulio, pausing at the gate on horseback, watched them all pass. He looked back to me. "I shall return for you, Luciana," he called, putting his fist to his chest like it was a pledge.

I nodded and he left. Two men closed the gates and barred them. The courtyard was eerily quiet after all the hubbub a moment before. With one glance, Nico and I turned and gathered everyone into the villa. We had to move quickly, or we might not be able to follow behind. I was reasonably sure that Castello Romano would be the next big structure along the road to Siena, but I wasn't one hundred percent sure. We'd taken a different road to Siena before. This road was on the northern border, connecting each outpost of the republic to the next. It had to be like connect the dots, right?

Still, if there were enemies about, it'd be best if we weren't really far away from our people. Nico shouted for the main house servant, Paulo, a man of about fifty, while I grabbed two stableboys and told them to get our horses saddled.

"Yes, m'lord?" Paulo appeared in the doorway.

Nico put a hand on his shoulder and gestured toward the hallway that led to the fortified corridor. "Lord Greco asked us to get all the servants in the corridor. You are to bar the doors and wait inside until Lord Greco or another from Castello Forelli comes to free you. Wait for the stable boys, take in some supplies, and then secure yourselves. Be certain that Lady Adri and Chiara are among you."

"Yes," the man said gravely. "We shall at once. But did he not intend—"

My brother grabbed my arm and hustled me away before the man finished. I supposed he thought it was better to ignore him than lie to his face. "What if they are too far ahead of us, Nico? What if we get lost?"

"I don't think that will happen." He shut the door of the main house behind us. "They just took off. And a bunch of galloping horses will leave a pretty obvious trail for us to follow."

"What if we get separated? Surrounded?"

Or stabbed again? My hand moved to my right pectoral, remembering the pain of those stitches. I thought of the red-hot iron rod, searing my flesh. The smell. The agony. Even now, it was just healing . . .

He grabbed my elbow as we were about to enter the stables. "Luci. Are you having second thoughts?"

"No." I furiously pulled my arm from his grip, despite the fact that I was very much having second thoughts.

They needed every single person they could get on that battlefield, and we could handle ourselves. We could help.

Hadn't we already proven that?

TILIANI

We rode hard for Castello Romano, and memories of the Perugian attack on Castello Forelli flooded back. We had so narrowly deflected them. Had we not been able to get messengers out to Monteriggioni and Siena in time, we would have been forced to surrender. Even with all those knights coming to aid us, we had lost many men, and many more had been wounded. And Ercole had been behind it. Was he behind this too? Had he planted the seed of doubt with Lord Beneventi?

Were the Romanos facing the same dire circumstances as a result, even at this moment?

In my mind's eye, I could see Lord Romano, his charming young wife, Anselma, and their four stair-step children. Were those small children huddling in fear? Anselma was no woman to carry a sword, though she had expressed interest in learning how to wield a bow. I could not imagine her out on the wall alongside the men, however. Like I had been, when Valentino had so narrowly saved me from that death blow . . .

"Tiliani!" Giulio called, jolting me back to the present as the castle came into sight. "With me!" Giulio led half of the men, my father the other. I followed him, as directed, but he glanced at me under his armpit as he galloped.

He had caught me lost in memory, and my face warmed. I could only be glad that the men were too focused on the coming battle to note it. In another moment, we pulled up on a curve in the road—which afforded a brief view of the castle—to confer on how we might best assist our friends.

"They are taking heavy blows to their gates," my father said, after a moment.

"Mayhap we can distract them?" Giulio suggested.

"We can do better than that." Papa glanced at my uncle, mother, and aunt. "Do you recall the battle at Castello Nozzoli?"

Mama spread her arms wide for a visual. "Half of us swept around and came in from one side, half from the other, with the aim to cross paths, turn, and sweep again, like ocean waves meeting in the middle, crushing our adversaries."

Zia Gabi nodded. "Let us get to it, then."

"You heard the She-Wolves," my uncle growled. "Captain, give us a few minutes' lead in order to get in position."

"Yes, m'lord," Giulio said.

We fell back among the trees, hoping no Fiorentini had yet spied us. Surprise was key to this plan. I prayed for the Lord's protection of our elders as they rode off with my cousins and half the men. I was unaccustomed to skirmishes—let alone battles—with them amongst us. While they had proven themselves indispensable when we battled the Perugians, that had been the first time in my memory that I had seen them pick up weapons in anything but daily exercises.

Despite the legends, the stories, it had become more lore than reality in my mind. Here again, I witnessed that the Forellis were a family that commanded respect, as they unsheathed swords and bows. I felt a rush of pride.

You can poke at a She-Wolf's den—or her friends—for only so long, before she will rise. And her husband will be behind her. Together, we would remind these Fiorentini that we were not to be trifled with.

We were to be feared.

And yet we were far outnumbered. The orderly troops below were not a raid but rather an organized attack, led by an astute leader. Their focus was on the gates, and if they managed to breach them, they would enter in methodical fashion. They seemed unharried by Castello Romano's archers. Was that because they had poor aim?

"Get into formation," Giulio ordered.

I moved my mount between his and Ilaria's, as we had trained. Other men flanked them, until we were a line of ten, ready to sweep down below when Giulio told us it was time. I pulled the bow from my shoulder, nocked an arrow, and brushed my fingers through the feathers of the others in the quiver. Felt for the hilt of my sword on my back. Atop my mount, I could do far more damage with an arrow than with my short sword. But I would need my sword if an enemy managed to unseat me.

I had just wrapped Cardo's reins around the horn of my saddle, giving him enough room to move as he saw fit—and knowing I could rely on his battle training to stay with the others until we reached the fray—when Giulio lifted his arm. When all looked his way, he dropped it.

We set off.

A mere squeeze of my calves sent my excited mount up and over the hill alongside the others. There was no trumpet, no unfurling of our family banner. This was a mission of surprise, and I smiled as I lifted my bow, thinking of the Betarrini twins. What had they called it? *Shock and awe.* I hoped we would so utterly surprise those below that some would turn tail and run.

If we could take enough down as we passed—and our elders did the same—we would have a chance at making this a fairer fight.

I sighted my first enemy, a man turning toward us, lifting his head to shout an alarm.

My first arrow pierced his neck before the shout left his throat.

I nocked the second, and chose the man right behind him,

who met my gaze and ducked in terror. I mentally calculated his movement, his likely stopping point, and let my arrow fly.

My arrow sliced through his chest, and he crumpled to his side.

The third arrow pierced a man helping push a heavy, wheeled battering ram toward the gates. My fourth missed. My fifth grazed a man's temple. And when I pulled my sixth across my bowstring, we were nearly upon the knights below. I dropped the first man I could find, knowing time was short for me to prepare for defensive moves.

But I saw with relief that our other group was drawing similar attention. Below us, men scattered, confused as to which way to run, turn, defend, ignoring their captain's call. As planned, we crossed paths, moving through the enemy and up the opposite hill, sowing seeds of bewilderment. I slashed at men with my short sword but inflicted little damage. I was best used by getting to the far side, turning, and taking aim again.

I winced as a man wielding the longest sword I had ever seen brought it down on me and Cardo as we passed. At the last moment, I used my heel to push Cardo to sidestep. He obeyed, but I was a hair too late. The tip of the man's sword cut through the side of my calf.

I felt the wounding as if from a distance. And then as I had to dodge another enemy, I pushed it aside. We regrouped, down a few of our men. A quick glance to the field told me they were battling below. They were best aided by another pass.

"Tiliani! Otello! Baldarino!" Giulio shouted. "Take position halfway down and use the remainder of your arrows before you join us!" With no further word, he raised his arm, brought it down, and they were off again for another pass, just as our other group did the same from the other side.

We archers did our best to pick off men below as we settled into position. All three of us aimed for those taking on our companions who had been unseated on our first pass. It was with some pleasure that I sent an arrow through the neck of one who was viciously striking at Falito.

My friend staggered to a stop, followed the path of the arrow, gave me a crooked grin and quick wave of thanks, then turned to find his next opponent.

But the men operating the battering ram continued at their task. I saw, then, why the archers had been fairly ignored. While men pulled and pushed the ram, others covered them with shields.

"Let us see if we can get beneath those shields," I muttered.

32

LUCIANA

We were approaching a hill on the road when we saw a knight ride across it and disappear. Then two more. One glanced our way, and Nico veered off the road and into the trees. I followed. He slowed to a canter and then a trot, climbing a hill. We dismounted and led our horses deeper into the wood.

"Do you think they saw us?"

"No," Nico said. "Or if they did, they're focused on bigger prey. We have to get to a place where we can see what's comin' down."

"Let's go," I said.

We meandered through the wood until we could peek between the trees at the top of a hill.

And what we saw took my breath away.

About a hundred Fiorentini rode south, most of them in formation. Toward the battle at Castello Romano?

A shiver ran down my back, and I glanced over my shoulder. "Nico, do you think scouts are surrounding us, even now?" My eyes darted from one tree to the other.

He shook his head. "They don't care about us, Luci. They're focused on Castello Romano."

"Why?"

"I heard Luca say if they sack this one, then turn toward Castello Forelli—they can take out this whole corner of Siena's protection.

If they capture Romano, Castello Forelli will be somewhat cut off. The forces at Castello Paratore could then close in and meet others from the north."

"But Aurelio wouldn't do that, would he?"

"He probably doesn't want to, but what choice would he have if Firenze demands it?"

"So this could get messy," I said with a sigh. "Fast."

"Very messy." He paused. "Luci."

I followed his gaze. More troops approached from the east—in Paratore crimson.

We receded further into the trees as they passed below us on the road. "Maybe he's here to intervene?" I asked.

"Maybe," Nico responded, doubt lacing his tone.

"Most of the people we love are down there, Nico." Giulio. Ilaria. Tiliani. The Forellis.

"Then we had better find a way to help them out," he grunted, mounting his horse again.

"Would we be better off riding for Monteriggioni? Or Siena? To try and bring back reinforcements?"

He shook his head. "Luca sent messengers from the villa. With luck, they will send reinforcements. But it's going to take hours."

We shared a grim look. Our people did not have hours.

And if we did not have our people here, did we have anything at all?

We mounted up and followed the Paratore troops from a distance, knowing there was little chance for us to get ahead of them. Our intent was to find out what Aurelio would do, then aid our friends and family the best we could from there.

"They will set up archers among the rocks," I said quietly. "Maybe we could take them out, one by one, guerrilla-warfare style."

"I like the way you think."

Once they turned south, we dared following them on the road for a time. As the castle rose on the hill in front of us—the melee of battle before it—we turned and rode hard for a neighboring hill, covered with swaying grain. We hobbled our horses and climbed the last bit, hunched over. From there we could see all that was happening and take stock. Consider where we might best aid our friends.

Aurelio and Sir Valeri rode directly into the fray, one carrying the Paratore herald flag, the other a small white flag. "Be at peace!" Aurelio bellowed. "Lay down your arms!"

Gradually, the Fiorentini did as he asked, and the Sienese followed.

"Why is it you are attacking this castle?" he asked, directing his question to the nobleman near the battering ram.

The man turned and furiously strode over to him. "Not that I must explain myself to you, *brother*, but this house has stolen a treasure chest of taxes from the southern border gate. We have come to reclaim it and make certain they never dare such action again!"

His men shouted their approval, lifting swords to the sky.

"We did not steal the treasure!" called a man from the wall. "For years we have lived to your south and never attempted something so brazen. Why would we do so now?"

"Open up your gates, then!" called the lord on the ground. "We shall search your house for the treasure chest, and if we do not find it, be on our way."

"I shall be cold and dead in the grave before I allow a *Fiorentini* in my keep!"

The nobleman lifted a hand to Aurelio as if to say, *You see?*

"Why is it you believe that Lord Romano stole the treasure?" Aurelio's gelding danced underneath him, feeling the tension.

"Six men in green tunics were seen stealing away from the treasury the night before last."

"Well *that* sounds familiar," Nico muttered.

"Ercole again?" My wounds twinged in memory.

"Seems obvious, right?"

"All our men are accounted for each eve, as they have been for weeks!" called Lord Romano to those below.

"Even if they snuck out after dark, you are responsible! The fact is this—my treasure has been stolen, and your men were seen. Now either open your gates and allow us to search for what is ours or prepare to be conquered."

He turned to Aurelio, jabbing a finger toward him. "And are you truly Fiorentini? Truly? You *stink* of wolves. To arms!" he called over his shoulder.

"To arms!" his men answered. Immediately, the battle resumed.

Aurelio caught up again to Lord Beneventi, trying to reason with him, but the man shook his head in disgust, sending a wad of spit to the dust at his side. We were too far away to make out any more among the commotion. Aurelio and Valentino rode back up the hill and circled up with the other men. To do what? Would they join the attack? Or simply observe?

We spotted the Forellis, entering formation together. Marcello and Gabi were still on their horses. Lia and Tiliani were halfway up the hill, with the other archers. On the opposite side, we glimpsed Fiorentini archers amongst the rocks and, using the natural shield, emerging to take aim at our people.

"C'mon, Luci," Nico said.

"Right behind ya," I muttered.

Hunched over, we returned to our horses and rode around to the far side of the other hill. We tied our mounts to a low branch of an oak tree and scurried back up the incline. We ducked down as two knights passed perilously close, apparently on guard duty but distracted by the battle below. My heart hammered in my chest.

"Let's go save some of our people," Nico said.

"Yes. Let's."

"Keep to my side."

"Like you're my good arm," I returned.

We dared to creep forward, staying low, until we could see the first archer on the left. He rose, took aim, shot, then immediately crouched down.

Nico gave me a meaningful look. We'd have a second, maybe two, to intervene.

The archer nocked a new arrow and rose. We scurried forward and dropped into the little pocket between the boulder and hillside.

"Hey, hi!" Nico said in English, swiftly punching the surprised man in the belly. He doubled over, and I used my knee to meet his nose. He straightened, gasping, blood spurting, and Nico took him down before anyone spotted us.

We caught our breath, and I grabbed hold of an errant arrow as Nico hooked a thumb over his shoulder. I nodded and we eased around the rock. He counted down silently with his fingers—*three, two, one*—and then he surged into motion. For this new adversary, we didn't know what to expect.

He caught him just as he drew back his arrow, aiming.

"Uh-uh," Nico said, grabbing the bow and wrenching it from his hands. "Those are *our* friends you're trying to kill." He whacked the man across the head with the bow, knocking him out cold.

I felt the person behind me before Nico's eyes widened. I whirled and leapt, blindly stabbed him in the neck with the arrow in my hand, just as I knew he was bringing down his sword to decapitate me. The knight staggered back, stunned. His sword teetered in his hand and then clattered to the rocks just over my right shoulder. Two others below spotted us and shouted an alarm.

"So much for covert ops," Nico said. "Let's go!"

I followed his lead as he slid over the rounded face of a boulder and dropped between two archers. Grabbing hold of the first one's shoulders as he took aim, Nico swiveled and pulled the man's bowstring-hand farther. Mouth agape, the man let go of the string, and the arrow went winging past me and into a knight chasing us, catching him beneath the chin. He wheeled backward, into a second man behind him.

"Lucky shot." I jumped onto the second archer's back and brought my good arm around his chin, choking him. Nico grabbed a dagger from the first archer's belt and stabbed him. He lurched forward but kept his feet.

"Luci!" Nico shouted, ducking.

I released my adversary and dropped to the ground as an arrow sang past my head.

"C'mon." He hauled me up, and we scrambled over the dead and dying men. "Back-to-back," he said.

I immediately turned and faced my opponents, as he did his.

"So much for you being my right-hand man," I said over my shoulder.

"We're kinda between a rock and a hard place," he quipped.

We were in a literal crevice, forcing the men coming for me into a line. The first lowered his sword and, with a growl, drove toward me, intending to send the tip of his blade through my belly. I rammed my left arm against one side of the rock, my right foot to the other and twirled into him, landing mostly on his shoulders.

I turned, wincing as we bounced off the rock and my right arm took a hit. I locked his head between my legs, and lurched back into the second man. We fell down in a heap, the first man clawing at my legs as I strangled him.

I shifted as he choked, holding on tight. I had to be done with him if I was to have half a chance at the second and third.

The second wriggled out from under us. He grabbed hold of my hair and pulled. "Release him, witch!"

I stubbornly held onto the first man until he slumped.

Nico arrived and stabbed my assailant with a dagger and broke the nose of another with the palm of his hand.

I scrambled backward, my scalp on fire, hoping to knock my attacker backward too. Abruptly, he released me. My tailbone met rock, and I felt it shiver up my spine. But I regained my feet, determined not to get separated from my brother. Now more than ever, I knew my life depended on it. In that unstoppable momentum, we ran toward the next group of men.

I dropped the first archer with a roundhouse kick and pummeled the second, startled man with my left fist. He fell to his butt, cradling his nose. Nico was finishing off his second opponent when two burly knights entered our small arena, one carrying one of those spiky balls. A *battle flail*, I thought I'd heard it called. The same kind of thing that knight caught in my skirts in the battle outside Castello Forelli and rendered me utterly incapacitated.

But I was more worried about my head at the moment than my skirts.

He whirled the evil ball through the air, smiling wickedly as he approached. The circumference of the chain would keep me from kicking or striking him.

I glanced around. Nico fell partially into me and righted himself in the midst of his own battle, but I kept my eyes on my adversary. I knew I was in trouble.

I snatched a stick from the ground, seriously wishing it was a lot thicker.

At least it's something.

The man advanced, and the metal ball whipped past me, narrowly missing my chest as I leaped backward, bumping into Nico. "Incoming!" I cried, turning my head as it swept past again.

The next time, the flail nicked my cheek. I grabbed hold of my stick with both hands and rose, trying to figure out my best move in order to capture the chain and have it roll around, rather than make hamburger of my head.

"Nico," I muttered as the first wave of my bravado slipped.

"Wish I could help," he said under his breath and then grunted, taking a blow. He fell against me, and I kept him upright while concentrating on my advancing opponent. I rammed upward again with my stick on the next round and missed. A spike caught my left shoulder and then rolled off. The ball had to be a good ten pounds. Maybe twenty?

But the man wielding it looked up to the task. He was perhaps six feet, well over two hundred pounds. Arms the size of logs. As if he twirled this flail in his free time like the guys at NYU did pull-up wars to show off for girls walking by.

My coach always said that when facing a much larger adversary obeying no rules, the only rule was to fight to survive. And this was definitely a fight-to-survive moment.

I ducked low as the flail swung past my head, tucked my leg as he leaned back, and kicked as hard as I could to his groin.

He cried out and staggered away. I belatedly recognized he had some sort of protection there beneath his chain mail.

But I'd made him mad.

I rolled to the left as the metal ball arced toward me again. It glanced off the stone behind my shoulder.

He growled and hurled it again, and I ducked to the right, ignoring the pain in my shoulder. This time it came so close it bounced into me. I shoved off the stone and charged into him as hard as I could.

My move surprised him, and he staggered back. But then, startlingly fast for a man of his size, he grabbed hold of my throat.

I grasped at his thick, sausage-like fingers, but he lifted me—almost off my toes—then tossed me against the boulder.

His fingers clenched my neck again, so hard that my vision began to cloud.

Distantly, I thought about gouging his eyes with my thumbs. But as I lifted my hands, he rammed my head against the rock.

Then again.

✣   ✣   ✣

from a distance i felt him lift my head yet again

ram it to the rock

and then

i felt nothing at all

✣   ✣   ✣

TILIANI

"Do you see them?" I cried, as the Betarrini twins disappeared behind the rock face.

Giulio grabbed the reins of a Fiorentini mare skittering about, as lost as her master in the fray. "I know where they are. With me!" He swung up into the saddle and reached down. I grabbed hold of his arm and arced behind him, and we rode hard for the hill, ignoring the *whish* of passing arrows, dodging men wielding swords. He dug his heels in hard, and we climbed fast, the mare eager to burn off her fear.

He leaped off at once, wading into the swordfight. He bested one with a single blow, but the next gave him more of a challenge. I took his place in the saddle and nocked an arrow, seeking my first adversary. I could not charge into the fray around this field of boulders, potentially landing myself in a nest of vipers.

I picked off a man sighting his arrow on me, a second before he let it loose, easily ducking his last, futile volley. I shot at a third and a fourth, not waiting to see what came of my targets. Because I was getting close to the Betarrinis, and I knew their time was likely short.

I jumped from the horse to the knight facing Domenico, about to deal him a death blow. I clasped onto his head and neck, wrapping my legs around his waist and fiercely hanging on. I reached back to my belt and grasped a dagger and plunged it into his chest, again and again, hoping I would hit a lung.

He fell, and I rolled off and got to my feet, wiping the man's blood from my blade.

But my eyes were on Giulio.

Killing the man who had bludgeoned Luciana against the rock.

The man fell to the ground, but Luciana lay motionless before Giulio on the boulder. And there was blood, so much blood.

He lifted her in his arms. Looked to me, terror and tears in his eyes. Never, ever had I seen him so.

She was limp. Bleeding from the back of her head. Her cheek. Her shoulder. If I didn't see the subtle rise and fall of her chest, I would've believed her dead.

He stared at me, and I knew what he was silently asking me. *The tomb?*

Was that our only recourse? But there had been talk of that man, Manero, doing damage to the tomb wall. Would it even work any longer? "My grandmother! I shall take her to the villa!"

If we could get her there at all. More men circled around. Closing in.

I thought of Aurelio and Valentino at the top of the hill, watching. Observers with men at their back. Unable to wade in as either adversaries or aid. Paralyzed.

To come to our aid would sever their ties with Firenze.

And yet to *not* come to our aid would forever sever their ties with us.

33

TILIANI

We were hopelessly outnumbered. I knew that Luciana's only chance was to get clear of the madness and to Nona. So did Giulio. She would know if Luci's only chance was the tomb.

Giulio ran a hand through his sweat-drenched hair, his face telling me how torn he felt. As captain of the guard, he had to remain with our knights, here. I put a hand on his arm. "We shall get her to Nona. Trust me."

My eyes met Aurelio's across the field, desperate. He immediately set off down the hill on his horse, Valentino beside him. Four others followed. Valentino raised a white flag. They pulled up short beside us and took in the gravity of the situation. When three knights moved in on us, he turned and said coldly, "You shall hold. They must take the woman to seek aid."

"That woman killed several of our men!"

"You shall hold," Aurelio gritted out, hands on the hilt of his sword.

Valentino dismounted and handed his mare's reins to me. "Take her," he said. "You do not have time to fetch Cardo. Every moment counts."

Giulio had removed his shirt, ripped a portion off, and attempted to wind it around Luciana's head. Immediately, the blood seeped through. I knew head wounds bled a great deal, but 'twas terrible to witness.

"Tiliani." Valentino gestured to me. "You must be away."

More knights gathered on Aurelio's other side. Captain Beneventi strode up the hill, fuming.

Domenico went to Luciana and gathered her in his arms from Giulio, dazed. I recognized the delirium, the blank expression in his eyes. *Shock*, Nona called it. *Nona.* If she deemed that the tomb was Luciana's only hope, she'd need Domenico there too.

"Nico!" I slapped his blood-splattered cheek. "You must take her back to the villa!" I pulled my shoulder sword, aware that someone slipped over the boulder above us. I whirled and narrowly parried a Beneventi knight's strike.

Valentino stabbed our attacker, and he fell roughly to his butt, gripping his belly in surprise. Grimacing, I turned to Domenico. "You must go. *Now!*"

More of Beneventi's men descended upon us in a circle.

And the term *melee* was not enough to touch what was coming.

Valentino took Luciana from Domenico's arms and, with a tilt of his head, nodded to the mare. Domenico mounted and reached for his sister. Valentino had only a moment to help settle her.

"Try and hold her tightly!" he cried, pulling up his sword to meet another's strike. "Keep her head against yours!"

Domenico blinked slowly, as if trying to make sense of it all. But we were out of time. I swatted the mare's rump, and the startled horse jumped to the only clear spot and up the hill.

The castello's gate splintered. Our enemies closed in.

The Fiorentini outnumbered us three to one. Reinforcements had not arrived. The moment was at hand. And we were falling.

Men circled us, a nightmarish force of twenty behind twenty more.

I fought and fought, wiping my eyes of my enemies' blood, striking, blindly striking, when a gloved hand caught my arm.

"Tiliani," Papa said. "'Tis me."

I turned and blocked the next strike of my next adversary, driving him back, but then my knees buckled. Never had I been so utterly spent as I was right then.

"Get up!" Papa gripped my hand, thumbs interlocked. "Rise!" Over my head, he blocked a strike.

I grasped his hand, wondering if I could truly do so without fainting, but looking into his eyes—not daring to look away—I obeyed.

"Take heart. Some of Aurelio's men have joined us." He turned to meet the attack of the next knight. "Stay behind me."

Aurelio Paratore, Valentino, and six men stood in formation, driving forward, with us behind. They were giving us a moment's reprieve, a chance to catch our breath and gather ourselves. A moment to reclaim hope.

"Traitor!" Beneventi screamed at Aurelio, trying to reach him. "I shall have your head for this!"

I glanced up the hill. More of Aurelio's men came down the hill to aid him, but more than half remained on their horses, watching. They were unwilling to pick up arms against their fellow Fiorentini, and yet unwilling to pick up arms against their master or captain either.

Mama dashed for another vantage point on the hill, followed by four of our archers. Together they took aim, aiding us in making a path to rejoin the remnants of our own knights. Across the field before the castle, men were wearying, slower with each strike, gasping for breath. Those at the battering ram had turned away from it to join their comrades on the field when the Paratore knights waded into the fray and came for them.

Ten paces away, Zio Marcello and Fortino fought back-to-back, surrounded. Papa and I made it through the thick of the crowd. I raced for a bow and quiver on the ground, diving to my belly beside a dead knight as three arrows came my way. I rolled his body to his side as a shield. Two pierced him, one extending all the way through to me. My mother took down one archer, and I let my own arrow fly and pierced the second's hand as he drew again. The third ducked behind a rock. I immediately turned and brought down three other men on the field in quick succession.

"Cease this madness!" Aurelio yelled at Lord Beneventi. "Have not enough died this day?"

"It could have been over by now," Lord Beneventi cried, shoving aside one of his men to lift his sword toward Aurelio. "Had you not intervened!" He brought his sword down against Aurelio's, his face lined with rage.

"I tell you again," Aurelio said, driving him back, "that you are beginning a war with Siena. Committing the entire republic to backing you. And without just cause. 'Tis a setup, my brother. I know who is behind it! Andrea Ercole!"

"I know no Ercole!" Lord Beneventi struck at him, then again, Aurelio parrying every blow, but refusing to go on the offensive. Gradually, the rest of the field stilled, all eyes turning to these two.

"Call a truce, brother," Aurelio said as they circled, each plainly spent.

"You are not my brother. You are a traitor!" With each phrase, he struck at Aurelio. "You bear the burden of every dead man on this field!"

"I did not lead them into this false battle."

"Regardless of how it began, we could have captured this castle by now, had you come to *our* aid rather than your *Sienese* friends." His eyes cut to me and Benedetto as Ilaria and Mama joined us. "We could have sacked not only Castello Romano, but Castello Forelli too! Seized this entire corner for the republic!"

"And begun a war that would take hundreds, if not thousands, of lives." Aurelio's blade came up a second later each time, his pushback a little less bold. Lord Beneventi, so clearly enraged, seemed to forget his own lagging vigor. My uncle and father strode toward them, my aunt too. Then Valentino and Giulio and Ilaria. We silently surrounded the duo, sword tips to the ground. Aurelio's knights did the same.

"Surrender, Lord Beneventi," Zio Marcello said. "Go home. If you kill Lord Paratore, you will not return to your wife, your children. We shall allow you to leave because you were deceived. Lord Romano was set up to appear the thief. We do not wish to be at war with Firenze again."

"And what do I tell the wives and children of all these men?" Lord Beneventi gestured to the dead and dying Fiorentini. "If I had been able to do as I ought, they would at least have a portion of the bounty to see them through the coming year."

"'Tis a tragedy for each household," Zio Marcello said. "But you shall see them through, just as we shall see our Sienese friends through. We have all lost this day. *All* of us."

Lord Beneventi drew in a deep breath through his nose, considering my uncle from beneath his glowering brow. His breath emerged as a heavy sigh, and he lowered his sword. Aurelio did the same.

They surveyed the field.

Beneventi turned to leave. Too late, I saw it. He tucked the blade under his arm and then stepped back toward Aurelio, stabbing him clean through.

"Nay!" Valentino screamed as Aurelio fell, mouth agape, hand against his wound.

I might have screamed the same, but in the moment, I could not seem to hear anything. The field erupted again, each man picking up his weapon as Valentino killed Lord Beneventi with three swift blows.

LUCIANA

It was the headache that I noticed first.

Migraine, I thought distantly.

But I didn't get migraines anymore. Not here in medieval Tuscany. The time tunnel had healed me, freed me.

And yet this, this one was murderous. I couldn't seem to open my eyes, and it felt like I was on a horse . . . with Nico. I could feel his warm chest behind my back. One strong arm across my clavicle, his hand pressing my head beside his. His other arm was around my waist, holding the reins.

I tried to blink my eyes, terrified when they didn't seem to work. Nico trotted, urging his mare forward as fast as he dared. Because of me? Was I hurt?

The battle, I remembered. The big knight's fingers closing around my neck. Ramming my head against the rock . . .

"*Nico,*" I tried to say, but no sound left my mouth. I wasn't even sure I'd formed the word. Had I forgotten how to speak as well as how to open my eyes? In my dark world, my head spun, dizziness overtaking me, threatening to make me vomit.

I'd had migraines that bad before. Headaches that sent me into tilt-a-whirl orbit until I was vomiting my guts out in the toilet. Maybe this was just another.

Just another. Wasn't it?

Or was it something much, much worse?

34

Valentino cradled Aurelio in his arms as his friend, his brother, struggled to breathe. I fell to my knees beside them, holding Aurelio's hand, weeping as Valentino rocked and rocked him, looking to the sky as anguished tears swept down his dust-lined and blood-spattered face. My family and friends now formed a circle around us, protecting us, but refusing to fight further. Periodically my father would shout, "Peace! Be at peace! Enough have died this day!"

But those who followed Aurelio into the battle now fought with the last of their vigor. As if the dozen or so still on their feet could bring the young lord back from the brink of death by defeating their last assailant.

Valentino and I shared a knowing, tortured look.

Aurelio had moments left.

Valentino slowed his rocking and took hold of Aurelio's other hand.

Aurelio's eyes—an even more brilliant green in that moment—glanced from him to me. His lips opened, trying to form words, but no sound emerged.

"Forgive me, brother," Valentino said, his voice choked. "I did not see it coming. I should have seen it coming."

"You are a fine man," I said. I looked into Aurelio's eyes and swallowed back the lump in my throat, tears dripping down my face. "A fine friend. We shall speak of you forever in our family as a Paratore we loved. Thank you for coming to our aid. Thank you for trying to stop the bloodshed, the battles."

Aurelio lifted my hand—his breath coming at a shallow pant now—and then he placed Valentino's hand over mine. My eyes met Valentino's. Was he blessing our relationship? Encouraging us, even in his final moments? Did he know that coming to our aid had already severed Valentino and his men from the rest of the Fiorentini?

Our eyes met across him for a moment. Then we both looked back to Aurelio, and in that second, we saw his eyes grow terribly still. His desperate attempt to breathe ceased, and his spirit left us.

Valentino groaned and wept anew, shaking his head slowly back and forth as if he could wake from this nightmare.

I shook my head, too, as I brought up Aurelio's hand and kissed it, my tears falling to his lifeless fingers. What was to become of them all now? The castello would be seized. His fighting men charged with treason.

"'Tis over!" my father called to those still wearily battling. "Lord Paratore is dead!"

But it was the men who had hung back on the ridge that brought the fighting on the field about us to a halt. They took up my father's call, urging their comrades to cease as they rode down the hill.

"Lord Paratore wanted this to stop. Honor his last wishes!"

"Peace be among you!"

"Lay down your swords!"

Gradually all did as they demanded. Then Aurelio's men circled past in single file, hands to their chests, bowing to their dead lord as they departed. When the last rode up and over the hill, I turned to Valentino. "Will they ride for Castello Paratore? Or Firenze?"

"Both." He wearily wiped his face of tears with both palms.

"Then Castello Forelli may soon be in danger," Zio Marcello said tightly. "They may summon others among Beneventi's men. Incite them with a call for vengeance."

"'Tis likely," he returned dully. Valentino laid Aurelio gently to the ground, crossing his arms atop his chest. "There shall be repercussions all along the border in the coming days and weeks."

"Then we best return home." Papa put a hand on his shoulder. "And you with us. We are in your debt, Captain Valeri. You and your men shall have a place with us."

Valentino wearily rose and offered me a hand. But there was no pleasure, no romance, no hope in the moment. Only tearing, ripping, loss. The horribly heavy burden of grief.

I looked about. Took in all the dead or dying. Thought about the families mentioned, until I could think about it no more, lest I dissolve into tears again.

I trudged up the hill with my mother and aunt, who were too spent themselves to offer me their customary soothing ministrations.

Zio Marcello called to Lord Romano, now coming through the battered gates. "We must return to Castello Forelli to defend her! Siena shall soon arrive to aid you and see to your reparations. Might you gather our injured and dead inside your gates? We shall return as soon as we can to carry them home!"

"Of course, my brother! We shall see to them as our own."

I looked again to the hills all about us. Many men were down, unmoving. Many more sat or lay prone, bleeding, crying out for help. New tears ran down my face. For those of Siena.

And for those of Firenze too.

My attention returned to Aurelio Paratore.

Four of Aurelio's faithful men lifted him gently to a blanket then somberly carried him toward the castello gates, Valentino silently leading them. His other men made way for them, taking a knee, sword tip to the soil, heads bowed.

Their somber procession amplified the breath-stealing sorrow inside my own chest.

"Come, Tiliani," Mama said, pulling at my arm. "You can do no more for him. But you can help us keep watch over our own."

LUCIANA

I awakened to the muffled sound of someone praying. Drops hit my arm. Water? No . . . tears. I knew the warmth of the hand that held mine.

Domenico.

I tried to say his name but couldn't seem to make my lips form the word, nor make any sound leave my mouth other than breath. I tried to open my eyes and thought I had. But I could see nothing. Nothing but darkness. Were we in some protected room without torch or candle?

Again I tried to say his name but failed.

Panic rose in my chest. I gripped his hand as hard as I could. Concentrated on the syllables of his name. *Ni-co.*

"She moved a little!" he exclaimed. "Lady Adri!"

I felt a woman at my other side and knew a moment of relief. It was coming back to me now. The battle. The massive knight. The rock.

"It was faint, but I felt it!" Nico said. "Luciana!" He stroked my arm, squeezed my hand. "Luci, we are here."

"If you can hear us," Adri said, taking my other hand in hers, "try squeezing our hands."

My headache threatened to make me sick with how it sent me tilting in the darkness. But I squeezed as hard as I could.

"Good, good." I heard the smile in Adri's voice even as Nico sputtered a broken laugh through what sounded like tears.

I seemed to remember how to speak, to form words then as I felt my eyelids flutter on my cheeks. "I-I can't see," I whispered to Adri, my voice ragged. My throat was terribly dry. It surprised me, to hear the words leave my mouth, as if my brain was catching up to them.

"Here, drink." Nico put the edge of a waterskin to my lips. Water dribbled into my mouth, and I swallowed gratefully.

"Did she say . . .?" Nico asked Adri, as he gave me another mouthful.

"She can't see," Adri said quietly.

He sucked in his breath. Adri's slim fingers tightened around mine. "Luciana, you took some terrible blows to your occipital lobe," she said in English. "I've seen it a number of times here, after battle, this type of blindness. Try and not panic. Sometimes it is temporary."

Sometimes. Her word echoed in my aching head.

Sometimes it's temporary.

Sometimes.

Meaning other times it was not.

I could feel my eyelids flutter on my cheeks again. *Try and not panic,* she'd said. I was absolutely on the edge of panic.

The door creaked open, and I heard several people come in. "Giulio! Ilaria!" my brother cried. "She has just awakened!"

Giulio. I was so anxious to feel his hand on mine, know that he was okay after the battle. But Nico rose, swift in his movement. On defense. Why?

"Giulio!" Adri cried.

"Nay! *Giulio!*" cried Ilaria.

But there were only sounds of struggle, scuffling, my brother's breath leaving his chest. A thud of flesh on stone.

"Why . . . were . . . you . . . there?" Giulio gritted out.

"Giulio, stop!" Ilaria yelled.

"We told you . . . to . . . stay here!" Giulio continued.

"Let me go!" Nico growled.

"Do you see her?" Giulio asked, half enraged, half grief-stricken.

"Let me *go*," Nico warned again. Then, when Giulio obviously did not, I heard three short sounds. A soft *oof* from Giulio, hand against flesh, a grunt. Another strike.

"That is *enough*," Ilaria said. I assumed she had gotten between them. Oh, how my head ached. I quit trying to see and closed my eyes.

"Does it hurt a great deal?" Adri asked, as if my boyfriend had not just tried to beat up my brother.

"Worse than any migraine ever. And I think I might be sick."

"You are battle weary as well," she said. A cork popped from a bottle. "Undoubtedly feeling the ache of blows and effort from your head to your toes. Inhale through your nose."

I did as she asked and smelled the clean, acrid scent of alcohol. A little stunned, I felt my stomach settle.

"What was that?"

"Just a bit of alcohol. Or as close as I can approximate it. Old nurses' trick for nausea."

"We had to come to your aid!" Nico said. It sounded like his back was to me. "We had to come to your aid," he repeated, more calmly. "Had we not, many more of our friends would likely be dead or injured. Mayhap *you*."

"'Tis true, Giulio," Ilaria said. "They managed to take down a number of archers before they were laid low."

"*You* both could have been killed," Giulio growled. "And I do not believe even your tunnel brings back the dead," he added in a whisper.

Everyone went silent.

"Giulio." I lifted my hand, knowing he could not refuse me.

It took a moment, but eventually his presence settled beside my pallet, and he took my hand in both of his. "Is it terrible, my love? Your pain?"

"It is terrible," I admitted. "But worse, I cannot see."

He sucked in his breath. His palpable terror made my own all the worse.

"We hope it will return," Adri said quickly. "With rest."

All were silent a moment. Then Giulio asked, "Why, Luciana? Why were you there? You promised to remain here."

"Nay. We promised to get everyone into the tunnel," Nico said.

"We could do no other than come to your aid," I intervened softly, feeling Giulio's grip tighten with rage. "Just as you would have done for us. Especially if you had seen how many were closing in. We could not stand aside and watch you all perish."

"And yet now . . . your eyes, my love . . ." he whispered. I felt his forehead against the back of my hand.

"If we are to remain here, be a part of your family, your life, we cannot remain behind the battle lines. You cannot relegate me to some pedestal, hide me away forever."

"You were injured in Firenze, Luciana. Still healing. There was no dishonor in remaining behind. And now . . ."

"Now I am injured and healing in new ways." I squeezed his hand. "I do not regret my decisions. And it *was* my decision. Not only Nico's. We were together in it. We go where you and the Forellis go. God brought us here. He alone will decide if we die here."

Giulio brought my hand to his lips, kissing the knuckles, one by one. "My stubborn, brave, She-Wolf."

There were shouts outside, someone running through the halls. A man appeared at the door. "We must be off to Castello Forelli, Lord Greco. Scouts say there are Fiorentini closing in on both Castello Forelli and Paratore."

"Word from Siena?"

"Troops are a few hours behind us. But they are coming."

"What has happened?" I asked, blinking again, wishing I could see. Wishing I could rise. "Castello Paratore? Where is Aurelio?"

Everyone fell silent again. "He is dead," Giulio said regretfully.

"Oh," I mouthed, tears rising in my dark eyes. "How? When?"

But they ignored my questions, pulled by the more urgent matters at hand.

"She cannot be moved, Giulio," Adri said as he rose. "If we are to have a chance at saving her eyesight, she needs to remain as still as possible."

"The fortified tunnel," Nico said. "We can hole up there. And this time, we shall stay put," he pledged.

The room was silent as Giulio thought it through. "Leave them mounts at the cavern exit," he directed. "As well as six knights. Seal them in yourself, Ilaria, before you follow."

He leaned back toward me and tenderly kissed my brow. "My love, I would stay with you if I could, but—"

"I know." There was not one castle at risk, but two. And Castello Romano was so badly damaged. "You have to go. You must. The Forellis need you."

He turned away. "You shall remain by her side? All of you?"

"Of course," Adri said.

"Yes," Chiara said.

"I give you my word," Nico said.

I breathed a sigh of relief, knowing they would not leave me.

"I will pray for you unceasingly, beloved," Giulio said, kissing my forehead. "And your eyesight. We shall return for you all."

"I shall be eager to see you. And Castello Forelli. Go."

With one more tender kiss between my brows, he strode out of the room, along with the man—or men—who had entered. I could hear him barking orders as they walked down the hall.

"Let us get you situated in the tunnel," Ilaria said.

"I am going to strap your head down, Luci," Adri said. "You're on a stretcher atop a pallet, so we'll be ready to move you. We need to keep your head as stable as possible. Please keep your eyes shut. Rest is what your brain needs most and trying to see will only tax it further."

"Okay."

"Try not to talk either. Again, brain rest is what you need most. Understood? I have stitched your head wound and there is poultice packed against it. I've seen to your other wounds as well. Now drink this tincture. It shall help you sleep."

I tried not to laugh at her litany of rapid orders and obediently drank from her tiny vial of medicine. It tasted foul, but I was thinking about her directive.

Brain rest. No problem.

If only my boyfriend was not wading into another battle that threatened to become an all-out war.

If only I wasn't blind.

And if only we were not about to be sealed up in a narrow, damp tunnel, praying we would not be discovered by an enemy who wanted us all dead.

35

Valentino galloped beside me for the first couple of miles, which kept us from any conversation, but as our mounts wearied, we slowed to a walk. He did not look left or right. Never at me. Only ahead.

"Valentino," I said.

He ducked his head but still did not look my way.

"Are you . . . are you angry with me?"

"Nay," he grunted. "Only myself. 'Twas I who suggested we come to your aid." He finally glanced my way, torture within his eyes. "We could see you were losing, Tiliani. Overwhelmed." He swallowed hard. "Luciana, bleeding so."

"We would have *all* been lost," I said to him, grave. "We would have all died had you and Aurelio and your men not come to our aid. And we would never have gotten Luciana away."

His mouth trembled, and he looked to his side, as if he fought back tears again.

"Aurelio would not have agreed if he had not believed it the right choice," I said. "You did not force him to enter the fray. He wanted to stop the carnage. Stop Beneventi from beginning a war."

He shook his head back and forth, as if silently chastising himself. "And yet here we are. Riding toward what most certainly will be more battle. Mayhap all-out war. What is the point, Tiliani?

What is the point of it all if we only find ourselves back at this place, again and again?"

I gazed at him, mute, unable to come up with a suitable answer to meet his despair. We rode on in silence for a while.

"Our priest tells me that we are to hope for the best," I said, "pray for the best, work for the best. All our lives, we are to follow where God leads us and trust that he does not abandon us, no matter how it *feels*. We live in a broken world. You, more than most, have experienced it, even as a small child. But, Valentino, hope is not lost. It may seem distant this day, but 'tis never lost."

He said nothing, but I sensed him turning over my words.

"I have utterly failed," he murmured at last, then eyed me grimly. "All my life, I wished only to protect Aurelio, follow him, serve him. Honoring the gift his family gave me in taking me in, making me a knight."

I reached out and put a hand on his arm, and he stiffened. I ignored what felt like a rebuff. "And you did that. To the best of your ability. To the end." I paused. "What brought you to the field, Valentino?"

"A scout reported the skirmish. Beneventi asked for reinforcements. When we arrived and discovered *you* were there, aiding Lord Romano . . ."

I shook my head. "Aurelio would not have imagined Beneventi doing what he did. None of us did. You cannot punish yourself for lacking the gift of foresight."

As we rode on, I thought about Beneventi, and how his mind had been poisoned against Lord Romano. It stunk of Ercole. How long would the man continue to torment us? Until he had what he had hinted at in Firenze?

Castello Forelli herself?

LUCIANA

Trickling water and damp chill were my tunnel companions.

I'd been awake for several minutes, but only now dared to speak after gathering my memories. "Adri?" I whispered. "Nico?" I felt about for someone, hating being strapped to the stretcher. I needed to move. Turn over. The tunnel seemed to be closing in on me.

"I am here," Adri whispered, pulling a blanket back over me. I heard gravel scatter beneath her. She took my hand. "How is your head?"

"It still aches." Feeling her hand in mine helped me breathe, focus, rather than give in to panic. "But it is not as terrible as it was . . . yesterday? What day is it? How long has passed? What time is it?"

"You have slept for almost twenty-four hours, which is good. Most of the others are asleep. Only the guards are awake. Can you see anything?"

"No." I fought the despair in that single word.

"Not even shadows?"

I swallowed hard. "No. Tell me the truth, please. Do you think it will come back?"

She paused. "Honestly, I have no idea. When I said that sometimes it does, that was the truth. But head injuries . . ."

I sighed. "They're tricky even in our time."

"Yes. All we can do is wait. And pray."

I thought about that for a while. "Do you think it makes a difference, prayer?"

"I do. What I have seen over the years here has made me a person who believes." She paused, lifted a skin to my lips, and let me drink. "Back at home, in our own time," she went on, "most rely on themselves. We are secure in our lives only when we believe we have some semblance of control. Until we struggle with illness or a crisis, we can fool ourselves into thinking we are our own gods, holding our lives in our own hands. Here, faced with mortal danger and illness—and no semblance of the medical power we have at home—we are forced to recognize that God is God, and we are not."

I considered her words. "Do you think . . . do you think that if God's plan was to bring us here, just as he did you . . . is it part of his plan to leave me blind?"

She sighed and brushed the hair from my face. "I believe that no pain is wasted, if we trust God to make something good of it. Through pain, we become stronger, deeper, somehow. Which allows us to tackle the next bout of pain better. Like a knight getting stronger with his sword with each battle."

"I heard once that broken bones grow stronger as they heal."

She gave me another drink of water. "They do."

"Awesome." I huffed a laugh. "If only this was just a broken bone."

She laughed softly with me. "Right. None of us really want breaks, pain. But we get what we get. And it's how we negotiate the pain, deal with it, that helps define our lives."

I paused, thinking about all she had lost. Ben. Grandsons. Friends. Even her career as a famous archeologist. Yet she had found a way to manage it, which gave me hope.

"Adri, can I . . . can people . . ." I paused, wondering if I really wanted to know. "How do people in medieval Italy handle blindness?" All I could picture were beggars on the streets.

She covered my hand with hers. "If that is your fate, we shall tackle it together. It will be all right. But I am praying that it is *not* your fate. Do not give in to fear. Do you hear me? Do not give in to fear. You are a She-Wolf, Luciana Betarrini. *A She-Wolf.*"

They were good words. Righteous words.

In the moment, I took heart in them.

But when I next awakened, it was to the awful pounding of something against the iron door that led to the cavern. On our side, men shouted. Footsteps raced across the floor above us. A woman let out a muffled cry. Children whimpered.

Our hiding place had been discovered. We were under attack.

The cold chill of fear slipped back in from an unanticipated angle. I still could not see. I was still strapped to the stretcher, immobilized. Frantically, I felt for the bandage around my torso, my head, wondering how I might untie myself.

"Nico!" I cried. "Adri!"

"I'm here." Nico took my hand.

"They know we're down here?" I asked.

"It appears so," he returned grimly.

"And the Forellis? The Grecos?"

"A messenger arrived. They are defending Castello Forelli and attempting to reclaim Castello Paratore before Fiorentini reinforcements arrive."

"The Sienese?" I said desperately. "Are they not yet at Castello Romano?"

"Yes. Seeing to the wounded and shoring her back up. Sending others onward. But it's chaos out there, Luci."

"Can you untie me?" I reached for the cloth around my head. I had to get up. Be loose. *Move.*

"Adri wants you to—"

"Nico! I need to be free if we're about to be in a fight!" My fingers tugged at the cloth. I was getting frantic, claustrophobic, giving into panic.

"Here, stop." He pulled my hands away. "Let me do it."

I tried to steady my breathing as he worked on the knot. Tried to shut out the banging at the iron door that seemed to reverberate through my head. At least my headache was not quite so beastly as it had been.

"Why are they here? Why bother with us?"

He remained quiet while he moved to the cloth that was tied around my torso.

"Nico."

"Word has it that it's Ercole up there."

"*Ercole*? Why?"

"Think, Luci. Why would he want us?"

My mouth went dry. "To use us as bait?"

"Or trade. Ransom, maybe."

"That's better than just wanting to kill us to make the Forellis and Grecos mad."

"True." He got the knot out at my waist next. "Now take it easy. Not too fast." He took my hand and I slowly sat up.

I took in a deep breath, then another, swaying from nausea and dizziness.

"Whoa," Nico said. "Want to lie back?"

"No." I panted, trying to get enough oxygen in my system to find my equilibrium again. If I could only see. *Please, Lord, let me see! Bring back my eyesight!*

We heard a screech of metal, a bending sound, and my heart seemed to pause for a moment, then pound painfully. "Was that—"

"I'll be right back," Nico said, rising. "You stay here."

"No. Nico. You can't—"

"You'll be safe here. You're in a side cavern. It's kind of hidden. Everyone else is out in the main one."

We heard more pounding, the shouts of men. Another terrible screech.

"No, Nico!" I cried, hearing him surge into motion. I tried to reach for him but felt only the brush of his tunic as he ran toward the cavern entrance.

"Stay here! I'll be back!" he whispered.

My ears pulsed with my blood as I tried to hear anyone else nearby. They'd squirreled me away somewhere? A side cavern?

"Adri? Anyone? Is anyone here?" I whispered.

I rose, tentatively. Taking hold of the rock wall to make sure I wouldn't fall. The last thing I needed was to hit my head again. I shuffled my way forward.

Swords clashed. Women screamed. Children cried. Could I help them? Could I help anyone? Not without being able to see. I squinted, straining to make out anything, even the shadows.

Please, Lord, let me see even shadows!

I reached the mouth of my tiny cavern and could better hear what was happening. Men were cursing, shouting, arguing to my right, out where I imagined the water and outer wall were. Where we had been breached.

But to my left, they still worked on the fortified villa door, trying to get at us from both sides.

"Calm yourselves!" shouted a man. "We do not intend to maim or kill any of you unless you continue to fight us! Surrender and take a knee! Put down your weapons! You cannot fight your way out of here!"

There was a slowing in the battle, and it sounded as if our knights might agree with the attacker. After all, it was better to kneel than die. Live for another day to fight. And since there was no avenue of retreat and the bulk of the people here were servants, women, and even some kids . . .

"Friends, stand down!" Adri called. "We surrender! Everyone take a knee! Lay down your weapons! Do not be afraid," she said to the others. "They shall not harm us."

I swallowed hard. We were surrendering? I mean, it made sense, but what about me? I took a tentative step backward. Could I hide? But then what? Wait another night, see if my eyesight came back? Then go after them all? Without a horse? Without Nico?

No. I wasn't going to stay behind. I stepped forward.

"An excellent choice, Lady Betarrini," purred a man at the cavern entrance near Adri. "I would much prefer to deliver you to your daughters unharmed and unmolested."

Ercole.

I took a step back.

"Now, where are the younger Betarrinis? Ahh, there is Domenico. What of Luciana?"

I stilled. He knew our names?

"Come now. Where is your sister?" His voice came closer with the progression of slow, threatening footsteps. Nico did not respond.

"I am here," I said, my voice faint, raspy. I coughed. "I am here!" I said more firmly.

Nico groaned.

Someone moved toward me at once, about twenty feet down the cavern passageway. "Ahh, my dear. I see you are injured." Ercole's voice came from mere inches away. "And this time, not by my hand. You are quite . . . formidable. Was *this* why the Grecos left you behind? Because of your injury?"

I refused to respond. I must be quite a sight, with my head swaddled in bandages.

"They thought they could leave you in safety. But they did not account for my spies. Come, m'lady. Take my arm."

"She should be returned to her stretcher," Adri said. "She should not be up at all."

"Very well." Ercole snapped his fingers. "You there—find it. We shall carry her."

"To where?" I dared. "Where are you taking us?"

I could sense his pleasure. "To claim my birthright."

"Your birthright?"

"Indeed. With Lord Paratore dead, I am next in line. My great-grandmother was a Paratore. And all of Firenze shall support me in taking the castello as my own."

36

TILIANI

We could not allow Castello Paratore to fall into any Fiorentini lord's hands that they chose. The Grecos had given her over in the effort to assure peace, in partnership with Aurelio—not to allow Firenze to be on our threshold with some diabolical man in charge again. So we were both defending our own home while attacking Castello Paratore. She was protected by a thin retinue of men—those who had refused to follow Aurelio's lead outside Castello Romano, and those who had remained behind on guard duty.

Otello and I picked off our fourth archer from the wall, while hiding behind the trunks of two massive oaks. Mama and her archers did similar damage from the western side. Captain Fiore and Gaspare from the north.

"How many do you figure remain?" I asked Otello as I nocked another arrow.

"Twenty? Mayhap twenty-five? I have taken five or more. You?"

"About the same." I pulled back my string, waiting for the next man to dare show his face.

Giulio and Ilaria each led contingents of men, holding off Fiorentini forces on the far side of the castello. Scouts had informed us that Sienese troops had secured Castello Romano and were moving our way. Men from Monteriggioni approached from the north, which would double our fighting numbers, ahead of the Fiorentini arriving. Castello Paratore would have to surrender. She was without her lord and down to little more than a score of men.

Make that nineteen, I thought grimly, as I shot a man when he peeked out from around a pillar again. He staggered back, overcorrected, then stumbled forward, tumbling over the parapet and to the ground before us with a sickening sound. I grimaced and looked away.

"Baldarino!" I yelled. He looked my way after letting his arrow fly. "Find Captain Mancini! Bring the siege ladders! Let us see if we can take them!"

The man left at once to do as I bid.

"Let us get higher!" I said to Otello, reaching for the lowest tree branch and hauling myself upward. Mayhap from another angle, we could catch the remaining defenders off guard.

He shouldered his bow and took to his own tree.

Once I reached an open area of the branches, affording me some protection from the wall above but still lean out and take a shot, I settled into my perch. I nocked an arrow, shutting out the sounds of battle from numerous locations all about the castle.

I tried to do the same with my thoughts. Were my mother, aunt, father, and uncle all right? Could we really be close to taking Castello Paratore again? And would doing so bring the wrath of all of Firenze down upon our heads?

I spotted a knight on the parapets, searching the ground where Otello and I had been situated before. When he dared to lean further out, I sent my arrow winging his way, estimating how he would lean backward when he heard it.

It landed true.

"I suggest you cease killing my knights," said a voice from below.

My eyes met Otello's, and we searched the forest floor. I had not thought any Fiorentini were nearby.

"I suggest you show yourself," I returned.

"Swear you shall set down your bow. Your companion too."

I looked to Otello again and nodded once. We lowered our bows. "For a moment. Show yourself and say what you must."

My mouth went dry when Andrea Ercole walked out of the brush, arms outstretched. He cast me a cheeky grin.

"How dare you show your face here," I said.

"How dare you murder my men."

"Your men? Those are Paratore guards."

"And I am a Paratore."

I paused. Did he jest? "We are taking the castello back until we can agree on a suitable man to take Lord Paratore's place."

Ercole lifted his hands higher. "And I am that man. All of Firenze is behind me."

My grip on my bow tightened. "Never. You are the last man who should take Aurelio's place."

"And yet I have a family claim on the castle as well as the Grandi's support."

My mind raced. *This* had been the castle he had spoken of when Luciana overheard him? He had not had designs on Castello Forelli but rather Castello Paratore?

Likely both, knowing him.

"M'lady," Otello grunted, asking permission.

"Take him!" I cried, hoping he'd already nocked an arrow. I heard the thrum of Otello's bowstring. But Ercole had disappeared into the brush again.

"Show yourself!" I cried, nocking my own arrow.

"I think not!" he returned.

I sent my arrow into the bush in which I thought he might be hiding. He dodged behind a clump of three small trees, an effective barrier. "Kill me, and you shall never see your grandmother again!"

My heart paused and then pounded. Nona? He had captured her? Then . . . what of the Betarrini twins? Chiara?

"Ahh, yes. You are thinking now, are you not? We have captured them all. Servants. Women and children. The newest Betarrini wolves, and your grandmother. Captain Greco's elder sister too. Now come down, Tiliani. We shall speak in proper fashion."

Otello shook his head furiously.

"How do I know you have them?"

He paused and then tossed something in the air. It landed in a deep green patch of moss near the base of my tree.

Oh, nay, I thought. *Nay, nay, nay!*

'Twas my grandmother's necklace. Etruscan beads.

"If you have harmed them—"

He scoffed. "Why would I harm them? Hostages are of little use if they are not whole. Though Lady Luciana seems to be struggling with her eyesight. Lady Adri seems to think she must get to the castello soon and have a proper rest if she has hope of recovery."

How had they found them in the hidden cavern? It was a terrible blow.

"Come down, Tiliani." Ercole's tone lost all semblance of play. He was deadly intent.

"You shall address her as Lady Forelli," Otello growled.

"Forgive me." He sidled from behind the trees and bowed. "Lady Forelli." There was no honor in the way he said *lady.* "Know that if I do not return to my men within the hour, they have orders to begin killing your loved ones. One for each hour I am detained."

I grimaced, shouldered my bow once more, and climbed down. Otello did the same and hurried to stand beside me as I dropped to the soft forest floor.

Ercole was ten paces away. He tossed his cape over his shoulder, revealing the Paratore crimson. "Do not shoot!" he called to the archers on the walls. "I have these two in hand!"

I shook my head at him. "There is no way my elders shall let you take control of this castello. Not after all you have done to harm us."

He shrugged his shoulders. "We have long hovered at the edge of war. I merely escalated the process. With my knowledge of Castello Forelli's strengths and weaknesses, and a familial tie to the Paratores, the decision to have me take Aurelio's place shall be unanimous among the Grandi."

I squinted at him. "Was this your plan all along? Or are you late to recognizing your familial bloodlines?"

"I was aware. I simply did not yet see how they might benefit me, with Aurelio in the way. Now . . ." He lifted his hands and one brow, and cocked his head. "All has come together."

"You came to us as a spy?"

"I came to you as a collector. Of information. I had not yet determined how I might best benefit." He waved upward at the castle. "And here at last I have found it." He took a step forward. "You considered one Paratore. Mayhap in time, you shall consider another."

"I would rather be drawn and quartered."

He sniffed and gave a sidelong smile. "That can be arranged. But I believe we shall find our way—as enemies or lovers."

"You overstep," Otello said, drawing an arrow.

Ercole ignored him. "I merely have stated the obvious. But for now, we must stop this battle, Lady Tiliani. And you shall help me do so. After all, time is of the essence for your loved ones."

LUCIANA

We had come to a stop. My stretcher was set down on the forest floor, the Fiorentini knights summoned to speak with their captain.

Adri and Nico came to my side, each taking one of my hands.

"I feel so helpless," I said in English.

"You are wounded, recovering," Adri responded. "You must be gentle with yourself and your capabilities. Stress will only delay your healing." I started to shake my head, but she hissed. "Stay still. You have already endured jostling I'd rather not see. Do not exacerbate it."

I took a deep breath, trying to keep from crying. I supposed that, too, might cause me further harm.

"If it wasn't for me, you might be fighting back. Or trying to escape," I said forlornly.

"Nay," Adri said. "We would not endanger our people. There are more than a dozen captives here."

"If your eyesight doesn't come back in a few days," Nico said, "there's always the tunnel."

"If we can escape Ercole," I said.

"He does not wish to keep us," Adri said. "He wishes to use us to press our loved ones."

"Even if we do escape him, what about Manero?" I said. "What if he's done something to damage the wall—the tunnel itself—in his efforts to find out what happened?"

"It's likely been only an hour or two for them," Nico said.

"Time enough to start digging. Or laying a trap for us."

"There's the other tunnel," Adri said. "Near Firenze."

"But you do not know where it is for sure?"

"Wouldn't be hard to trace it. People here are a superstitious lot. They would likely speak of it because of the other Betarrinis who appeared once, in its mouth."

"What did they do to them?"

"Imprisoned them. Accused them of witchcraft. We had to rescue them."

"And they never returned?"

"Never. But then, one of them almost died."

"I'm beginning to understand that decision," Nico said.

"And we'd have to slip across the border," I said, "just as the border is heating up."

"We'll find a way, if necessary," Nico said.

His words heartened me. We would find a way. If we had to.

But being blind? I did not feel nearly as confident as I had, arriving full-sighted. And Giulio? He would not want a blind bride. That would be like saddling him with challenges before we ever began.

"Hey, Luci," Nico said, leaning down.

I looked toward him—or at least *faced* him.

"Don't get ahead of yourself. Remember what Mom always said. How do you eat an elephant?"

"One bite at a time."

"Exactly. Just focus on the next bite. Which is to get you home to Castello Forelli and resting, properly."

"That sounds nice. But I don't think these guys nabbed us just to escort us back."

"Yeah. Probably not," he admitted.

"They're going to use us as ransom, huh?"

"Most likely," Adri said with a sigh.

"Maybe we'll help avoid some bloodshed at least."

"There you go." Nico's tone held none of the cheer his words did.

The Fiorentini knights returned then. Judging from the sounds of birds all around us, we were still deep in the forest.

"We wait here," said a deep voice.

"How much longer does she have?" asked another.

"A half an hour, if that," said the first.

I frowned. "What is he talking about?" I whispered.

"Assassination," Adri replied grimly. "It sounds as if Andrea Ercole's demands are not met, they intend to kill us. One at a time."

"Perfect," I returned. "I have to tell you that I'm going to give this field hospital a bad review. It smells like manure, the bed is terrible, and there are constant threats of violence."

Nico laughed, mirthlessly. "Good one, baby sis."

Adri took my hand and covered it with her other one. "This is not the end of you, She-Wolf. Nor shall it be the end of me."

37

I swallowed back the bile that rose in my throat as I walked beside Andrea Ercole. He forced me to lay my hand atop his, as if we entered a fine hall, rather than to the forefront of one battle site after another. One by one, we captured the attention of fighting knights. One by one, seeing me, the Forelli forces laid down their arms, as did the Paratore knights and those Fiorentini that had entered the fray.

My family and friends followed behind, helpless to intervene with me in such a precarious position. Ercole had told them in no uncertain terms that they would be informed of "developments" as soon as we had circumvented the castello and reached the gates.

Valentino, battle-filthy and panting, was one of the last to lower his sword, standing beside my father.

My heart pounded in what felt like an empty chest. I was a pawn. A trophy. Ercole was masterful, seeking me out, knowing I might be the lone Forelli knight who could bring the rest to bay.

We paused before the gates of the castle, and it burned, knowing how very close we had been to overtaking her. With but a score of knights still standing within?

"Lord Forelli," Ercole said, nodding to my uncle. He looked around. "People of the land, Sienese and Fiorentini! Peace is at hand!"

Papa's cheek muscle clenched and released, then clenched

again. "How is *peace* at hand, Ercole? Other than you have my *daughter* at hand?"

Ercole smiled down at me and then over to him. "I am the lord-elect of this castle," he said, gesturing above. "Blessed by Firenze to take over where Lord Aurelio Paratore left off."

My father shook his head, as did my uncle and aunt. Mama lifted her chin, waiting for what came next.

"You shall retreat now, Lord Forelli," Ercole said. "And leave us in peace."

"Because you hold my niece?" Marcello said.

"Nay." Ercole drew himself up. "Well, yes. But I was long enough in your company to realize that she could fight her way out of this corner." He gave me a genteel nod. "But there are others you love that cannot."

My elders stiffened as one. As did the Grecos.

Andrea smiled. He lifted an arm. "Even now, my men hold your beloved Lady Adri, Lady Chiara, the newest Betarrinis, and many of your servants."

I watched as Giulio shared a long, slow look with Ilaria. His hand tightened on the hilt of his blade. *Nay.* He could not make a move. *Not now. Not here. 'Twould be disastrous.* I glanced upward. The sun hung low in the sky. How long did Nona have?

I stepped forward. "Papa. Uncle. Time is of the essence. I see no way forward other than to relinquish Castello Paratore to Sir Ercole."

Zio Marcello lowered his chin. "You support this?"

"I do not *support* it," I said. "I see no other way. He holds Nona's life in his hands. As well as the Betarrinis and multiple servants from the villa. And if we do not decide quickly, we might be too late. He has left orders to murder our people, one for each hour he is away."

Giulio stepped forward and spoke in my uncle's ear, then stepped back. The rest waited, holding their collective breath.

Zio Marcello drew himself up, closed his eyes, then shared a long look with my aunt. Zia Gabi nodded once, lips in a grim line.

"Release our loved ones," Marcello growled, looking toward Ercole. "Without delay."

"Then we are in agreement?" Ercole still held his arm aloft. "You shall retreat and allow us to take hold of Castello Paratore?"

"We shall," my uncle said. "But should any harm come to our family, you shall suffer the consequences."

"Understood. Pull back your men three hundred paces."

My uncle circled his hand in the air and pointed toward Castello Forelli. As one, those on foot or on horseback pulled back. When the bulk of them retreated down the hill toward the creek, Ercole made a gesture in the air and a group emerged from the forest's edge.

My heart caught as I saw the stretcher suspended between two horses, as well as the figures on either side—Nona and Domenico. Chiara. And the servants from the villa . . . women and children. Hands bound behind them.

I bit back my fury, fighting every urge within me to end Andrea Ercole's life there and then.

LUCIANA

"I really, really hate that guy," Nico said, as we listened to the conversation, passed backward in waves.

I took a deep breath, feeling it too. I hated that we were being used as bait. Hated that we had weakened our family's position. That our family felt trapped. Responsible to save us.

And yet, and yet . . . the feeling of connection, of value, left me short of breath.

We were worthy of bringing battle to a halt.

We were worthy of bringing our loved ones to the bargaining table.

We were worthy of sacrificing Castello Greco—again—if it meant our lives were forfeit.

That they already considered us family, as we did them.

"Why?" I whispered. Both Adri and Nico still held my hands, from either side. "Why would they not just let us die? When so much hangs in the balance?"

Adri squeezed my hand and leaned closer. "Because you are loved, Luciana. So loved. You are one of us. And no castle is worth the life of one you love. We shall find our way past Ercole, in time. But we would never get over missing you. You are one of us. Forever."

I smiled bleakly—trying not to nod. I wanted my blindness to recede. I wanted to find healing, freedom with this new family of ours.

"We are to go to the castello," said a man.

"Take the reins," said another. To Nico? "You are free to retreat to Castello Forelli."

No more words were exchanged, but I felt my stretcher lift, and we were off. After a few hundred paces, we stopped.

"What's happening?" I asked.

"Ercole is entering the castle," Nico muttered.

"Unbelievable," I said. "That guy . . ."

"He really is something else."

"Please tell me we can take him down in time."

"I hope so. I'd happily take part."

I sensed another approach the stretcher. I knew it was Giulio from his first touch. "Luciana?"

"I am well," I assured him. "That is, as well as I might be."

He brought my hand to his lips. "I am so sorry you were taken captive. We thought . . ."

"You thought we would be well, hidden away. 'Twas a good guess. And with so many needs in so many places, I understand. Please. Stop berating yourself."

"I cannot cease berating myself for leaving you vulnerable."

Because we became tokens? Ransom? Bait to accept Ercole's bribes, allowing him access to the castle?

"Giulio," I said. "You all were drawn in ten different directions. Everyone made the best decision they could."

He brushed the hair back from my eyes. "You are . . . Do you . . .?"

"I still cannot see a thing," I said miserably.

"We may need to go to the tunnel," Nico said. "If she does not improve in another few days."

"Then we shall get her there."

"Yes," said Ilaria. It sounded like she was at my brother's shoulder. "And if you two are going, so shall we."

I took that in. They were willing to travel with us? Hope surged. If they were with us, we might fight off anyone who awaited us.

"I have to say, I would not mind experiencing it again," Ilaria said. She leaned toward me. "And if it healed your eyes, Luciana? 'Twould be worth it."

I took a deep breath. "You two have already sacrificed so much on our behalf. On the Forellis'."

"And we shall sacrifice more, should it be required of us," Giulio said.

My stretcher was attached between two horses. We were turning—I could feel the warmth of the last vestiges of the setting sun move upon my face.

"It is over? Ercole has taken *full* control of Castello Paratore?" I asked.

"Ostensibly," Giulio said, walking beside me. "But it is far from over."

"Why did I know you were going to say that?" Nico asked.

"Because it is the way," Ilaria said wearily. "Until we oust him again, hold the castle as our own, battle shall again be our constant companion."

"But we are together," Giulio said, taking my hand again. "And that is the most important part."

"Yes," I said. But inside I thought, *Until we are not.*

"Let us get you to Castello Forelli. To tranquility. Quiet. Peace," Ilaria said. "Once there, after a few days, your eyesight shall return."

"I hope," I said.

"It shall," Giulio said, as if he could will it. "You need only believe."

Need only believe. His words rang through my mind. My heart.

I believe, Father, I prayed. *Help me in my unbelief. And please, please let my vision return. And this all to be okay. Somehow. Amen.*

I felt the steady, warm grip of Giulio's hand, all the way home. Heard the creak of the mighty gates as they opened for our weary forces. Felt Giulio's strong arms lift me from the stretcher and carry me toward my room. The chill of the stones enveloped me, but the warmth of homecoming kept it at bay.

He settled me on my cot, drew a blanket to my chest, and came down to my level. "You rest, beloved. Here, you shall find healing. You are home." He kissed me tenderly on the forehead.

I smiled, knowing it was what he needed most. The reassurance. The hope.

After all, I was home. Home, surrounded by people who would sacrifice anything—*anything*—for our good.

Even if the enemy was again at our very door.

ACKNOWLEDGMENTS

Many thanks to my editors, Nadine Brandes, Sarah Grimm and Megan Gerig, who helped this book shine. To my my jiu jitsu consultants—Amy Fisher, Abby and Nick Pugh, and Shane Duffy—thanks for helping out this couch potato. Faithful friends with eagle eyes—Cheryl Crawford and Melanie Stroud—bless you for helping me out with a final proof. Also to the Enclave team—Steve Laube, Lindsay Franklin, Jamie Foley and more—I love working with you all and so appreciate your investment in this book. Hugs and high fives all around!

ABOUT THE AUTHOR

Lisa T. Bergren is the author of over seventy books spanning a variety of genres, from children's picture books to women's historical fiction to supernatural suspense and time travel. She lives with her husband and three gradually-graduating-from-the-nest young adult children in Colorado Springs, Colorado. For more information, see LisaBergren.com.

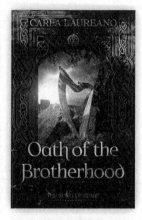

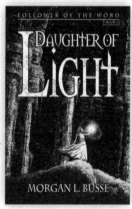